ONE OF THE MOST CRITICALLY ACCLAIMED BOOKS OF THE YEAR

"Edison Hark immediately joins the ranks of Philip Marlowe and Sam Spade in a smart, classic noir drenched in style and history."

– JAMES TYNION IV (DEPARTMENT OF TRUTH, *Batman*)

"The comic isn't just well-crafted, but also true to the history."

– *ASIAN REVIEW OF BOOKS*

"The gripping story of a detective who knows he'll have to lose a few battles if he's going to win a war."

– ROB THOMAS (*Veronica Mars, iZombie* showrunner)

"Fantastic."

– JEFF LEMIRE (GIDEON FALLS, *Sweet Tooth*)

"A book that swings for the fences and has managed to land in the stars."

– *BLACK NERD PROBLEMS*

"Like any good noir, a sense of dread hangs off every page of THE GOOD ASIAN, a brittle story that takes place during an unfamiliar time in our history that is tragically all too familiar now in our present."

– BRIAN AZZARELLO (*100 Bullets*, MOONSHINE*)*

"A stunning, layered noir in the tradition of Dashiell Hammett and Raymond Chandler."

– ALEX DE CAMPI
(DRACULA, MOTHERF**KER, *Madi: Once Upon a Time in the Future*)

"This is absolutely the best kind of comics noir."

– KIERON GILLEN (THE WICKED + THE DIVINE)

"Simply cannot be missed... It cannot be understated how gorgeous this book looks."
– *COMICS BEAT*

"THE GOOD ASIAN sits at the intersection of classic noir and contemporary understanding. There is a sharp truth at the center of the book that you don't realize is there until it's slipped between your ribs, and by then you're already a believer!"
– **VITA AYALA** (*The Wilds, New Mutants*)

"A stunning feat of comic book synthesis. I can't think of a more perfect comic for this imperfect moment."
– **W. MAXWELL PRINCE** (ICE CREAM MAN, HAHA)

"An unflinching look at the Chinese-American experience in 1930s Chinatown."
– *COMIC BOOK RESOURCES*

"A crime comic that stands among the very best of the modern era. People will be talking about this book for a long time — for good reason."
– **ALEX SEGURA**
(Anthony Award-winning author of *Blackout* and *Miami Midnight*)

"It's powerful, compelling Asian-American noir set in 1930s San Francisco. Give it a try — you'll be swept up in it."
– **KURT BUSIEK** (**ASTRO CITY**, *Avengers*)

"A timely and visually bold crime thriller...an assured classic entry into American noir subgenre."
– *THE POP BREAK*

"Stunning."
– **JOCK** (WYTCHES, *All-Star Batman*)

"THE GOOD ASIAN is so damn...well, GOOD. It's a fantastic noir tale with compelling mysteries, great characters, and dynamic art."

– **JOE HENDERSON** (SHADECRAFT, *Lucifer* showrunner)

"Edison Hark makes Philip Marlowe look like a p***y."

– **DIANE RUGGERIO-WRIGHT** (*iZombie* showrunner)

"One of the strongest debuts of 2021."

– ***COMICBOOK.COM***

"I was blown away by it. Such a smart, compelling, and gorgeous book. It feels more relevant than ever right now."

– **MATTHEW ROSENBERG**
(*4 Kids Walk Into a Bank, Batman: Urban Legends*)

"I'm hooked. Very interested to see how far this book goes with what it's set up, and I get the strong impression it's going to go all the way."

– **GREG PAK** (*Darth Vader, Incredible Hulk*)

"A phenomenal addition to the world of crime comics, a necessary and daring creation."

– ***COMICS BOOKCASE***

"This is an outstanding read about greed, class, moral decay and race supremacy... fucking fantastic crime book."

– **JOSHUA DYSART** (*Goodnight Paradise, Harbinger*)

"May very well spearhead a noir revival in comics, THE GOOD ASIAN feels beautifully classic and freshly modern at the same time."

– **JOHNNIE CHRISTMAS** (*Angel Catbird*, TARTARUS)

"More than just a gripping mystery and meticulously researched historical fiction, it's a thoughtful examination of identity and timely reflection of modern anxieties in the Asian-American community."

– ***FANBASE PRESS***

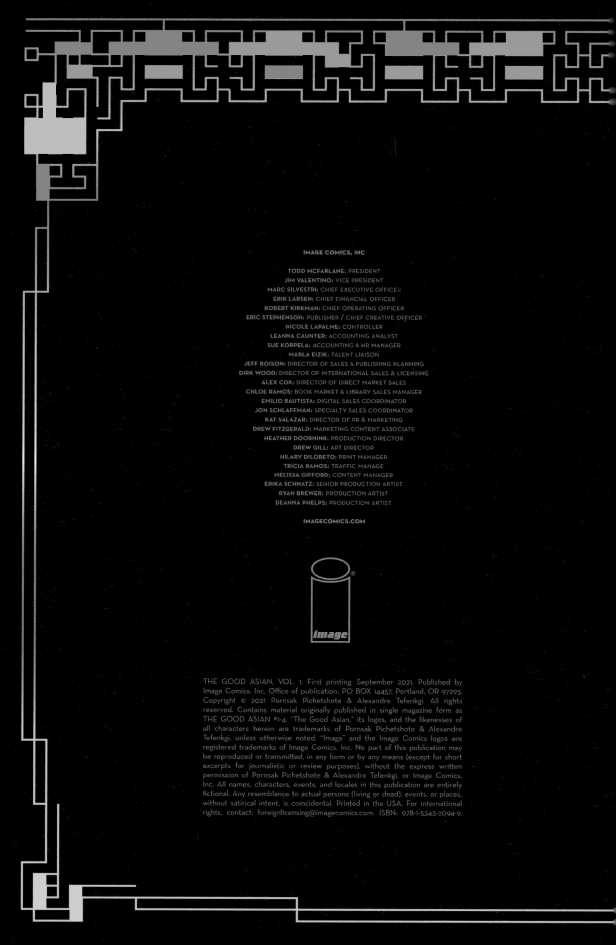

IMAGE COMICS, INC

TODD McFARLANE: PRESIDENT
JIM VALENTINO: VICE PRESIDENT
MARC SILVESTRI: CHIEF EXECUTIVE OFFICER
ERIK LARSEN: CHIEF FINANCIAL OFFICER
ROBERT KIRKMAN: CHIEF OPERATING OFFICER
ERIC STEPHENSON: PUBLISHER / CHIEF CREATIVE OFFICER
NICOLE LAPALME: CONTROLLER
LEANNA CAUNTER: ACCOUNTING ANALYST
SUE KORPELA: ACCOUNTING & HR MANAGER
MARLA EIZIK: TALENT LIAISON
JEFF BOISON: DIRECTOR OF SALES & PUBLISHING PLANNING
DIRK WOOD: DIRECTOR OF INTERNATIONAL SALES & LICENSING
ALEX COX: DIRECTOR OF DIRECT MARKET SALES
CHLOE RAMOS: BOOK MARKET & LIBRARY SALES MANAGER
EMILIO BAUTISTA: DIGITAL SALES COORDINATOR
JON SCHLAFFMAN: SPECIALTY SALES COORDINATOR
KAT SALAZAR: DIRECTOR OF PR & MARKETING
DREW FITZGERALD: MARKETING CONTENT ASSOCIATE
HEATHER DOORNINK: PRODUCTION DIRECTOR
DREW GILL: ART DIRECTOR
HILARY DILORETO: PRINT MANAGER
TRICIA RAMOS: TRAFFIC MANAGE
MELISSA GIFFORD: CONTENT MANAGER
ERIKA SCHNATZ: SENIOR PRODUCTION ARTIST
RYAN BREWER: PRODUCTION ARTIST
DEANNA PHELPS: PRODUCTION ARTIST

IMAGECOMICS.COM

THE GOOD ASIAN

AN EDISON HARK MYSTERY

PORNSAK PICHETSHOTE
WRITER

ALEXANDRE TEFENKGI
ARTIST

LEE LOUGHRIDGE
COLORIST

JEFF POWELL
LETTERER & DESIGNER

DAVE JOHNSON
COVER ARTIST

GRANT DIN
HISTORICAL CONSULTANT

ERIKA SCHNATZ
LOGO DESIGNER & PRODUCTION

WILL DENNIS
EDITOR

SPECIAL THANKS

Octavia Bray
Liz Choi Bubriski
Cliff Chiang
Jimmy Nguyen
Keith Chow
Tyler Jennes
Mel Judson
David Lei
Dawn Lee Tu
Cindy Wei

Jessica, Anaïs, Miles, Angelique,
Daniel, Leila, Steve, Niki, Eric, CC,
and our Moms for all their support
during a crazy pandemic

CHAPTER ONE

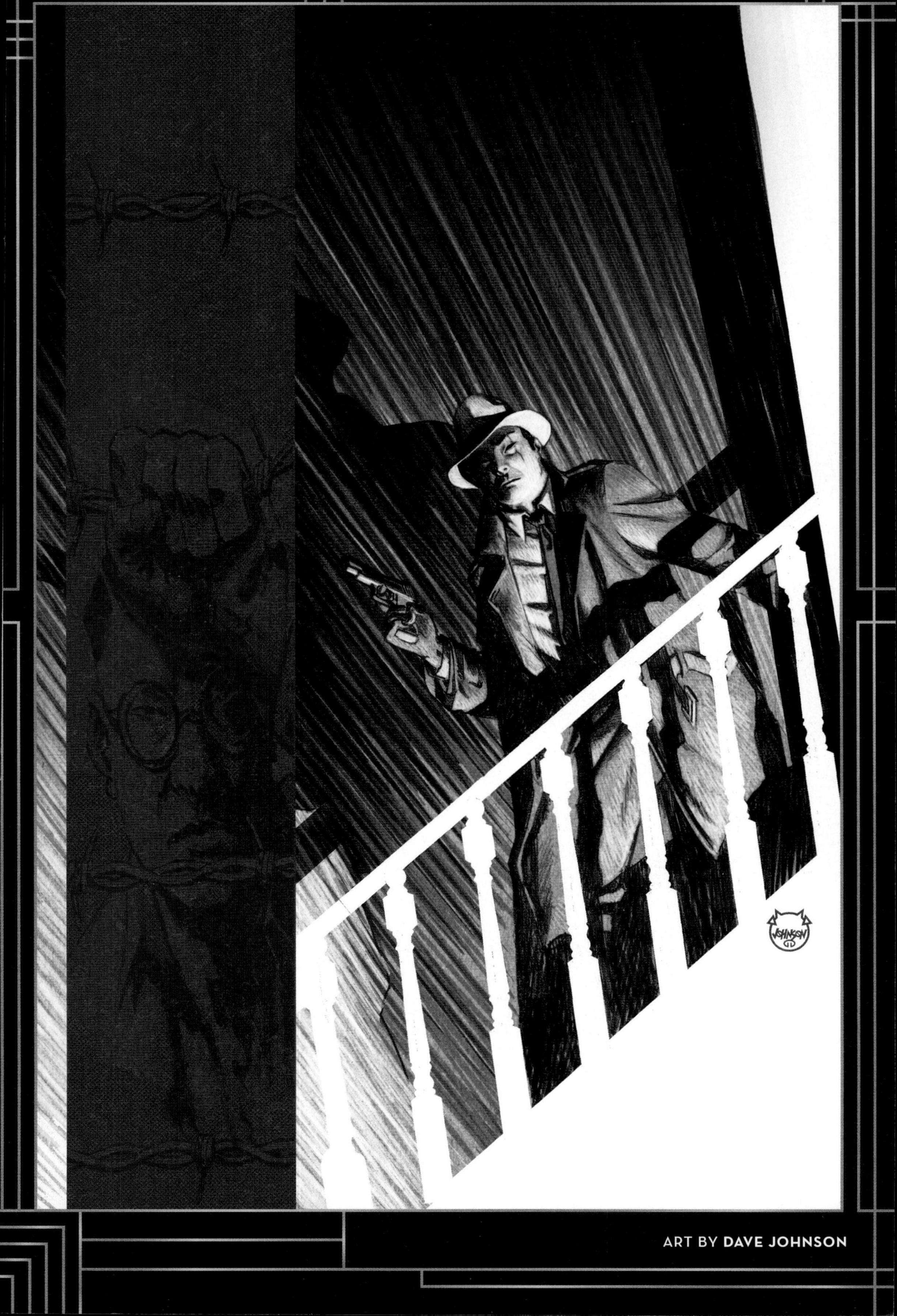

ART BY **DAVE JOHNSON**

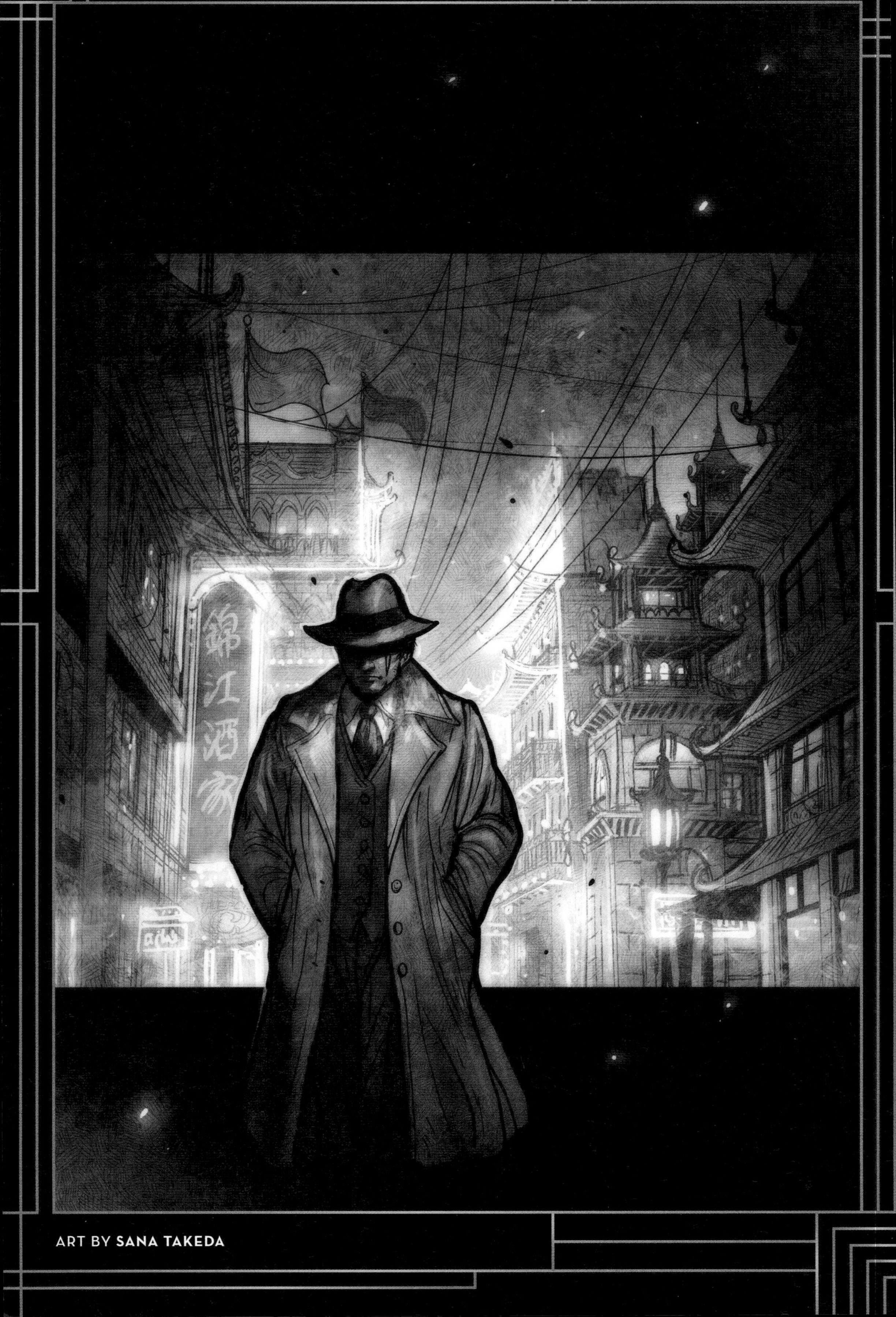
錦江酒家

ART BY **SANA TAKEDA**

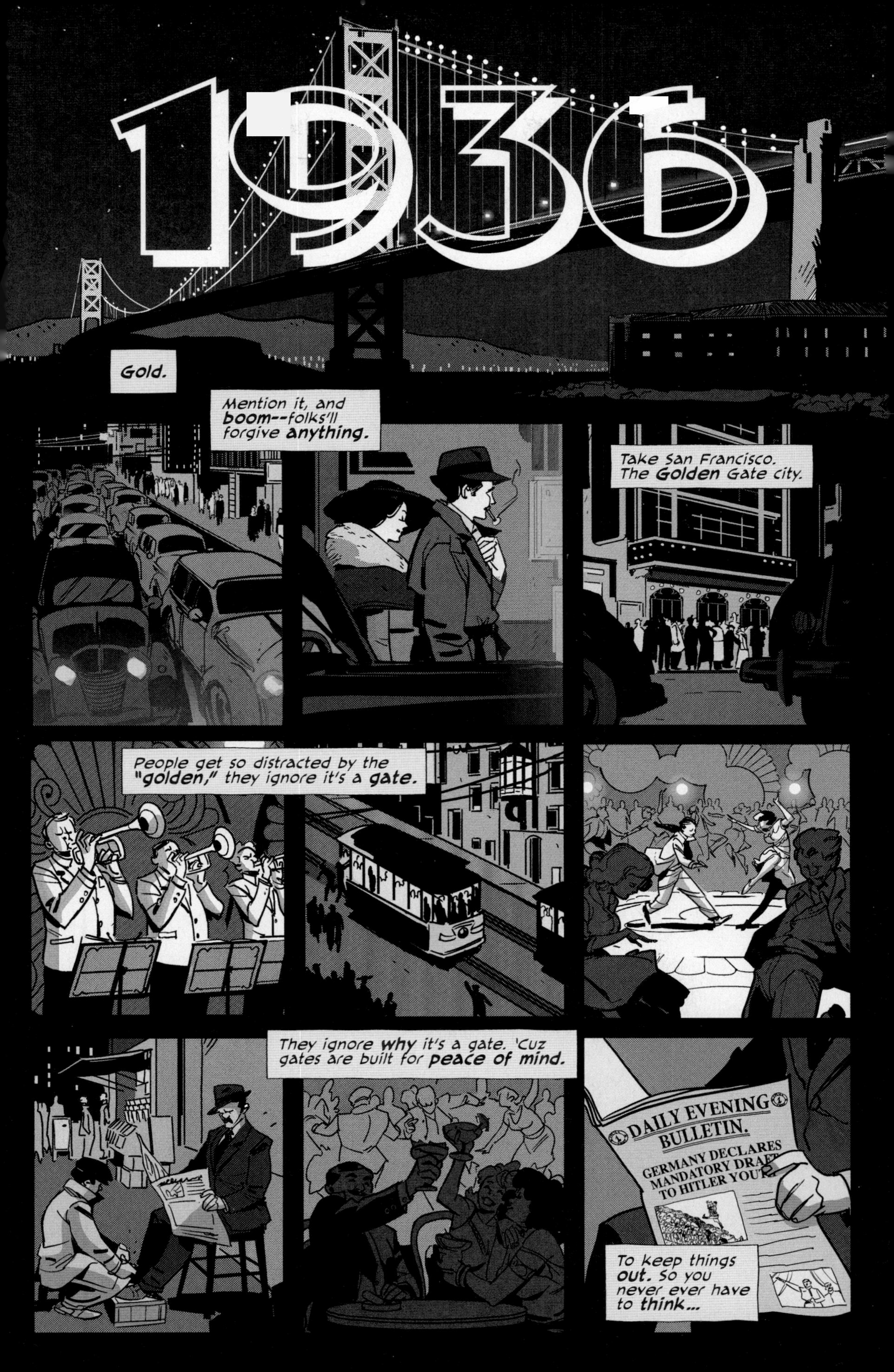
1936
Gold.
Mention it, and boom--folks'll forgive anything.
Take San Francisco. The Golden Gate city.
People get so distracted by the "golden," they ignore it's a gate.
They ignore why it's a gate. 'Cuz gates are built for peace of mind.
DAILY EVENING BULLETIN.
GERMANY DECLARES
MANDATORY DRAF
TO HITLER YOUT
To keep things out. So you never ever have to think...

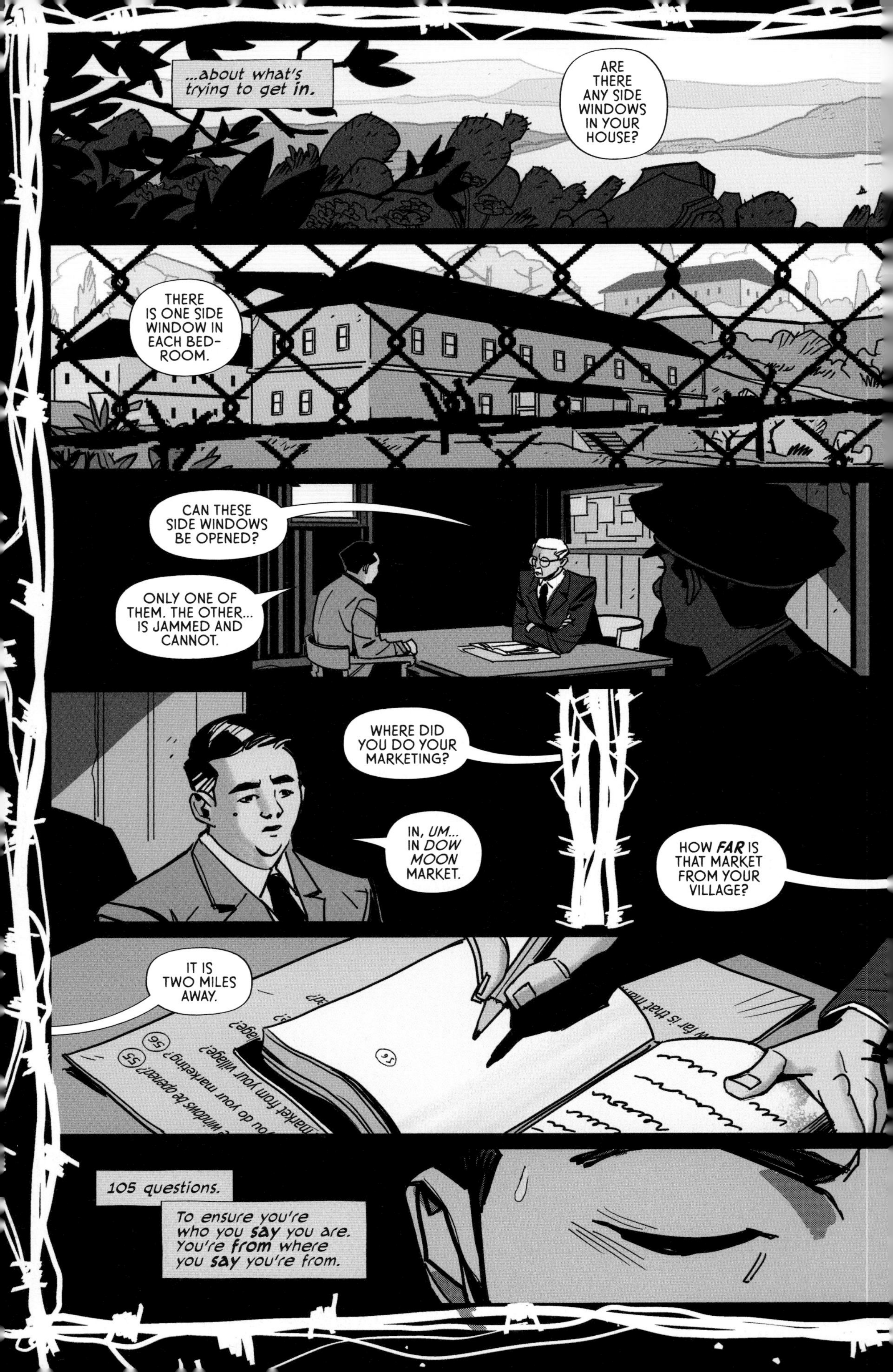
...about what's trying to get in.
ARE THERE ANY SIDE WINDOWS IN YOUR HOUSE?
THERE IS ONE SIDE WINDOW IN EACH BED-ROOM.
CAN THESE SIDE WINDOWS BE OPENED?
ONLY ONE OF THEM. THE OTHER... IS JAMMED AND CANNOT.
WHERE DID YOU DO YOUR MARKETING?
IN, UM... IN DOW MOON MARKET.
HOW FAR IS THAT MARKET FROM YOUR VILLAGE?
IT IS TWO MILES AWAY.
105 questions.
To ensure you're who you say you are. You're from where you say you're from.

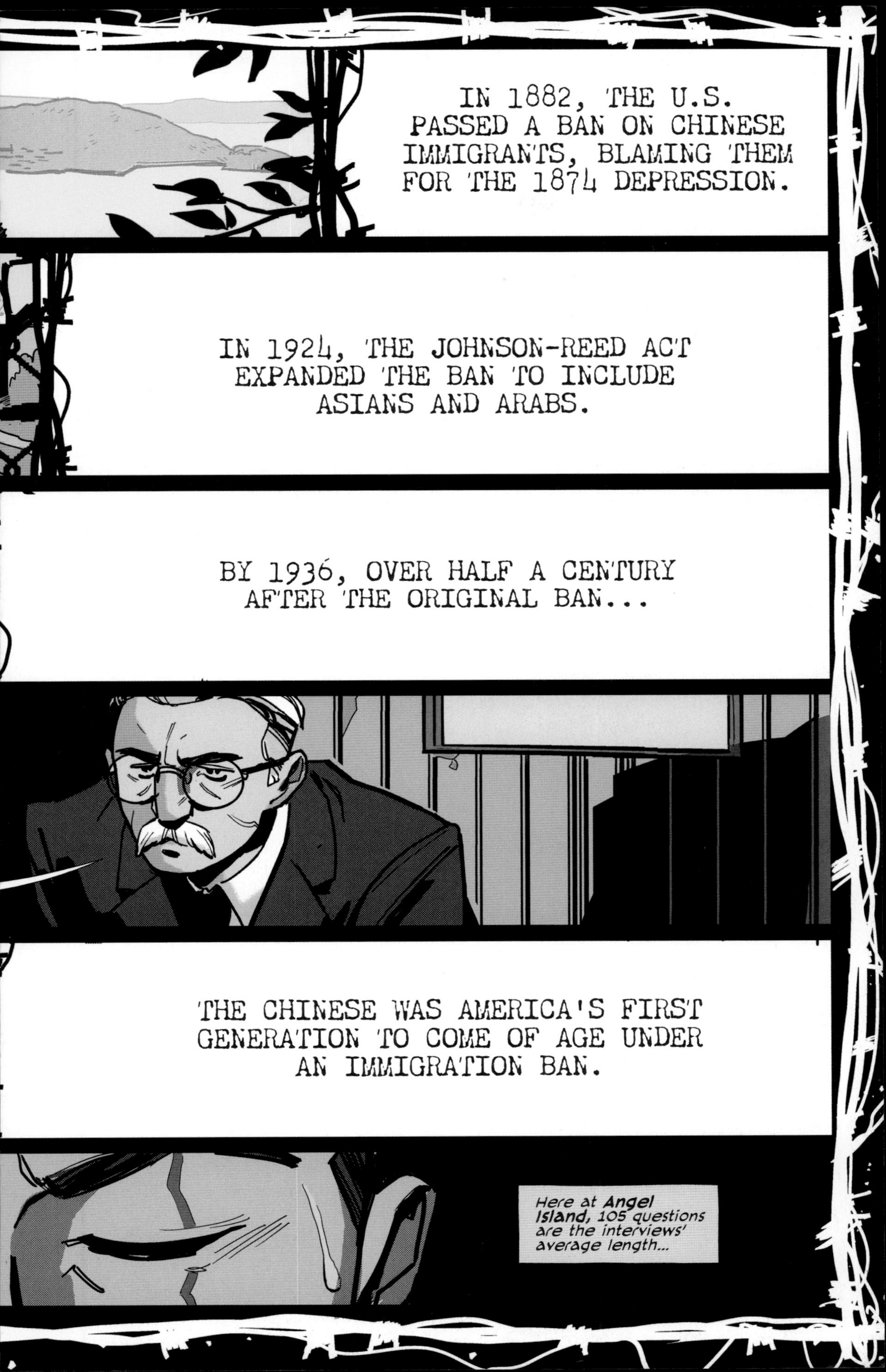
IN 1882, THE U.S. PASSED A BAN ON CHINESE IMMIGRANTS, BLAMING THEM FOR THE 1874 DEPRESSION.
IN 1924, THE JOHNSON-REED ACT EXPANDED THE BAN TO INCLUDE ASIANS AND ARABS.
BY 1936, OVER HALF A CENTURY AFTER THE ORIGINAL BAN...
THE CHINESE WAS AMERICA'S FIRST GENERATION TO COME OF AGE UNDER AN IMMIGRATION BAN.
Here at Angel Island, 105 questions are the interviews' average length...

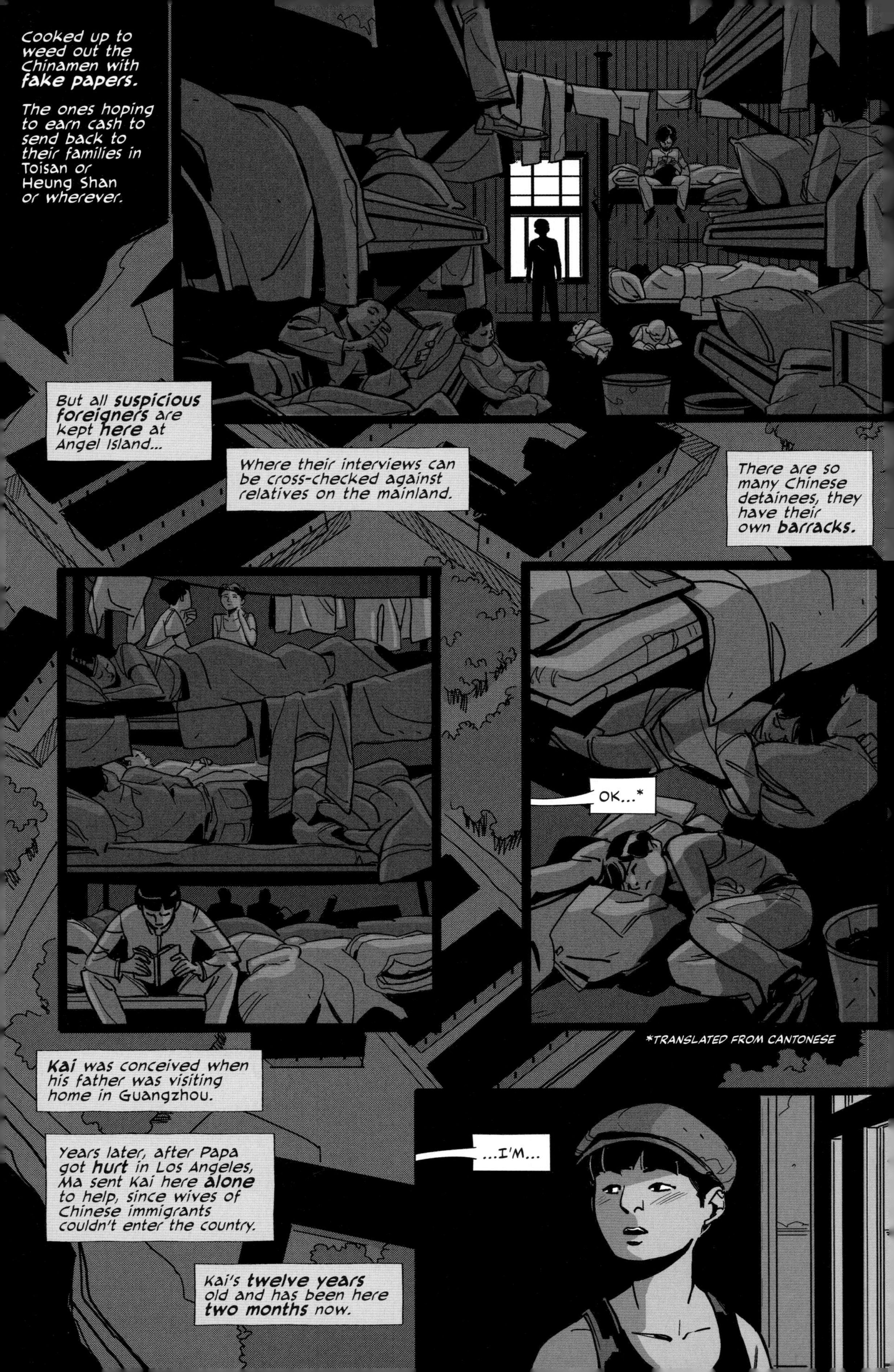
Cooked up to weed out the Chinamen with fake papers.
The ones hoping to earn cash to send back to their families in Toisan or Heung Shan or wherever.
But all suspicious foreigners are kept here at Angel Island...
Where their interviews can be cross-checked against relatives on the mainland.
There are so many Chinese detainees, they have their own barracks.
OK...*
*TRANSLATED FROM CANTONESE
Kai was conceived when his father was visiting home in Guangzhou.
Years later, after Papa got hurt in Los Angeles, Ma sent Kai here alone to help, since wives of Chinese immigrants couldn't enter the country.
...I'M...
Kai's twelve years old and has been here two months now.

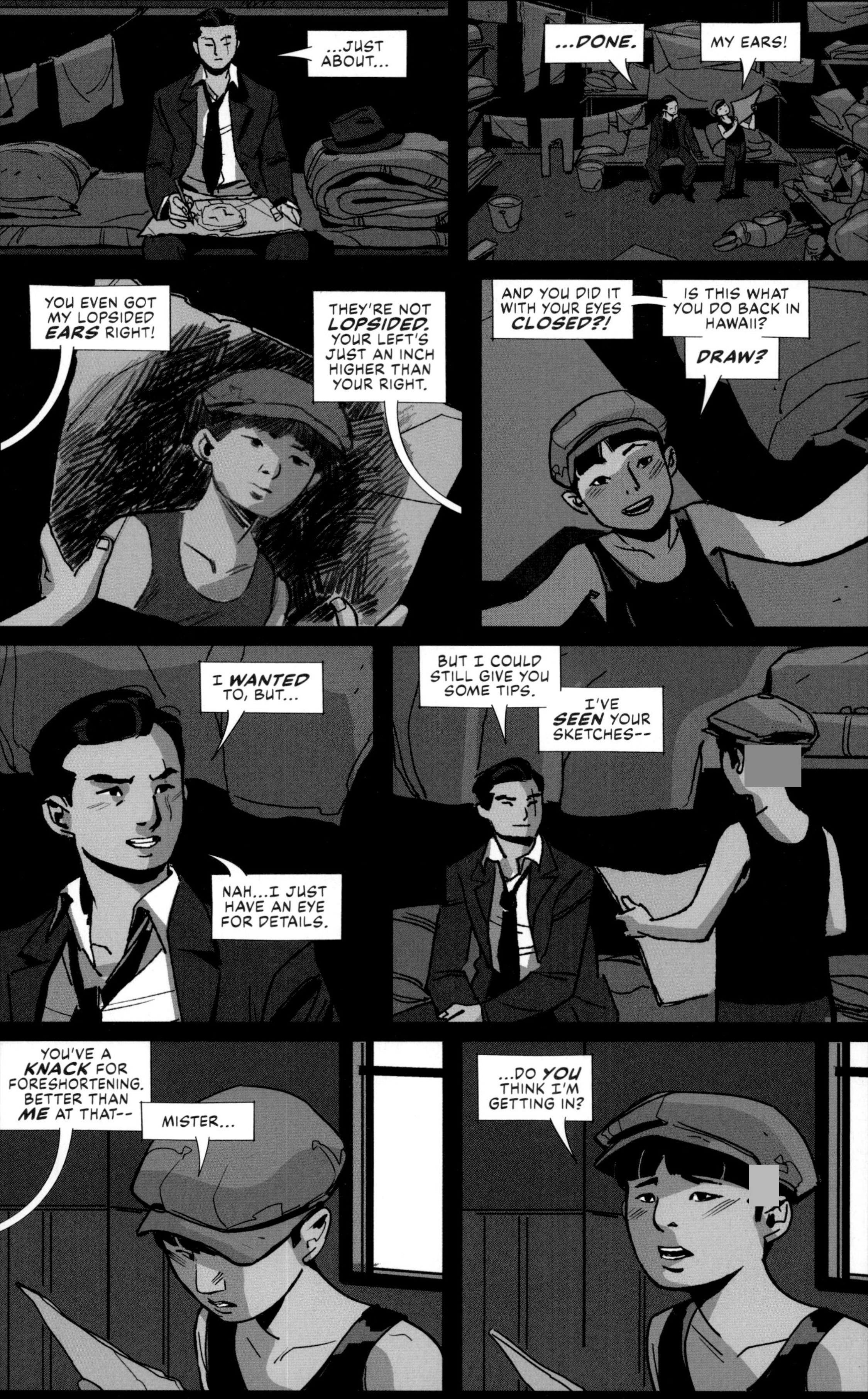
...JUST ABOUT...
...DONE.
MY EARS!
YOU EVEN GOT MY LOPSIDED EARS RIGHT!
THEY'RE NOT LOPSIDED. YOUR LEFT'S JUST AN INCH HIGHER THAN YOUR RIGHT.
AND YOU DID IT WITH YOUR EYES CLOSED?!
IS THIS WHAT YOU DO BACK IN HAWAII?
DRAW?
I WANTED TO, BUT...
NAH...I JUST HAVE AN EYE FOR DETAILS.
BUT I COULD STILL GIVE YOU SOME TIPS.
I'VE SEEN YOUR SKETCHES--
YOU'VE A KNACK FOR FORESHORTENING. BETTER THAN ME AT THAT--
MISTER...
...DO YOU THINK I'M GETTING IN?

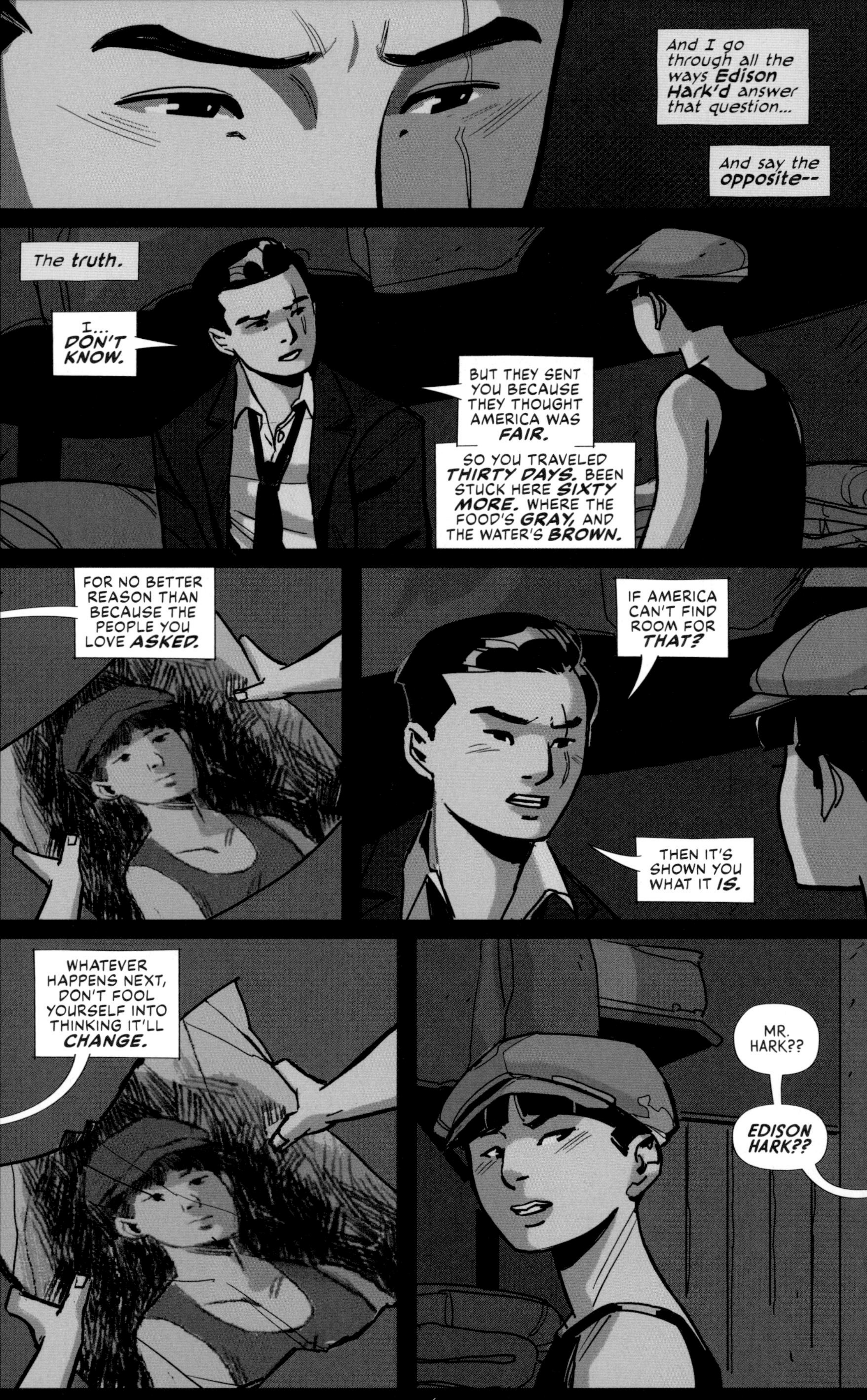

And I go through all the ways Edison Hark'd answer that question...
And say the opposite--
The truth.
I... DON'T KNOW.
BUT THEY SENT YOU BECAUSE THEY THOUGHT AMERICA WAS FAIR.
SO YOU TRAVELED THIRTY DAYS. BEEN STUCK HERE SIXTY MORE. WHERE THE FOOD'S GRAY, AND THE WATER'S BROWN.
FOR NO BETTER REASON THAN BECAUSE THE PEOPLE YOU LOVE ASKED.
IF AMERICA CAN'T FIND ROOM FOR THAT?
THEN IT'S SHOWN YOU WHAT IT IS.
WHATEVER HAPPENS NEXT, DON'T FOOL YOURSELF INTO THINKING IT'LL CHANGE.
MR. HARK??
EDISON HARK??

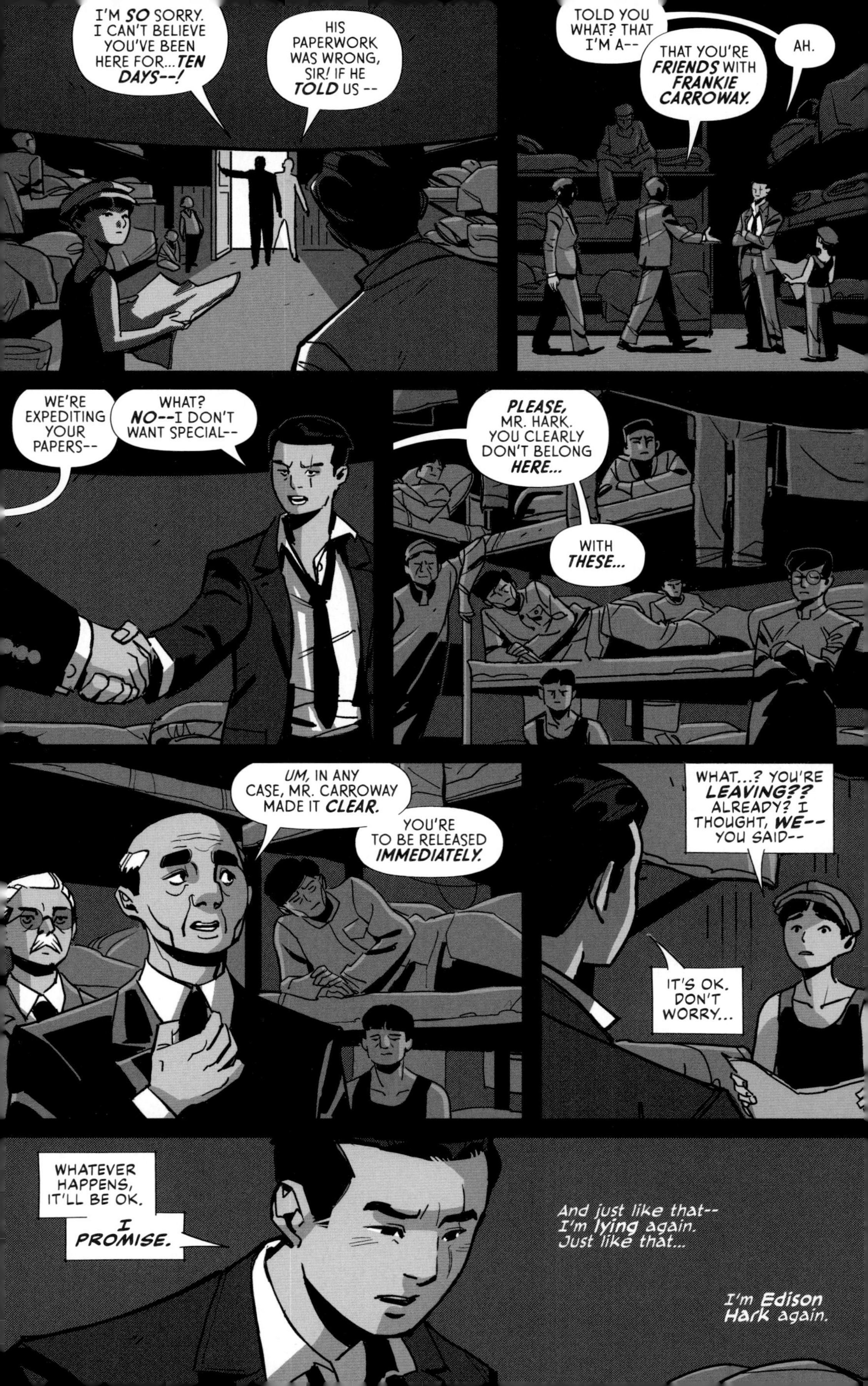
I'M SO SORRY. I CAN'T BELIEVE YOU'VE BEEN HERE FOR...TEN DAYS--!
HIS PAPERWORK WAS WRONG, SIR! IF HE TOLD US --
TOLD YOU WHAT? THAT I'M A--
THAT YOU'RE FRIENDS WITH FRANKIE CARROWAY.
AH.
WE'RE EXPEDITING YOUR PAPERS--
WHAT? NO--I DON'T WANT SPECIAL--
PLEASE, MR. HARK. YOU CLEARLY DON'T BELONG HERE...
WITH THESE...
UM, IN ANY CASE, MR. CARROWAY MADE IT CLEAR.
YOU'RE TO BE RELEASED IMMEDIATELY.
WHAT...? YOU'RE LEAVING?? ALREADY? I THOUGHT, WE-- YOU SAID--
IT'S OK. DON'T WORRY...
WHATEVER HAPPENS, IT'LL BE OK.
I PROMISE.
And just like that-- I'm lying again. Just like that...
I'm Edison Hark again.

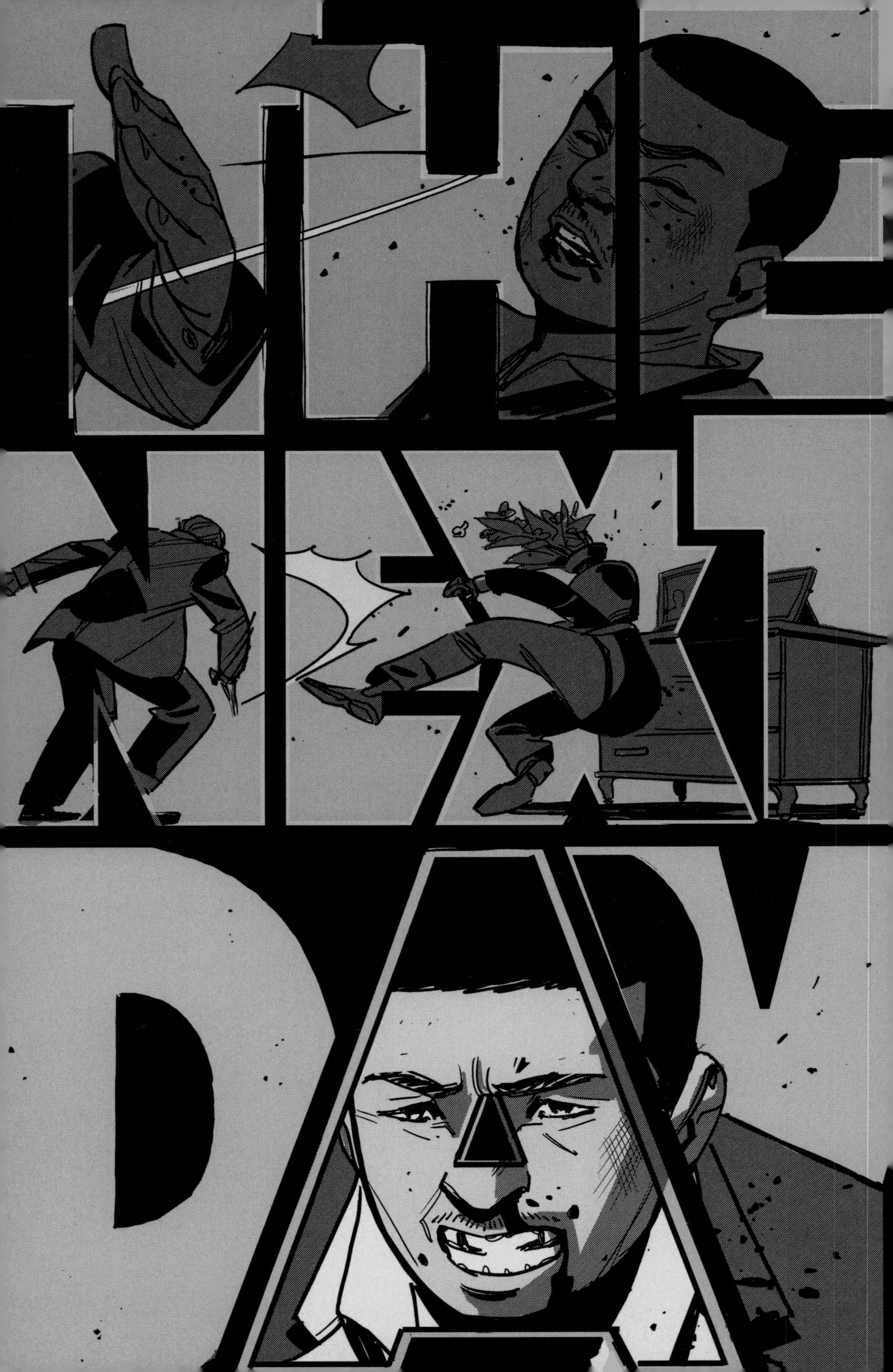
THE NEXT DAY

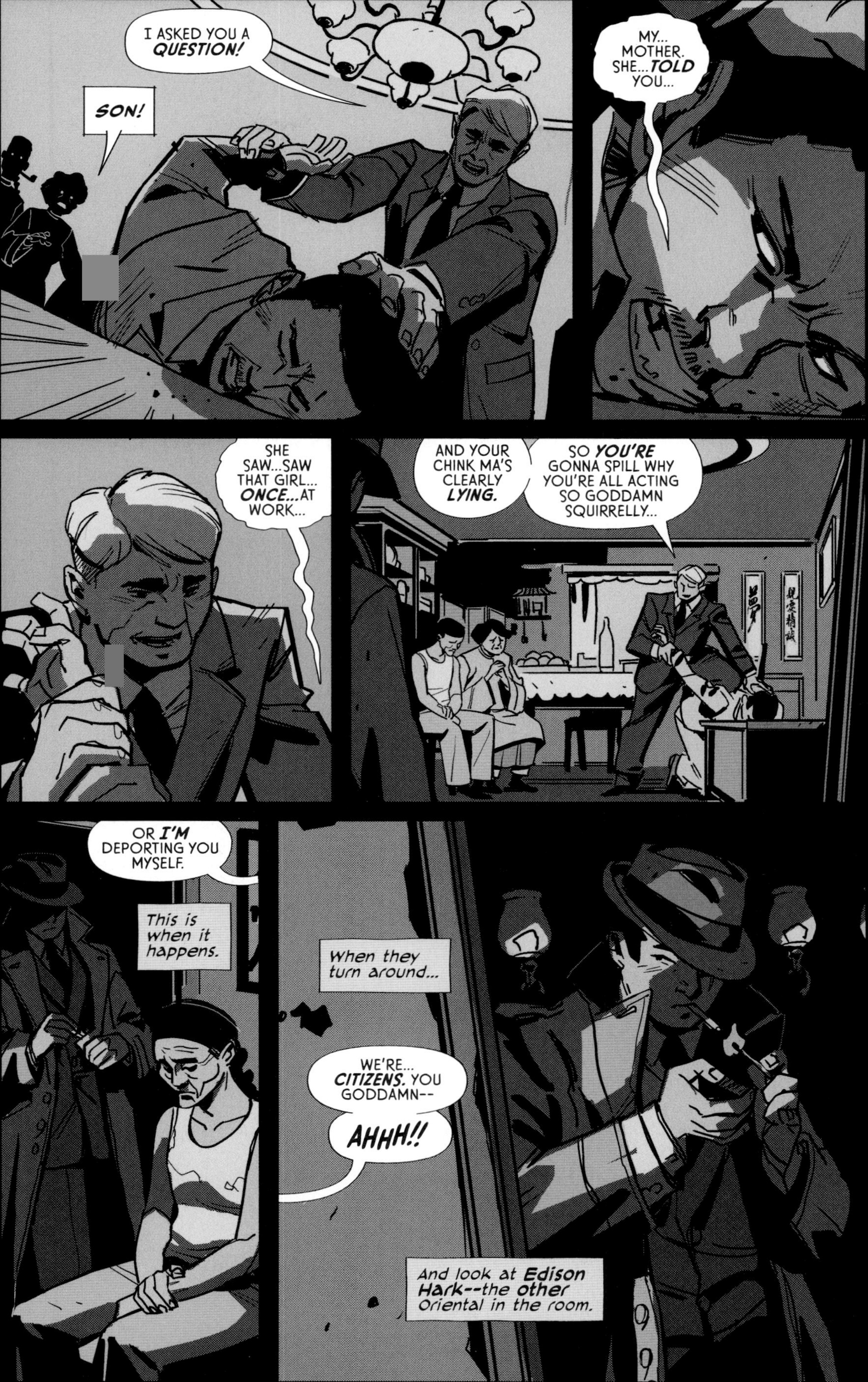
I ASKED YOU A QUESTION!
SON!
MY... MOTHER. SHE...TOLD YOU...
SHE SAW...SAW THAT GIRL... ONCE...AT WORK...
AND YOUR CHINK MA'S CLEARLY LYING.
SO YOU'RE GONNA SPILL WHY YOU'RE ALL ACTING SO GODDAMN SQUIRRELLY...
OR I'M DEPORTING YOU MYSELF.
This is when it happens.
When they turn around...
WE'RE... CITIZENS. YOU GODDAMN--
AHHH!!
And look at Edison Hark--the other Oriental in the room.

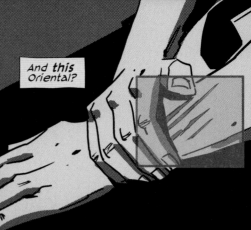

And *this* Oriental?

NAH, YOU'RE **COOLIES**.

SEE, MY BADGE MAKES ME *DETECTIVE O'MALLEY*.

AND IF *DETECTIVE O'MALLEY* DON'T SEE YOUR CITIZENSHIP CARDS?

SMK

YOUR CHINK KEISTER'S **GONE**.

SO AGAIN--

This Oriental's got an eye for **details**.

WHAT DO YOU KNOW 'BOUT A CHINK MAID NAMED *IVY CHEN*?

Which is how I know this family's in trouble...

If O'Malley finds what they're **really** hiding.

So I play the only play...

...PLEASE...

10

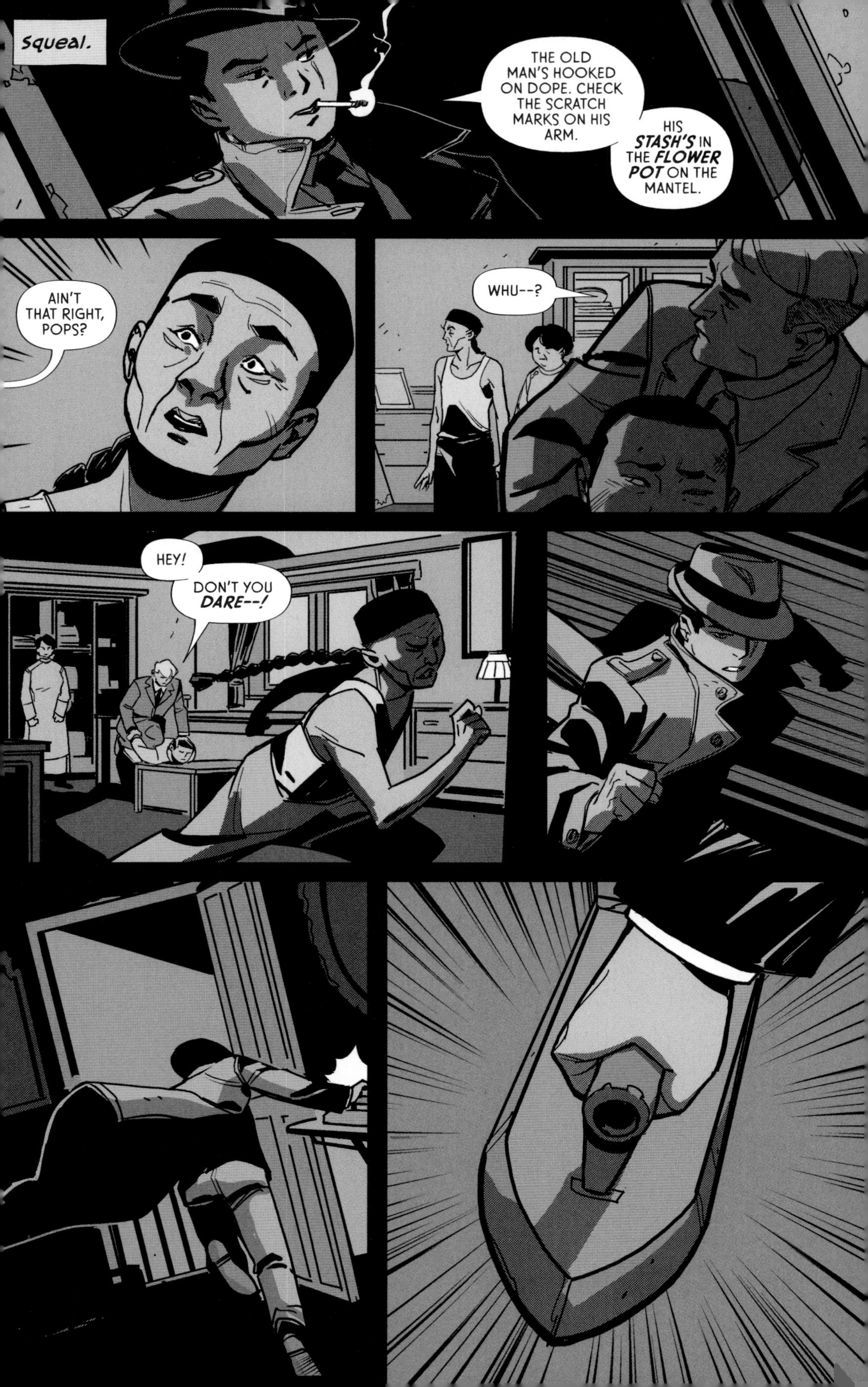
Squeal.
THE OLD MAN'S HOOKED ON DOPE. CHECK THE SCRATCH MARKS ON HIS ARM.
HIS **STASH'S** IN THE **FLOWER POT** ON THE MANTEL.
AIN'T THAT RIGHT, POPS?
WHU--?
HEY!
DON'T YOU **DARE--!**

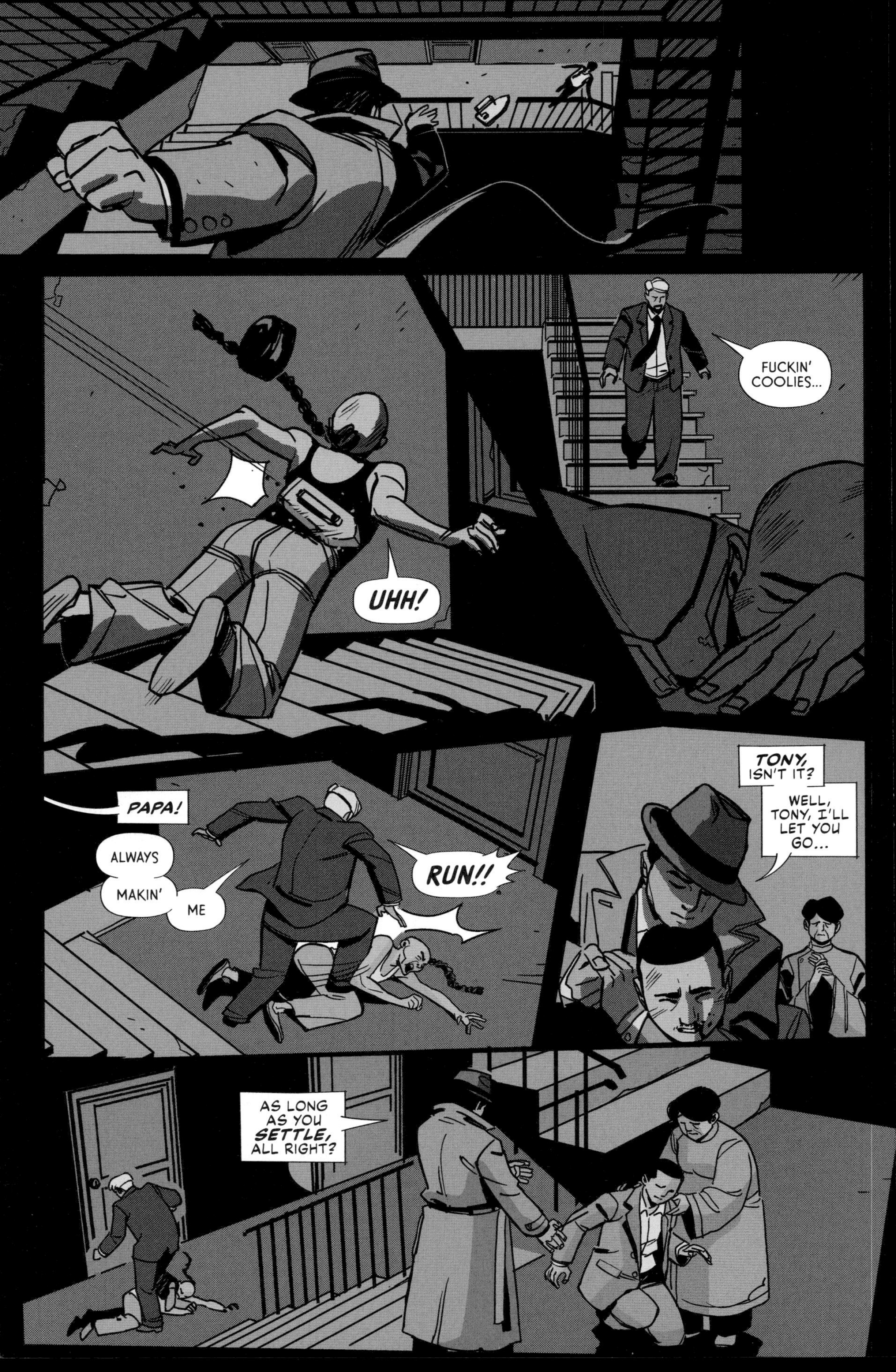
FUCKIN' COOLIES...
UHH!
PAPA!
ALWAYS
MAKIN'
ME
RUN!!
TONY, ISN'T IT?
WELL, TONY, I'LL LET YOU GO...
AS LONG AS YOU SETTLE, ALL RIGHT?

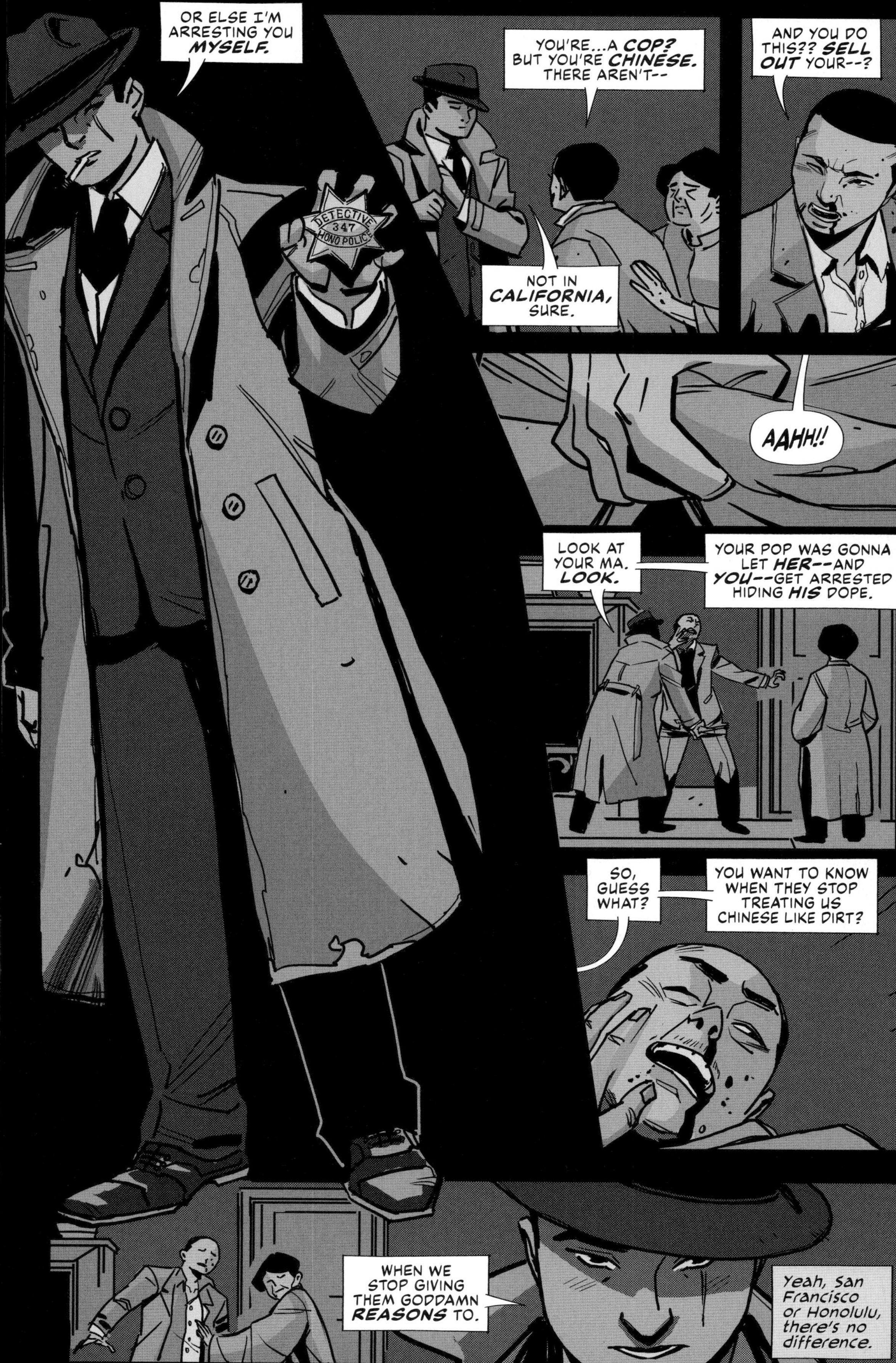
OR ELSE I'M ARRESTING YOU MYSELF.
DETECTIVE 347 HONO POLICE
YOU'RE...A COP? BUT YOU'RE CHINESE. THERE AREN'T--
NOT IN CALIFORNIA, SURE.
AND YOU DO THIS?? SELL OUT YOUR--?
AAHH!!
LOOK AT YOUR MA. LOOK.
YOUR POP WAS GONNA LET HER--AND YOU--GET ARRESTED HIDING HIS DOPE.
SO, GUESS WHAT?
YOU WANT TO KNOW WHEN THEY STOP TREATING US CHINESE LIKE DIRT?
WHEN WE STOP GIVING THEM GODDAMN REASONS TO.
Yeah, San Francisco or Honolulu, there's no difference.

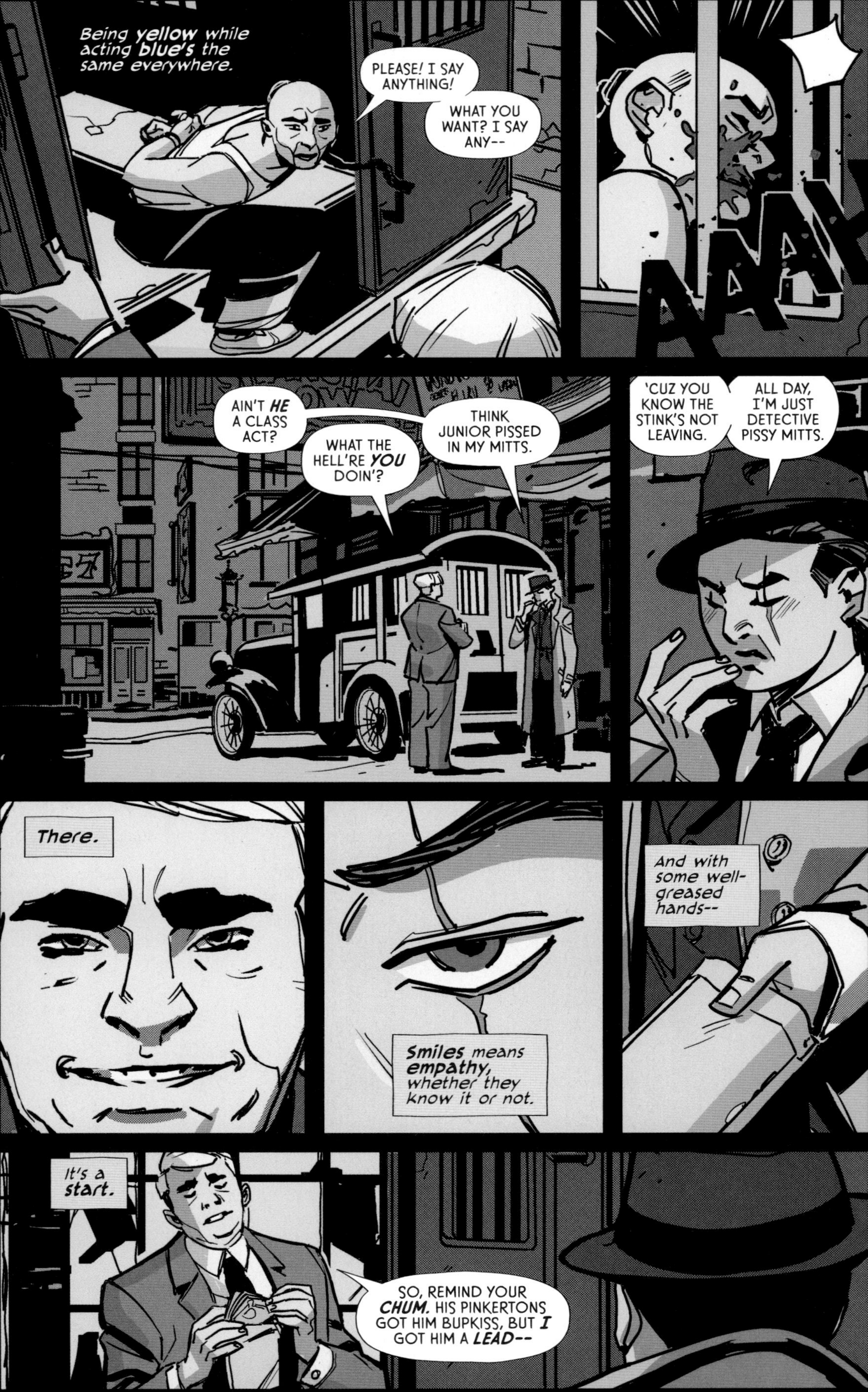
Being yellow while acting blue's the same everywhere.
PLEASE! I SAY ANYTHING!
WHAT YOU WANT? I SAY ANY--
AIN'T HE A CLASS ACT?
THINK JUNIOR PISSED IN MY MITTS.
WHAT THE HELL'RE YOU DOIN'?
'CUZ YOU KNOW THE STINK'S NOT LEAVING.
ALL DAY, I'M JUST DETECTIVE PISSY MITTS.
There.
Smiles means empathy, whether they know it or not.
And with some well-greased hands--
It's a start.
SO, REMIND YOUR CHUM. HIS PINKERTONS GOT HIM BUPKISS, BUT I GOT HIM A LEAD--

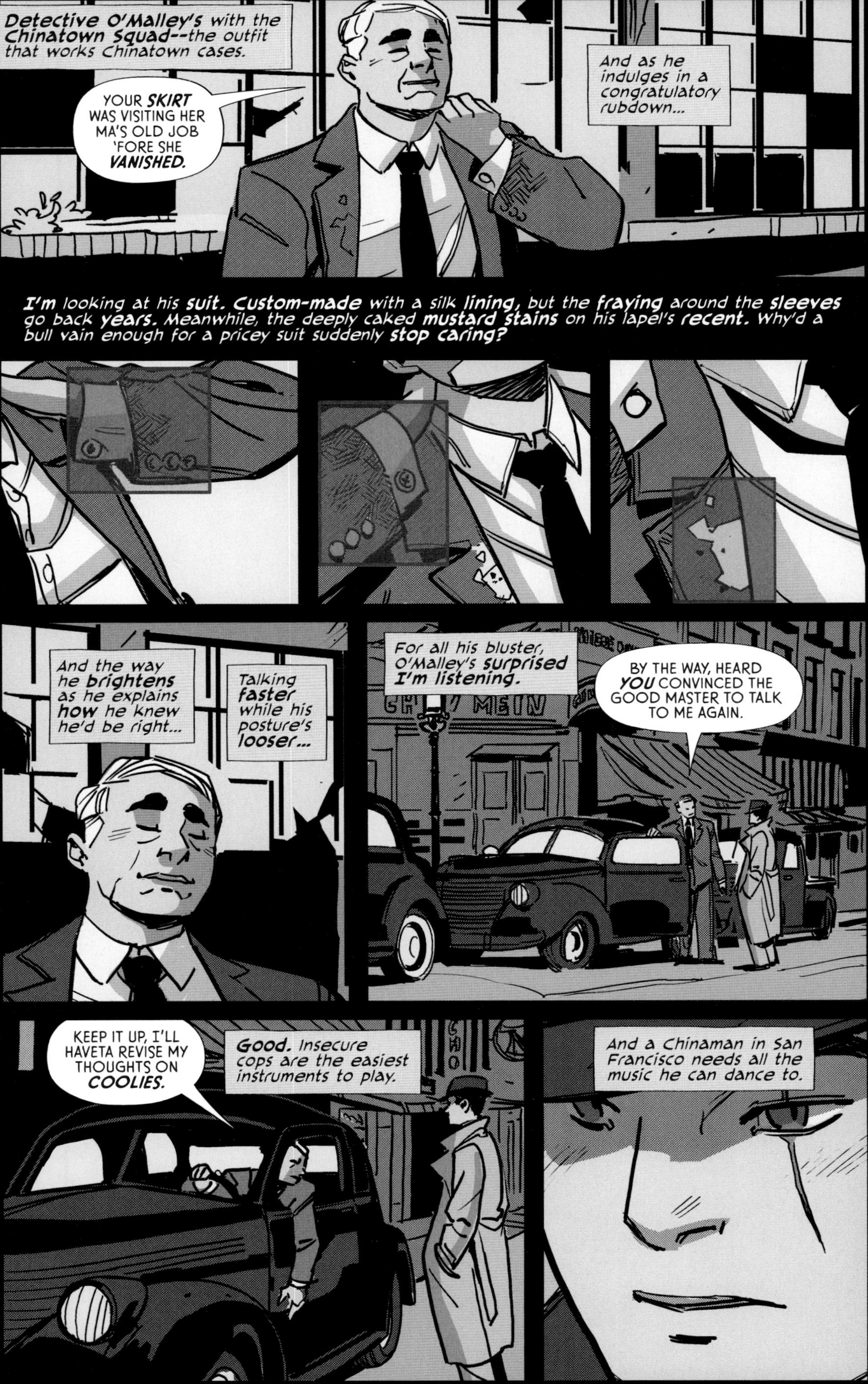

Detective O'Malley's with the Chinatown Squad--the outfit that works Chinatown cases.
YOUR SKIRT WAS VISITING HER MA'S OLD JOB 'FORE SHE VANISHED.
And as he indulges in a congratulatory rubdown...
I'm looking at his suit. Custom-made with a silk lining, but the fraying around the sleeves go back years. Meanwhile, the deeply caked mustard stains on his lapel's recent. Why'd a bull vain enough for a pricey suit suddenly stop caring?
And the way he brightens as he explains how he knew he'd be right...
Talking faster while his posture's looser...
For all his bluster, O'Malley's surprised I'm listening.
BY THE WAY, HEARD YOU CONVINCED THE GOOD MASTER TO TALK TO ME AGAIN.
KEEP IT UP, I'LL HAVETA REVISE MY THOUGHTS ON COOLIES.
Good. Insecure cops are the easiest instruments to play.
And a Chinaman in San Francisco needs all the music he can dance to.

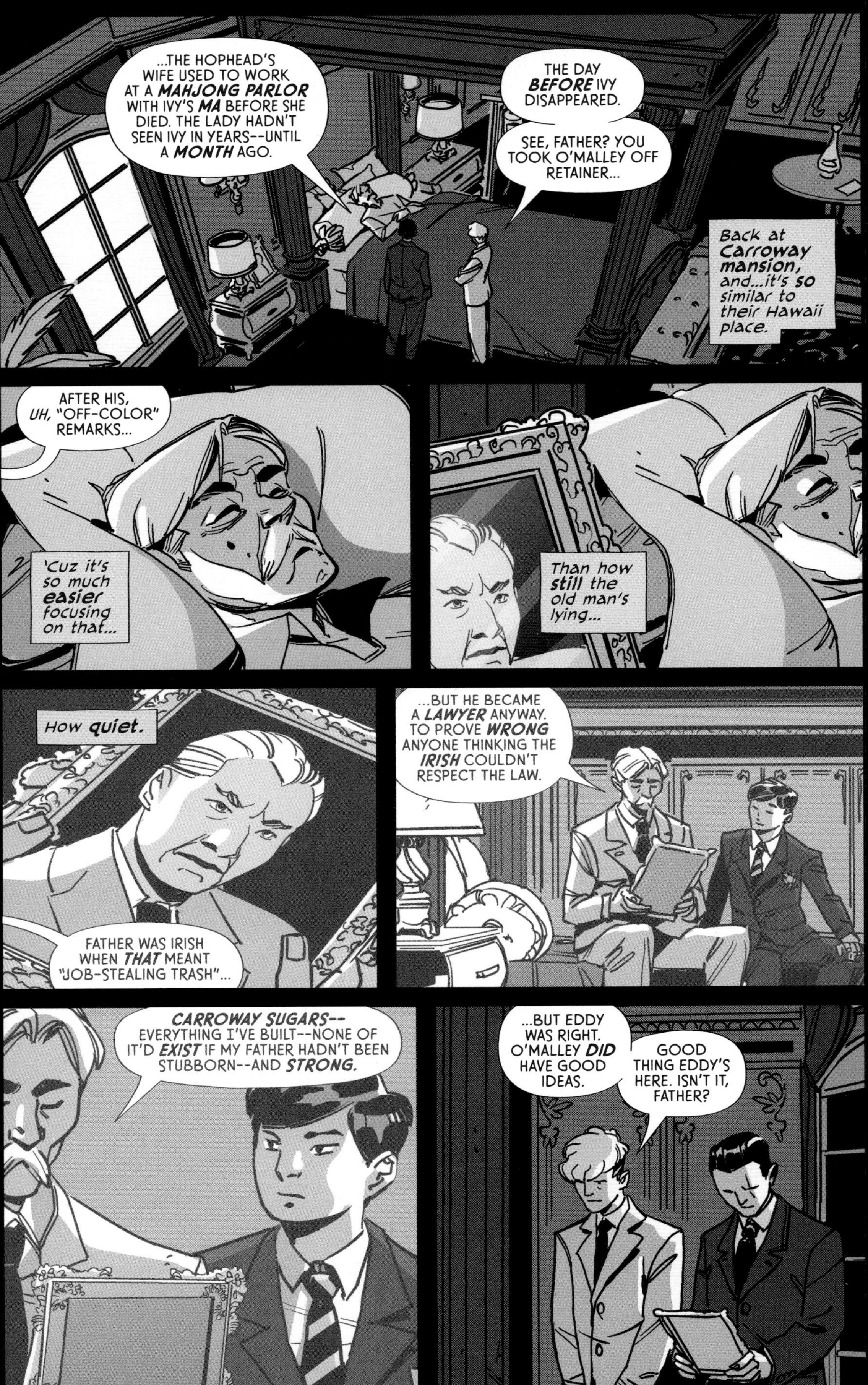
...THE HOPHEAD'S WIFE USED TO WORK AT A MAHJONG PARLOR WITH IVY'S MA BEFORE SHE DIED. THE LADY HADN'T SEEN IVY IN YEARS--UNTIL A MONTH AGO.
THE DAY BEFORE IVY DISAPPEARED.
SEE, FATHER? YOU TOOK O'MALLEY OFF RETAINER...
Back at Carroway mansion, and...it's so similar to their Hawaii place.
AFTER HIS, UH, "OFF-COLOR" REMARKS...
'Cuz it's so much easier focusing on that...
Than how still the old man's lying...
How quiet.
FATHER WAS IRISH WHEN THAT MEANT "JOB-STEALING TRASH"...
...BUT HE BECAME A LAWYER ANYWAY. TO PROVE WRONG ANYONE THINKING THE IRISH COULDN'T RESPECT THE LAW.
CARROWAY SUGARS-- EVERYTHING I'VE BUILT--NONE OF IT'D EXIST IF MY FATHER HADN'T BEEN STUBBORN--AND STRONG.
...BUT EDDY WAS RIGHT. O'MALLEY DID HAVE GOOD IDEAS.
GOOD THING EDDY'S HERE. ISN'T IT, FATHER?

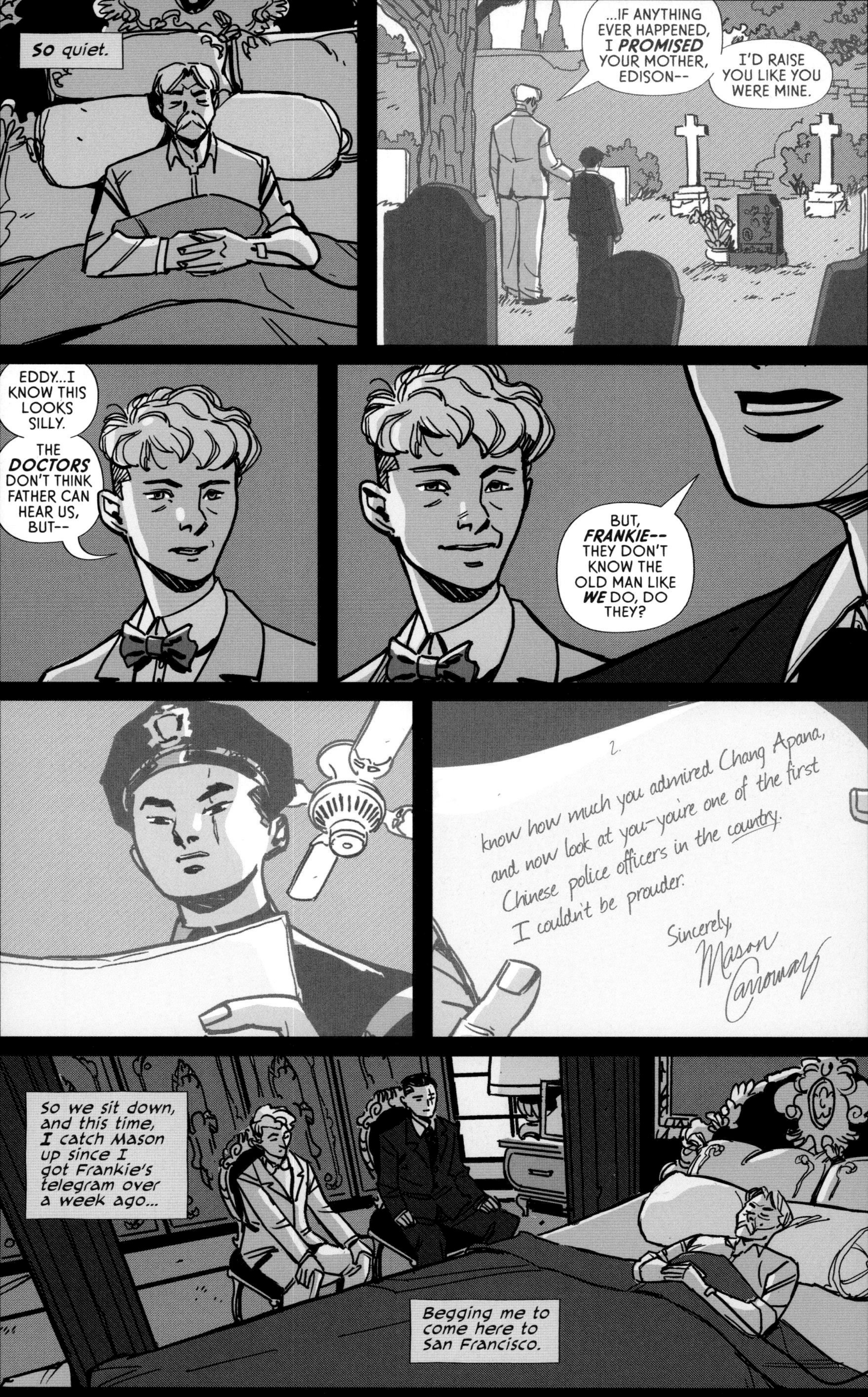
So quiet.
...IF ANYTHING EVER HAPPENED, I PROMISED YOUR MOTHER, EDISON--
I'D RAISE YOU LIKE YOU WERE MINE.
EDDY...I KNOW THIS LOOKS SILLY.
THE DOCTORS DON'T THINK FATHER CAN HEAR US, BUT--
BUT, FRANKIE-- THEY DON'T KNOW THE OLD MAN LIKE WE DO, DO THEY?
2.
know how much you admired Chang Apana, and now look at you-you're one of the first Chinese police officers in the country. I couldn't be prouder.
Sincerely,
Mason Carroway
So we sit down, and this time, I catch Mason up since I got Frankie's telegram over a week ago...
Begging me to come here to San Francisco.

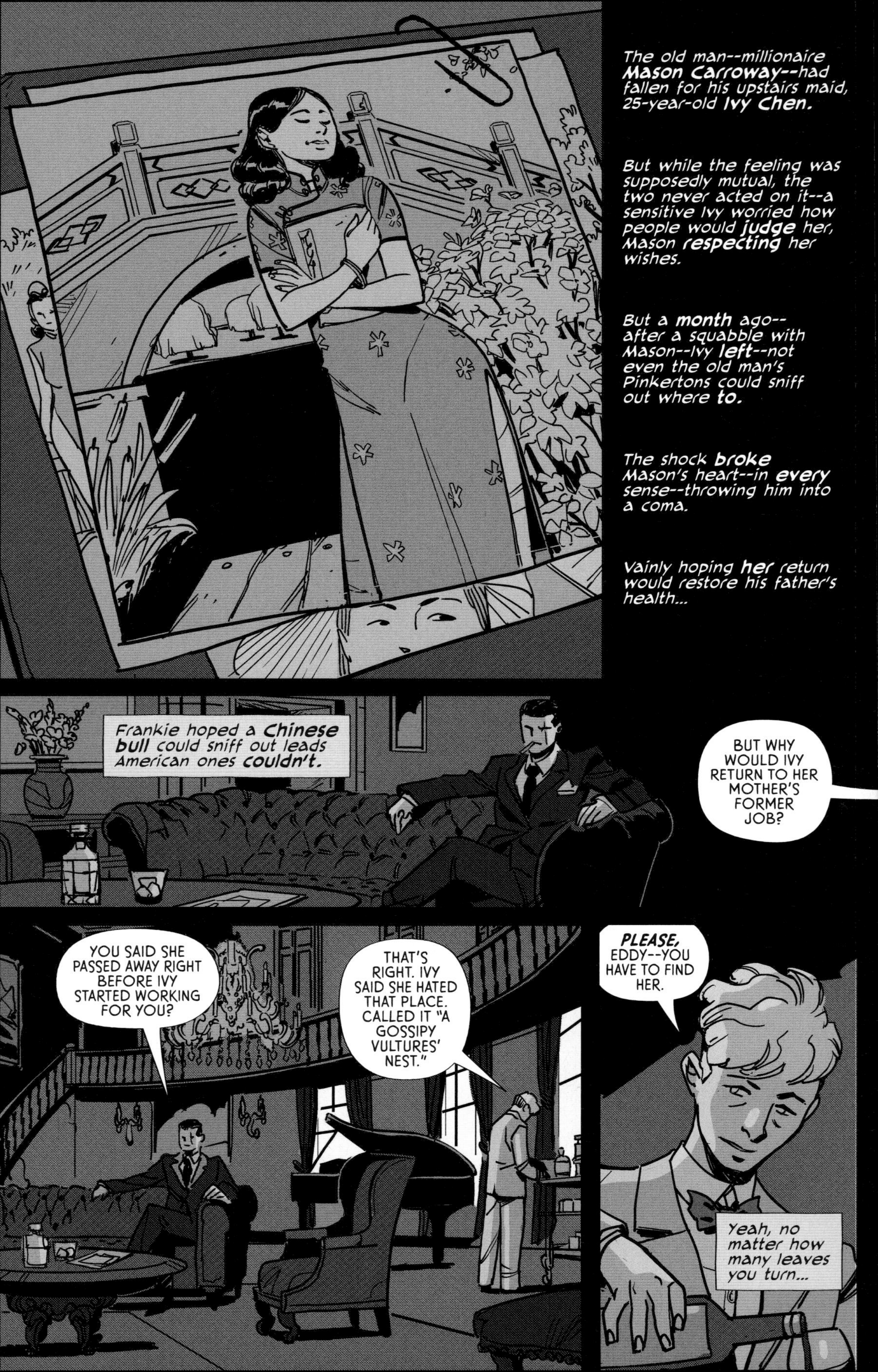
The old man--millionaire Mason Carroway--had fallen for his upstairs maid, 25-year-old Ivy Chen.
But while the feeling was supposedly mutual, the two never acted on it--a sensitive Ivy worried how people would judge her, Mason respecting her wishes.
But a month ago--after a squabble with Mason--Ivy left--not even the old man's Pinkertons could sniff out where to.
The shock broke Mason's heart--in every sense--throwing him into a coma.
Vainly hoping her return would restore his father's health...
Frankie hoped a Chinese bull could sniff out leads American ones couldn't.
BUT WHY WOULD IVY RETURN TO HER MOTHER'S FORMER JOB?
YOU SAID SHE PASSED AWAY RIGHT BEFORE IVY STARTED WORKING FOR YOU?
THAT'S RIGHT. IVY SAID SHE HATED THAT PLACE. CALLED IT "A GOSSIPY VULTURES' NEST."
PLEASE, EDDY--YOU HAVE TO FIND HER.
Yeah, no matter how many leaves you turn...

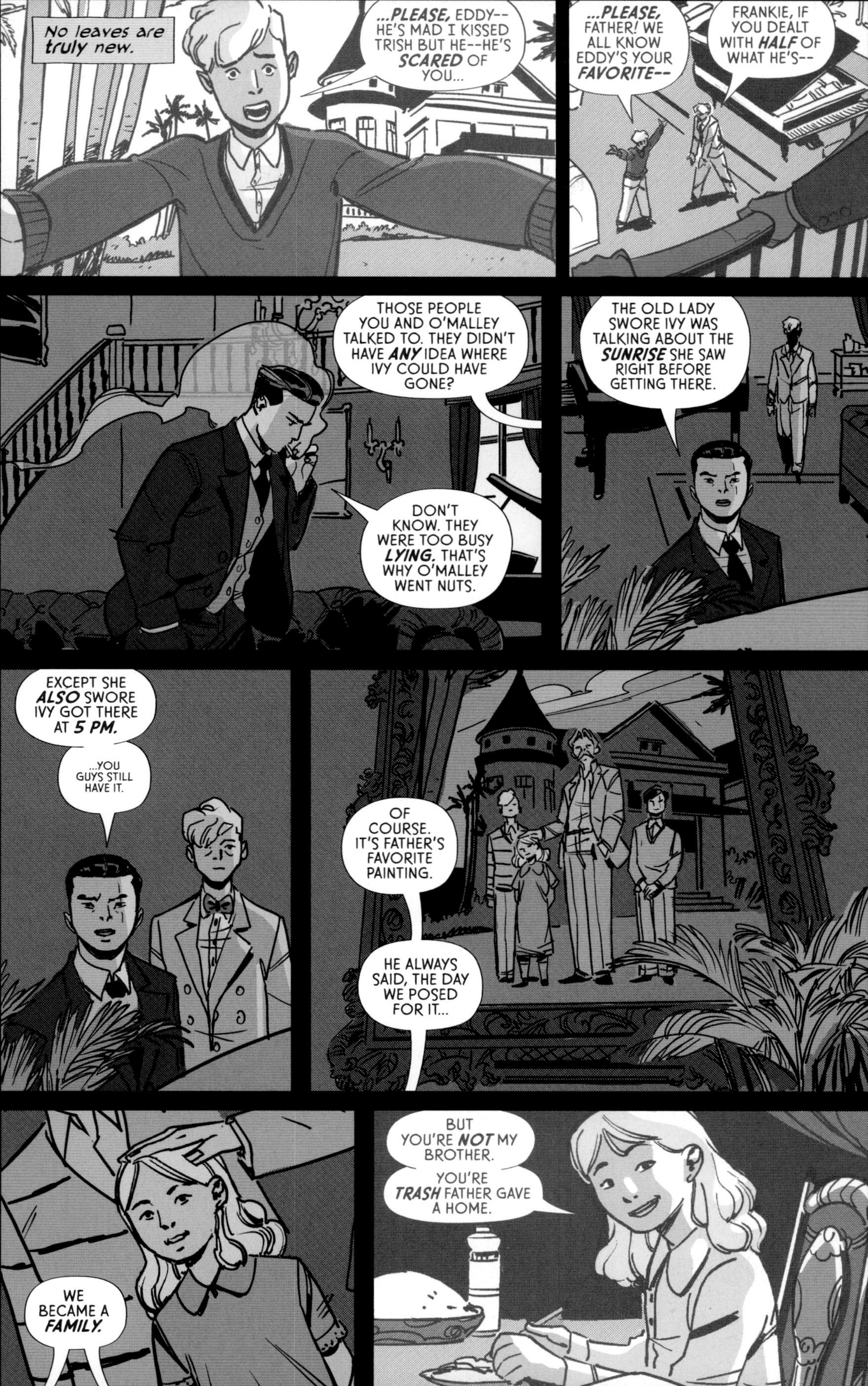
No leaves are truly new.
...PLEASE, EDDY--HE'S MAD I KISSED TRISH BUT HE--HE'S SCARED OF YOU...
...PLEASE, FATHER! WE ALL KNOW EDDY'S YOUR FAVORITE--
FRANKIE, IF YOU DEALT WITH HALF OF WHAT HE'S--
THOSE PEOPLE YOU AND O'MALLEY TALKED TO. THEY DIDN'T HAVE ANY IDEA WHERE IVY COULD HAVE GONE?
DON'T KNOW. THEY WERE TOO BUSY LYING. THAT'S WHY O'MALLEY WENT NUTS.
THE OLD LADY SWORE IVY WAS TALKING ABOUT THE SUNRISE SHE SAW RIGHT BEFORE GETTING THERE.
EXCEPT SHE ALSO SWORE IVY GOT THERE AT 5 PM.
...YOU GUYS STILL HAVE IT.
OF COURSE. IT'S FATHER'S FAVORITE PAINTING.
HE ALWAYS SAID, THE DAY WE POSED FOR IT...
WE BECAME A FAMILY.
BUT YOU'RE NOT MY BROTHER.
YOU'RE TRASH FATHER GAVE A HOME.

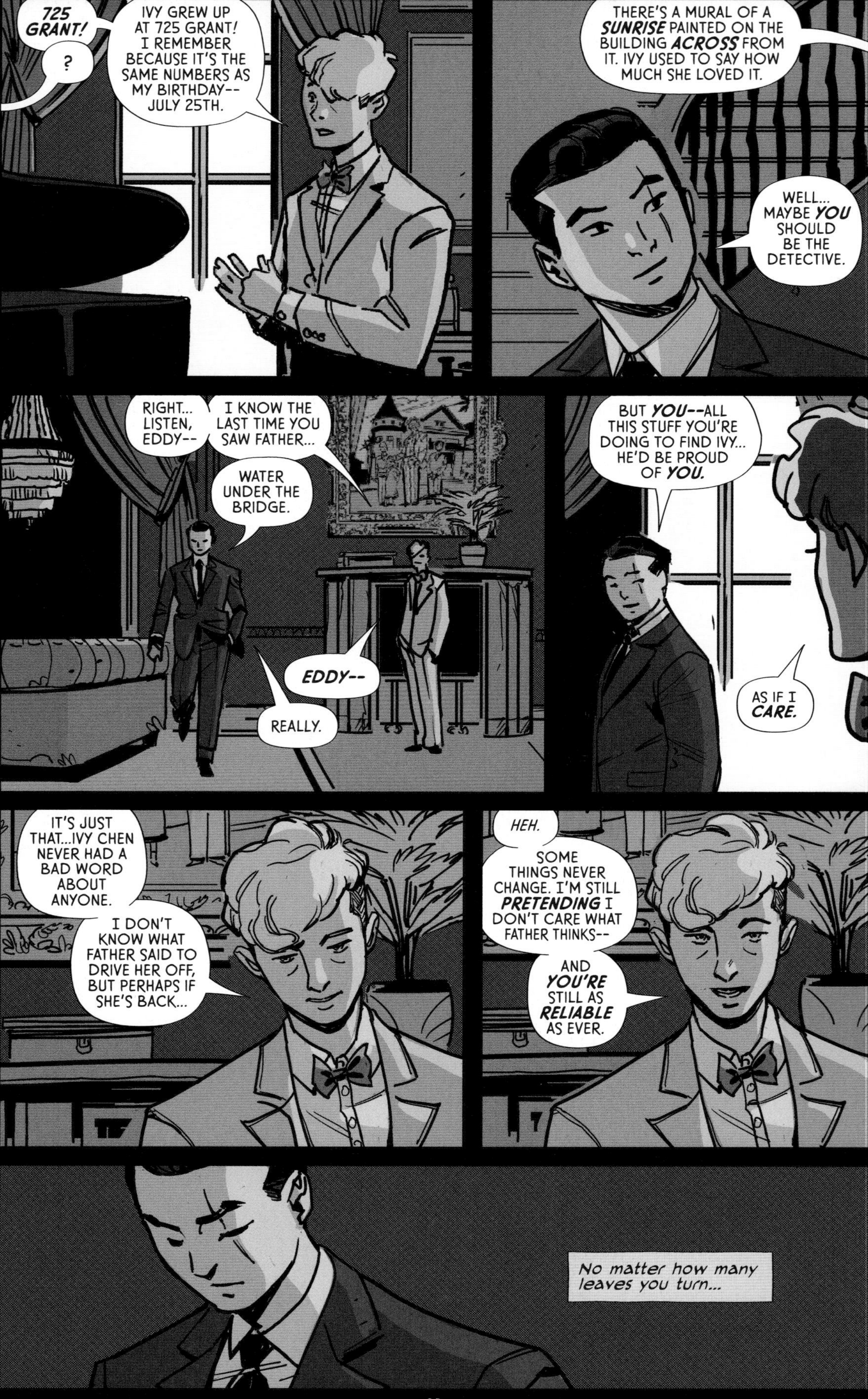

725 GRANT!
?
IVY GREW UP AT 725 GRANT! I REMEMBER BECAUSE IT'S THE SAME NUMBERS AS MY BIRTHDAY--JULY 25TH.
THERE'S A MURAL OF A SUNRISE PAINTED ON THE BUILDING ACROSS FROM IT. IVY USED TO SAY HOW MUCH SHE LOVED IT.
WELL... MAYBE YOU SHOULD BE THE DETECTIVE.
RIGHT... LISTEN, EDDY--
I KNOW THE LAST TIME YOU SAW FATHER...
WATER UNDER THE BRIDGE.
EDDY--
REALLY.
BUT YOU--ALL THIS STUFF YOU'RE DOING TO FIND IVY... HE'D BE PROUD OF YOU.
AS IF I CARE.
IT'S JUST THAT...IVY CHEN NEVER HAD A BAD WORD ABOUT ANYONE.
I DON'T KNOW WHAT FATHER SAID TO DRIVE HER OFF, BUT PERHAPS IF SHE'S BACK...
HEH.
SOME THINGS NEVER CHANGE. I'M STILL PRETENDING I DON'T CARE WHAT FATHER THINKS--
AND YOU'RE STILL AS RELIABLE AS EVER.
No matter how many leaves you turn...

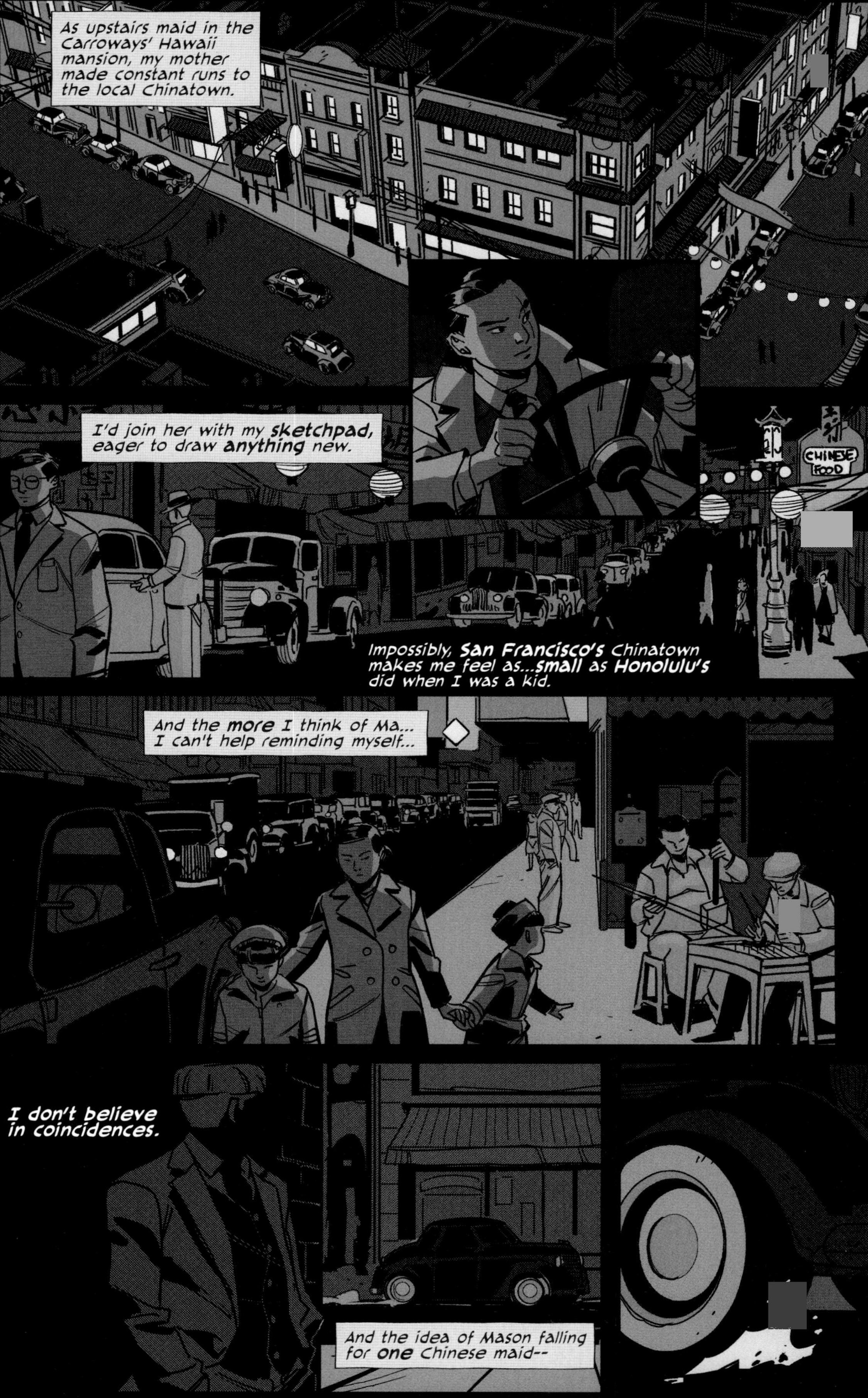
As upstairs maid in the Carroways' Hawaii mansion, my mother made constant runs to the local Chinatown.
I'd join her with my **sketchpad**, eager to draw **anything** new.
CHINESE FOOD
Impossibly, **San Francisco's** Chinatown makes me feel as...**small** as **Honolulu's** did when I was a kid.
And the **more** I think of Ma... I can't help reminding myself...
I don't believe in coincidences.
And the idea of Mason falling for **one** Chinese maid--

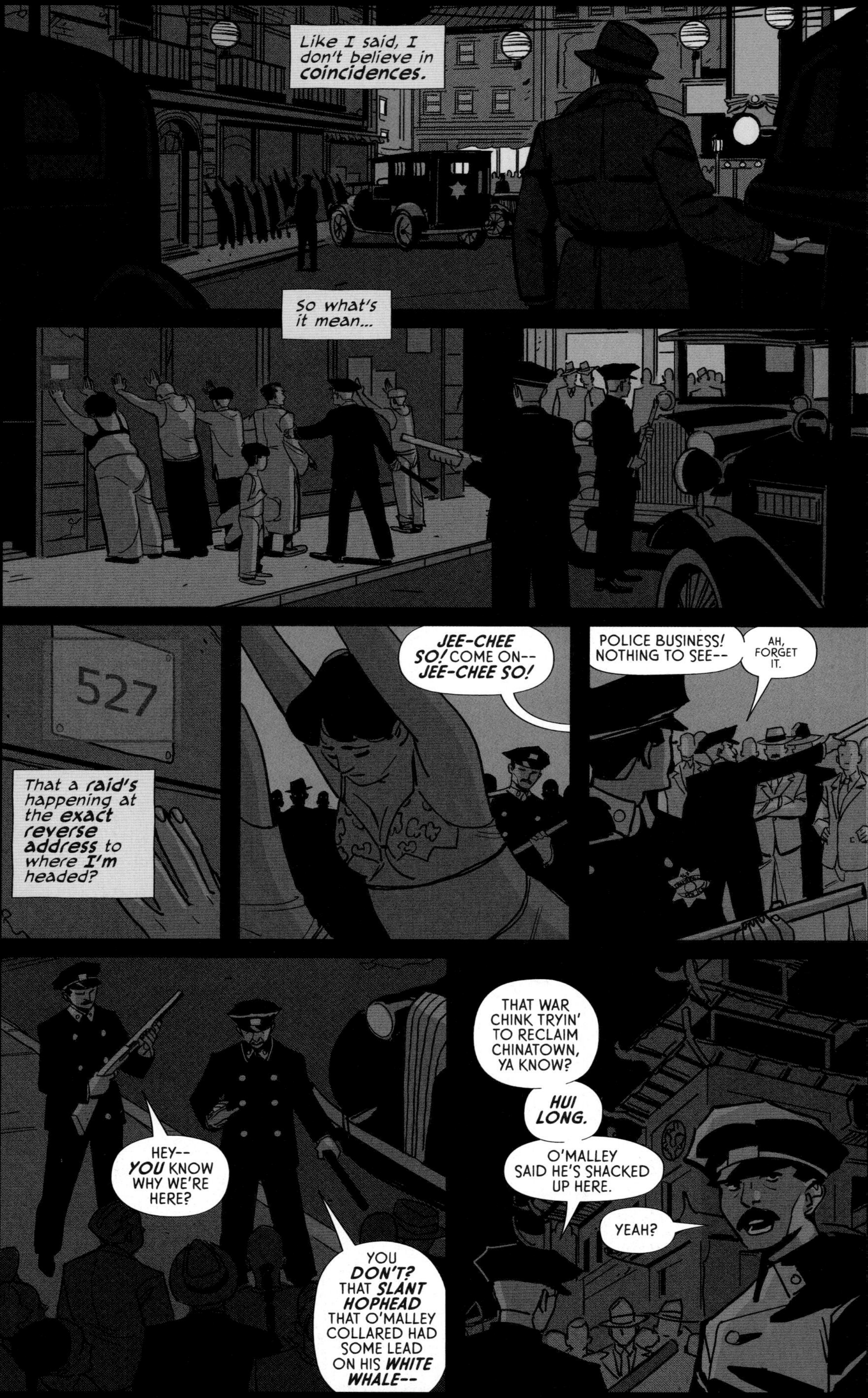

Like I said, I don't believe in coincidences.
So what's it mean...
527
That a raid's happening at the exact reverse address to where I'm headed?
JEE-CHEE SO! COME ON-- JEE-CHEE SO!
POLICE BUSINESS! NOTHING TO SEE--
AH, FORGET IT.
HEY-- YOU KNOW WHY WE'RE HERE?
YOU DON'T? THAT SLANT HOPHEAD THAT O'MALLEY COLLARED HAD SOME LEAD ON HIS WHITE WHALE--
THAT WAR CHINK TRYIN' TO RECLAIM CHINATOWN, YA KNOW?
HUI LONG.
O'MALLEY SAID HE'S SHACKED UP HERE.
YEAH?

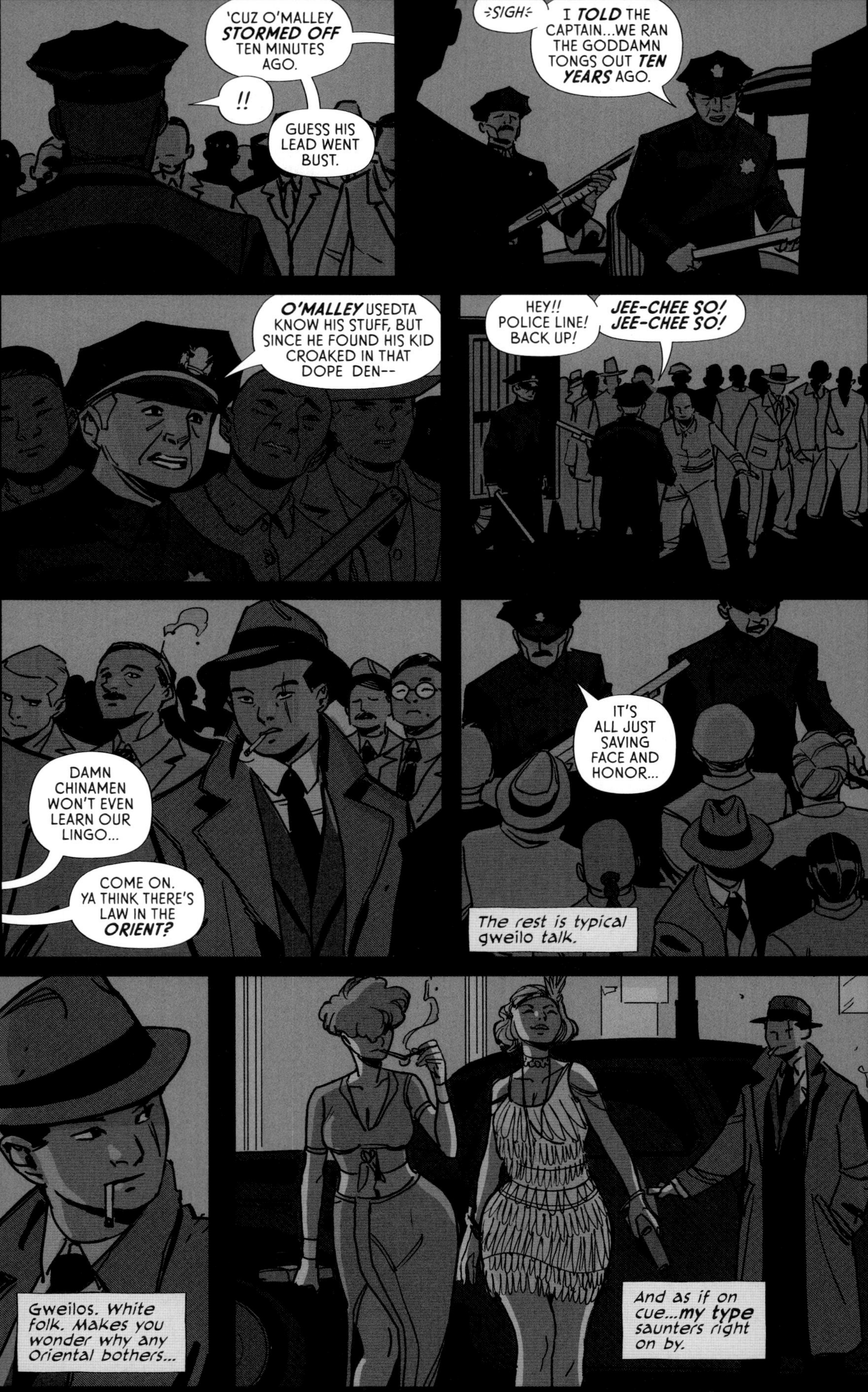

'CUZ O'MALLEY STORMED OFF TEN MINUTES AGO.
!!
GUESS HIS LEAD WENT BUST.
=SIGH=
I TOLD THE CAPTAIN...WE RAN THE GODDAMN TONGS OUT TEN YEARS AGO.
O'MALLEY USEDTA KNOW HIS STUFF, BUT SINCE HE FOUND HIS KID CROAKED IN THAT DOPE DEN--
HEY!! POLICE LINE! BACK UP!
JEE-CHEE SO! JEE-CHEE SO!
DAMN CHINAMEN WON'T EVEN LEARN OUR LINGO...
COME ON. YA THINK THERE'S LAW IN THE ORIENT?
IT'S ALL JUST SAVING FACE AND HONOR...
The rest is typical gweilo talk.
Gweilos. White folk. Makes you wonder why any Oriental bothers...
And as if on cue...my type saunters right on by.

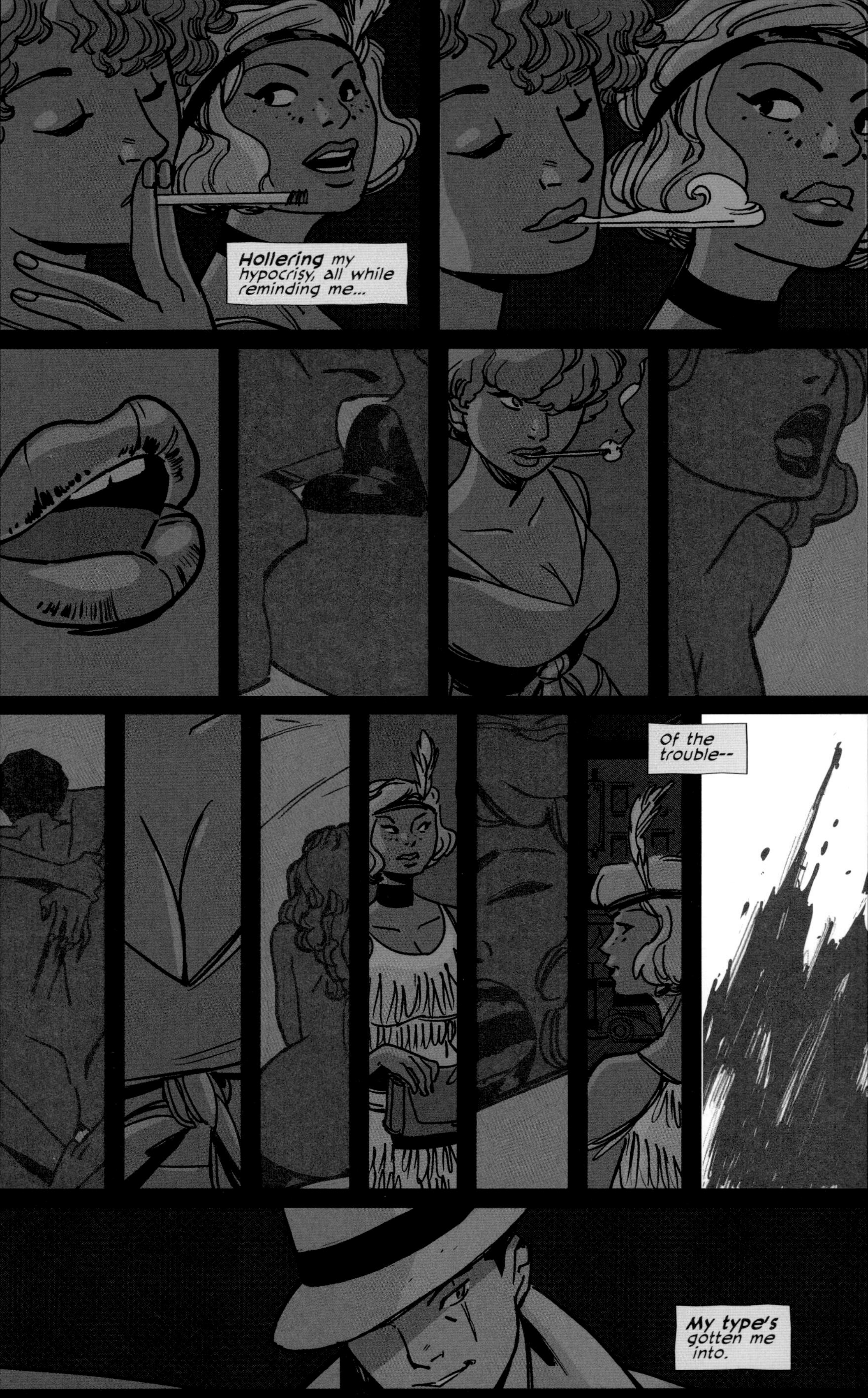
Hollering my hypocrisy, all while reminding me...
Of the trouble--
My type's gotten me into.

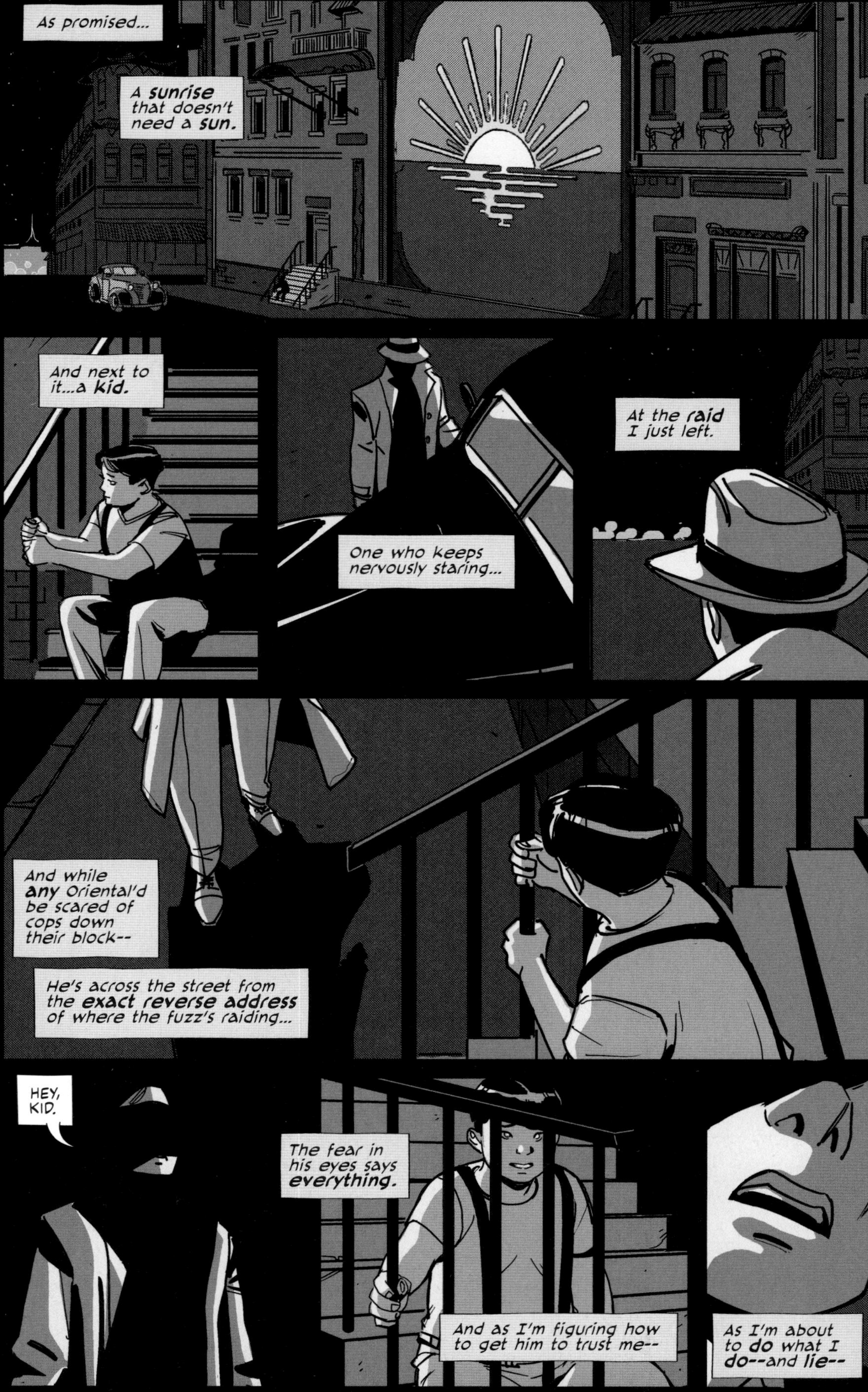
As promised...
A sunrise that doesn't need a sun.
And next to it...a kid.
One who keeps nervously staring...
At the raid I just left.
And while any Oriental'd be scared of cops down their block--
He's across the street from the exact reverse address of where the fuzz's raiding...
HEY, KID.
The fear in his eyes says everything.
And as I'm figuring how to get him to trust me--
As I'm about to do what I do--and lie--

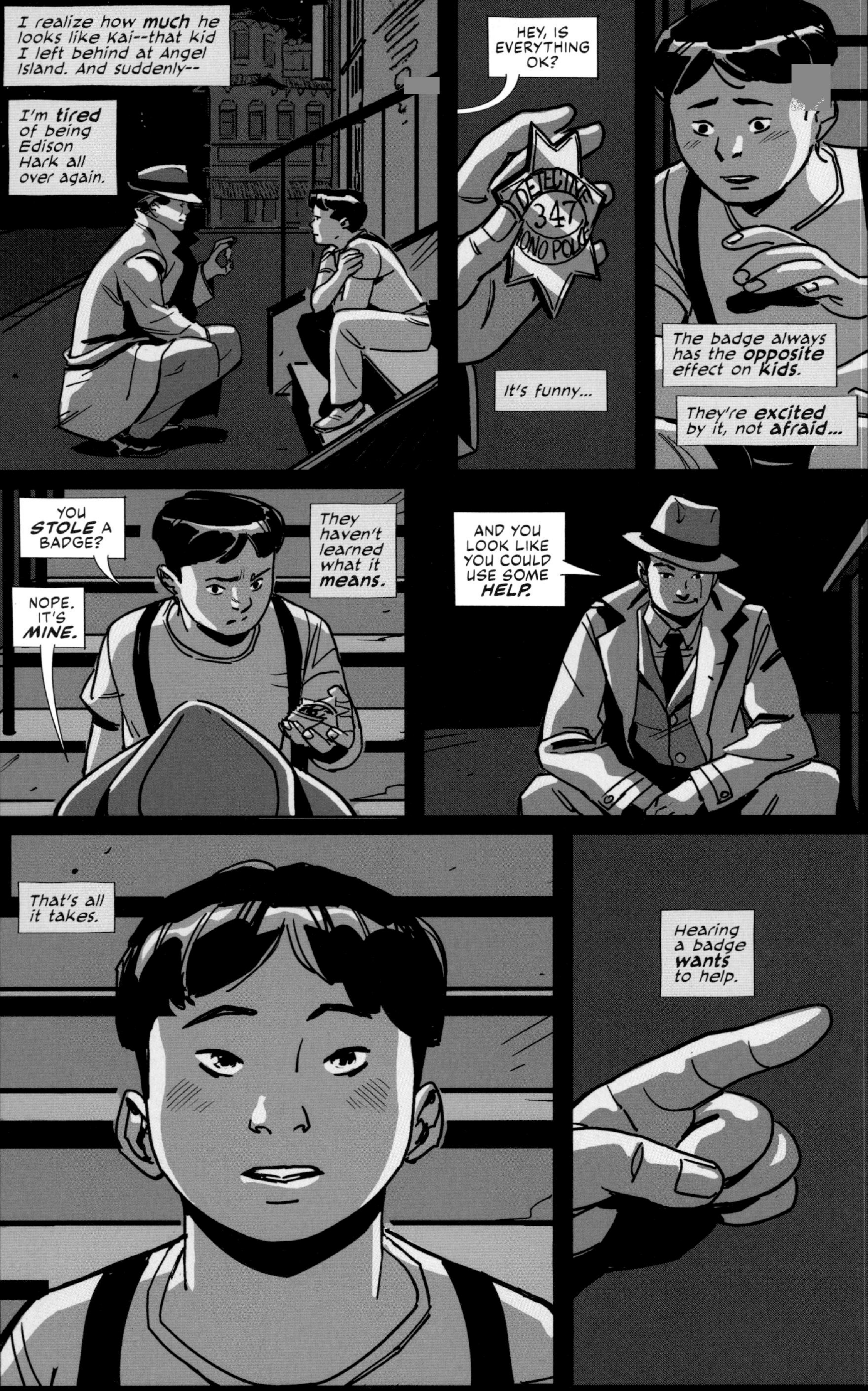
I realize how much he looks like Kai--that kid I left behind at Angel Island. And suddenly--
I'm tired of being Edison Hark all over again.
HEY, IS EVERYTHING OK?
DETECTIVE
347
It's funny...
The badge always has the opposite effect on kids.
They're excited by it, not afraid...
YOU STOLE A BADGE?
NOPE. IT'S MINE.
They haven't learned what it means.
AND YOU LOOK LIKE YOU COULD USE SOME HELP.
That's all it takes.
Hearing a badge wants to help.

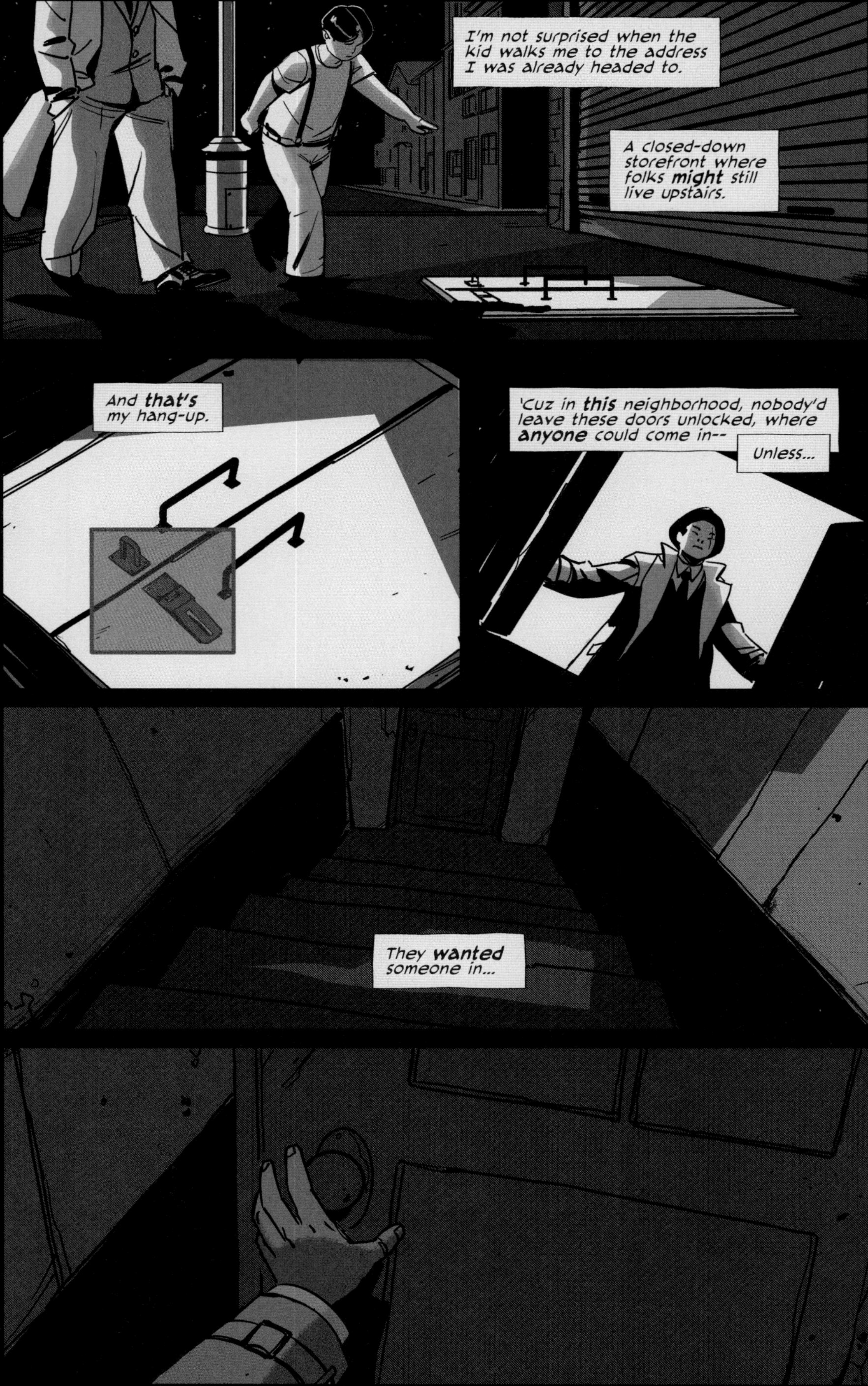
I'm not surprised when the kid walks me to the address I was already headed to.
A closed-down storefront where folks might still live upstairs.
And that's my hang-up.
'Cuz in this neighborhood, nobody'd leave these doors unlocked, where anyone could come in--
Unless...
They wanted someone in...

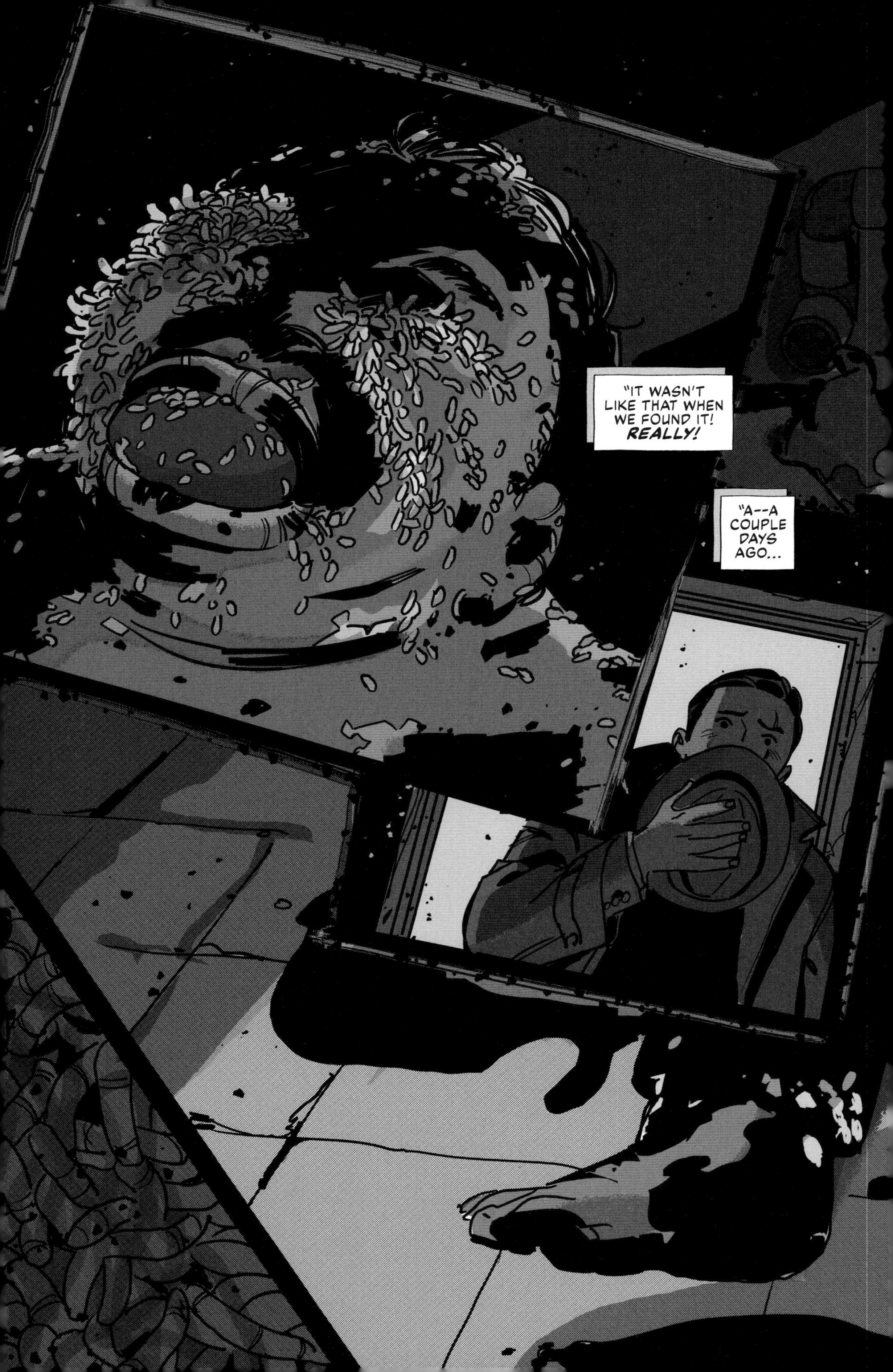
"IT WASN'T LIKE THAT WHEN WE FOUND IT! ***REALLY!***
"A--A COUPLE DAYS AGO...

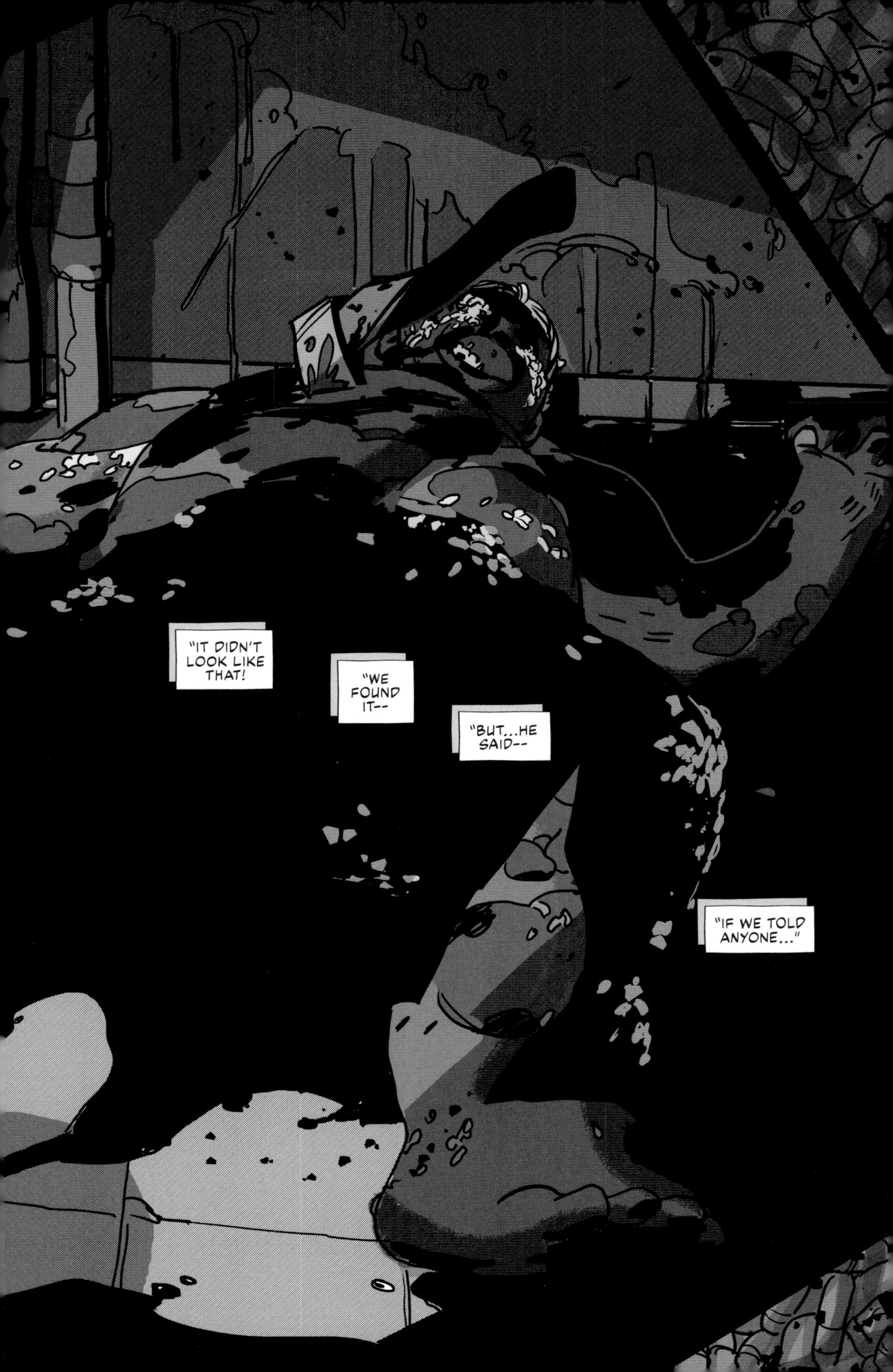
"IT DIDN'T LOOK LIKE THAT!
"WE FOUND IT--
"BUT...HE SAID--
"IF WE TOLD ANYONE..."

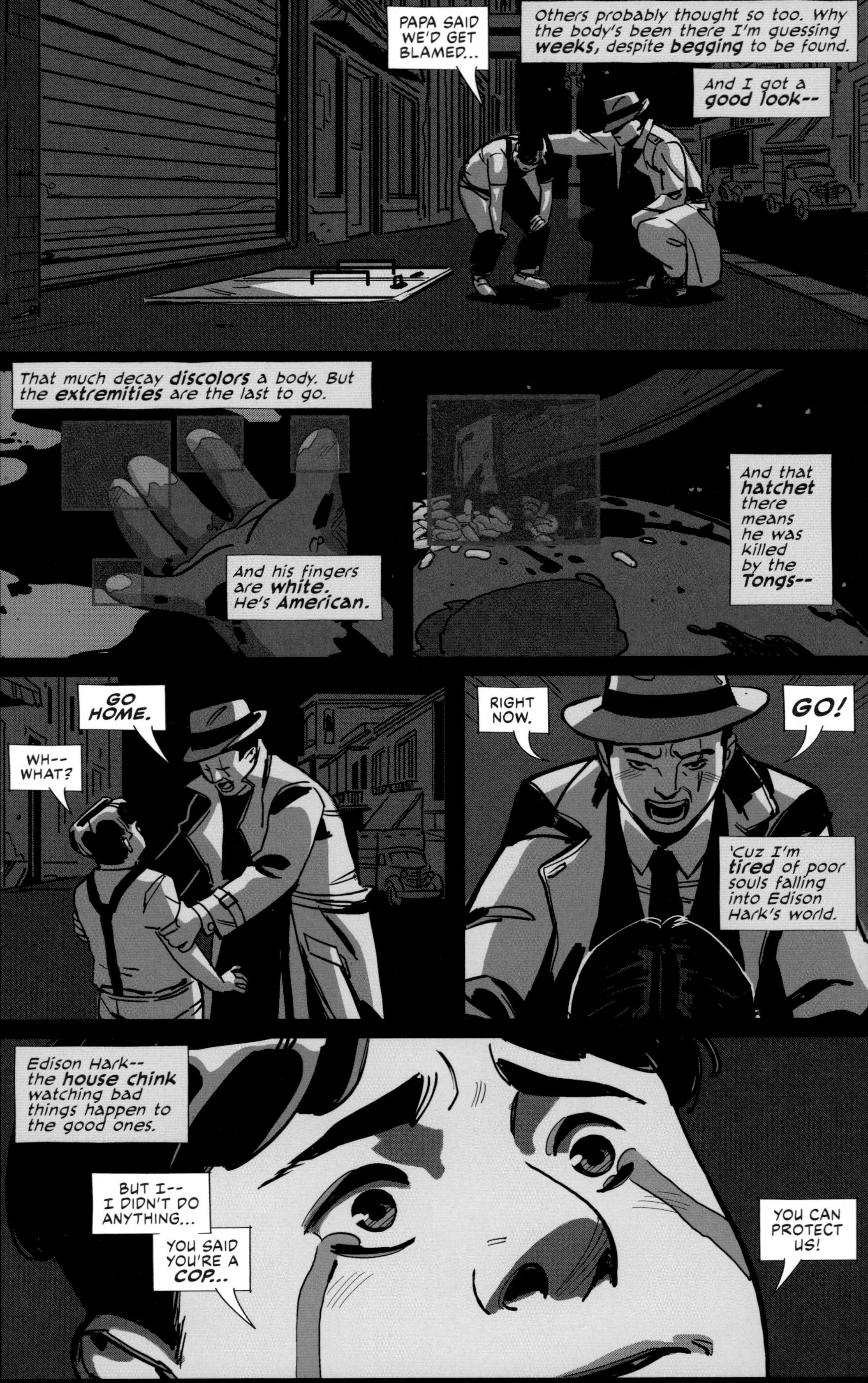

PAPA SAID WE'D GET BLAMED...
Others probably thought so too. Why the body's been there I'm guessing **weeks**, despite **begging** to be found.
And I got a **good look--**
That much decay **discolors** a body. But the **extremities** are the last to go.
And his fingers are **white.** He's **American.**
And that **hatchet** there means he was killed by the **Tongs--**
GO HOME.
WH-- WHAT?
RIGHT NOW.
GO!
'Cuz I'm **tired** of poor souls falling into Edison Hark's world.
Edison Hark-- the **house chink** watching bad things happen to the good ones.
BUT I-- I DIDN'T DO ANYTHING...
YOU SAID YOU'RE A COP...
YOU CAN PROTECT US!

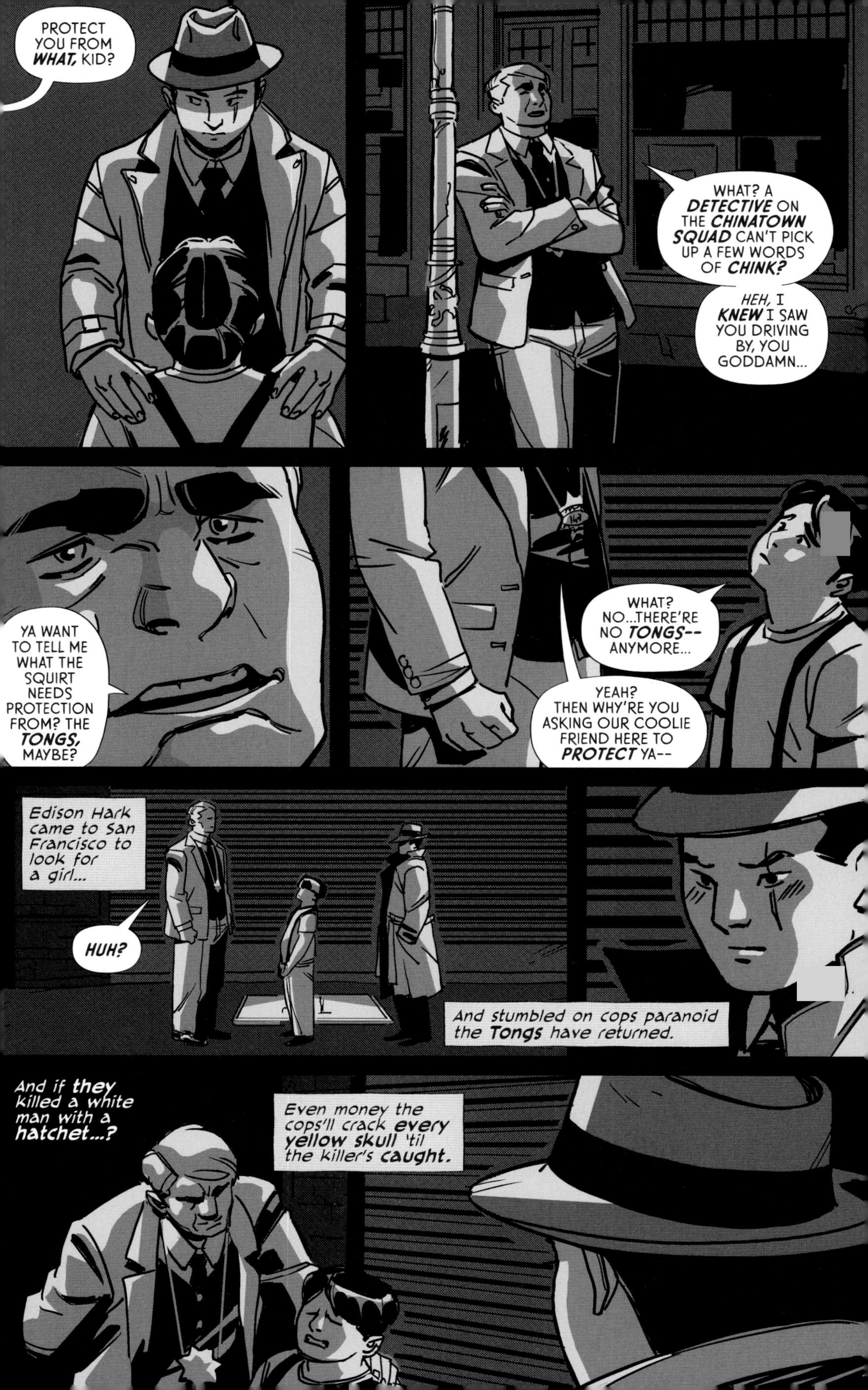
PROTECT YOU FROM WHAT, KID?
WHAT? A DETECTIVE ON THE CHINATOWN SQUAD CAN'T PICK UP A FEW WORDS OF CHINK?
HEH, I KNEW I SAW YOU DRIVING BY, YOU GODDAMN...
YA WANT TO TELL ME WHAT THE SQUIRT NEEDS PROTECTION FROM? THE TONGS, MAYBE?
WHAT? NO...THERE'RE NO TONGS-- ANYMORE...
YEAH? THEN WHY'RE YOU ASKING OUR COOLIE FRIEND HERE TO PROTECT YA--
Edison Hark came to San Francisco to look for a girl...
HUH?
And stumbled on cops paranoid the Tongs have returned.
And if they killed a white man with a hatchet...?
Even money the cops'll crack every yellow skull 'til the killer's caught.

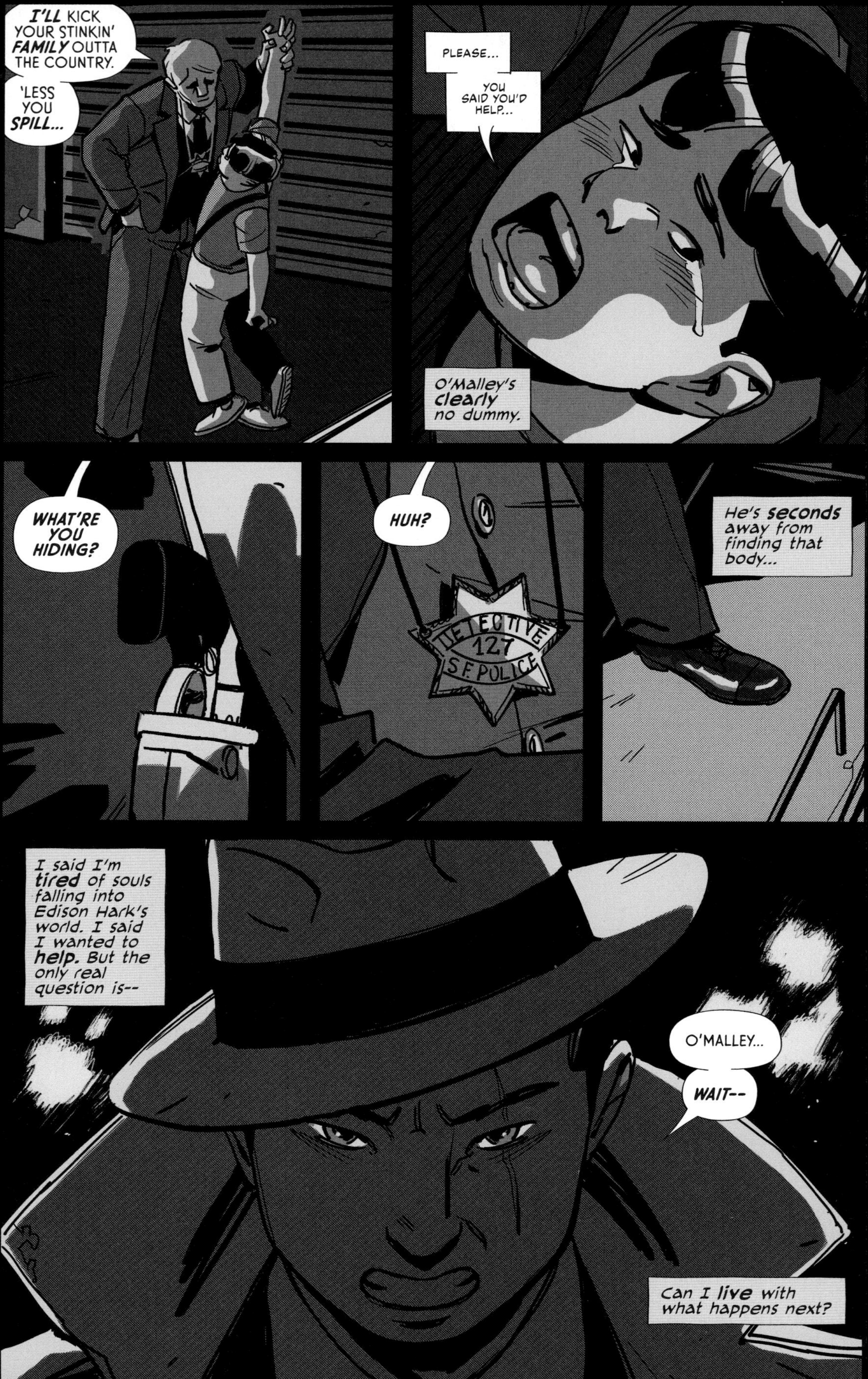
I'LL KICK YOUR STINKIN' FAMILY OUTTA THE COUNTRY.
'LESS YOU SPILL...
PLEASE...
YOU SAID YOU'D HELP...
O'Malley's clearly no dummy.
WHAT'RE YOU HIDING?
HUH?
DETECTIVE 127 S.F. POLICE
He's seconds away from finding that body...
I said I'm tired of souls falling into Edison Hark's world. I said I wanted to help. But the only real question is--
O'MALLEY...
WAIT--
Can I live with what happens next?

CHAPTER TWO

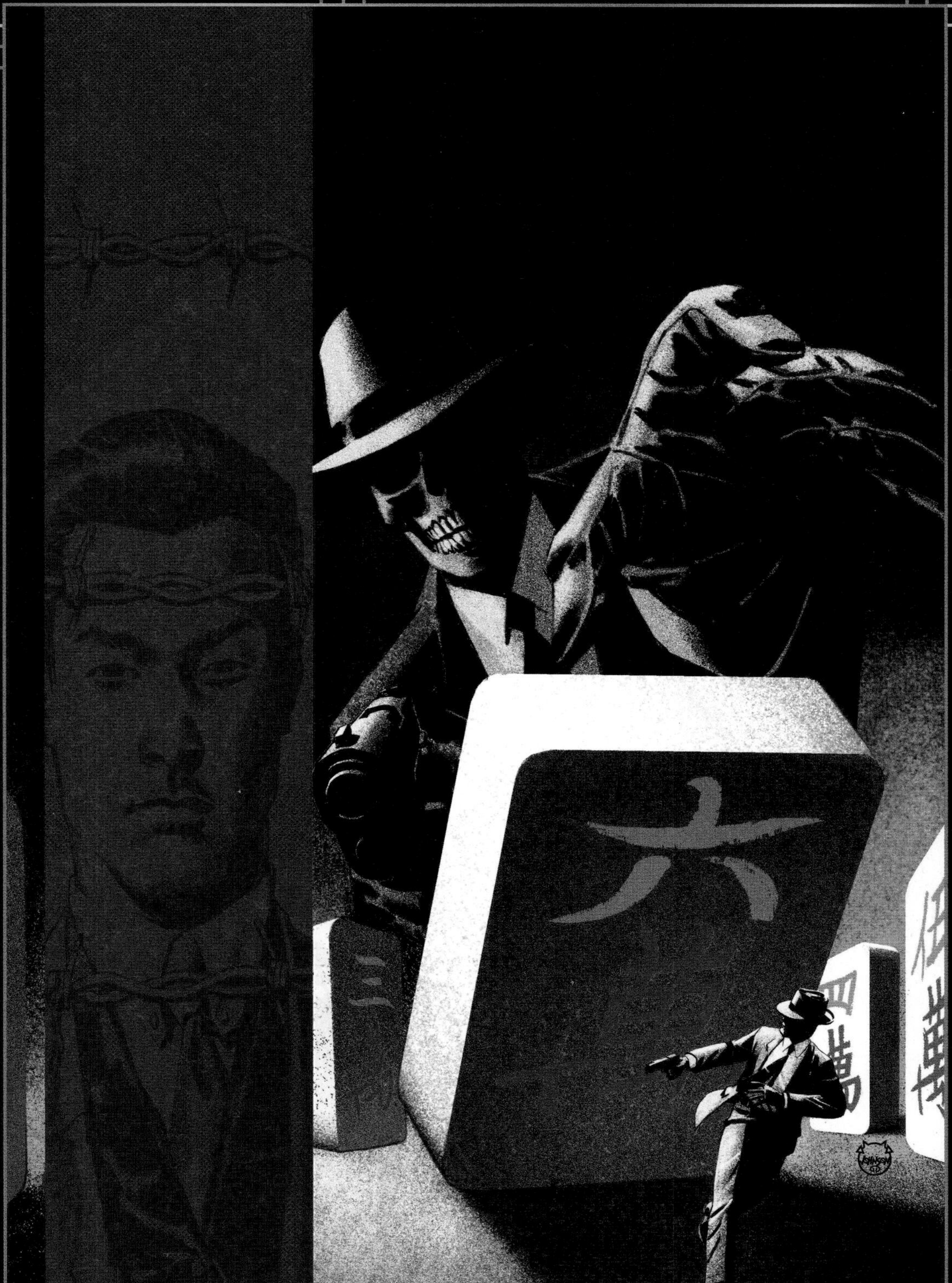
六
四萬

ART BY **DAVE JOHNSON**

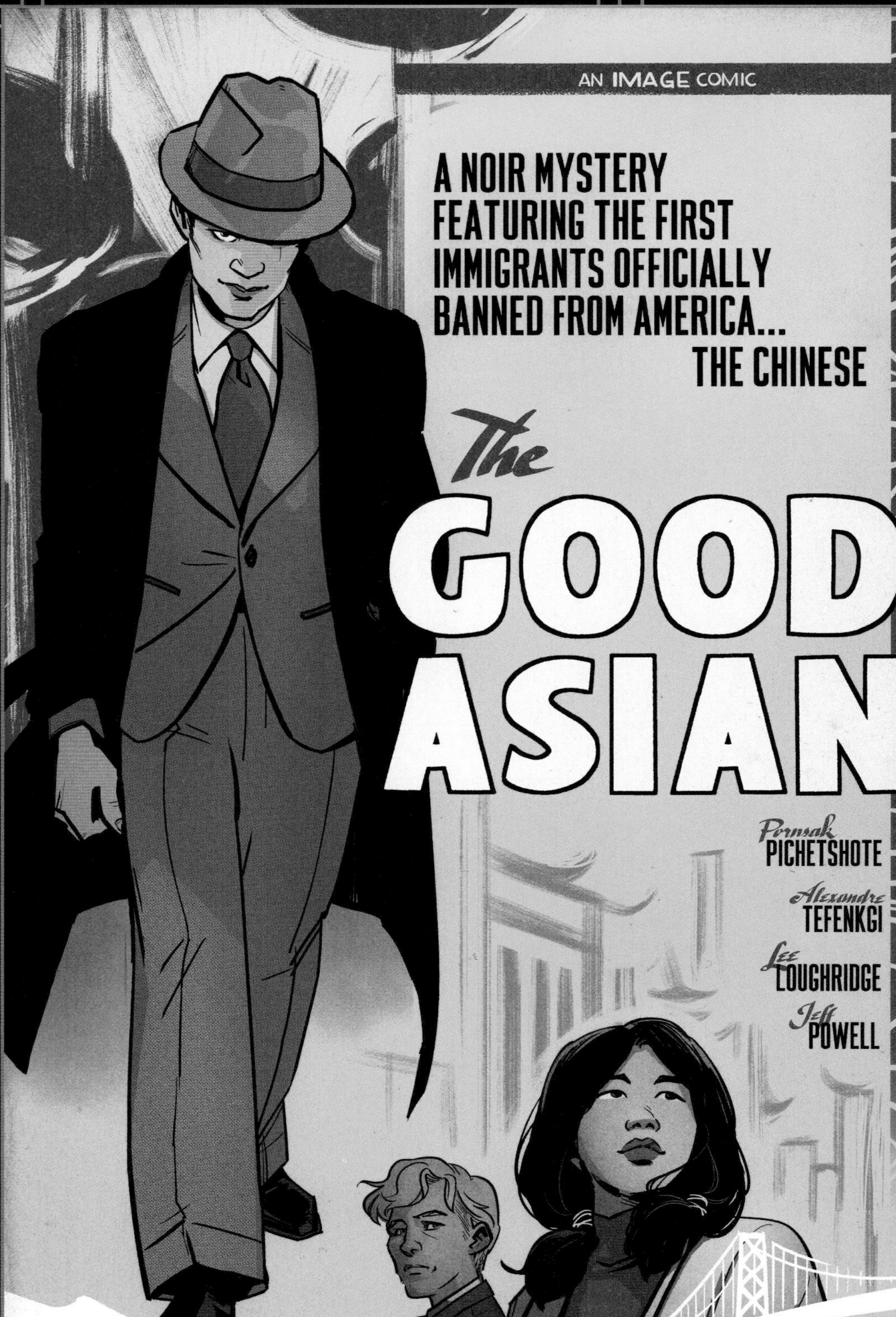

ART BY ANNIE WU

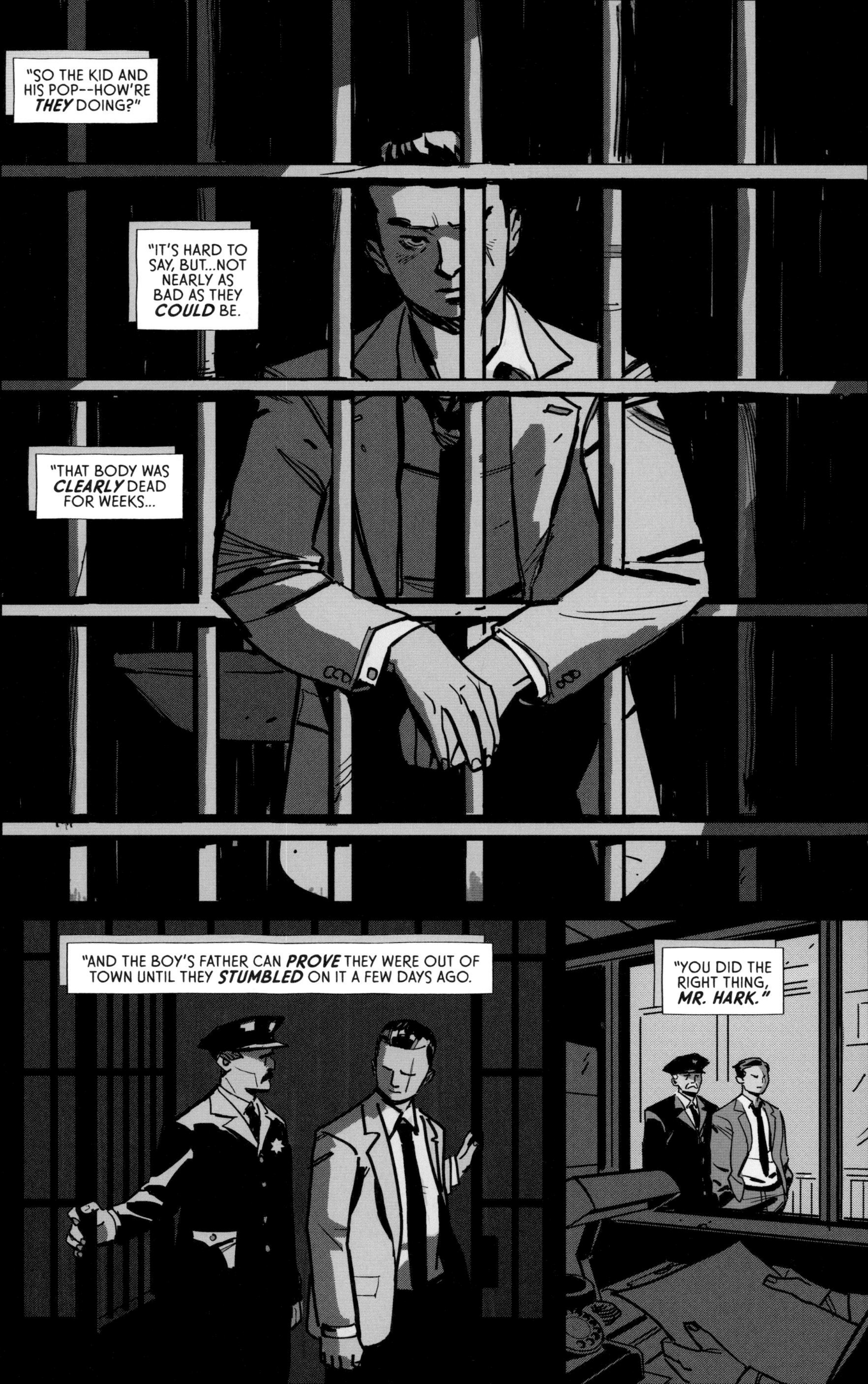
"SO THE KID AND HIS POP--HOW'RE *THEY* DOING?"
"IT'S HARD TO SAY, BUT...NOT NEARLY AS BAD AS THEY *COULD* BE.
"THAT BODY WAS *CLEARLY* DEAD FOR WEEKS...
"AND THE BOY'S FATHER CAN *PROVE* THEY WERE OUT OF TOWN UNTIL THEY *STUMBLED* ON IT A FEW DAYS AGO.
"YOU DID THE RIGHT THING, *MR. HARK.*"

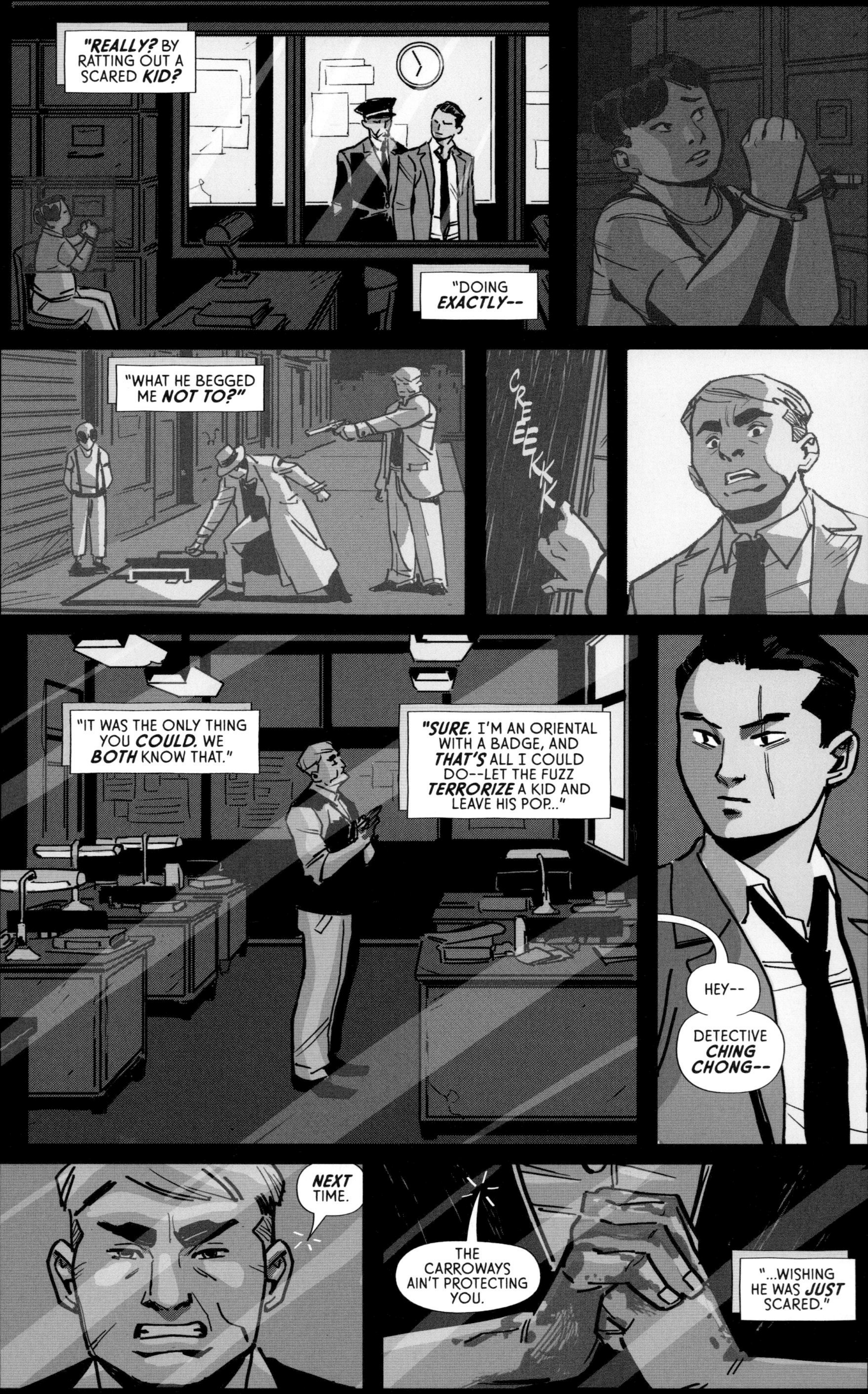
"REALLY? BY RATTING OUT A SCARED KID?
"DOING EXACTLY--
"WHAT HE BEGGED ME NOT TO?"
CREEKKK
"IT WAS THE ONLY THING YOU COULD. WE BOTH KNOW THAT."
"SURE. I'M AN ORIENTAL WITH A BADGE, AND THAT'S ALL I COULD DO--LET THE FUZZ TERRORIZE A KID AND LEAVE HIS POP..."
HEY--
DETECTIVE CHING CHONG--
NEXT TIME.
THE CARROWAYS AIN'T PROTECTING YOU.
"...WISHING HE WAS JUST SCARED."

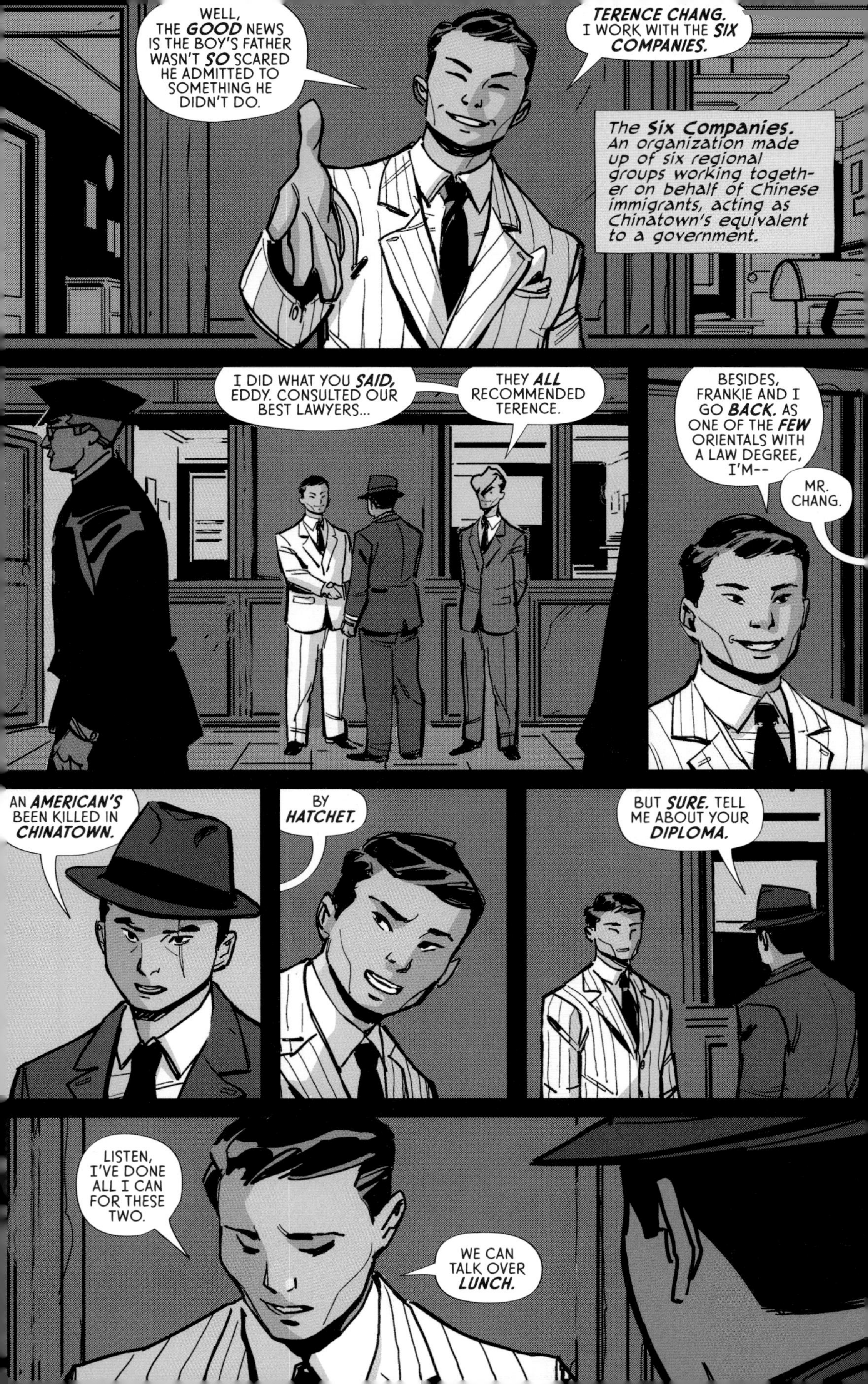
WELL, THE GOOD NEWS IS THE BOY'S FATHER WASN'T SO SCARED HE ADMITTED TO SOMETHING HE DIDN'T DO.
TERENCE CHANG. I WORK WITH THE SIX COMPANIES.
The Six Companies. An organization made up of six regional groups working together on behalf of Chinese immigrants, acting as Chinatown's equivalent to a government.
I DID WHAT YOU SAID, EDDY. CONSULTED OUR BEST LAWYERS...
THEY ALL RECOMMENDED TERENCE.
BESIDES, FRANKIE AND I GO BACK. AS ONE OF THE FEW ORIENTALS WITH A LAW DEGREE, I'M--
MR. CHANG.
AN AMERICAN'S BEEN KILLED IN CHINATOWN.
BY HATCHET.
BUT SURE. TELL ME ABOUT YOUR DIPLOMA.
LISTEN, I'VE DONE ALL I CAN FOR THESE TWO.
WE CAN TALK OVER LUNCH.

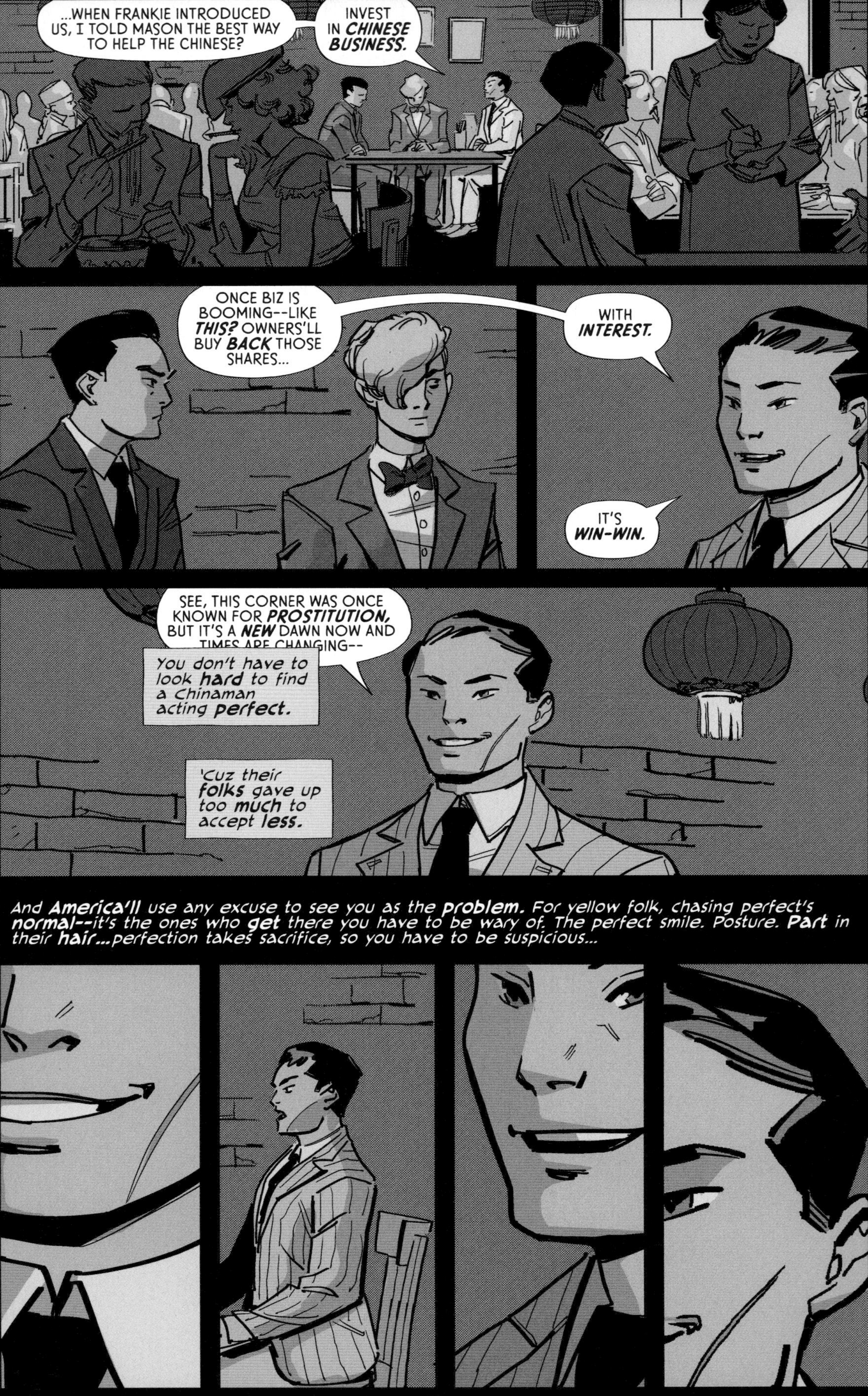

...WHEN FRANKIE INTRODUCED US, I TOLD MASON THE BEST WAY TO HELP THE CHINESE?
INVEST IN CHINESE BUSINESS.
ONCE BIZ IS BOOMING--LIKE THIS? OWNERS'LL BUY BACK THOSE SHARES...
WITH INTEREST.
IT'S WIN-WIN.
SEE, THIS CORNER WAS ONCE KNOWN FOR PROSTITUTION, BUT IT'S A NEW DAWN NOW AND TIMES ARE CHANGING--
You don't have to look hard to find a Chinaman acting perfect.
'Cuz their folks gave up too much to accept less.
And America'll use any excuse to see you as the problem. For yellow folk, chasing perfect's normal--it's the ones who get there you have to be wary of. The perfect smile. Posture. Part in their hair...perfection takes sacrifice, so you have to be suspicious...

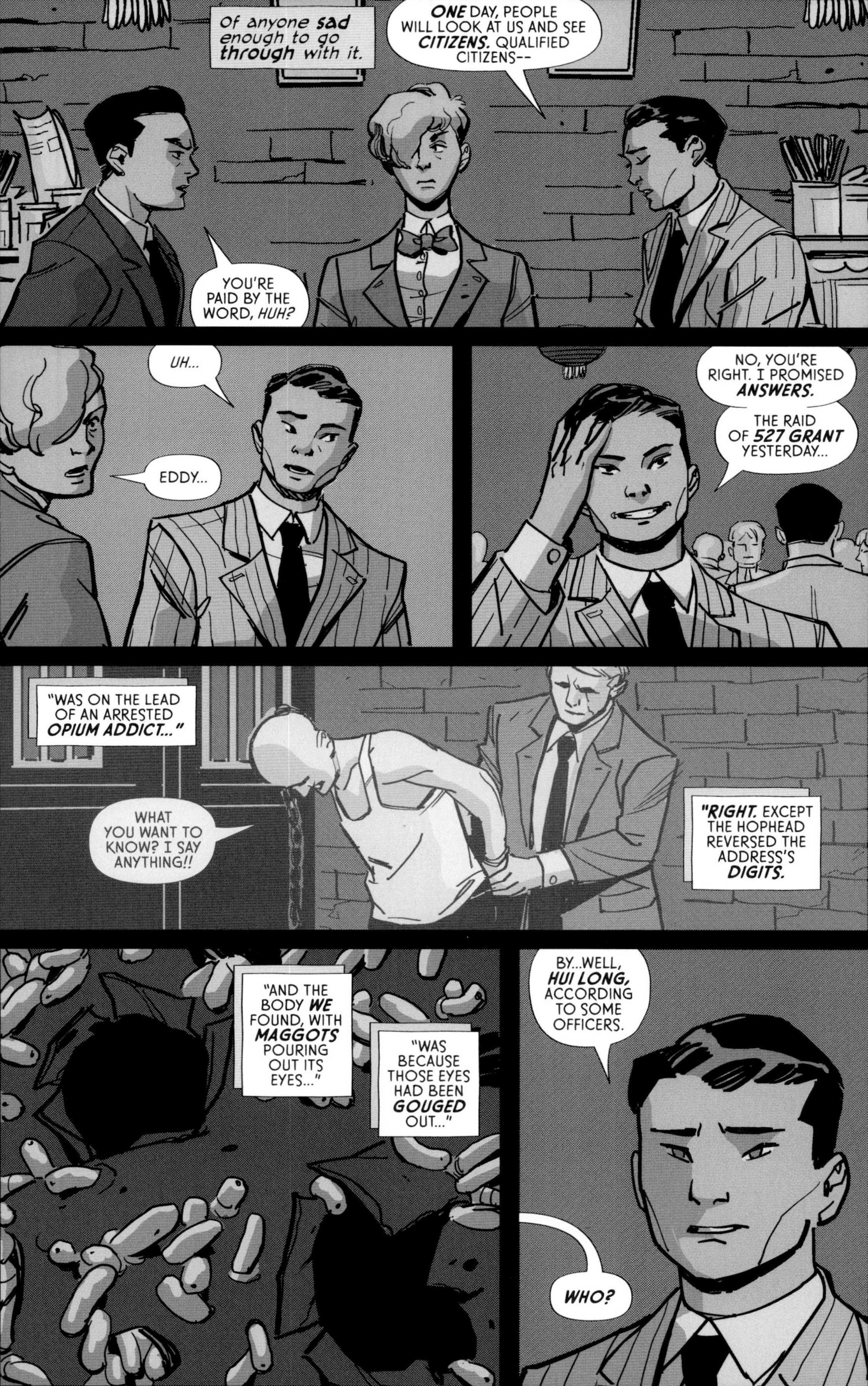
Of anyone sad enough to go through with it.
ONE DAY, PEOPLE WILL LOOK AT US AND SEE CITIZENS. QUALIFIED CITIZENS--
YOU'RE PAID BY THE WORD, HUH?
UH...
EDDY...
NO, YOU'RE RIGHT. I PROMISED ANSWERS.
THE RAID OF 527 GRANT YESTERDAY...
"WAS ON THE LEAD OF AN ARRESTED OPIUM ADDICT..."
WHAT YOU WANT TO KNOW? I SAY ANYTHING!!
"RIGHT. EXCEPT THE HOPHEAD REVERSED THE ADDRESS'S DIGITS.
"AND THE BODY WE FOUND, WITH MAGGOTS POURING OUT ITS EYES..."
"WAS BECAUSE THOSE EYES HAD BEEN GOUGED OUT..."
BY...WELL, HUI LONG, ACCORDING TO SOME OFFICERS.
WHO?

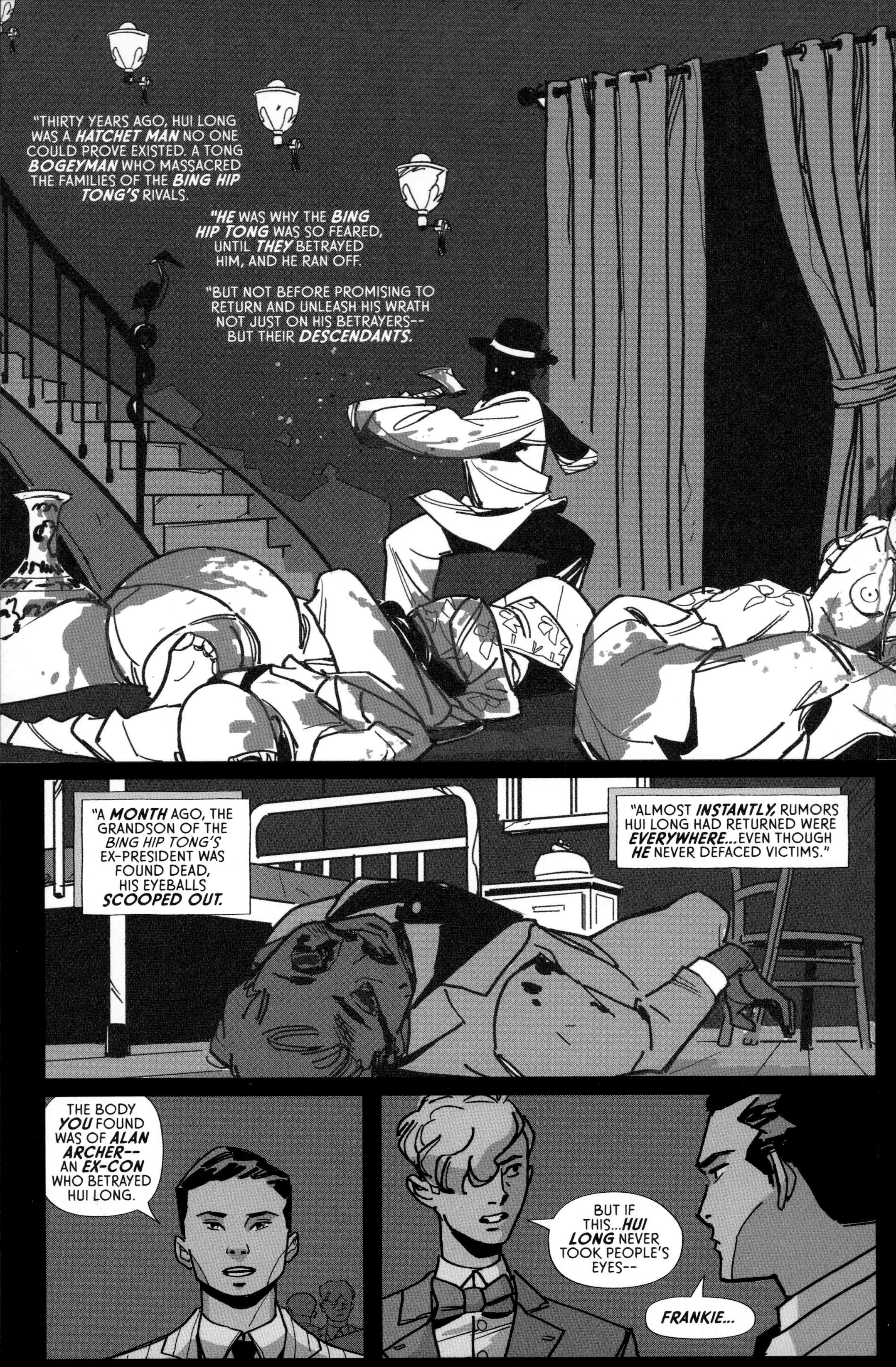
"THIRTY YEARS AGO, HUI LONG WAS A HATCHET MAN NO ONE COULD PROVE EXISTED. A TONG BOGEYMAN WHO MASSACRED THE FAMILIES OF THE BING HIP TONG'S RIVALS.
"HE WAS WHY THE BING HIP TONG WAS SO FEARED, UNTIL THEY BETRAYED HIM, AND HE RAN OFF.
"BUT NOT BEFORE PROMISING TO RETURN AND UNLEASH HIS WRATH NOT JUST ON HIS BETRAYERS-- BUT THEIR DESCENDANTS.
"A MONTH AGO, THE GRANDSON OF THE BING HIP TONG'S EX-PRESIDENT WAS FOUND DEAD, HIS EYEBALLS SCOOPED OUT.
"ALMOST INSTANTLY, RUMORS HUI LONG HAD RETURNED WERE EVERYWHERE...EVEN THOUGH HE NEVER DEFACED VICTIMS."
THE BODY YOU FOUND WAS OF ALAN ARCHER-- AN EX-CON WHO BETRAYED HUI LONG.
BUT IF THIS...HUI LONG NEVER TOOK PEOPLE'S EYES--
FRANKIE...

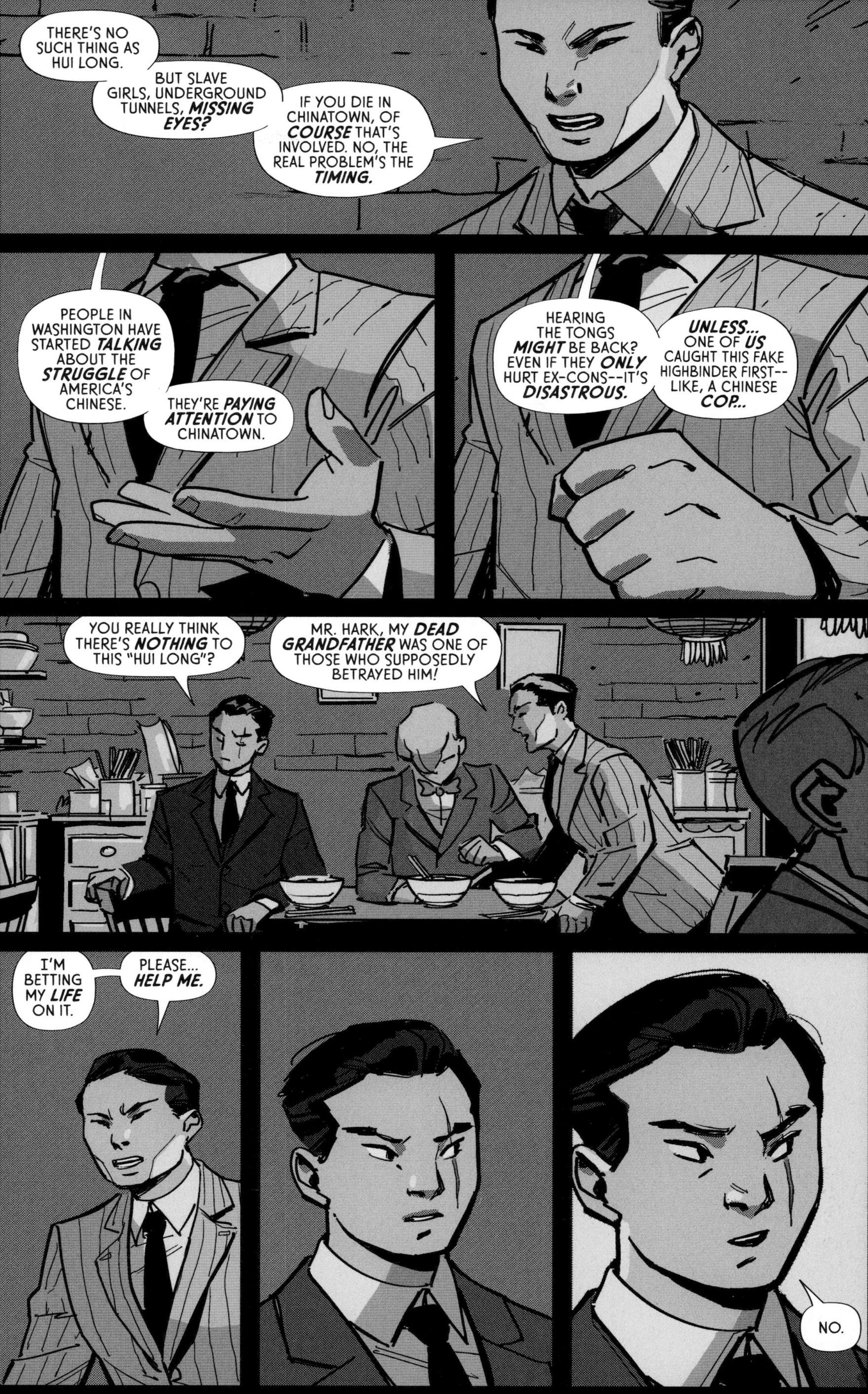

THERE'S NO SUCH THING AS HUI LONG.
BUT SLAVE GIRLS, UNDERGROUND TUNNELS, MISSING EYES?
IF YOU DIE IN CHINATOWN, OF COURSE THAT'S INVOLVED. NO, THE REAL PROBLEM'S THE TIMING.
PEOPLE IN WASHINGTON HAVE STARTED TALKING ABOUT THE STRUGGLE OF AMERICA'S CHINESE.
THEY'RE PAYING ATTENTION TO CHINATOWN.
HEARING THE TONGS MIGHT BE BACK? EVEN IF THEY ONLY HURT EX-CONS--IT'S DISASTROUS.
UNLESS... ONE OF US CAUGHT THIS FAKE HIGHBINDER FIRST--LIKE, A CHINESE COP...
YOU REALLY THINK THERE'S NOTHING TO THIS "HUI LONG"?
MR. HARK, MY DEAD GRANDFATHER WAS ONE OF THOSE WHO SUPPOSEDLY BETRAYED HIM!
I'M BETTING MY LIFE ON IT.
PLEASE... HELP ME.
NO.

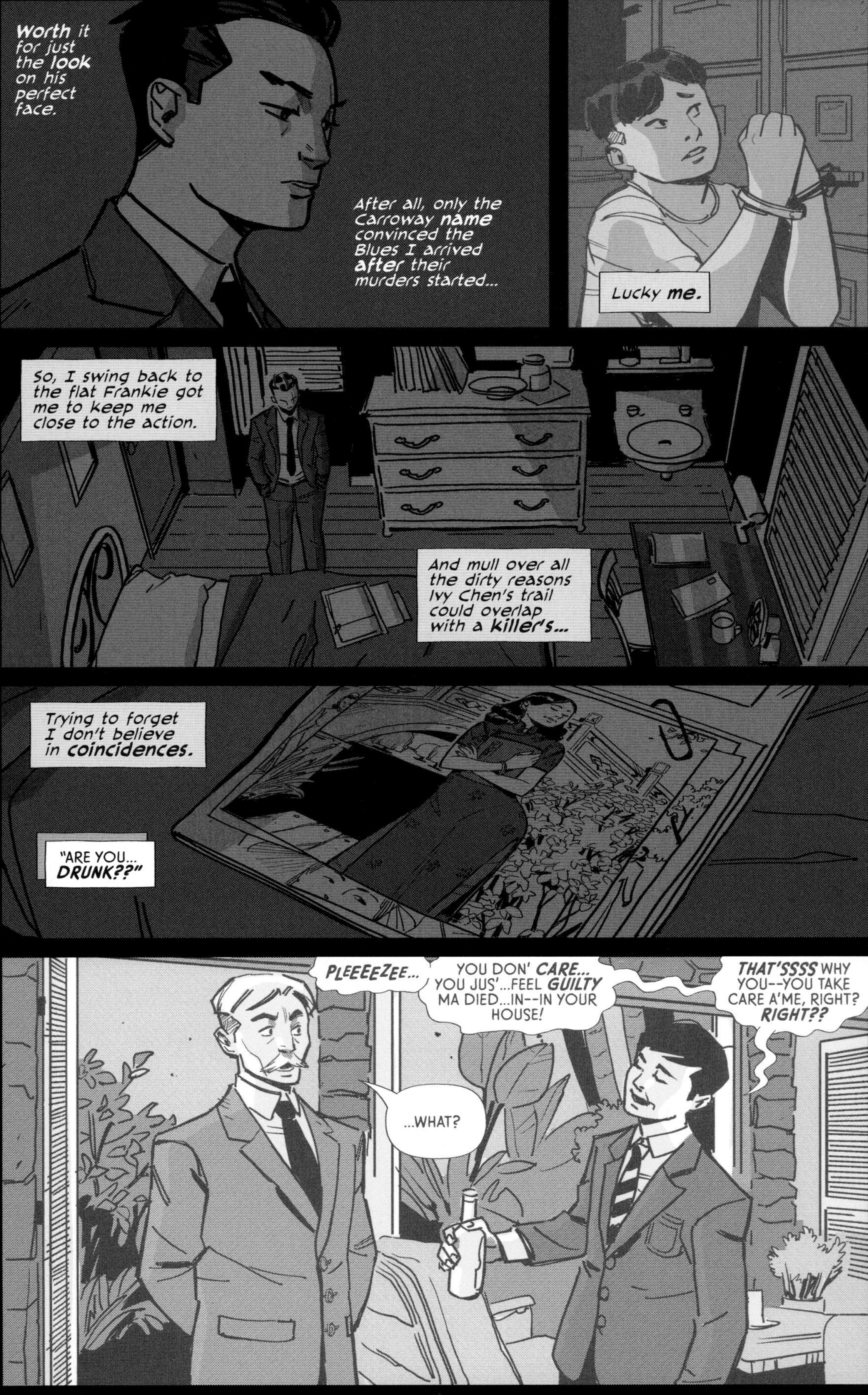

Worth it for just the look on his perfect face.
After all, only the Carroway name convinced the Blues I arrived after their murders started...
Lucky me.
So, I swing back to the flat Frankie got me to keep me close to the action.
And mull over all the dirty reasons Ivy Chen's trail could overlap with a killer's...
Trying to forget I don't believe in coincidences.
"ARE YOU... DRUNK??"
PLEEEEZEE...
YOU DON' CARE... YOU JUS'...FEEL GUILTY MA DIED...IN--IN YOUR HOUSE!
THAT'SSSS WHY YOU--YOU TAKE CARE A'ME, RIGHT? RIGHT??
...WHAT?

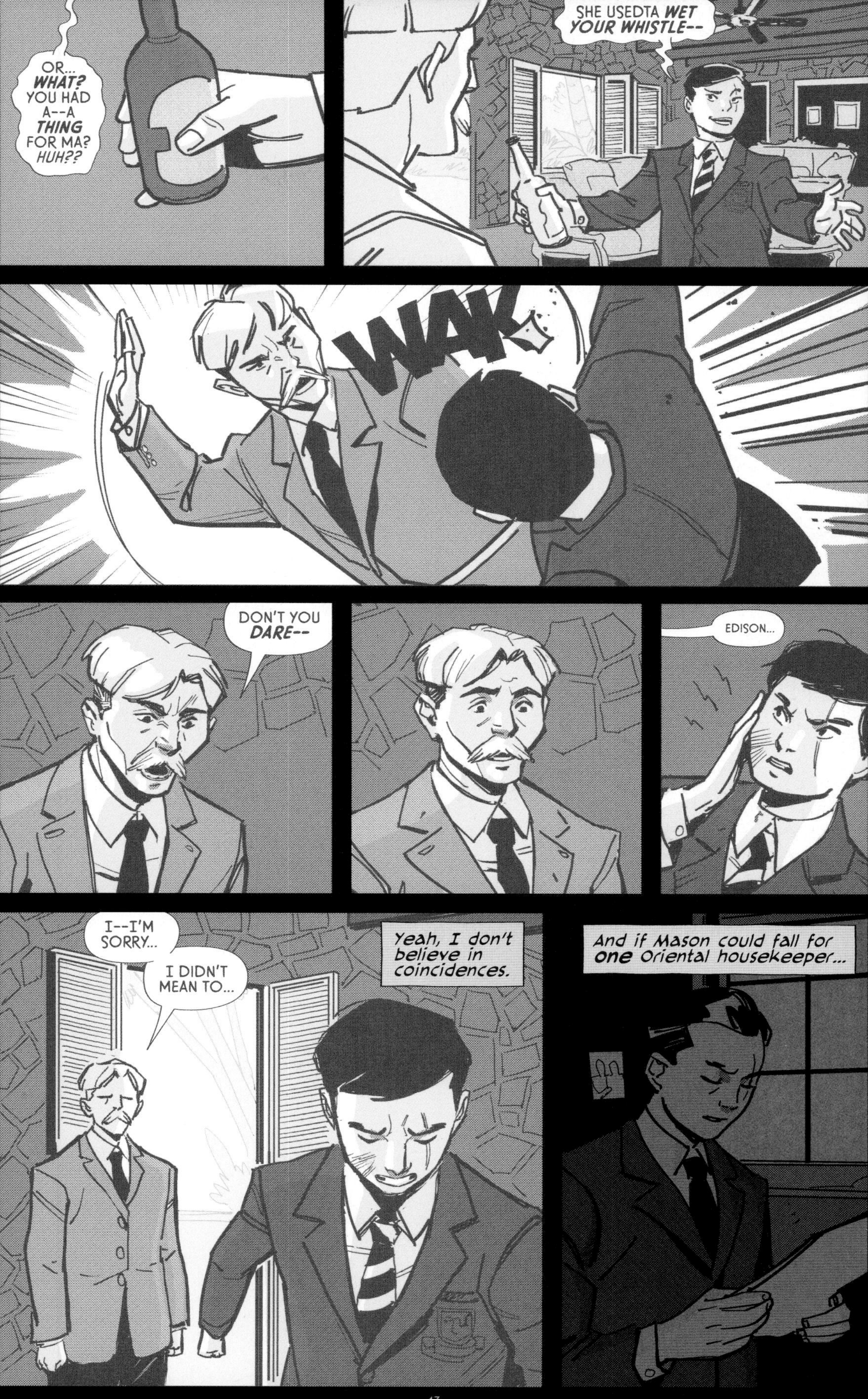

OR... WHAT? YOU HAD A--A THING FOR MA? HUH??
SHE USEDTA WET YOUR WHISTLE--
WAK
DON'T YOU DARE--
EDISON...
I--I'M SORRY...
I DIDN'T MEAN TO...
Yeah, I don't believe in coincidences.
And if Mason could fall for one Oriental housekeeper...

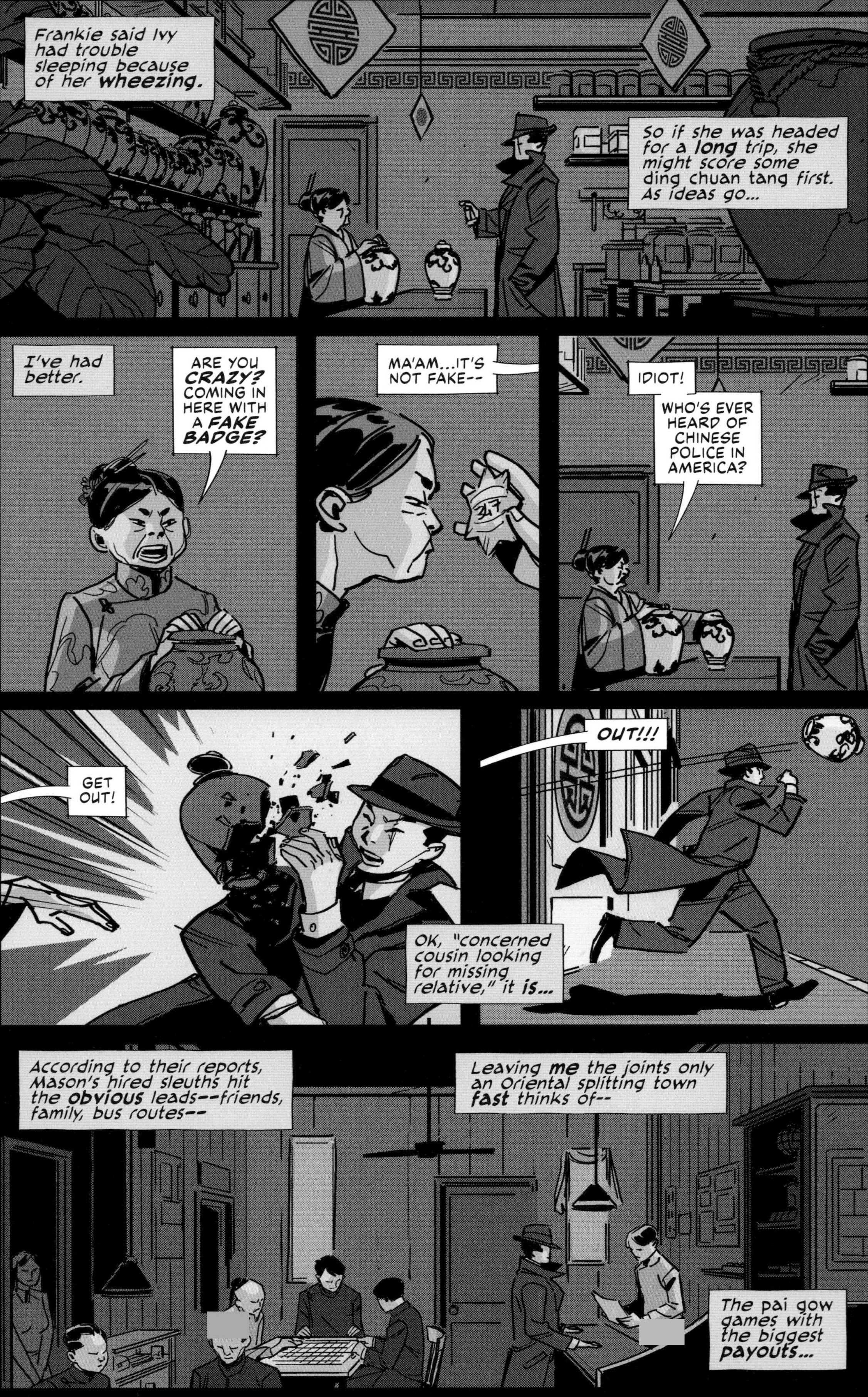
Frankie said Ivy had trouble sleeping because of her wheezing.
So if she was headed for a long trip, she might score some ding chuan tang first. As ideas go...
I've had better.
ARE YOU CRAZY? COMING IN HERE WITH A FAKE BADGE?
MA'AM...IT'S NOT FAKE--
IDIOT!
WHO'S EVER HEARD OF CHINESE POLICE IN AMERICA?
GET OUT!
OK, "concerned cousin looking for missing relative," it is...
OUT!!!
According to their reports, Mason's hired sleuths hit the obvious leads--friends, family, bus routes--
Leaving me the joints only an Oriental splitting town fast thinks of--
The pai gow games with the biggest payouts...

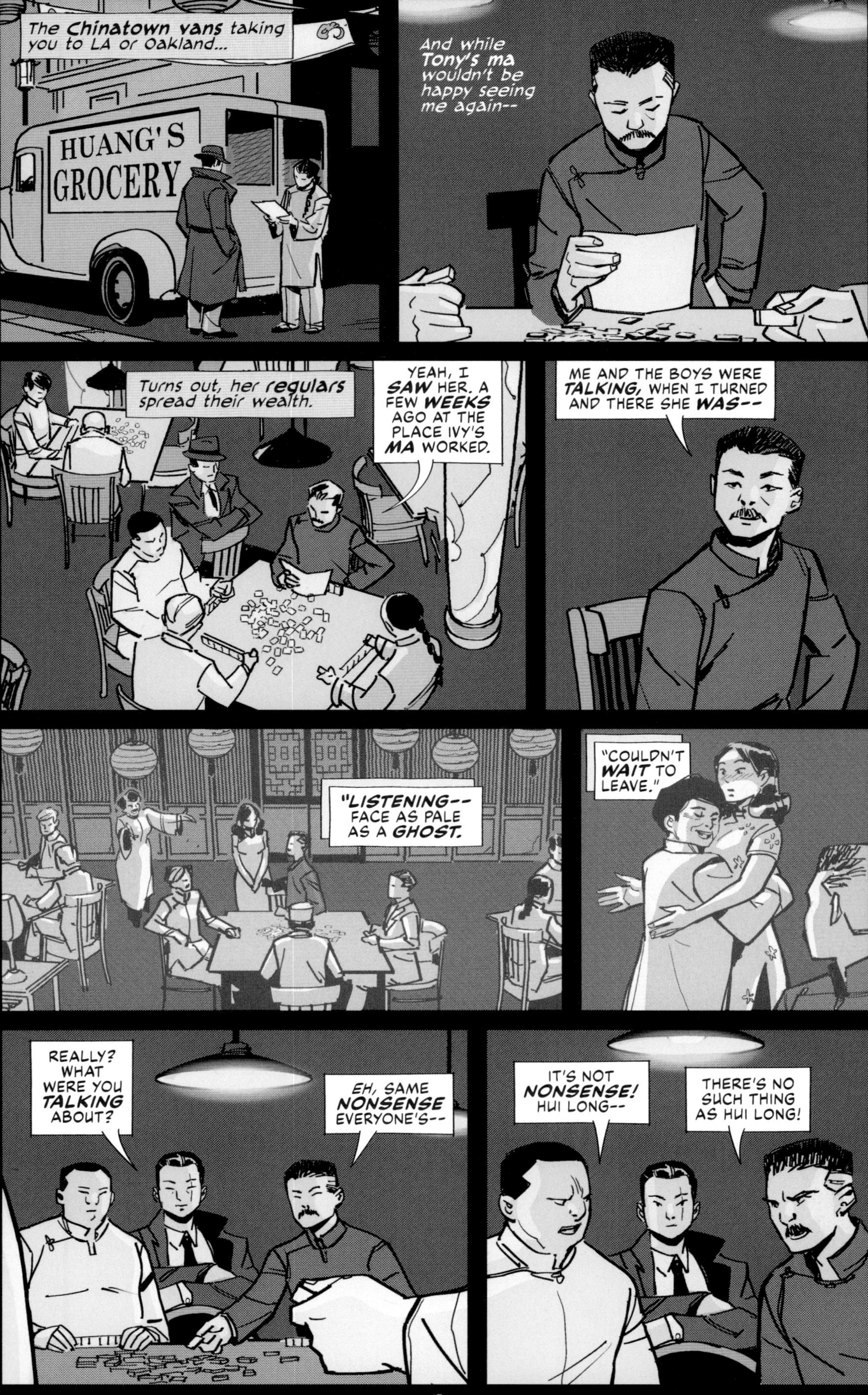
The Chinatown vans taking you to LA or Oakland...
HUANG'S GROCERY
And while Tony's ma wouldn't be happy seeing me again--
Turns out, her regulars spread their wealth.
YEAH, I SAW HER. A FEW WEEKS AGO AT THE PLACE IVY'S MA WORKED.
ME AND THE BOYS WERE TALKING, WHEN I TURNED AND THERE SHE WAS--
"LISTENING-- FACE AS PALE AS A GHOST.
"COULDN'T WAIT TO LEAVE."
REALLY? WHAT WERE YOU TALKING ABOUT?
EH, SAME NONSENSE EVERYONE'S--
IT'S NOT NONSENSE! HUI LONG--
THERE'S NO SUCH THING AS HUI LONG!

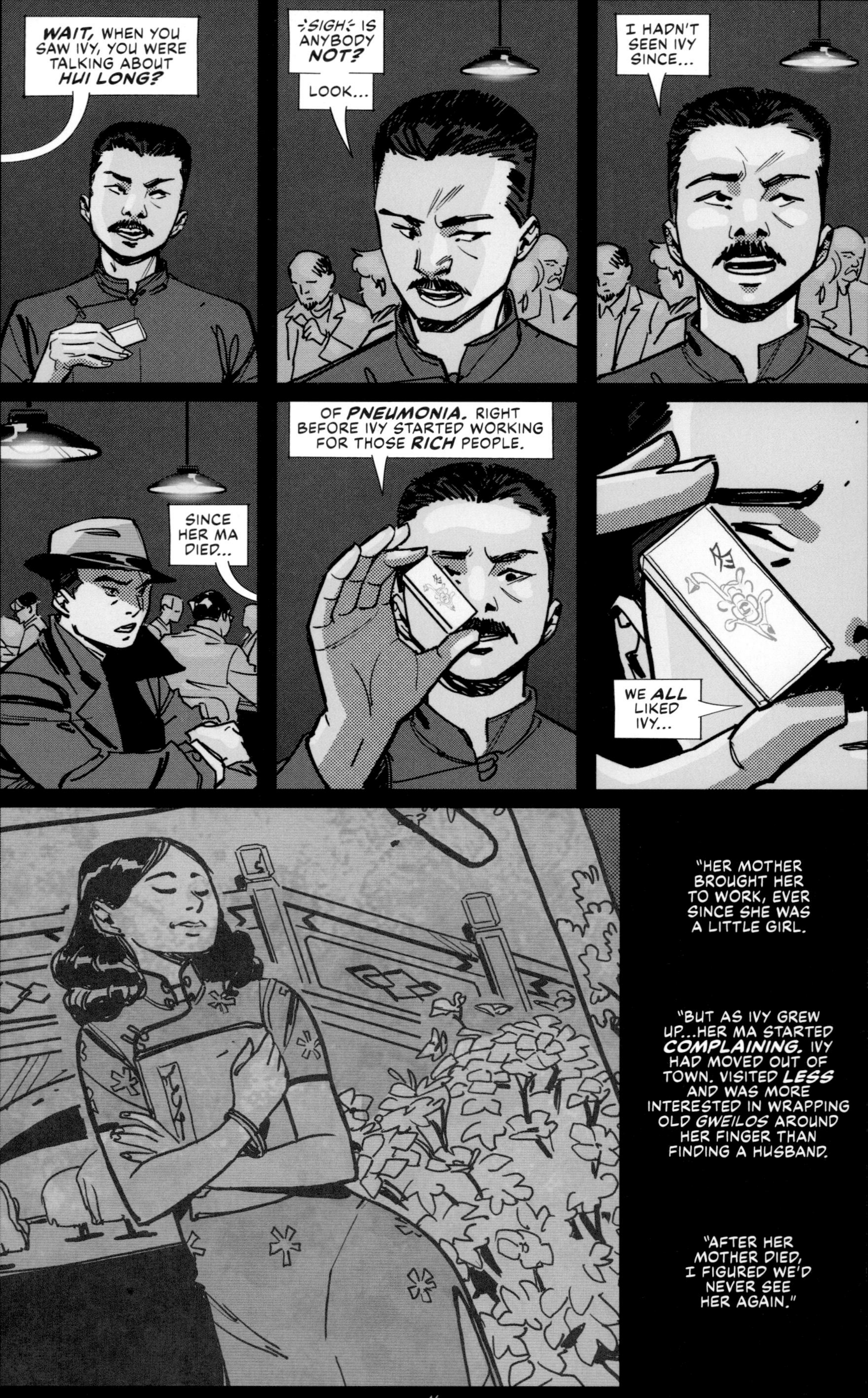

WAIT, WHEN YOU SAW IVY, YOU WERE TALKING ABOUT HUI LONG?
SIGH IS ANYBODY NOT?
LOOK...
I HADN'T SEEN IVY SINCE...
SINCE HER MA DIED...
OF PNEUMONIA. RIGHT BEFORE IVY STARTED WORKING FOR THOSE RICH PEOPLE.
WE ALL LIKED IVY...
"HER MOTHER BROUGHT HER TO WORK, EVER SINCE SHE WAS A LITTLE GIRL.
"BUT AS IVY GREW UP...HER MA STARTED COMPLAINING. IVY HAD MOVED OUT OF TOWN. VISITED LESS AND WAS MORE INTERESTED IN WRAPPING OLD GWEILOS AROUND HER FINGER THAN FINDING A HUSBAND.
"AFTER HER MOTHER DIED, I FIGURED WE'D NEVER SEE HER AGAIN."

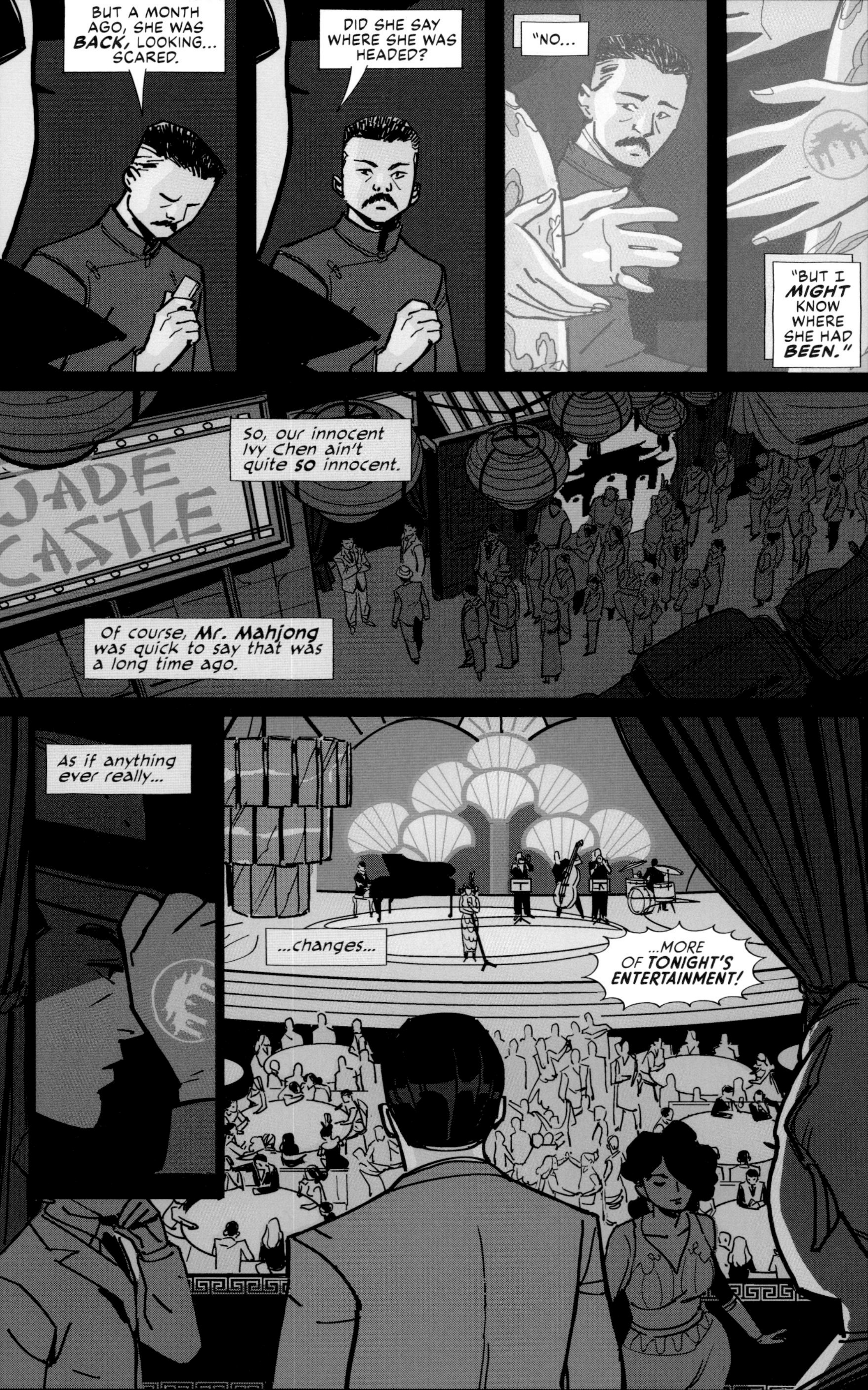
BUT A MONTH AGO, SHE WAS BACK, LOOKING... SCARED.
DID SHE SAY WHERE SHE WAS HEADED?
"NO...
"BUT I MIGHT KNOW WHERE SHE HAD BEEN."
So, our innocent Ivy Chen ain't quite SO innocent.
JADE CASTLE
Of course, Mr. Mahjong was quick to say that was a long time ago.
As if anything ever really...
...changes...
...MORE OF TONIGHT'S ENTERTAINMENT!

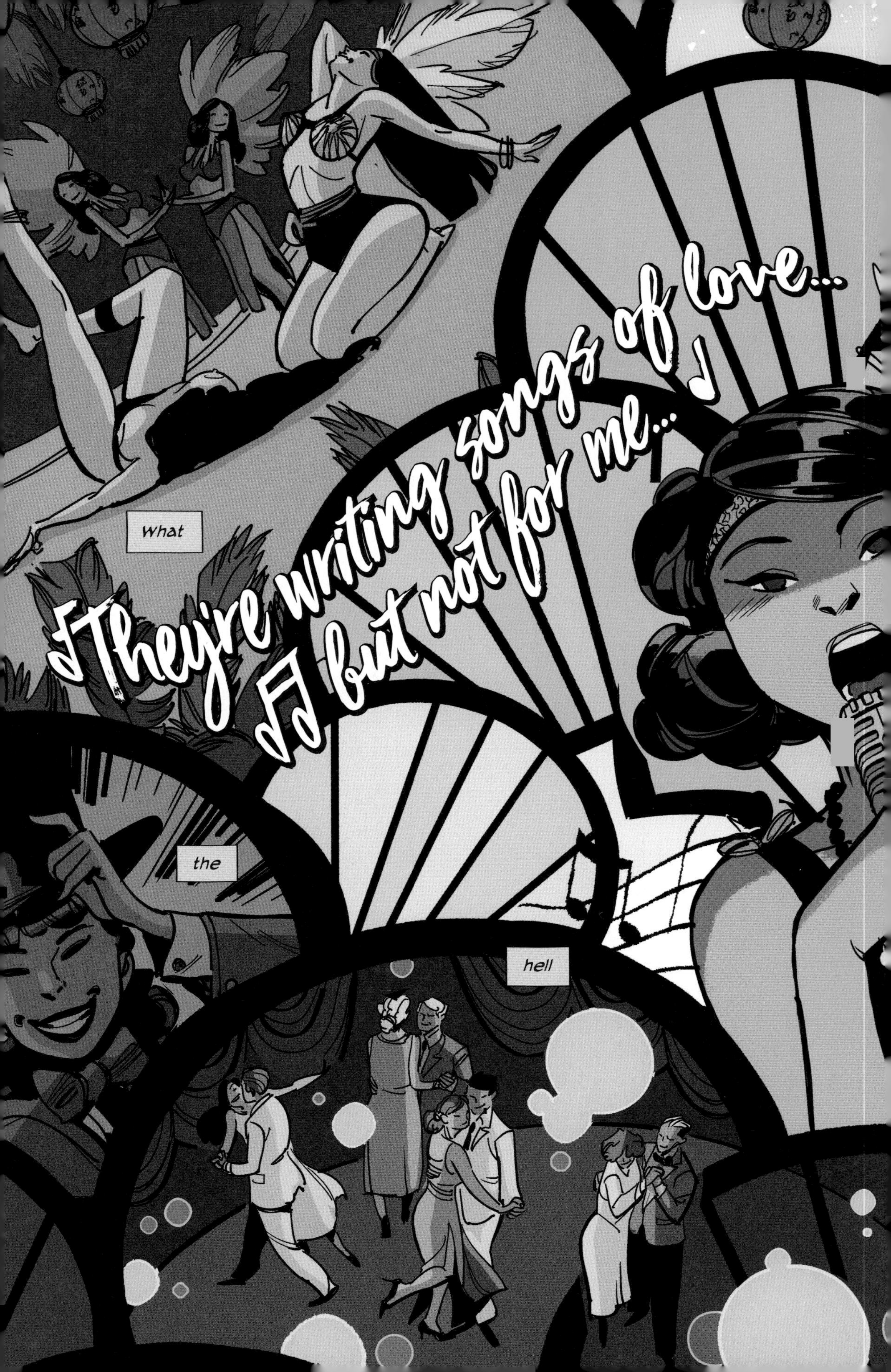
what
♩They're writing songs of love...
♫ but not for me... ♩
the
hell

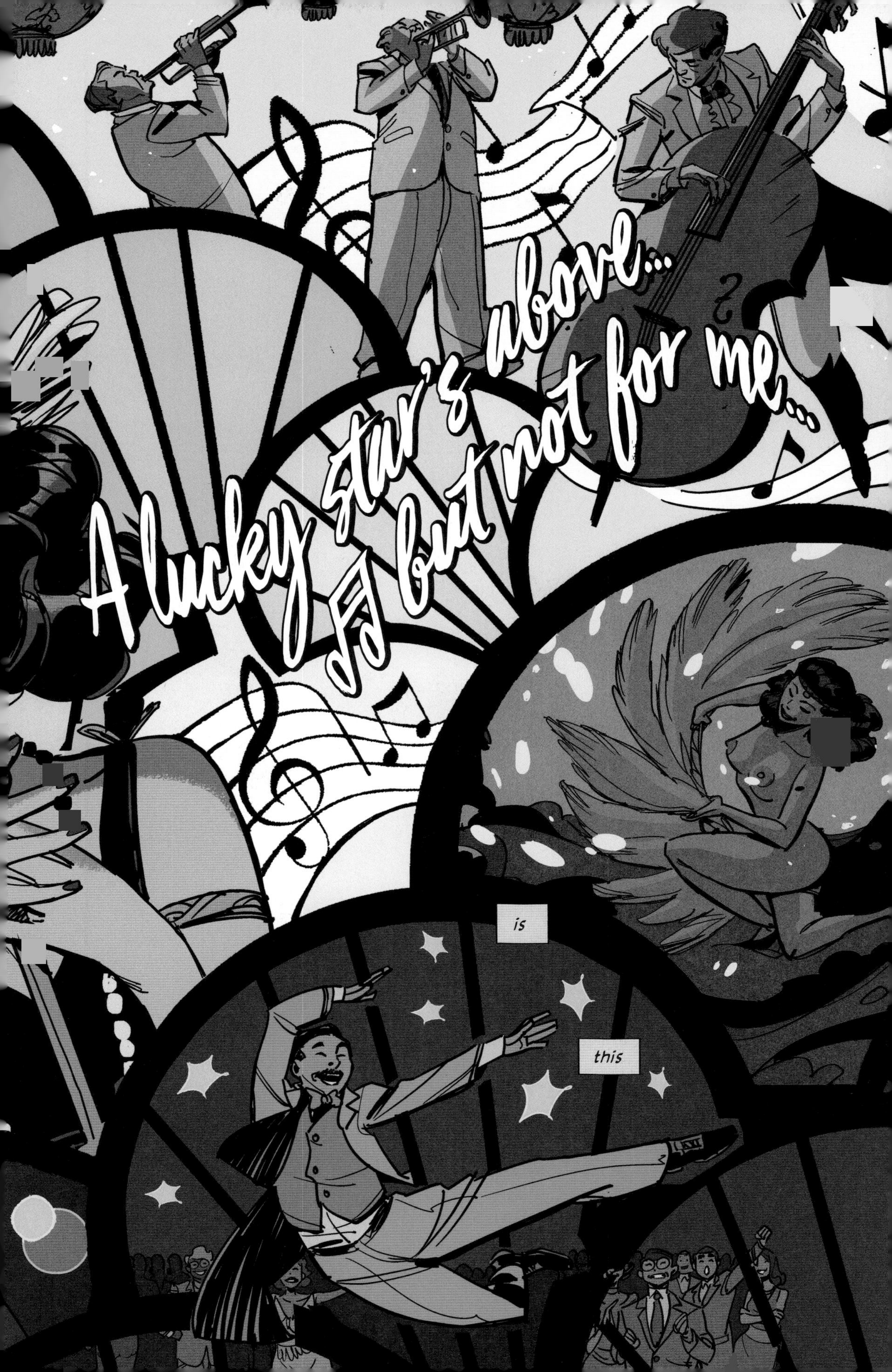

A lucky star's above...
but not for me...
is
this

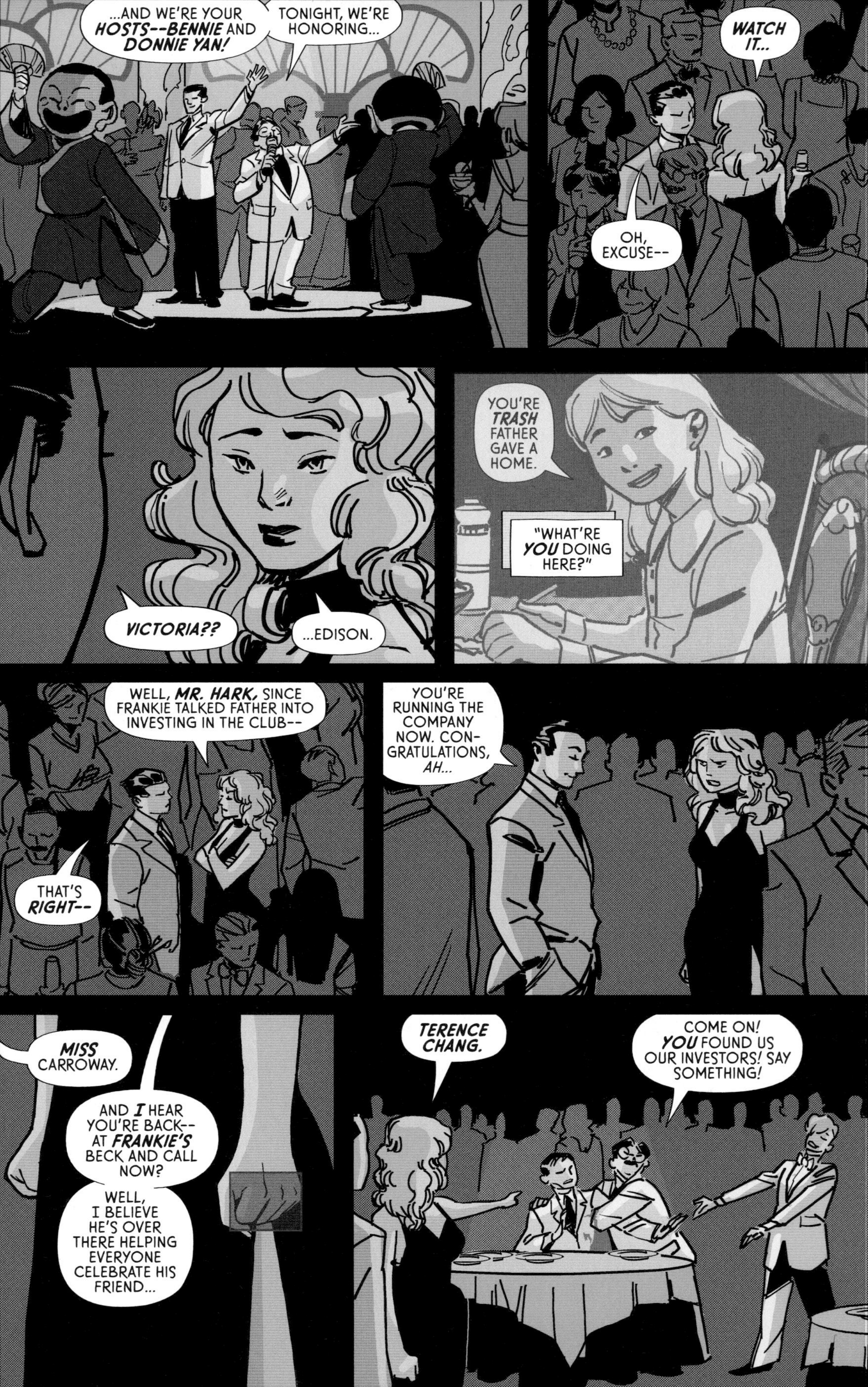
...AND WE'RE YOUR HOSTS--BENNIE AND DONNIE YAN!
TONIGHT, WE'RE HONORING...
WATCH IT...
OH, EXCUSE--
VICTORIA??
...EDISON.
YOU'RE TRASH FATHER GAVE A HOME.
"WHAT'RE YOU DOING HERE?"
WELL, MR. HARK, SINCE FRANKIE TALKED FATHER INTO INVESTING IN THE CLUB--
THAT'S RIGHT--
YOU'RE RUNNING THE COMPANY NOW. CONGRATULATIONS, AH...
MISS CARROWAY.
AND I HEAR YOU'RE BACK--AT FRANKIE'S BECK AND CALL NOW?
WELL, I BELIEVE HE'S OVER THERE HELPING EVERYONE CELEBRATE HIS FRIEND...
TERENCE CHANG.
COME ON! YOU FOUND US OUR INVESTORS! SAY SOMETHING!

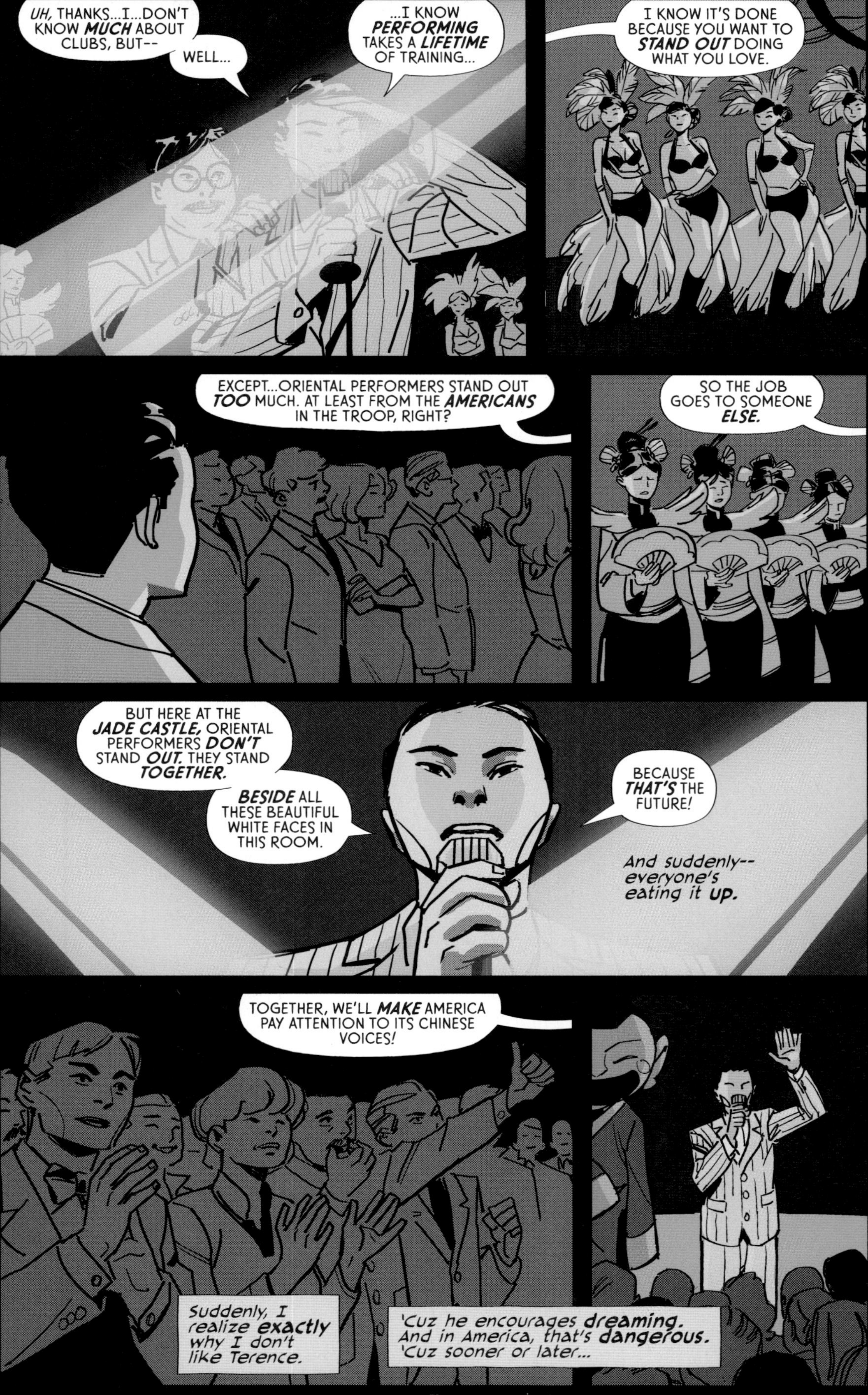
UH, THANKS...I...DON'T KNOW MUCH ABOUT CLUBS, BUT--
WELL...
...I KNOW PERFORMING TAKES A LIFETIME OF TRAINING...
I KNOW IT'S DONE BECAUSE YOU WANT TO STAND OUT DOING WHAT YOU LOVE.
EXCEPT...ORIENTAL PERFORMERS STAND OUT TOO MUCH. AT LEAST FROM THE AMERICANS IN THE TROOP, RIGHT?
SO THE JOB GOES TO SOMEONE ELSE.
BUT HERE AT THE JADE CASTLE, ORIENTAL PERFORMERS DON'T STAND OUT. THEY STAND TOGETHER.
BESIDE ALL THESE BEAUTIFUL WHITE FACES IN THIS ROOM.
BECAUSE THAT'S THE FUTURE!
And suddenly-- everyone's eating it up.
TOGETHER, WE'LL MAKE AMERICA PAY ATTENTION TO ITS CHINESE VOICES!
Suddenly, I realize exactly why I don't like Terence.
'Cuz he encourages dreaming. And in America, that's dangerous. 'Cuz sooner or later...

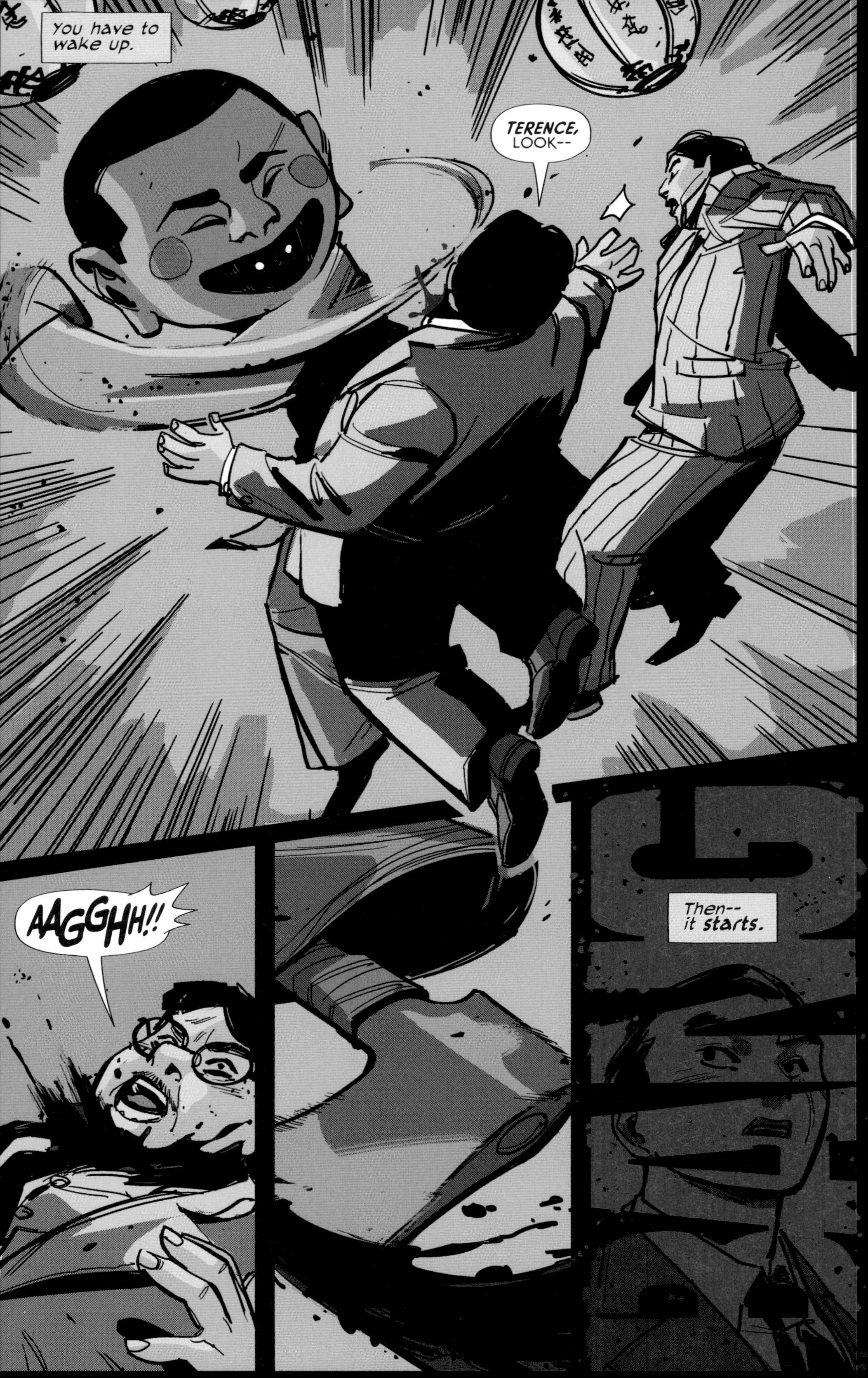
You have to wake up.
TERENCE, LOOK--
AAGGHH!!
Then-- it starts.

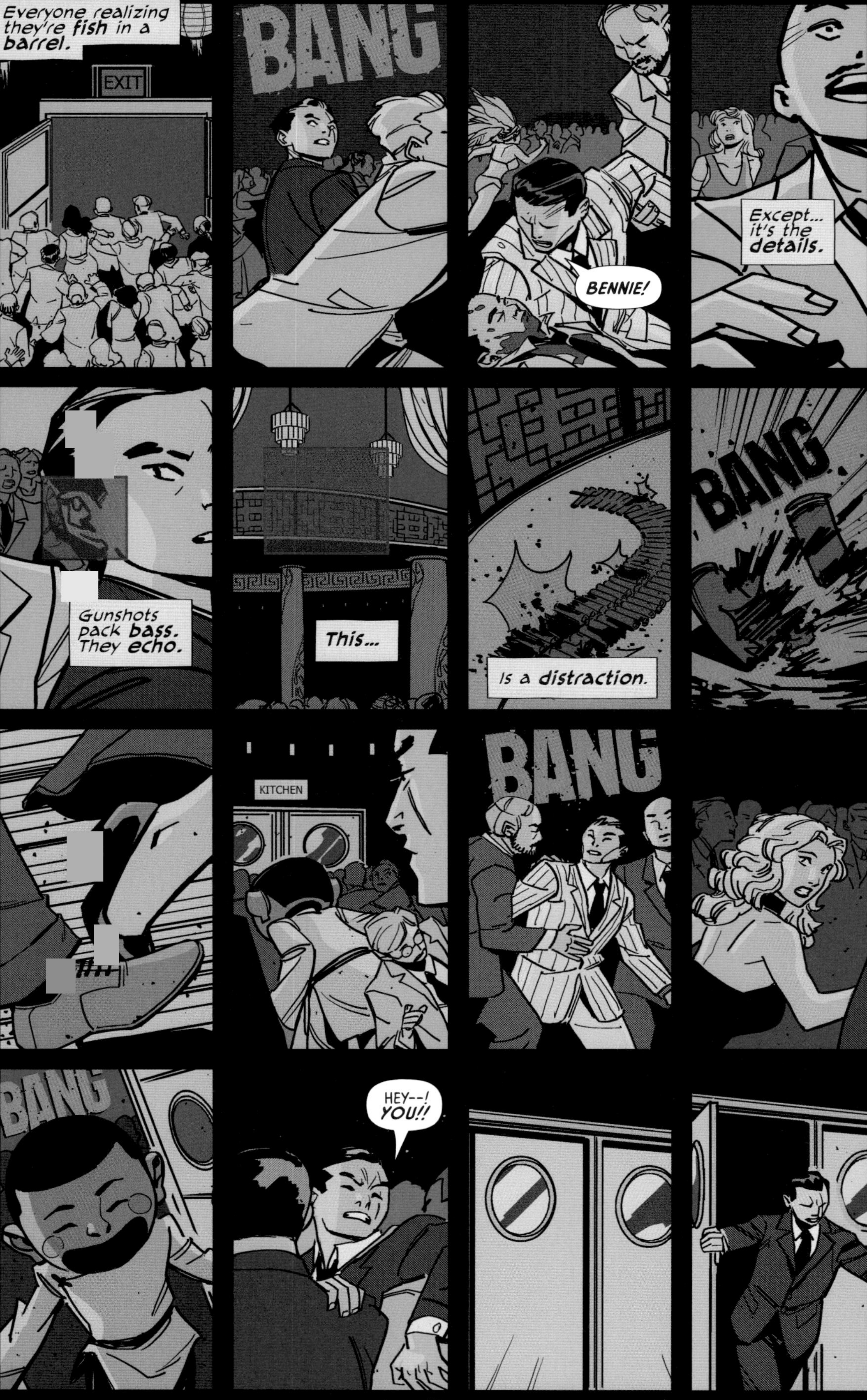
Everyone realizing they're fish in a barrel.
EXIT
BANG
BENNIE!
Except... it's the details.
Gunshots pack bass. They echo.
This...
Is a distraction.
BANG
KITCHEN
BANG
BANG
HEY--! YOU!!

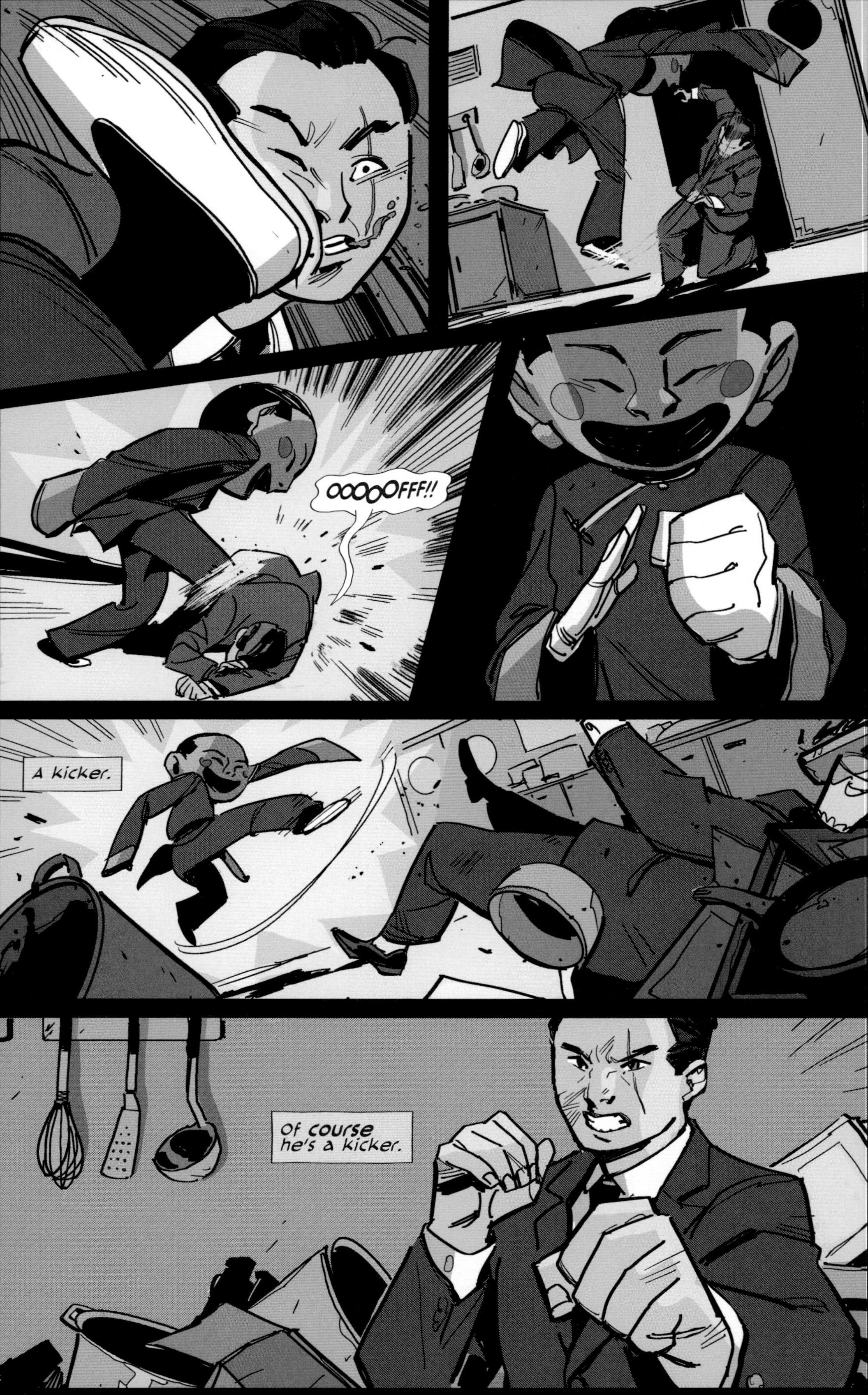
OOOOOFFF!!
A kicker.
Of course he's a kicker.

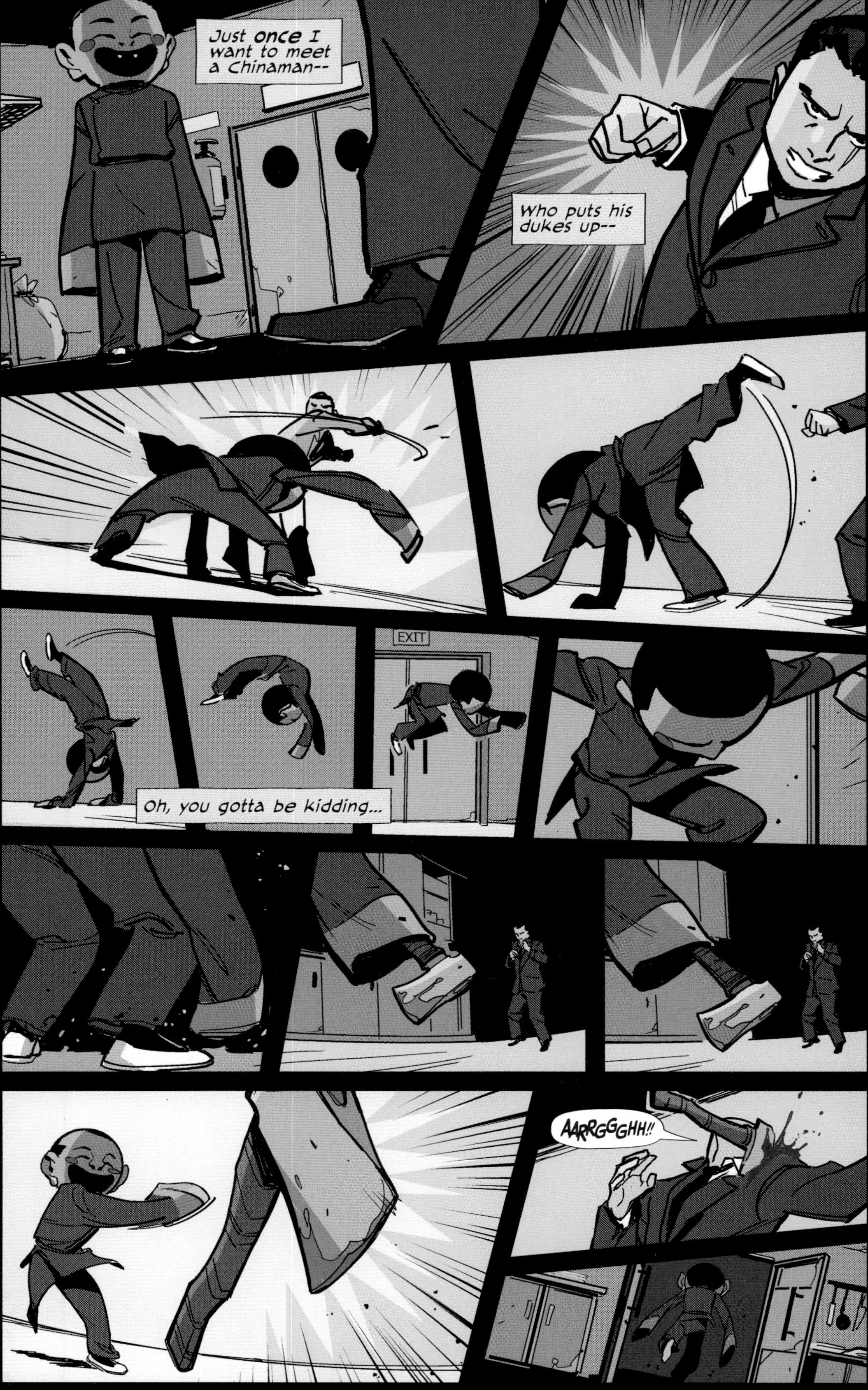
Just once I want to meet a Chinaman--
Who puts his dukes up--
Oh, you gotta be kidding...
AARRGGGHH!!

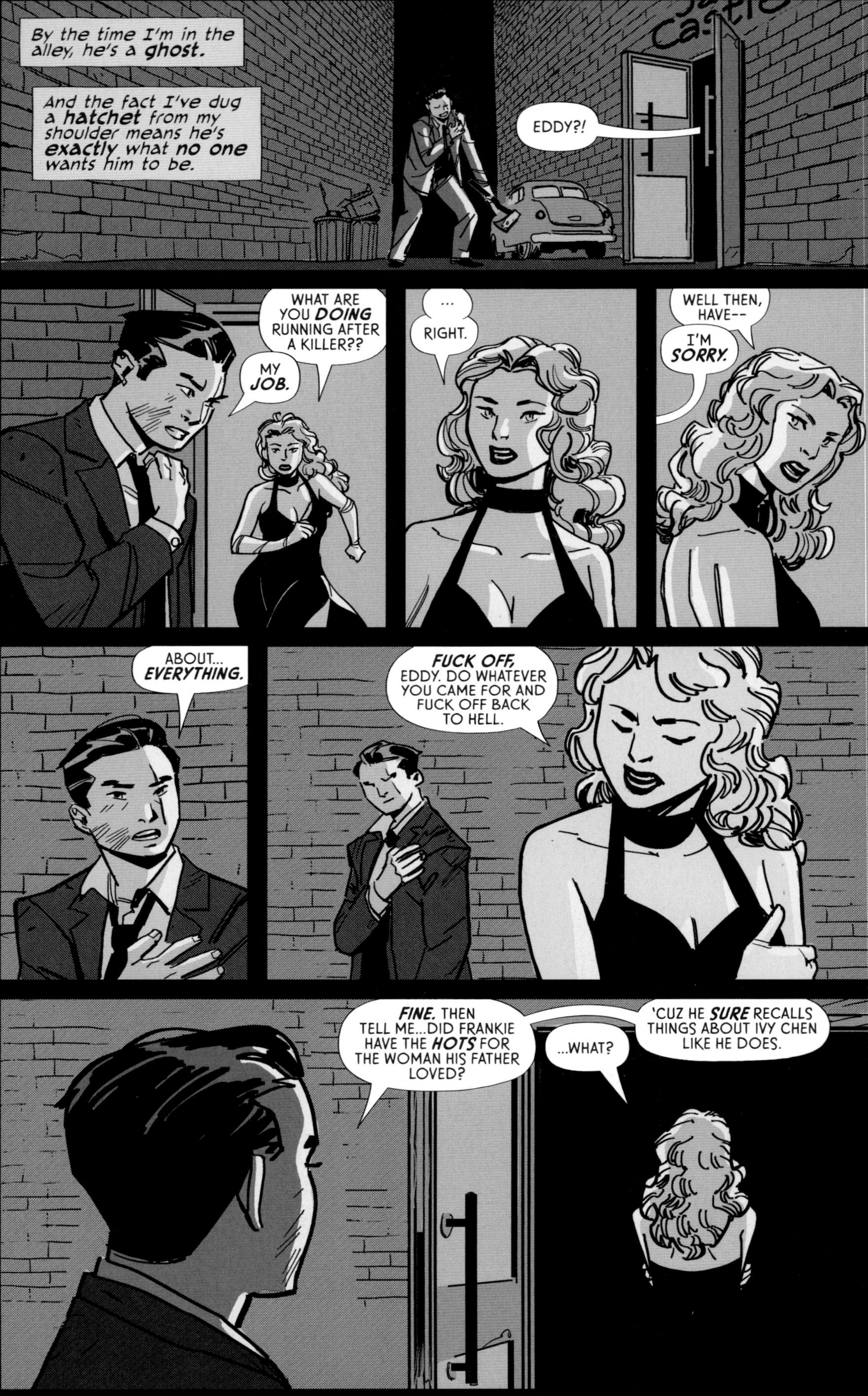

By the time I'm in the alley, he's a **ghost.**
And the fact I've dug a **hatchet** from my shoulder means he's **exactly** what **no one** wants him to be.
EDDY?!
WHAT ARE YOU ***DOING*** RUNNING AFTER A KILLER??
MY ***JOB.***
...
RIGHT.
WELL THEN, HAVE--
I'M ***SORRY.***
ABOUT... ***EVERYTHING.***
FUCK OFF, EDDY. DO WHATEVER YOU CAME FOR AND FUCK OFF BACK TO HELL.
FINE. THEN TELL ME...DID FRANKIE HAVE THE ***HOTS*** FOR THE WOMAN HIS FATHER LOVED?
...WHAT?
'CUZ HE ***SURE*** RECALLS THINGS ABOUT IVY CHEN LIKE HE DOES.

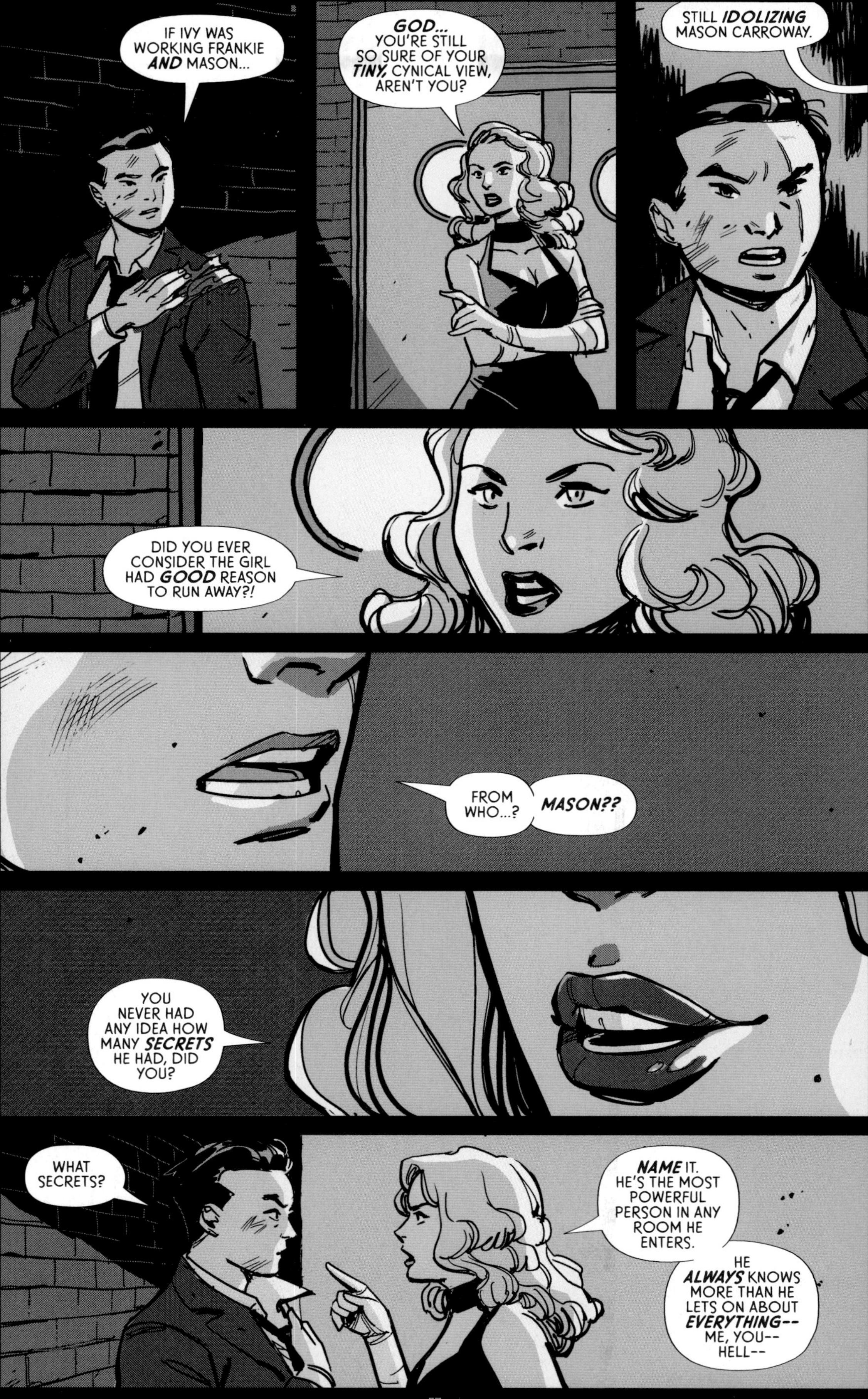
IF IVY WAS WORKING FRANKIE AND MASON...
GOD... YOU'RE STILL SO SURE OF YOUR TINY, CYNICAL VIEW, AREN'T YOU?
STILL IDOLIZING MASON CARROWAY.
DID YOU EVER CONSIDER THE GIRL HAD GOOD REASON TO RUN AWAY?!
FROM WHO...?
MASON??
YOU NEVER HAD ANY IDEA HOW MANY SECRETS HE HAD, DID YOU?
WHAT SECRETS?
NAME IT. HE'S THE MOST POWERFUL PERSON IN ANY ROOM HE ENTERS.
HE ALWAYS KNOWS MORE THAN HE LETS ON ABOUT EVERYTHING-- ME, YOU-- HELL--

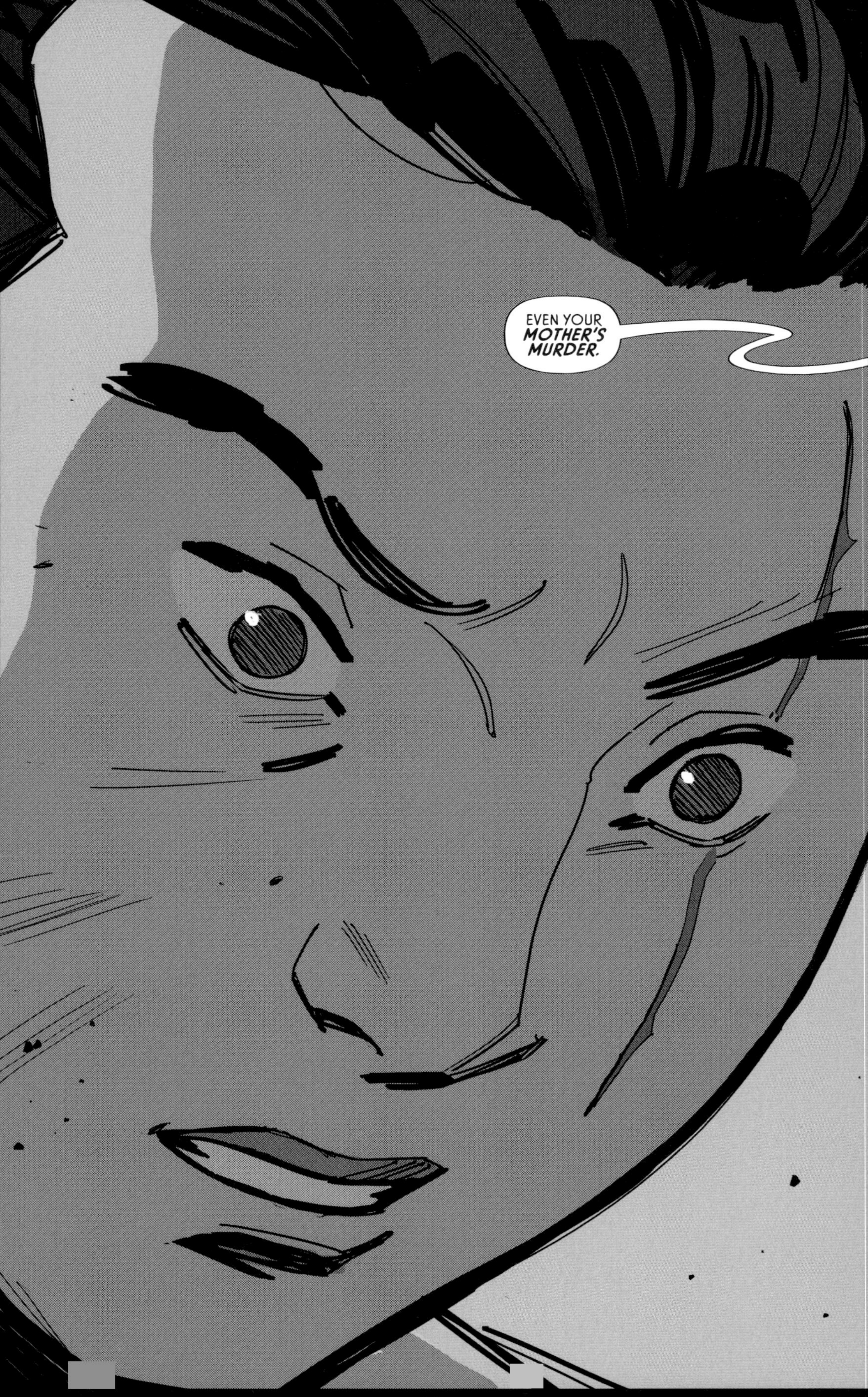
EVEN YOUR MOTHER'S MURDER.

HAPTER THRE

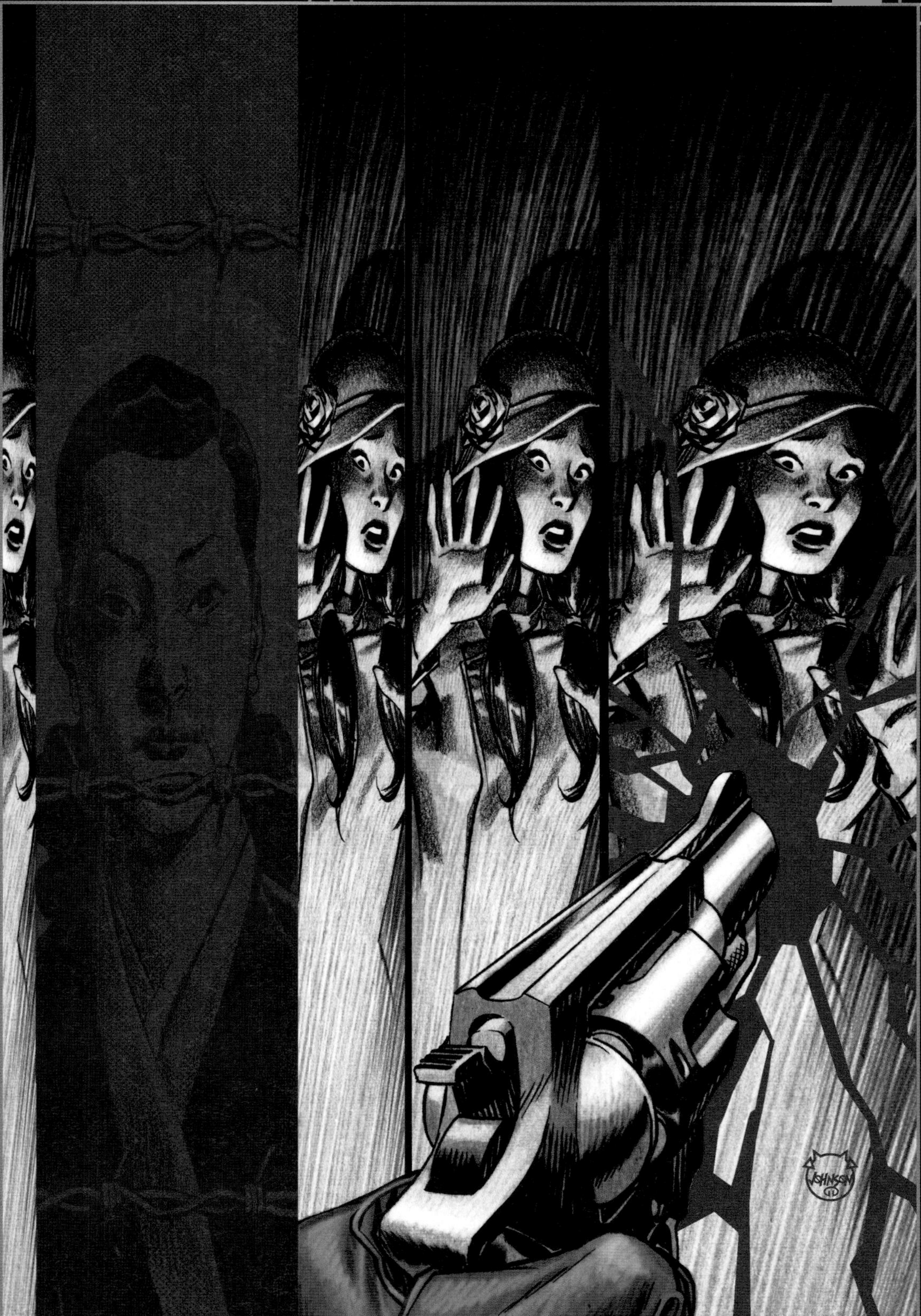

ART BY **DAVE JOHNSON**

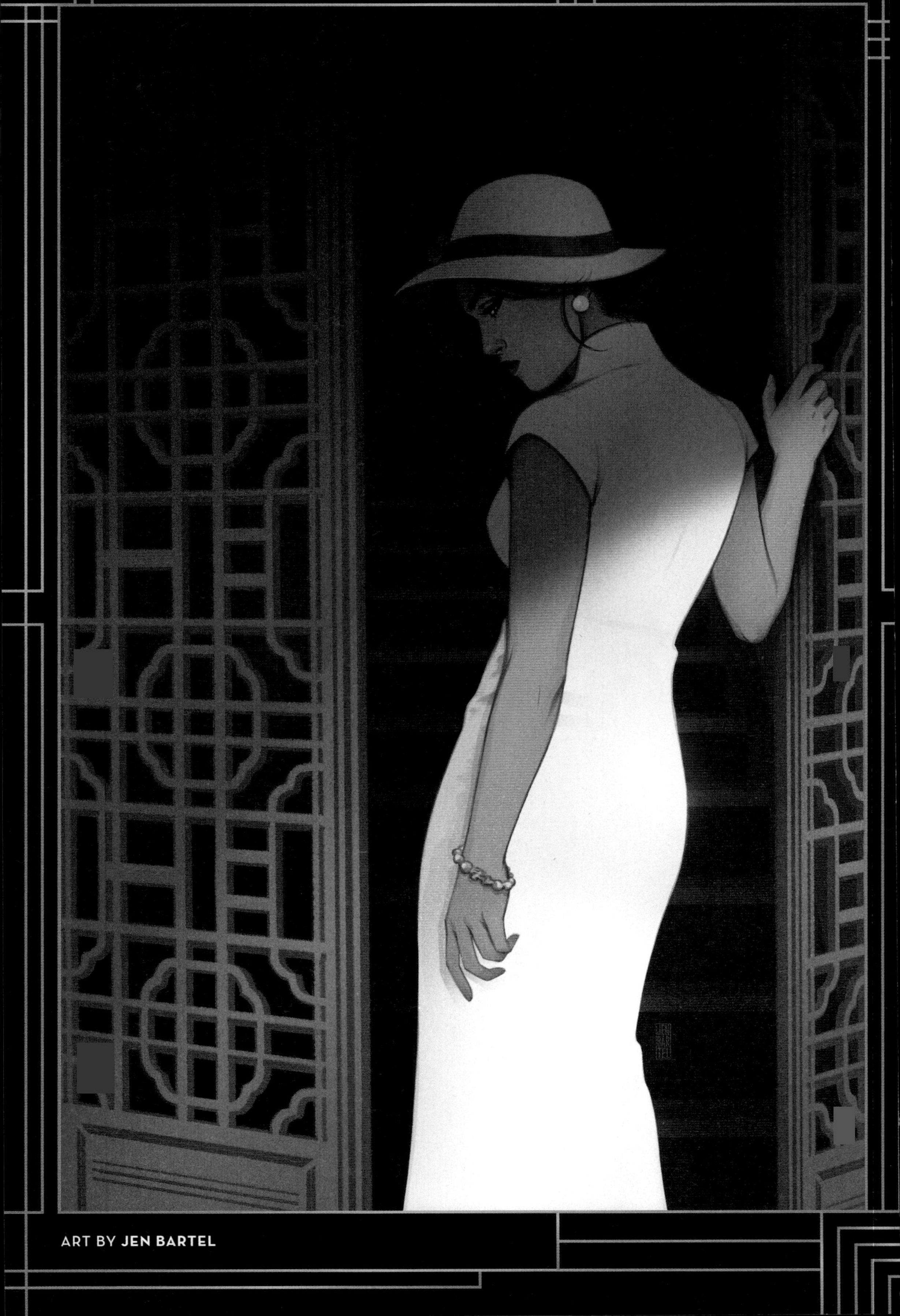
JEN BAR TEL

ART BY **JEN BARTEL**

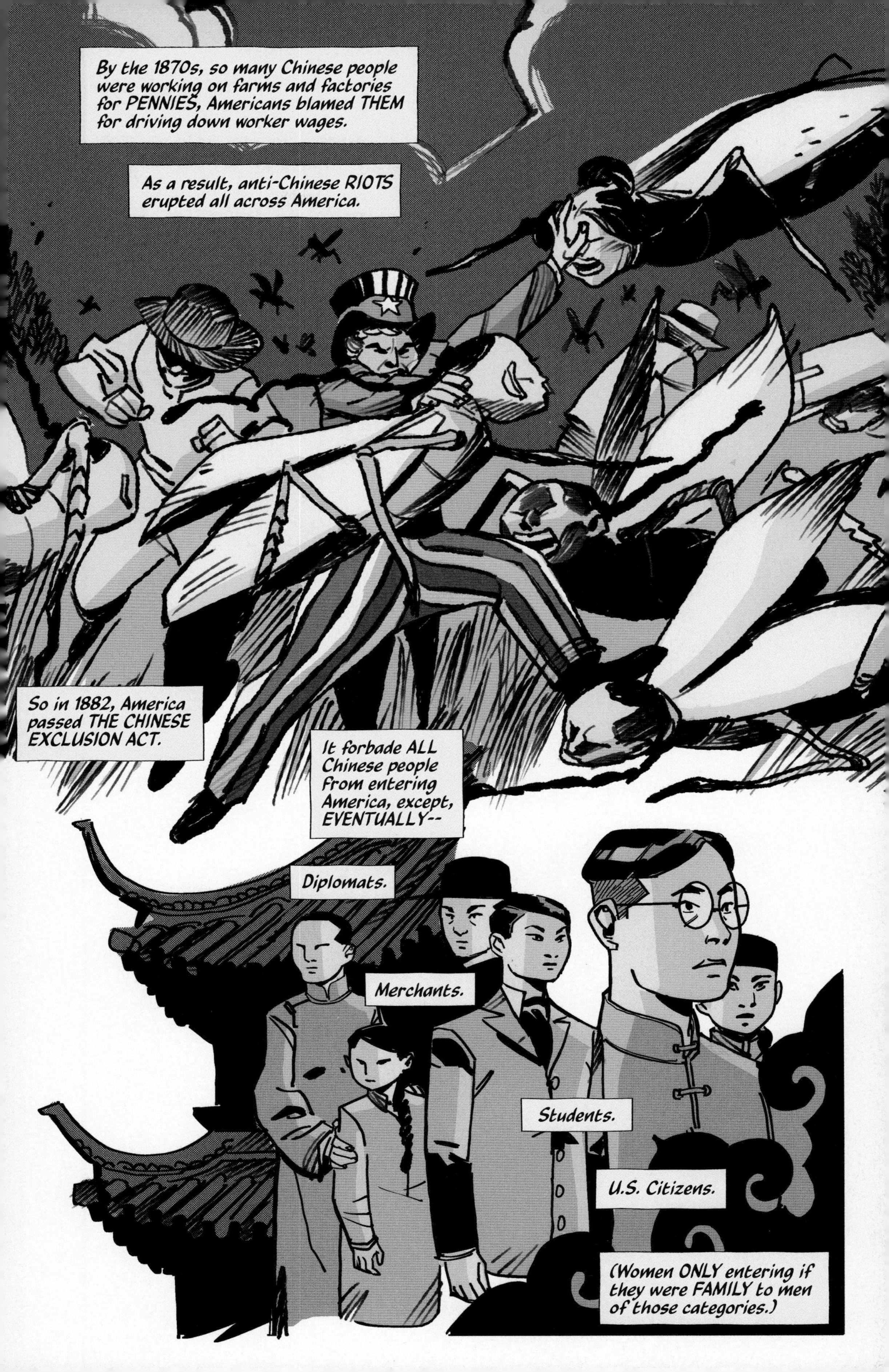
By the 1870s, so many Chinese people were working on farms and factories for PENNIES, Americans blamed THEM for driving down worker wages.
As a result, anti-Chinese RIOTS erupted all across America.
So in 1882, America passed THE CHINESE EXCLUSION ACT.
It forbade ALL Chinese people from entering America, except, EVENTUALLY--
Diplomats.
Merchants.
Students.
U.S. Citizens.
(Women ONLY entering if they were FAMILY to men of those categories.)

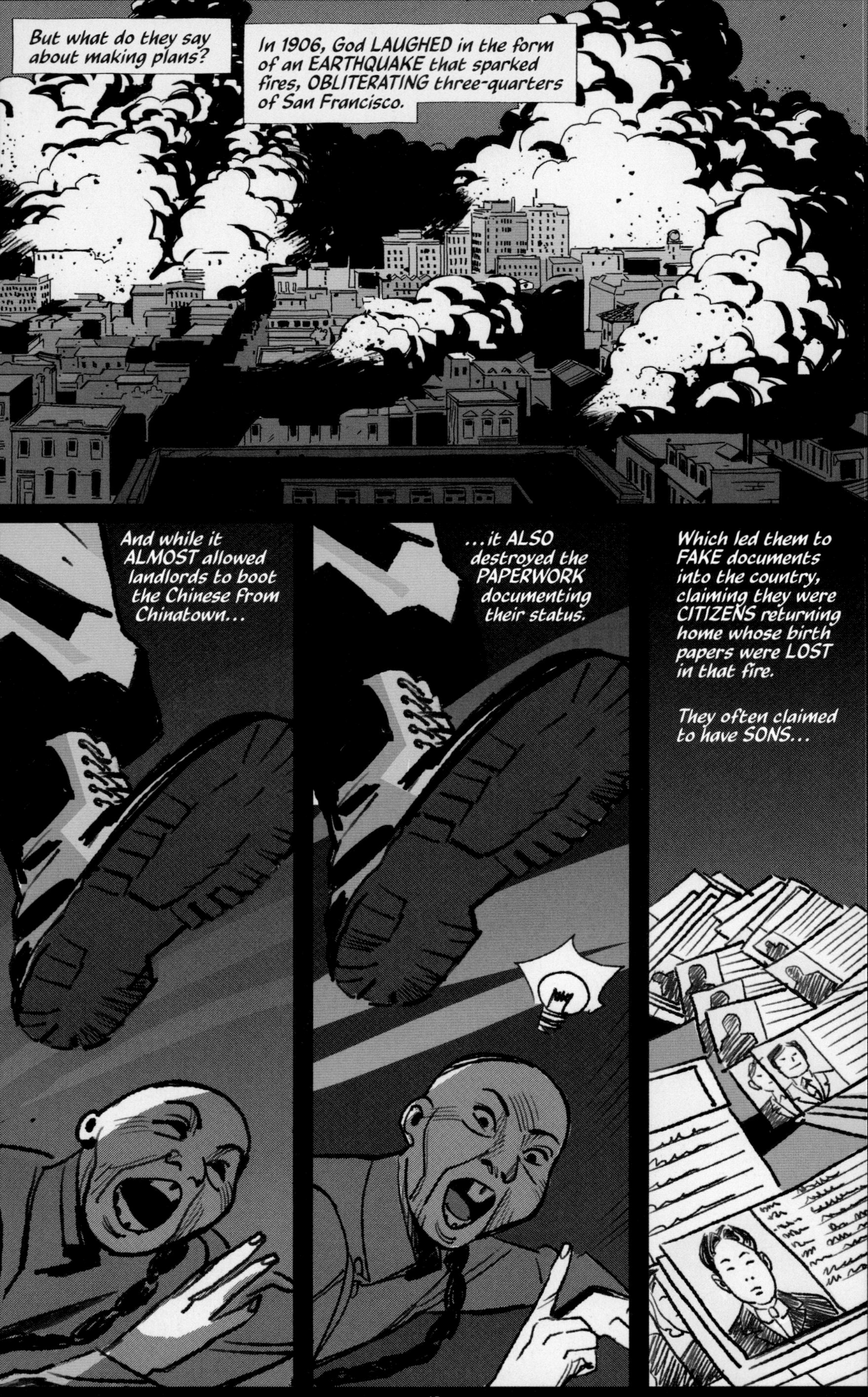
But what do they say about making plans?
In 1906, God LAUGHED in the form of an EARTHQUAKE that sparked fires, OBLITERATING three-quarters of San Francisco.
And while it ALMOST allowed landlords to boot the Chinese from Chinatown...
...it ALSO destroyed the PAPERWORK documenting their status.
Which led them to FAKE documents into the country, claiming they were CITIZENS returning home whose birth papers were LOST in that fire.
They often claimed to have SONS...

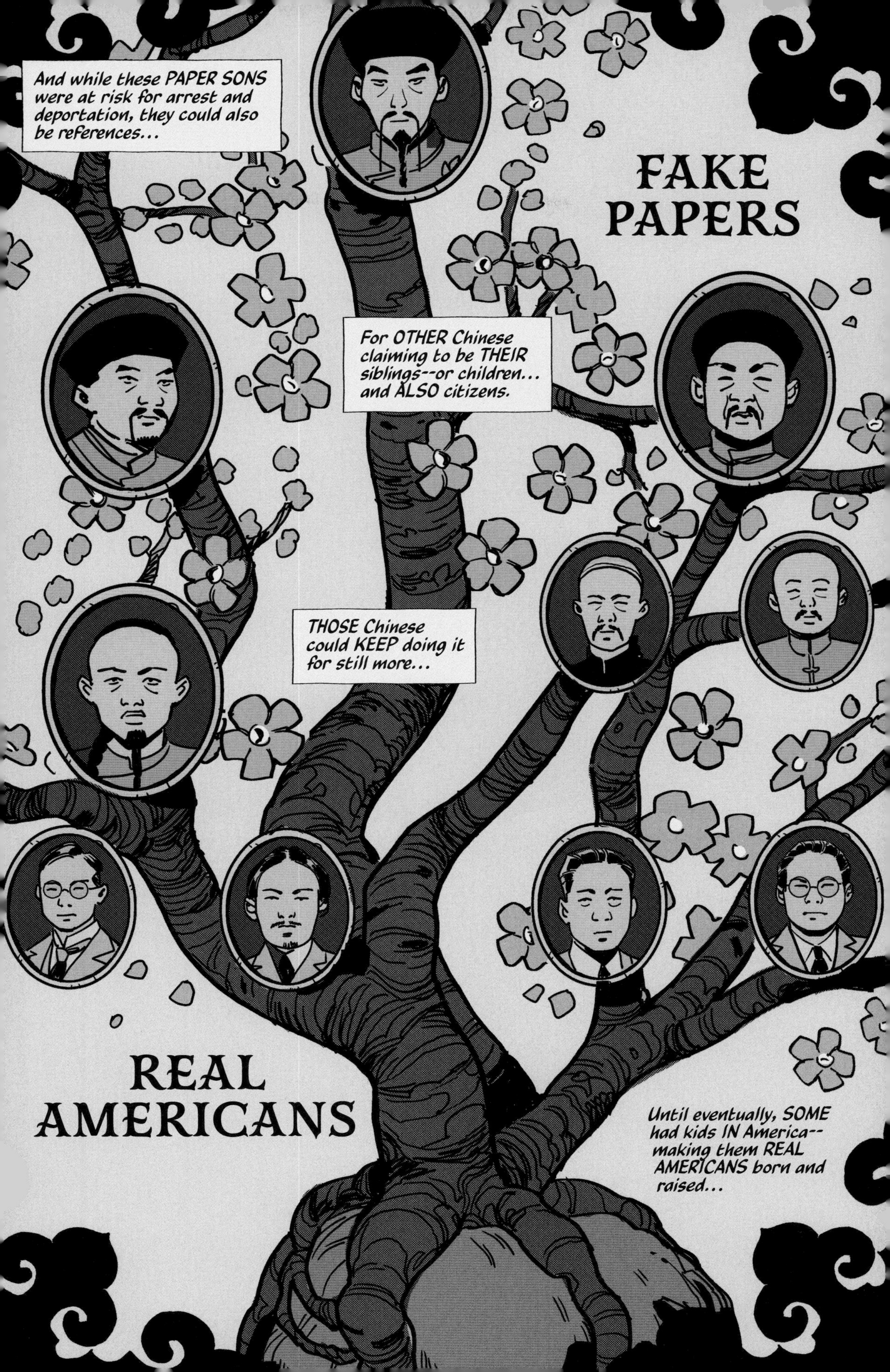
And while these PAPER SONS were at risk for arrest and deportation, they could also be references...
FAKE PAPERS
For OTHER Chinese claiming to be THEIR siblings--or children... and ALSO citizens.
THOSE Chinese could KEEP doing it for still more...
REAL AMERICANS
Until eventually, SOME had kids IN America--making them REAL AMERICANS born and raised...

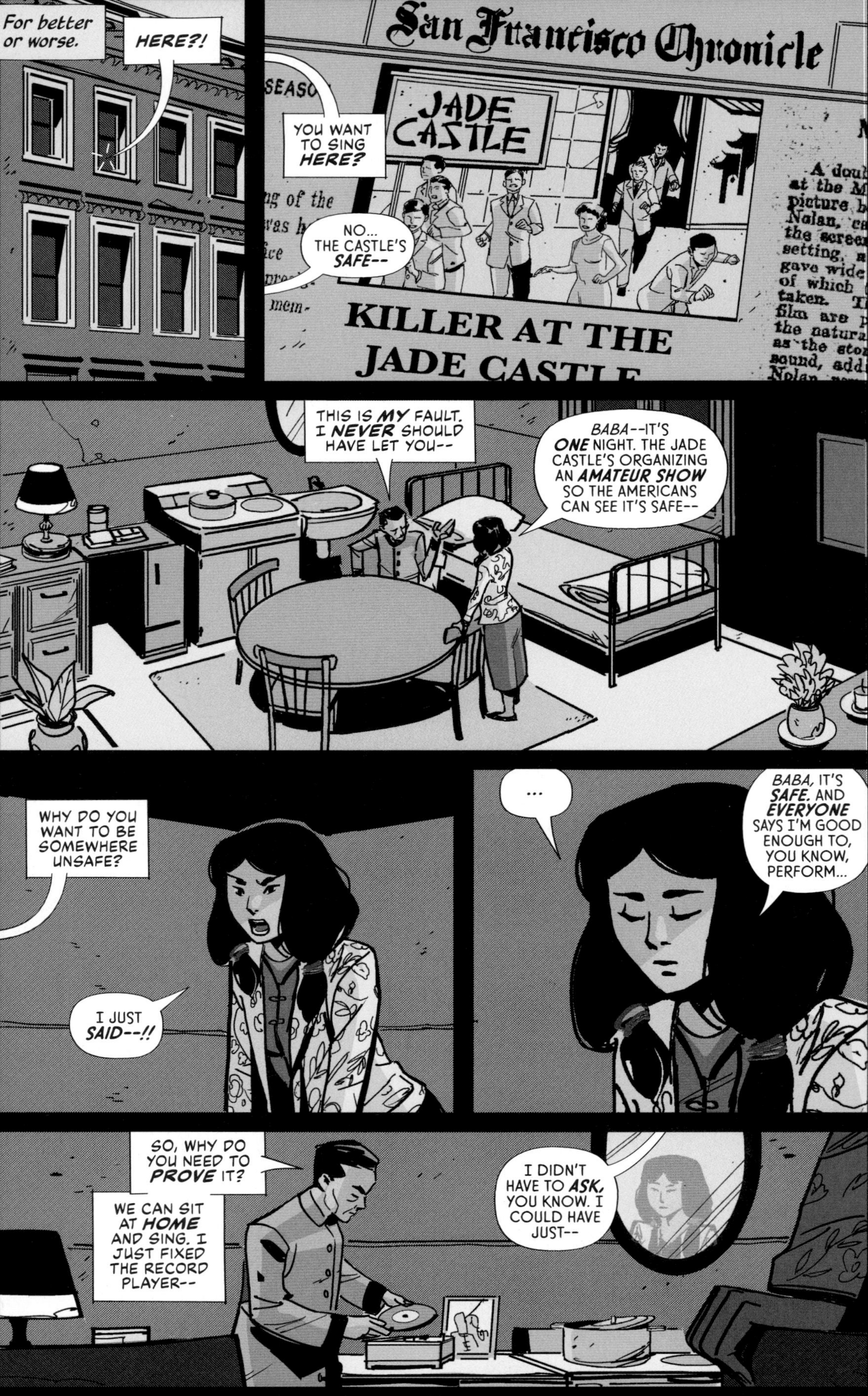
For better or worse.
HERE?!
San Francisco Chronicle
JADE CASTLE
YOU WANT TO SING HERE?
NO... THE CASTLE'S SAFE--
KILLER AT THE JADE CASTLE
THIS IS MY FAULT. I NEVER SHOULD HAVE LET YOU--
BABA--IT'S ONE NIGHT. THE JADE CASTLE'S ORGANIZING AN AMATEUR SHOW SO THE AMERICANS CAN SEE IT'S SAFE--
WHY DO YOU WANT TO BE SOMEWHERE UNSAFE?
I JUST SAID--!!
...
BABA, IT'S SAFE. AND EVERYONE SAYS I'M GOOD ENOUGH TO, YOU KNOW, PERFORM...
SO, WHY DO YOU NEED TO PROVE IT?
WE CAN SIT AT HOME AND SING. I JUST FIXED THE RECORD PLAYER--
I DIDN'T HAVE TO ASK, YOU KNOW. I COULD HAVE JUST--

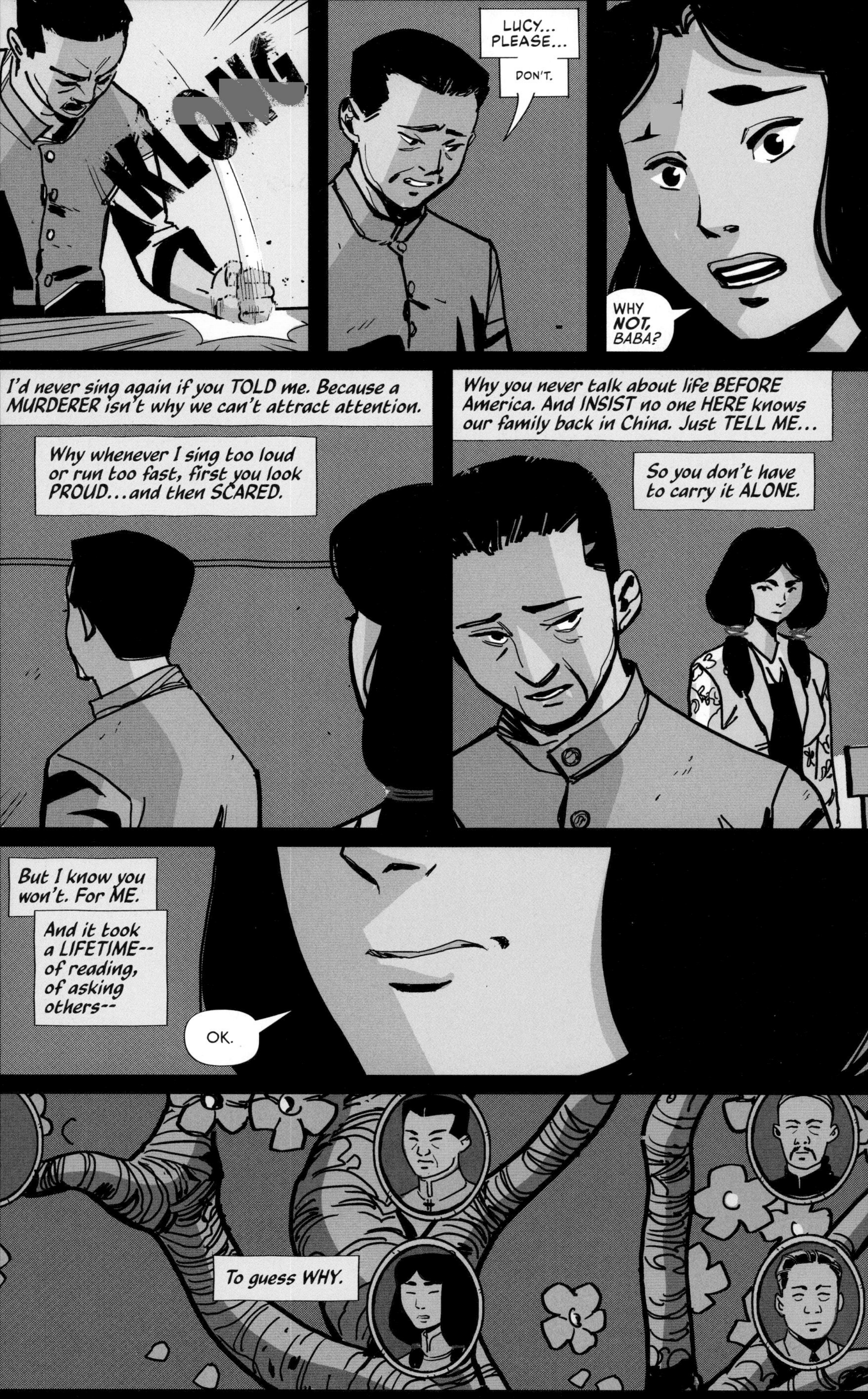
KLONG
LUCY... PLEASE...
DON'T.
WHY NOT, BABA?
I'd never sing again if you TOLD me. Because a MURDERER isn't why we can't attract attention.
Why whenever I sing too loud or run too fast, first you look PROUD...and then SCARED.
Why you never talk about life BEFORE America. And INSIST no one HERE knows our family back in China. Just TELL ME...
So you don't have to carry it ALONE.
But I know you won't. For ME.
And it took a LIFETIME-- of reading, of asking others--
OK.
To guess WHY.

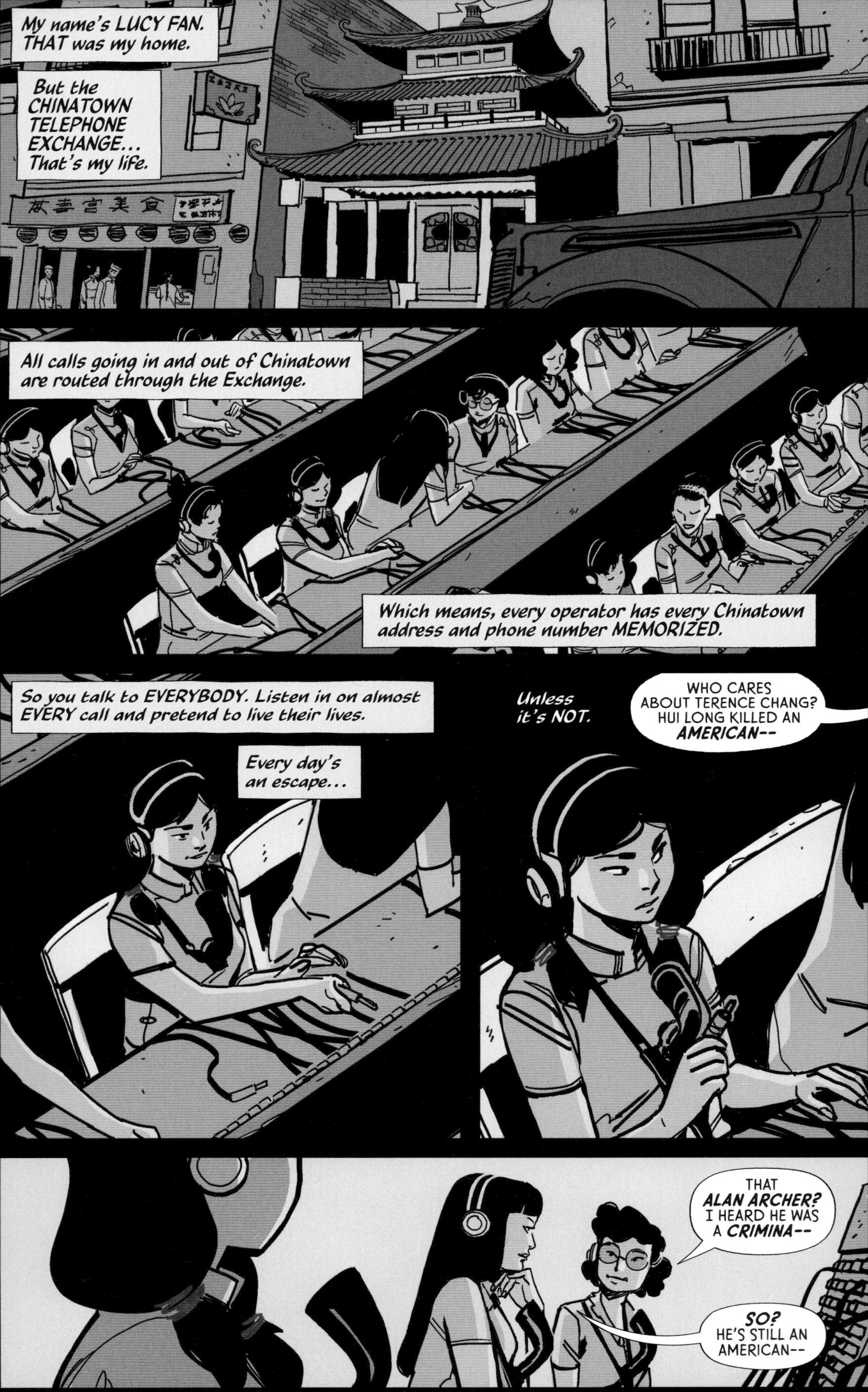
My name's LUCY FAN. THAT was my home.
But the CHINATOWN TELEPHONE EXCHANGE... That's my life.
All calls going in and out of Chinatown are routed through the Exchange.
Which means, every operator has every Chinatown address and phone number MEMORIZED.
So you talk to EVERYBODY. Listen in on almost EVERY call and pretend to live their lives.
Every day's an escape...
Unless it's NOT.
WHO CARES ABOUT TERENCE CHANG? HUI LONG KILLED AN AMERICAN--
THAT ALAN ARCHER? I HEARD HE WAS A CRIMINA--
SO? HE'S STILL AN AMERICAN--

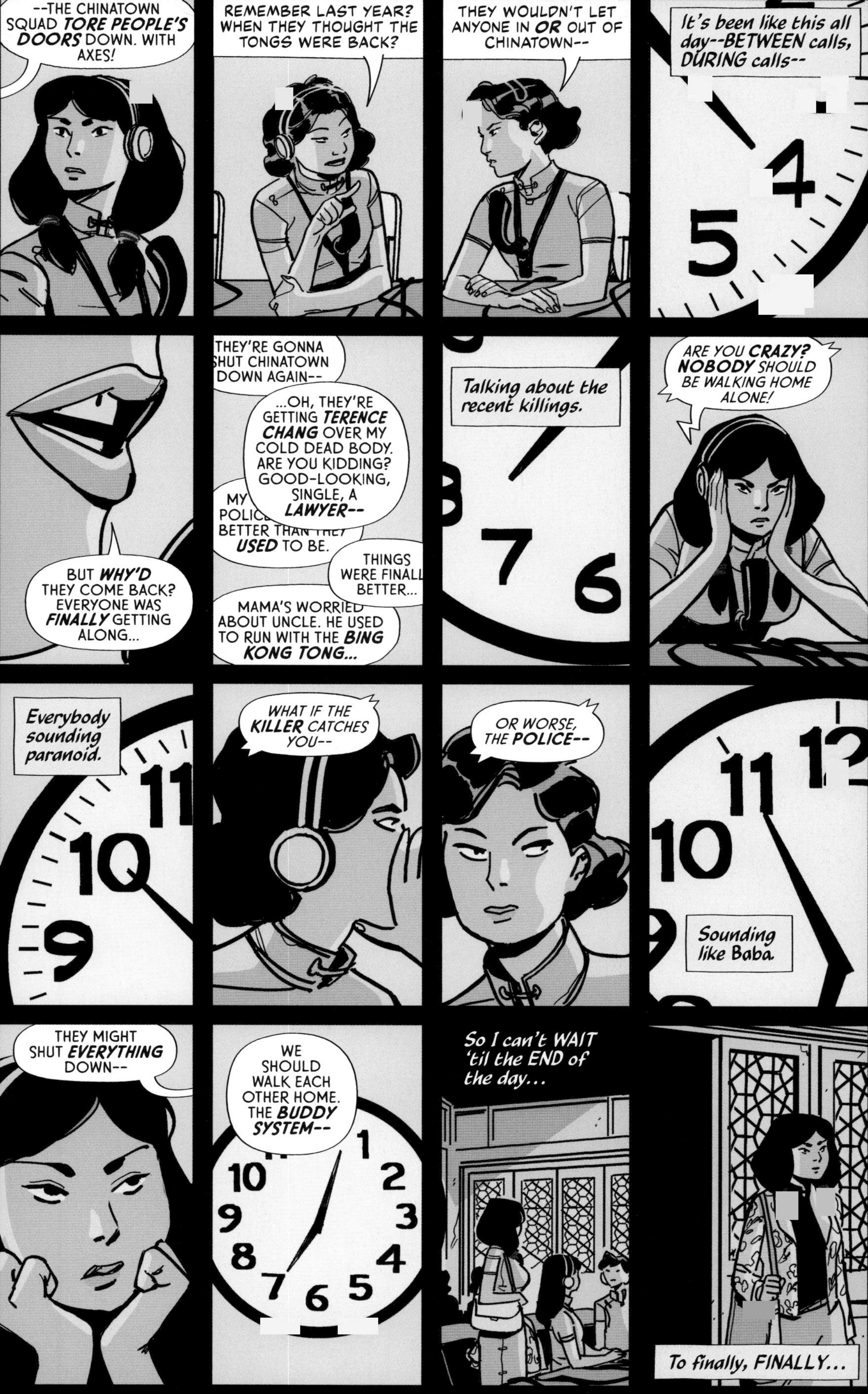
--THE CHINATOWN SQUAD TORE PEOPLE'S DOORS DOWN. WITH AXES!
REMEMBER LAST YEAR? WHEN THEY THOUGHT THE TONGS WERE BACK?
THEY WOULDN'T LET ANYONE IN OR OUT OF CHINATOWN--
It's been like this all day--BETWEEN calls, DURING calls--
BUT WHY'D THEY COME BACK? EVERYONE WAS FINALLY GETTING ALONG...
THEY'RE GONNA SHUT CHINATOWN DOWN AGAIN--
...OH, THEY'RE GETTING TERENCE CHANG OVER MY COLD DEAD BODY. ARE YOU KIDDING? GOOD-LOOKING, SINGLE, A LAWYER--
MY POLIC BETTER THAN USED TO BE.
THINGS WERE FINALL BETTER...
MAMA'S WORRIED ABOUT UNCLE. HE USED TO RUN WITH THE BING KONG TONG...
Talking about the recent killings.
ARE YOU CRAZY? NOBODY SHOULD BE WALKING HOME ALONE!
Everybody sounding paranoid.
WHAT IF THE KILLER CATCHES YOU--
OR WORSE, THE POLICE--
Sounding like Baba.
THEY MIGHT SHUT EVERYTHING DOWN--
WE SHOULD WALK EACH OTHER HOME. THE BUDDY SYSTEM--
So I can't WAIT 'til the END of the day...
To finally, FINALLY...

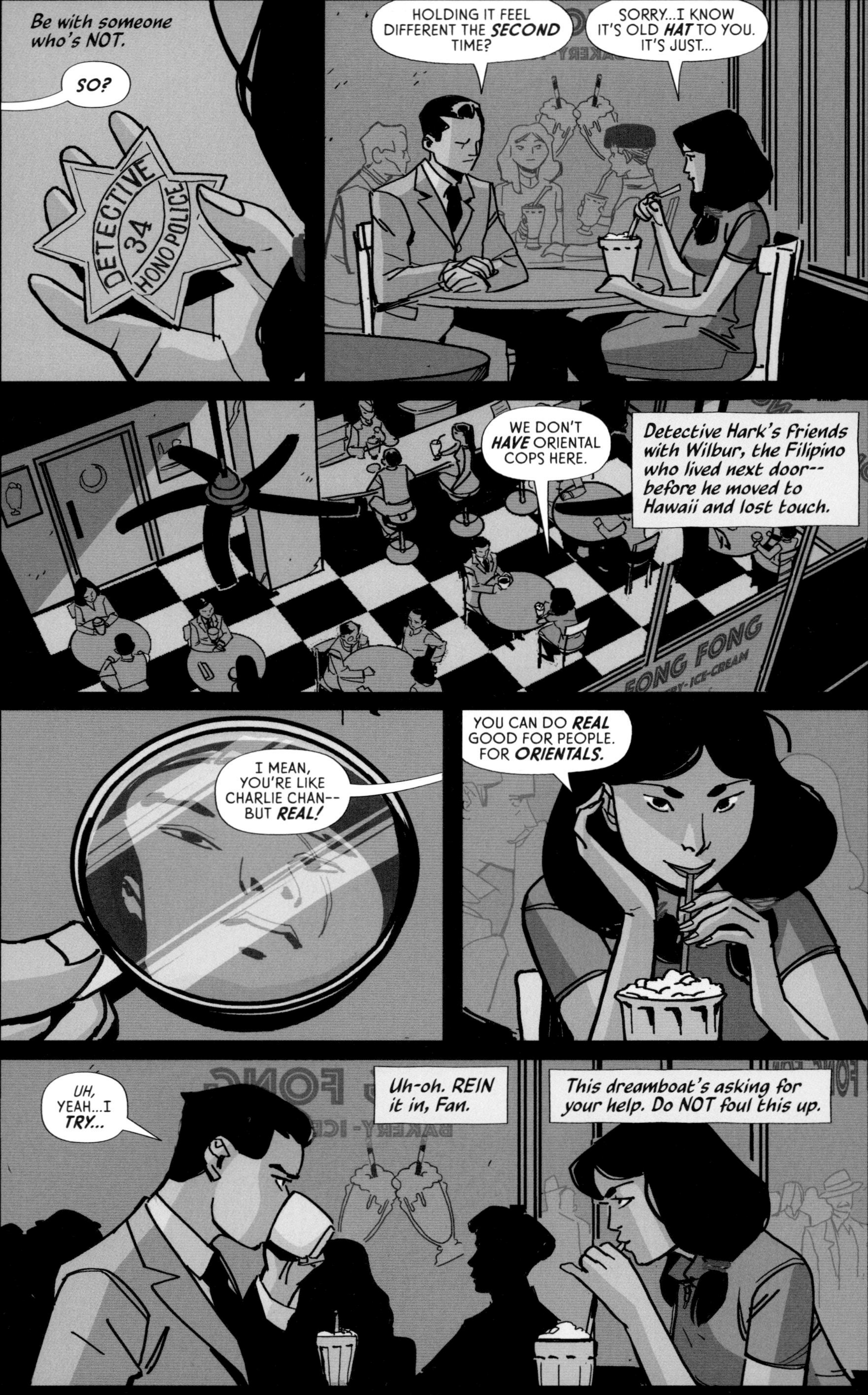

Be with someone who's NOT.
SO?
DETECTIVE 34 HONO POLICE
HOLDING IT FEEL DIFFERENT THE SECOND TIME?
SORRY...I KNOW IT'S OLD HAT TO YOU. IT'S JUST...
WE DON'T HAVE ORIENTAL COPS HERE.
Detective Hark's friends with Wilbur, the Filipino who lived next door--before he moved to Hawaii and lost touch.
FONG FONG
I MEAN, YOU'RE LIKE CHARLIE CHAN--BUT REAL!
YOU CAN DO REAL GOOD FOR PEOPLE. FOR ORIENTALS.
UH, YEAH...I TRY...
Uh-oh. REIN it in, Fan.
This dreamboat's asking for your help. Do NOT foul this up.

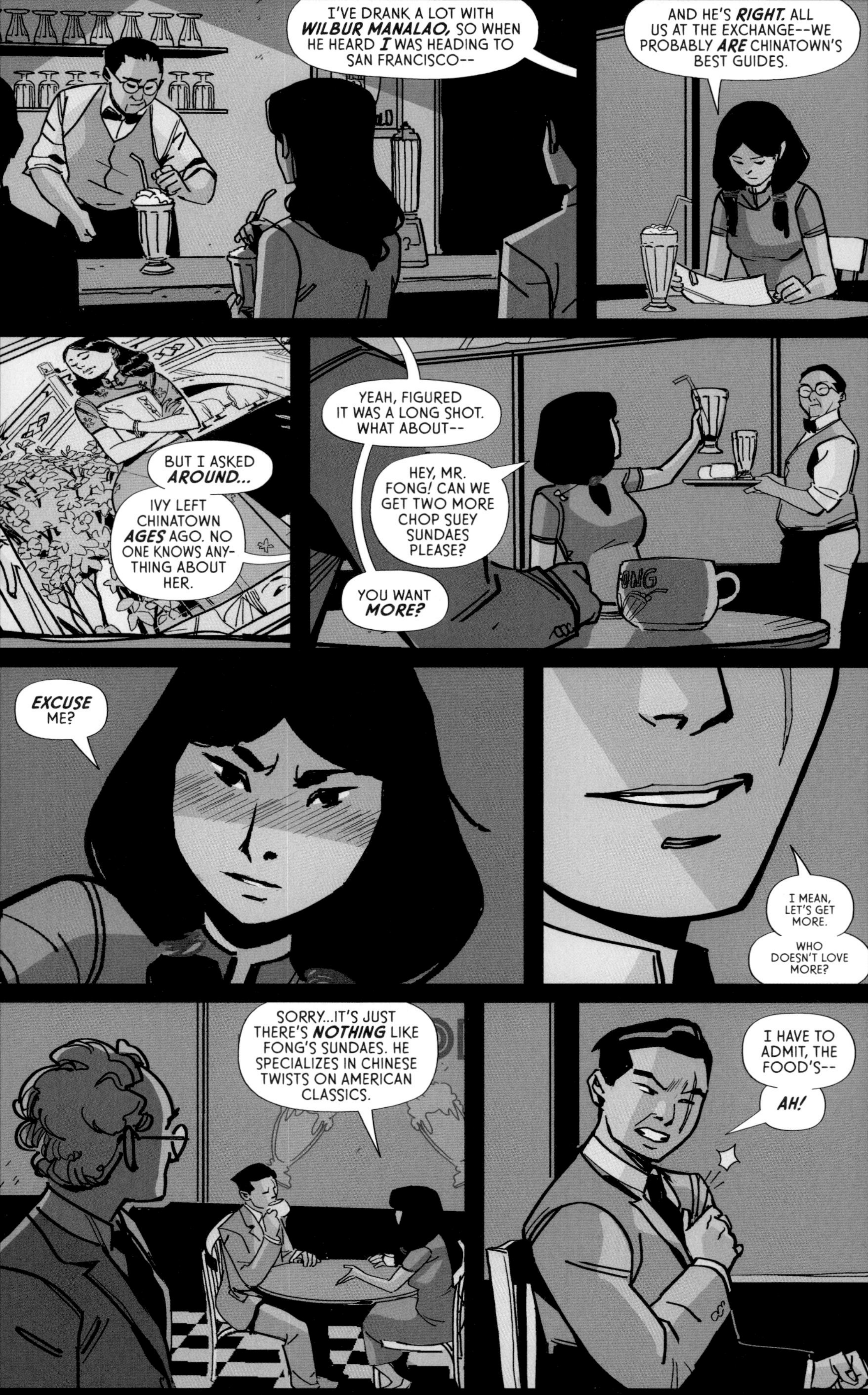
I'VE DRANK A LOT WITH WILBUR MANALAO, SO WHEN HE HEARD I WAS HEADING TO SAN FRANCISCO--
AND HE'S RIGHT. ALL US AT THE EXCHANGE--WE PROBABLY ARE CHINATOWN'S BEST GUIDES.
BUT I ASKED AROUND...
IVY LEFT CHINATOWN AGES AGO. NO ONE KNOWS ANYTHING ABOUT HER.
YEAH, FIGURED IT WAS A LONG SHOT. WHAT ABOUT--
HEY, MR. FONG! CAN WE GET TWO MORE CHOP SUEY SUNDAES PLEASE?
YOU WANT MORE?
FONG
EXCUSE ME?
I MEAN, LET'S GET MORE.
WHO DOESN'T LOVE MORE?
SORRY...IT'S JUST THERE'S NOTHING LIKE FONG'S SUNDAES. HE SPECIALIZES IN CHINESE TWISTS ON AMERICAN CLASSICS.
I HAVE TO ADMIT, THE FOOD'S--
AH!

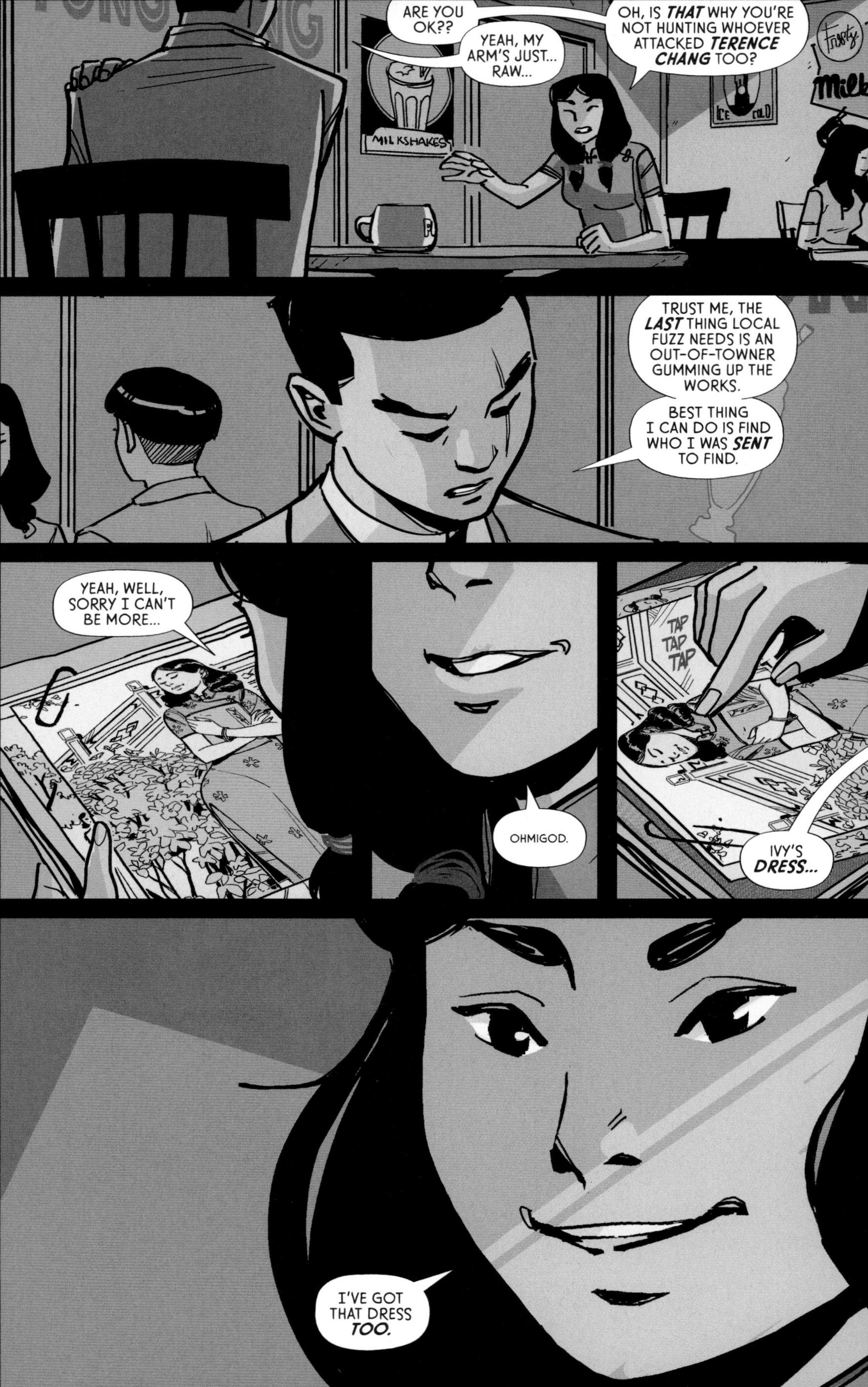
ARE YOU OK??
YEAH, MY ARM'S JUST... RAW...
OH, IS **THAT** WHY YOU'RE NOT HUNTING WHOEVER ATTACKED **TERENCE CHANG** TOO?
MILKSHAKES
TRUST ME, THE **LAST** THING LOCAL FUZZ NEEDS IS AN OUT-OF-TOWNER GUMMING UP THE WORKS.
BEST THING I CAN DO IS FIND WHO I WAS **SENT** TO FIND.
YEAH, WELL, SORRY I CAN'T BE MORE...
OHMIGOD.
TAP TAP TAP
IVY'S **DRESS...**
I'VE GOT THAT DRESS **TOO.**

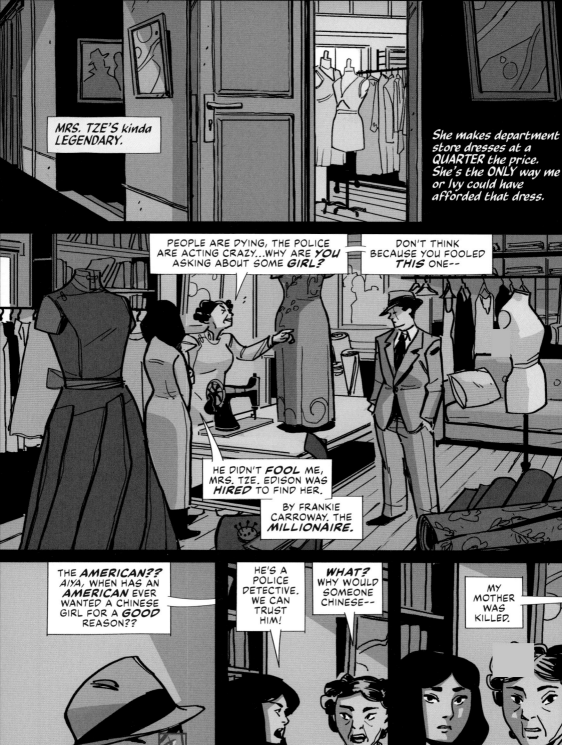

MRS. TZE'S kinda LEGENDARY.

She makes department store dresses at a QUARTER the price. She's the ONLY way me or Ivy could have afforded that dress.

PEOPLE ARE DYING, THE POLICE ARE ACTING CRAZY...WHY ARE *YOU* ASKING ABOUT SOME *GIRL?*

DON'T THINK BECAUSE YOU FOOLED *THIS* ONE--

HE DIDN'T *FOOL* ME, MRS. TZE. EDISON WAS *HIRED* TO FIND HER.

BY FRANKIE CARROWAY. THE *MILLIONAIRE.*

THE *AMERICAN??* AIYA, WHEN HAS AN *AMERICAN* EVER WANTED A CHINESE GIRL FOR A *GOOD* REASON??

HE'S A POLICE DETECTIVE. WE CAN TRUST HIM!

WHAT? WHY WOULD SOMEONE CHINESE--

MY MOTHER WAS KILLED.

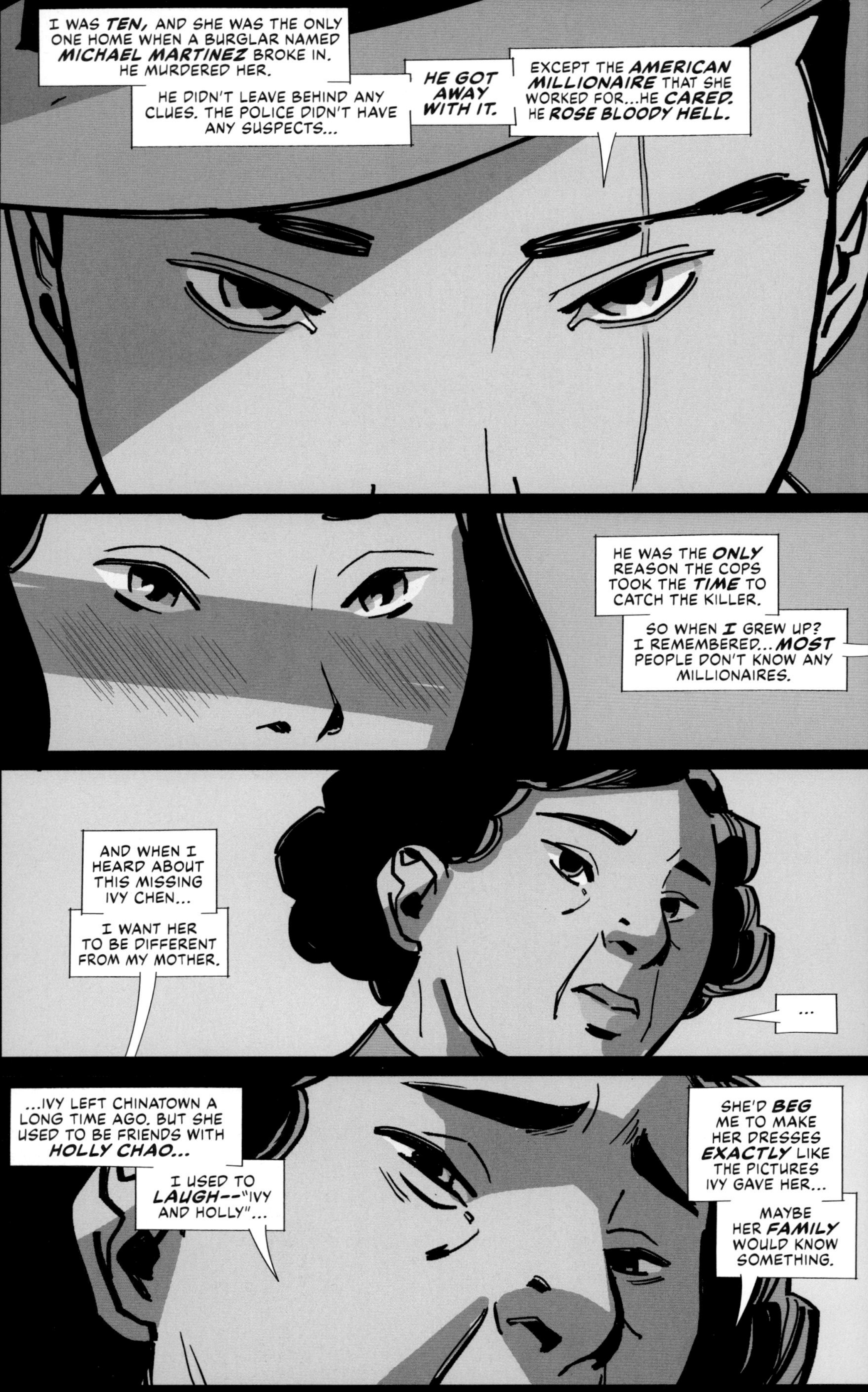
I WAS *TEN,* AND SHE WAS THE ONLY ONE HOME WHEN A BURGLAR NAMED *MICHAEL MARTINEZ* BROKE IN. HE MURDERED HER.
HE DIDN'T LEAVE BEHIND ANY CLUES. THE POLICE DIDN'T HAVE ANY SUSPECTS...
HE GOT AWAY WITH IT.
EXCEPT THE *AMERICAN MILLIONAIRE* THAT SHE WORKED FOR...HE *CARED.* HE *ROSE BLOODY HELL.*
HE WAS THE *ONLY* REASON THE COPS TOOK THE *TIME* TO CATCH THE KILLER.
SO WHEN *I* GREW UP? I REMEMBERED...*MOST* PEOPLE DON'T KNOW ANY MILLIONAIRES.
AND WHEN I HEARD ABOUT THIS MISSING IVY CHEN...
I WANT HER TO BE DIFFERENT FROM MY MOTHER.
...
...IVY LEFT CHINATOWN A LONG TIME AGO. BUT SHE USED TO BE FRIENDS WITH *HOLLY CHAO...*
I USED TO *LAUGH*--"IVY AND HOLLY"...
SHE'D *BEG* ME TO MAKE HER DRESSES *EXACTLY* LIKE THE PICTURES IVY GAVE HER...
MAYBE HER *FAMILY* WOULD KNOW SOMETHING.

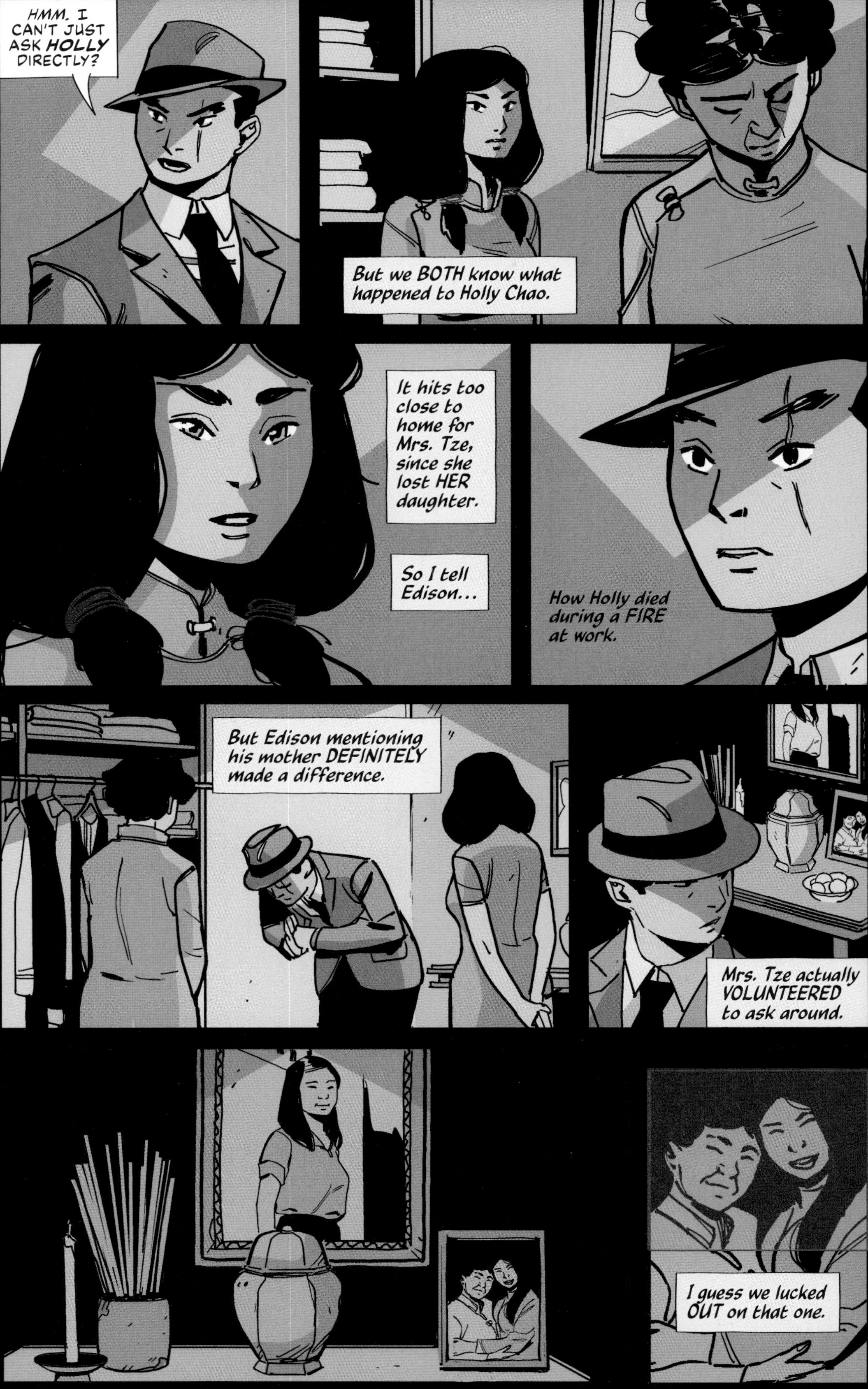
HMM. I CAN'T JUST ASK HOLLY DIRECTLY?
But we BOTH know what happened to Holly Chao.
It hits too close to home for Mrs. Tze, since she lost HER daughter.
So I tell Edison...
How Holly died during a FIRE at work.
But Edison mentioning his mother DEFINITELY made a difference.
Mrs. Tze actually VOLUNTEERED to ask around.
I guess we lucked OUT on that one.

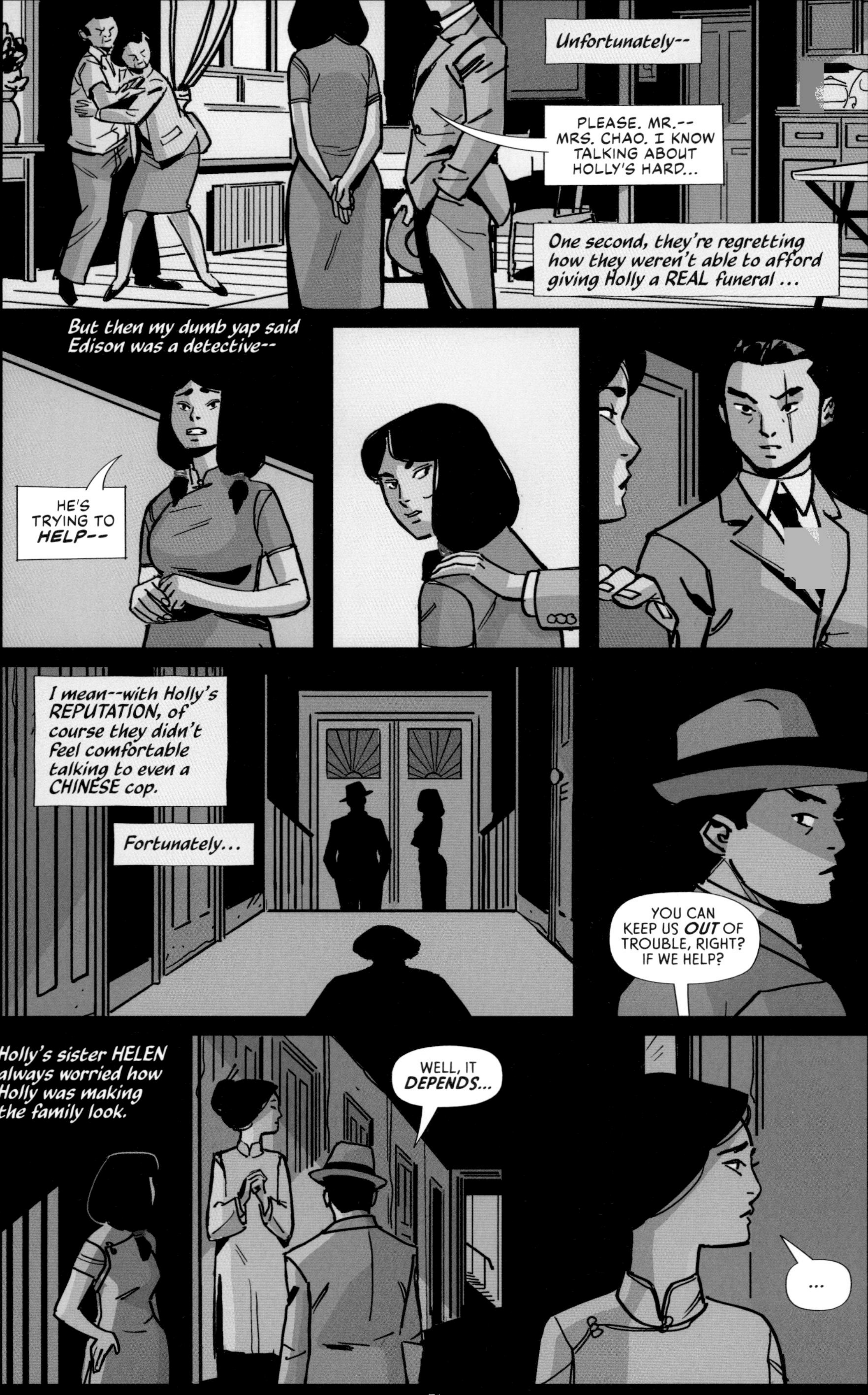
Unfortunately--
PLEASE. MR.-- MRS. CHAO. I KNOW TALKING ABOUT HOLLY'S HARD...
One second, they're regretting how they weren't able to afford giving Holly a REAL funeral ...
But then my dumb yap said Edison was a detective--
HE'S TRYING TO HELP--
I mean--with Holly's REPUTATION, of course they didn't feel comfortable talking to even a CHINESE cop.
Fortunately...
YOU CAN KEEP US OUT OF TROUBLE, RIGHT? IF WE HELP?
Holly's sister HELEN always worried how Holly was making the family look.
WELL, IT DEPENDS...
...

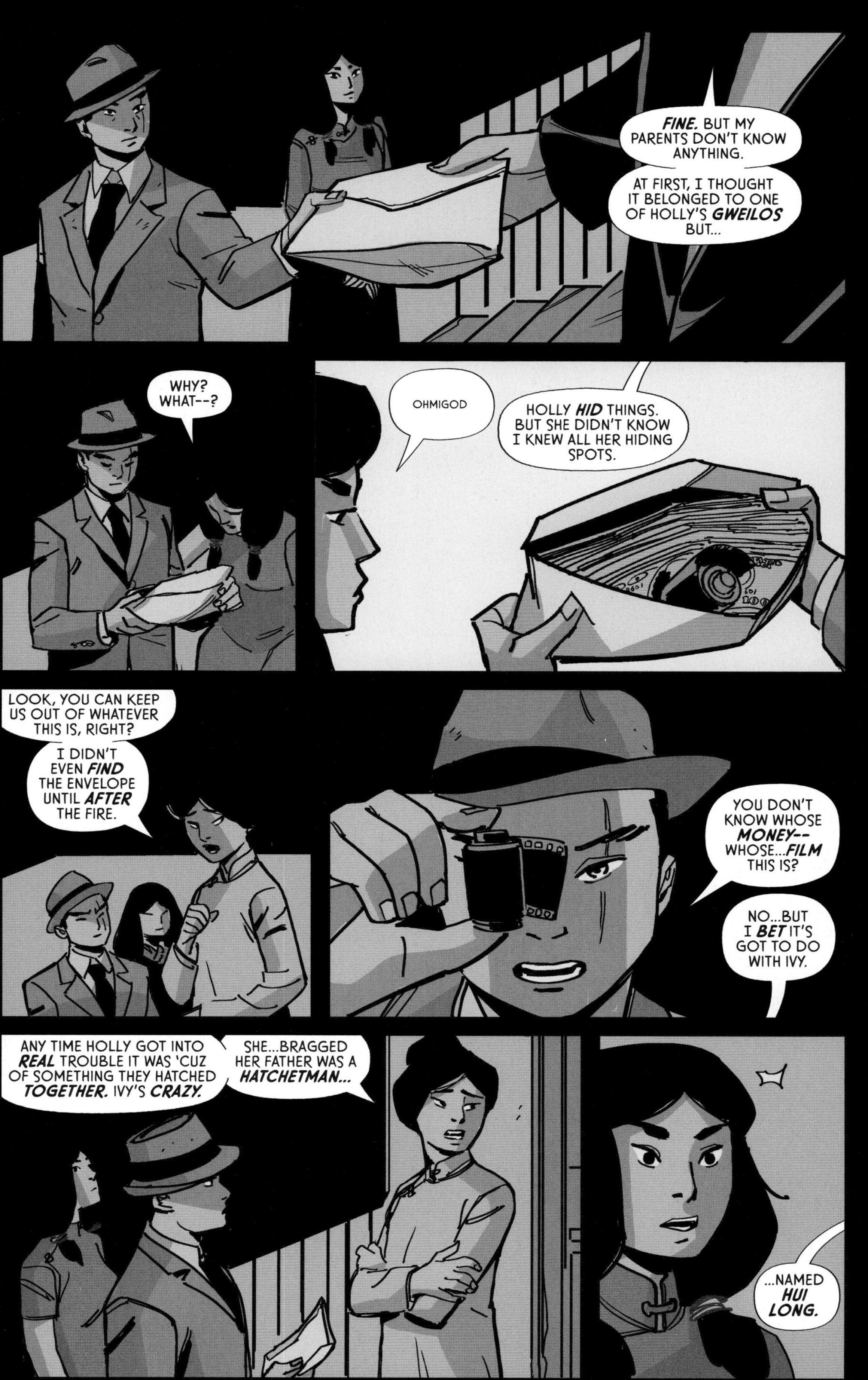
FINE. BUT MY PARENTS DON'T KNOW ANYTHING.
AT FIRST, I THOUGHT IT BELONGED TO ONE OF HOLLY'S GWEILOS BUT...
WHY? WHAT--?
OHMIGOD
HOLLY HID THINGS. BUT SHE DIDN'T KNOW I KNEW ALL HER HIDING SPOTS.
LOOK, YOU CAN KEEP US OUT OF WHATEVER THIS IS, RIGHT?
I DIDN'T EVEN FIND THE ENVELOPE UNTIL AFTER THE FIRE.
YOU DON'T KNOW WHOSE MONEY-- WHOSE...FILM THIS IS?
NO...BUT I BET IT'S GOT TO DO WITH IVY.
ANY TIME HOLLY GOT INTO REAL TROUBLE IT WAS 'CUZ OF SOMETHING THEY HATCHED TOGETHER. IVY'S CRAZY.
SHE...BRAGGED HER FATHER WAS A HATCHETMAN...
...NAMED HUI LONG.

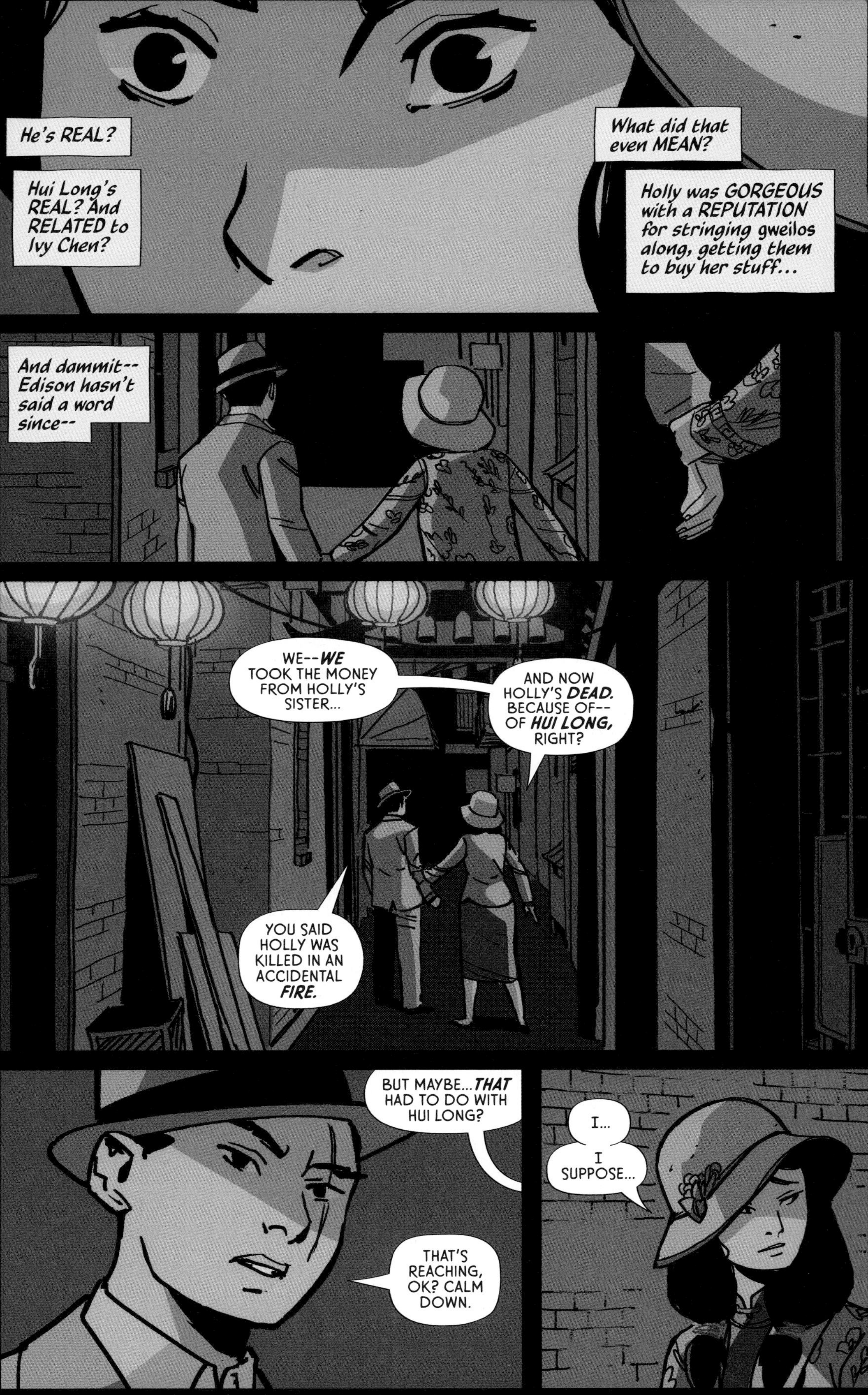
He's REAL?
Hui Long's REAL? And RELATED to Ivy Chen?
What did that even MEAN?
Holly was GORGEOUS with a REPUTATION for stringing gweilos along, getting them to buy her stuff...
And dammit-- Edison hasn't said a word since--
WE--WE TOOK THE MONEY FROM HOLLY'S SISTER...
AND NOW HOLLY'S DEAD. BECAUSE OF-- OF HUI LONG, RIGHT?
YOU SAID HOLLY WAS KILLED IN AN ACCIDENTAL FIRE.
BUT MAYBE...THAT HAD TO DO WITH HUI LONG?
THAT'S REACHING, OK? CALM DOWN.
I...
I SUPPOSE...

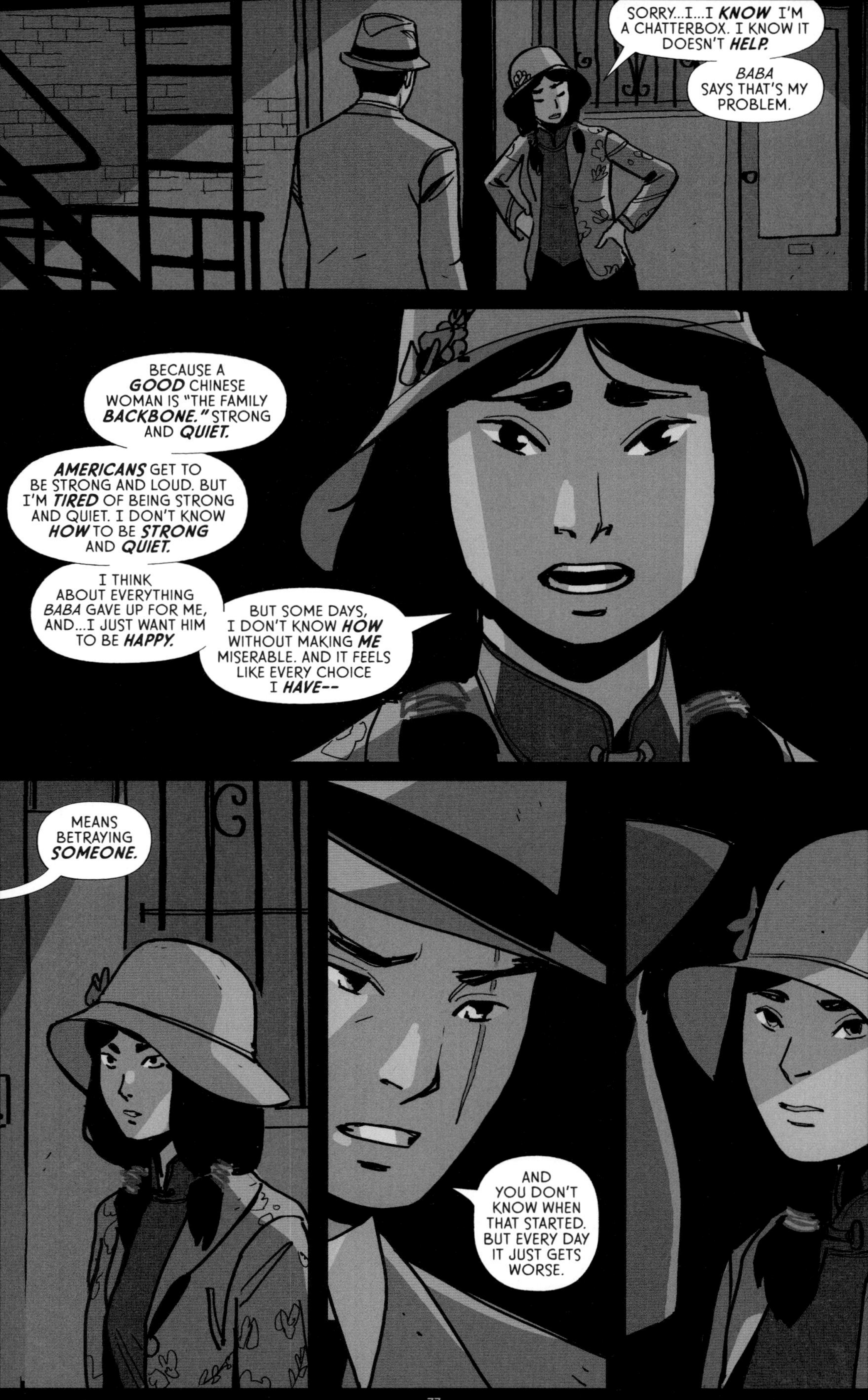
SORRY...I...I KNOW I'M A CHATTERBOX. I KNOW IT DOESN'T HELP.
BABA SAYS THAT'S MY PROBLEM.
BECAUSE A GOOD CHINESE WOMAN IS "THE FAMILY BACKBONE." STRONG AND QUIET.
AMERICANS GET TO BE STRONG AND LOUD. BUT I'M TIRED OF BEING STRONG AND QUIET. I DON'T KNOW HOW TO BE STRONG AND QUIET.
I THINK ABOUT EVERYTHING BABA GAVE UP FOR ME, AND...I JUST WANT HIM TO BE HAPPY.
BUT SOME DAYS, I DON'T KNOW HOW WITHOUT MAKING ME MISERABLE. AND IT FEELS LIKE EVERY CHOICE I HAVE--
MEANS BETRAYING SOMEONE.
AND YOU DON'T KNOW WHEN THAT STARTED. BUT EVERY DAY IT JUST GETS WORSE.

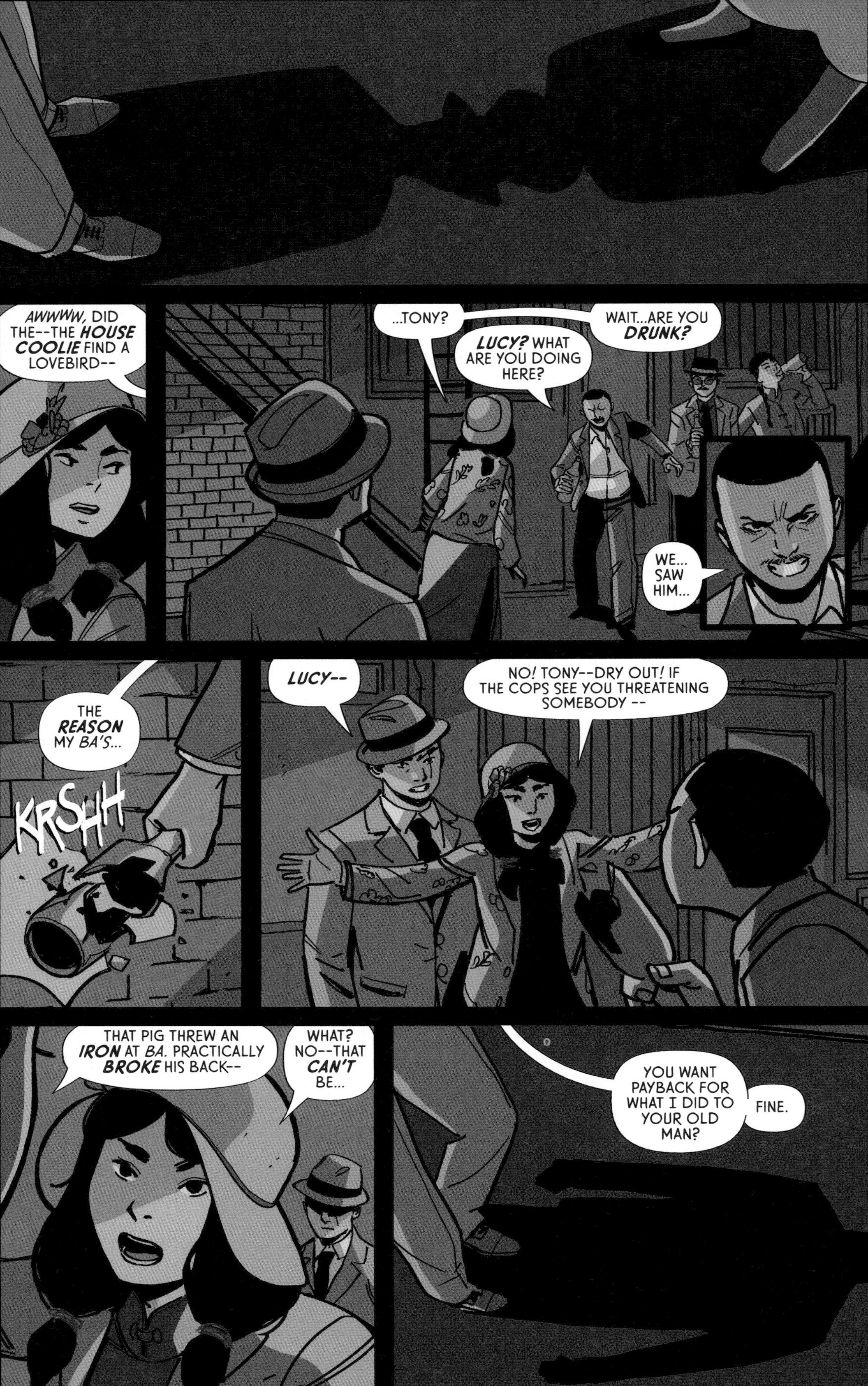
AWWWW, DID THE--THE HOUSE COOLIE FIND A LOVEBIRD--
...TONY?
LUCY? WHAT ARE YOU DOING HERE?
WAIT...ARE YOU DRUNK?
WE... SAW HIM...
THE REASON MY BA'S...
KRSHH
LUCY--
NO! TONY--DRY OUT! IF THE COPS SEE YOU THREATENING SOMEBODY --
THAT PIG THREW AN IRON AT BA. PRACTICALLY BROKE HIS BACK--
WHAT? NO--THAT CAN'T BE...
YOU WANT PAYBACK FOR WHAT I DID TO YOUR OLD MAN?
FINE.

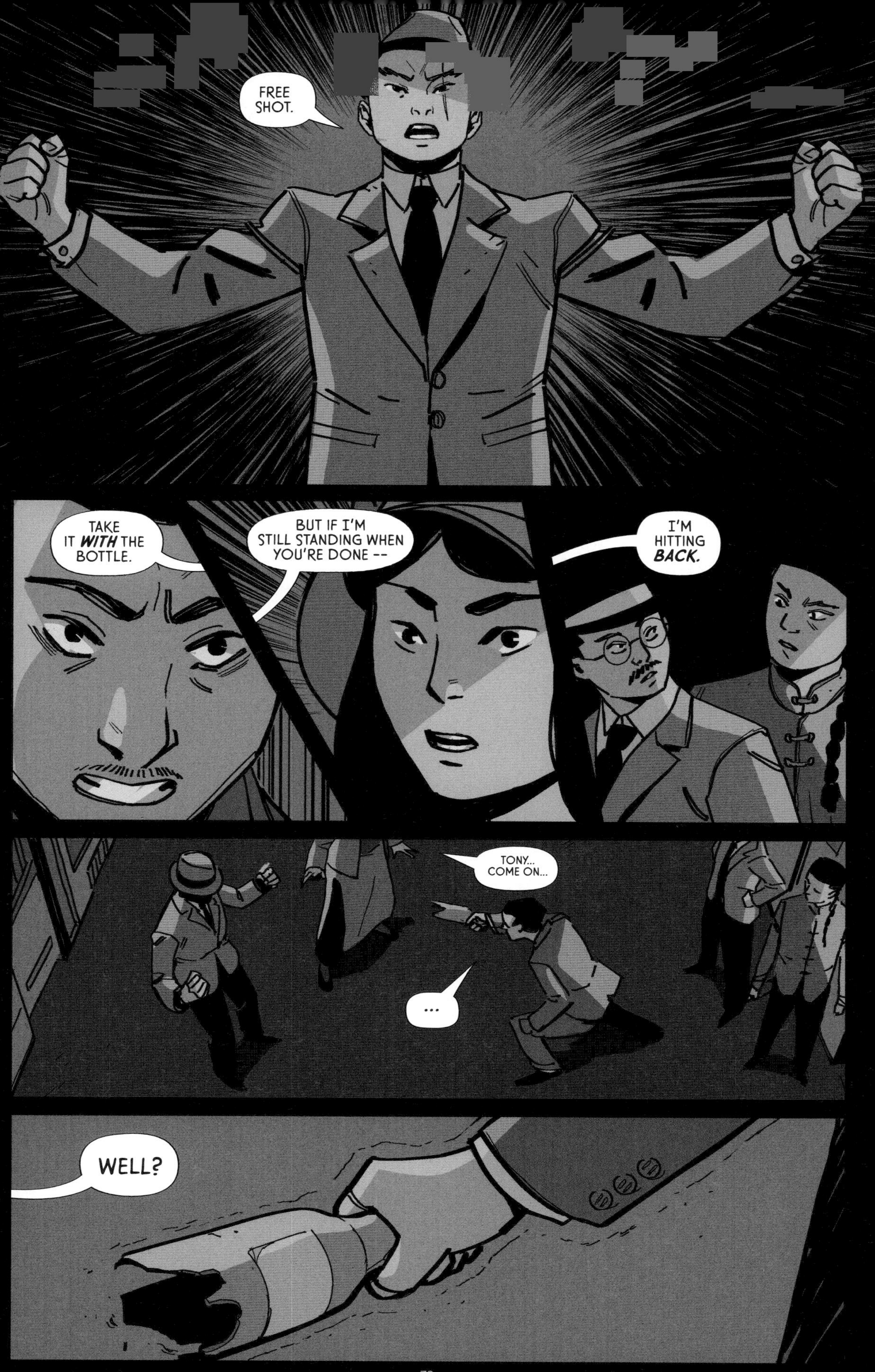
[redacted]
FREE SHOT.
TAKE IT *WITH* THE BOTTLE.
BUT IF I'M STILL STANDING WHEN YOU'RE DONE --
I'M HITTING *BACK.*
TONY... COME ON...
...
WELL?

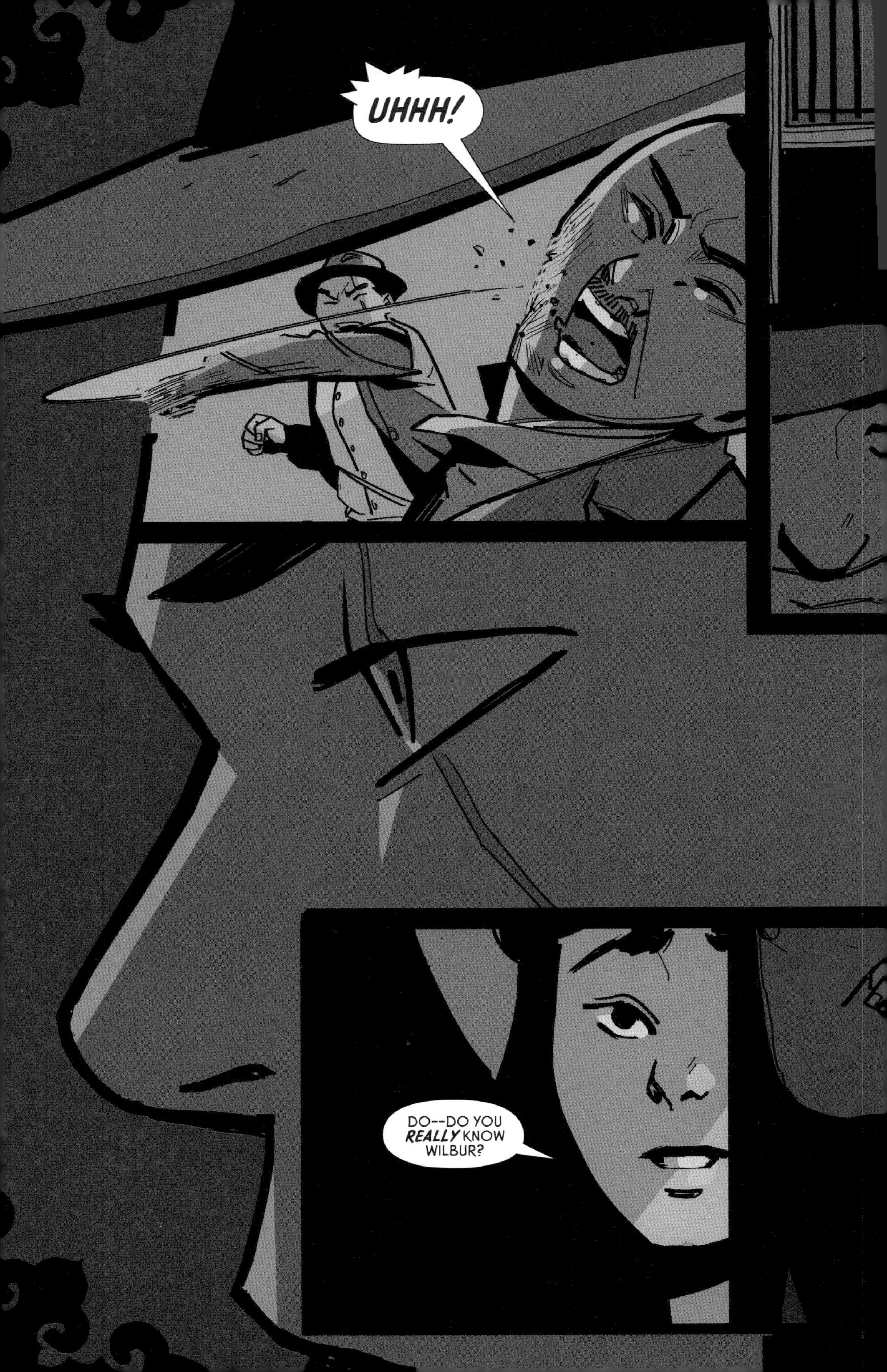
UHHH!
DO--DO YOU *REALLY* KNOW WILBUR?

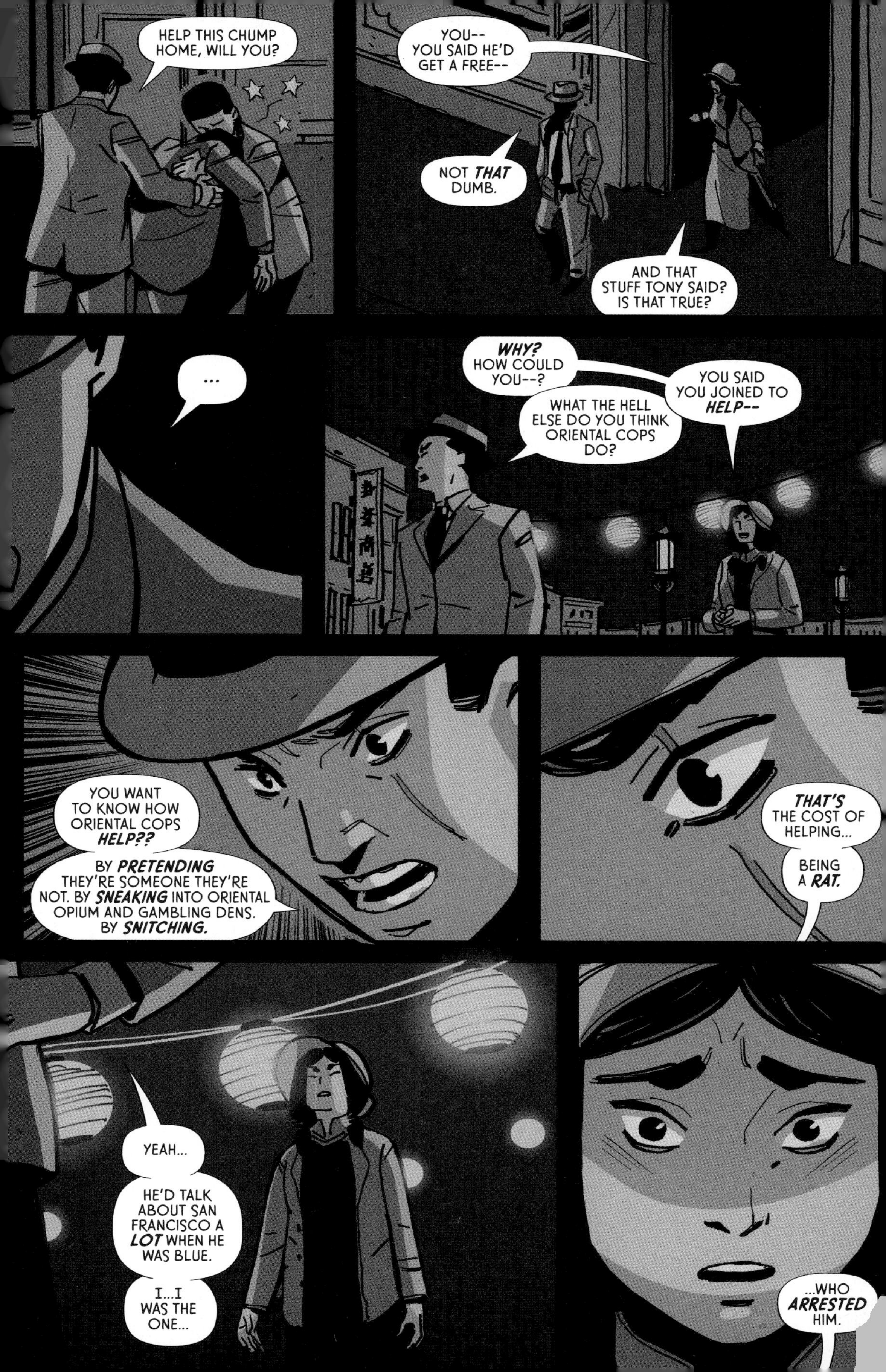
HELP THIS CHUMP HOME, WILL YOU?
YOU-- YOU SAID HE'D GET A FREE--
NOT *THAT* DUMB.
AND THAT STUFF TONY SAID? IS THAT TRUE?
...
WHY? HOW COULD YOU--?
YOU SAID YOU JOINED TO *HELP--*
WHAT THE HELL ELSE DO YOU THINK ORIENTAL COPS DO?
YOU WANT TO KNOW HOW ORIENTAL COPS *HELP??*
BY *PRETENDING* THEY'RE SOMEONE THEY'RE NOT. BY *SNEAKING* INTO ORIENTAL OPIUM AND GAMBLING DENS. BY *SNITCHING.*
THAT'S THE COST OF HELPING...
BEING A *RAT.*
YEAH...
HE'D TALK ABOUT SAN FRANCISCO A *LOT* WHEN HE WAS BLUE.
I...I WAS THE ONE...
...WHO *ARRESTED* HIM.

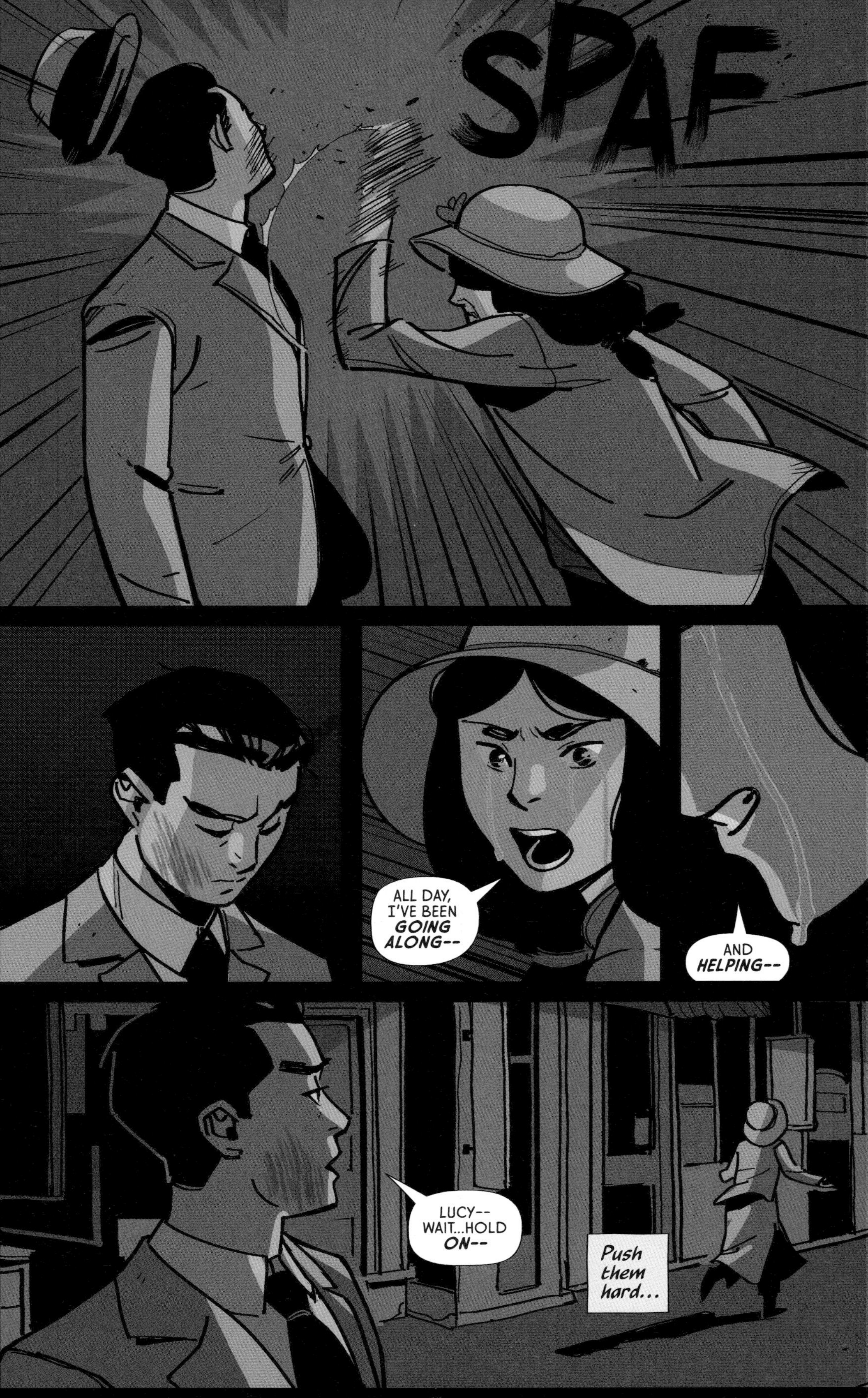
SPAF
ALL DAY, I'VE BEEN GOING ALONG--
AND HELPING--
LUCY-- WAIT...HOLD ON--
Push them hard...

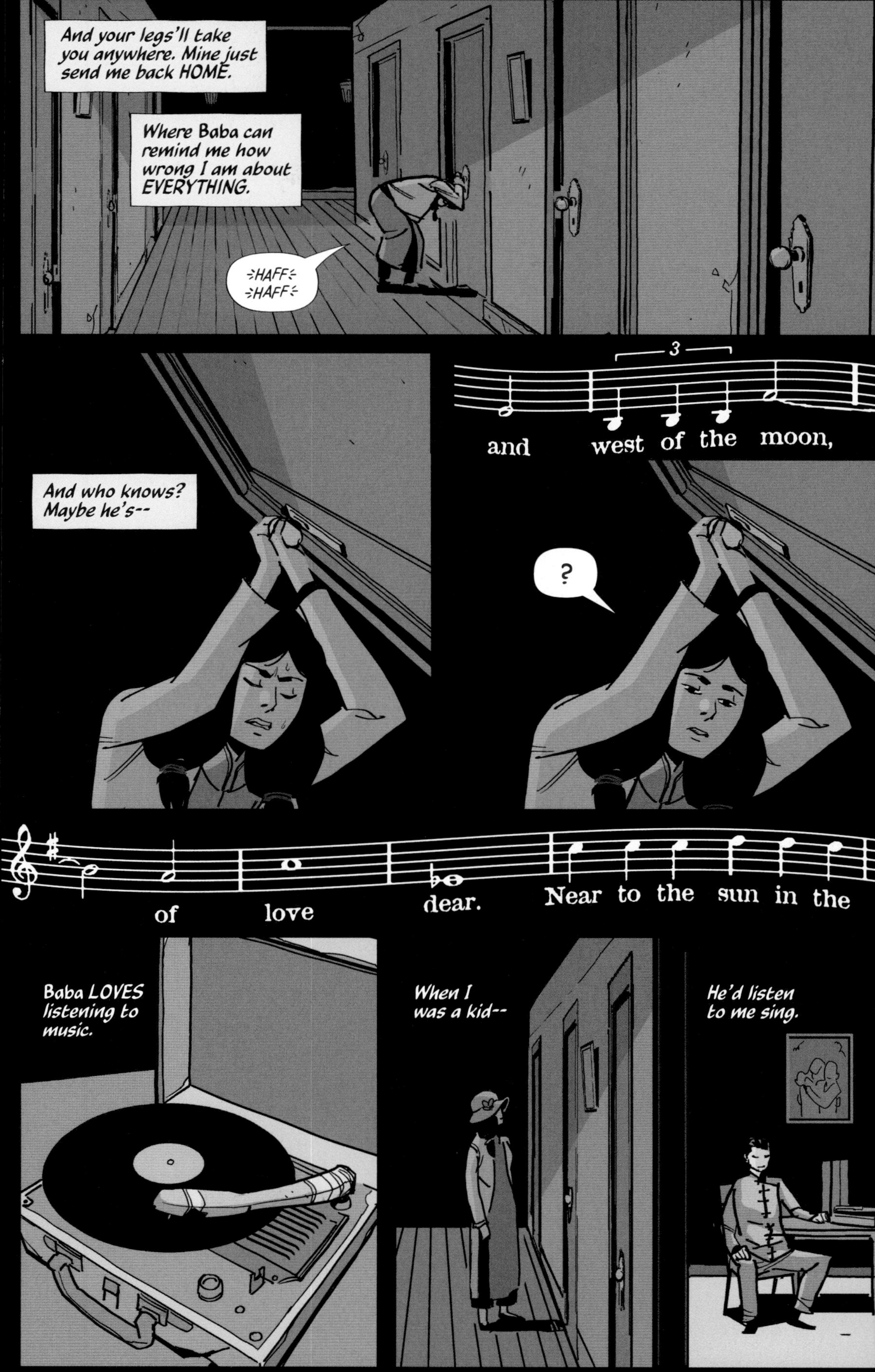

And your legs'll take you anywhere. Mine just send me back HOME.
Where Baba can remind me how wrong I am about EVERYTHING.
HAFF HAFF
3
and west of the moon,
And who knows? Maybe he's--
?
of love dear. Near to the sun in the
Baba LOVES listening to music.
When I was a kid--
He'd listen to me sing.

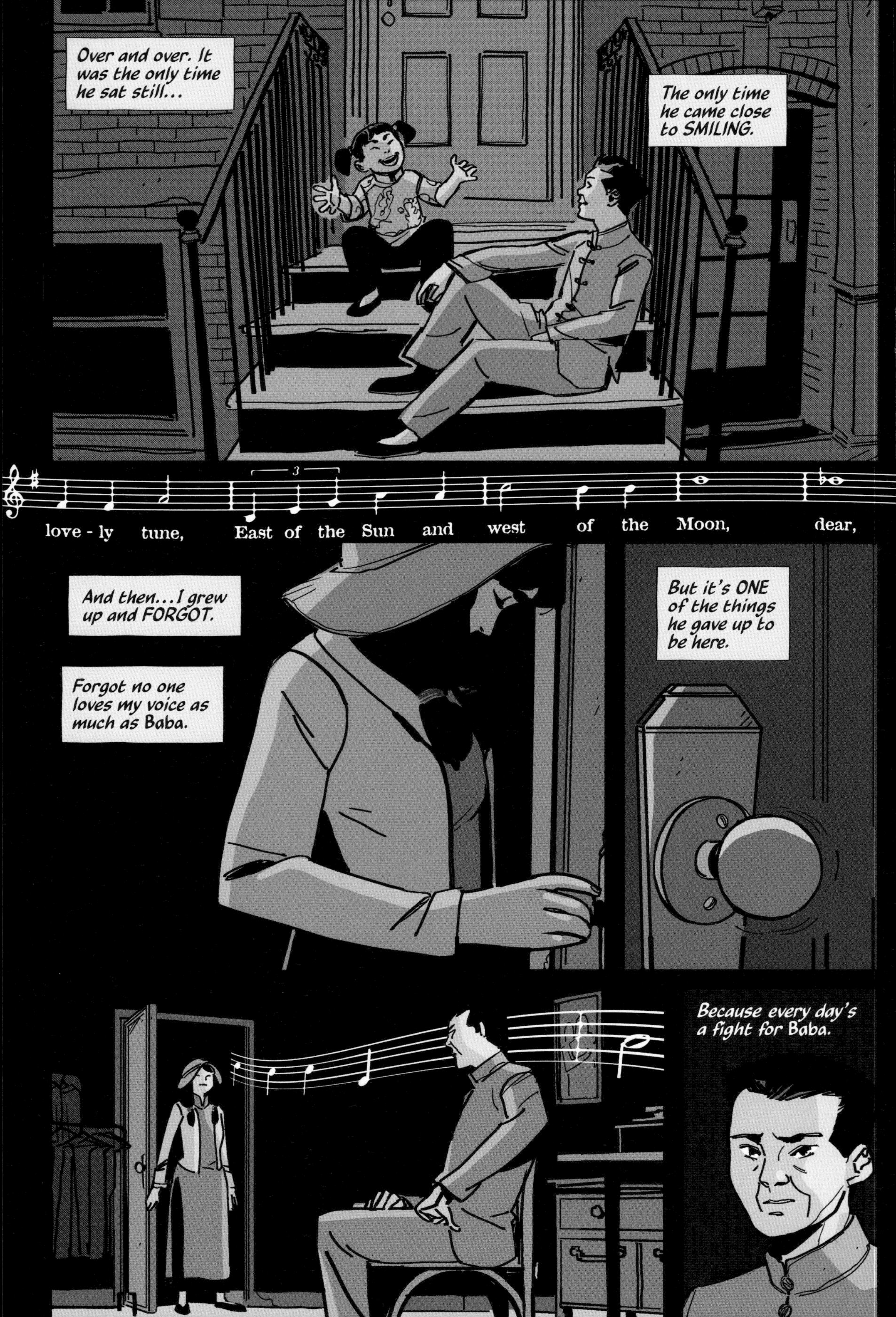

Over and over. It was the only time he sat still...
The only time he came close to SMILING.
love - ly tune, East of the Sun and west of the Moon, dear,
And then... I grew up and FORGOT.
Forgot no one loves my voice as much as Baba.
But it's ONE of the things he gave up to be here.
Because every day's a fight for Baba.

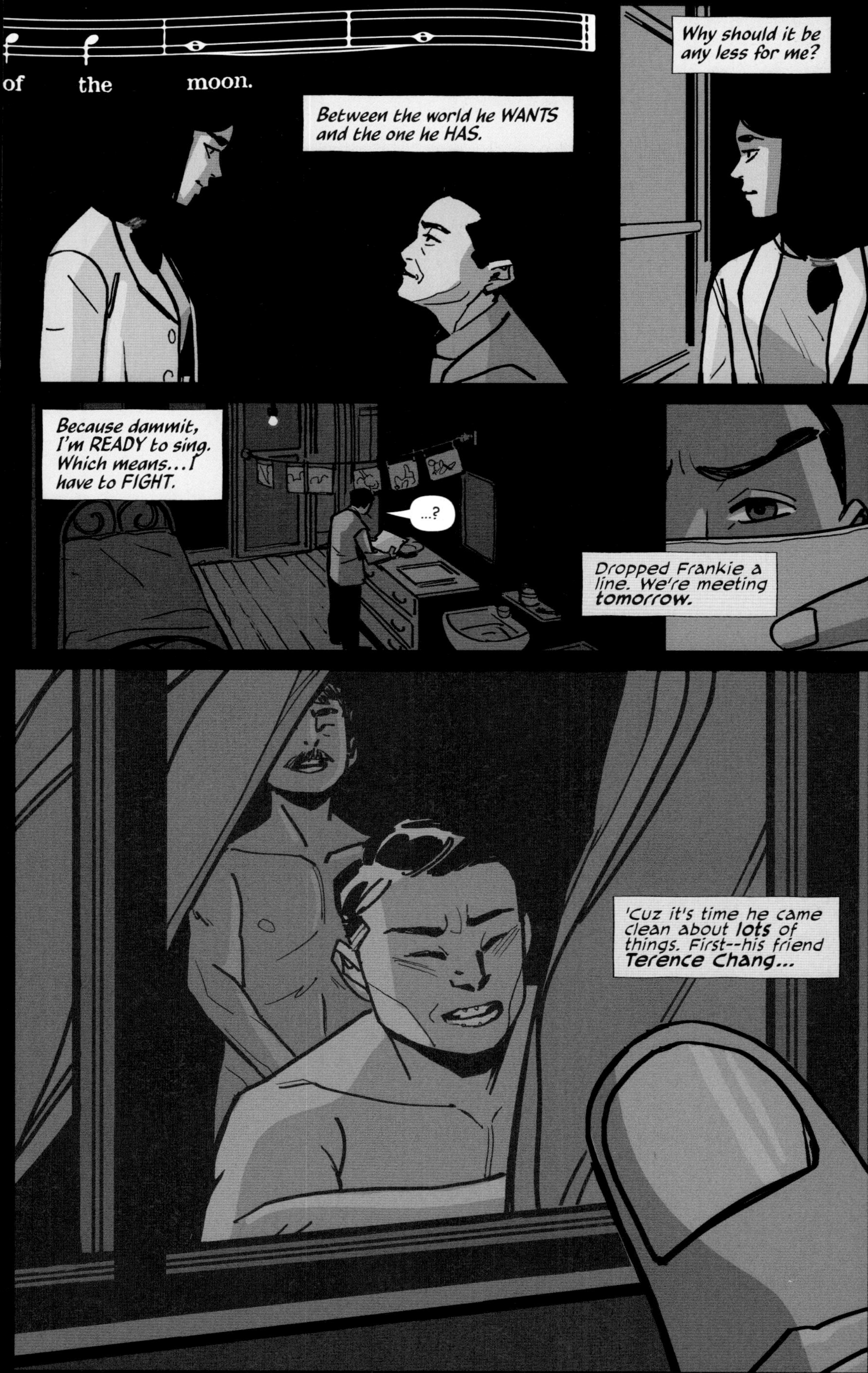
of the moon.
Between the world he WANTS and the one he HAS.
Why should it be any less for me?
Because dammit, I'm READY to sing. Which means... I have to FIGHT.
...?
Dropped Frankie a line. We're meeting tomorrow.
'Cuz it's time he came clean about lots of things. First--his friend Terence Chang...

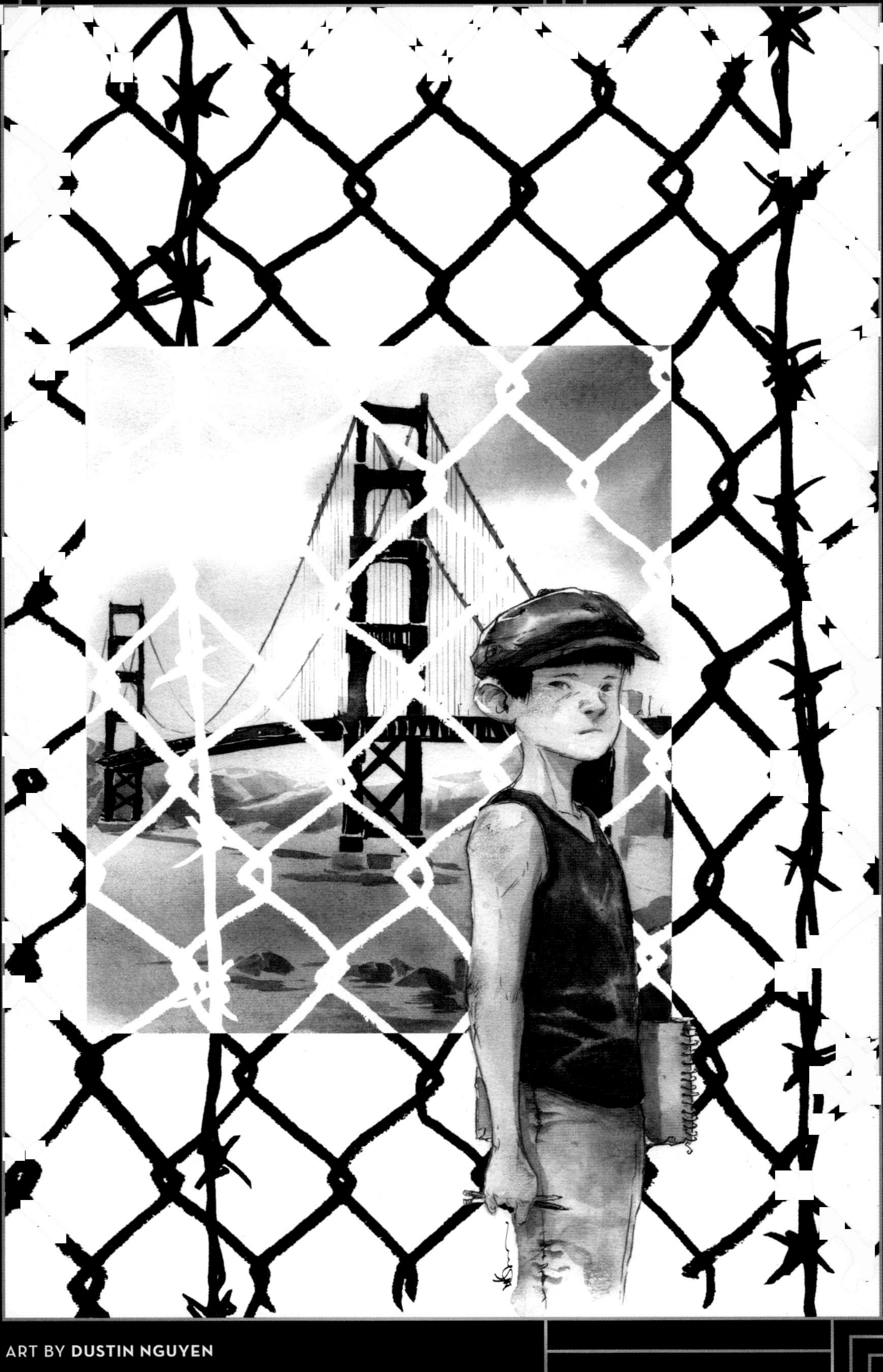

ART BY **DUSTIN NGUYEN**

CHAPTER FOUR

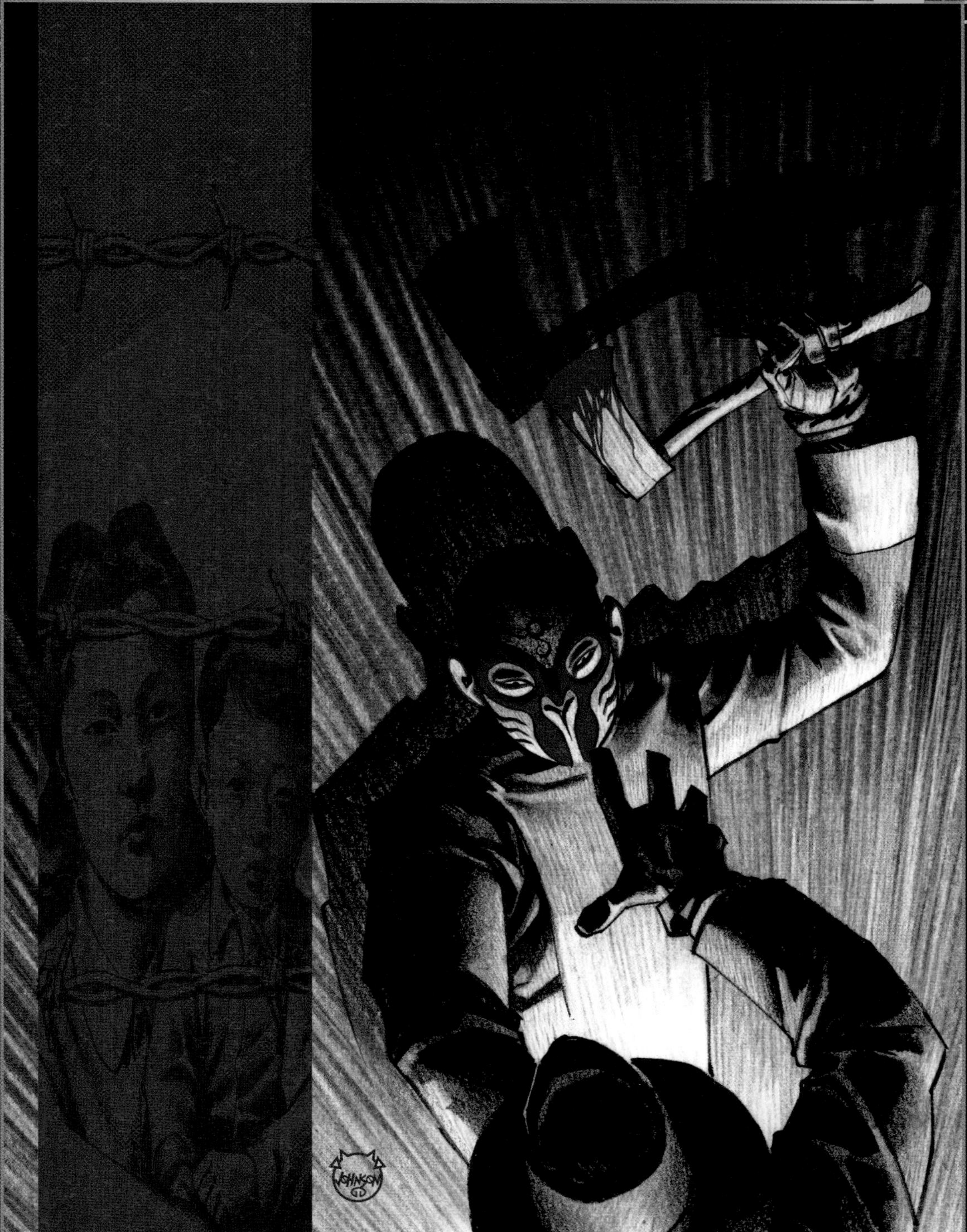

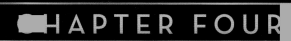

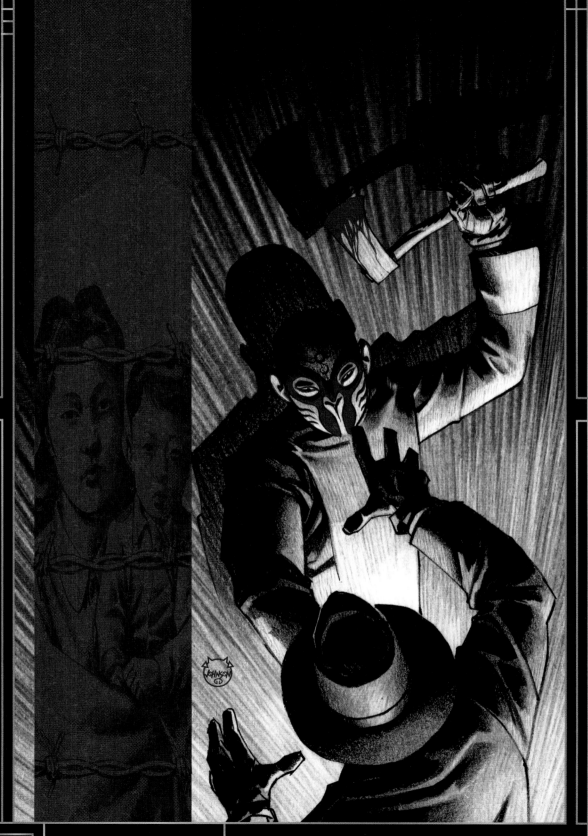

ART BY **DAVE JOHNSON**

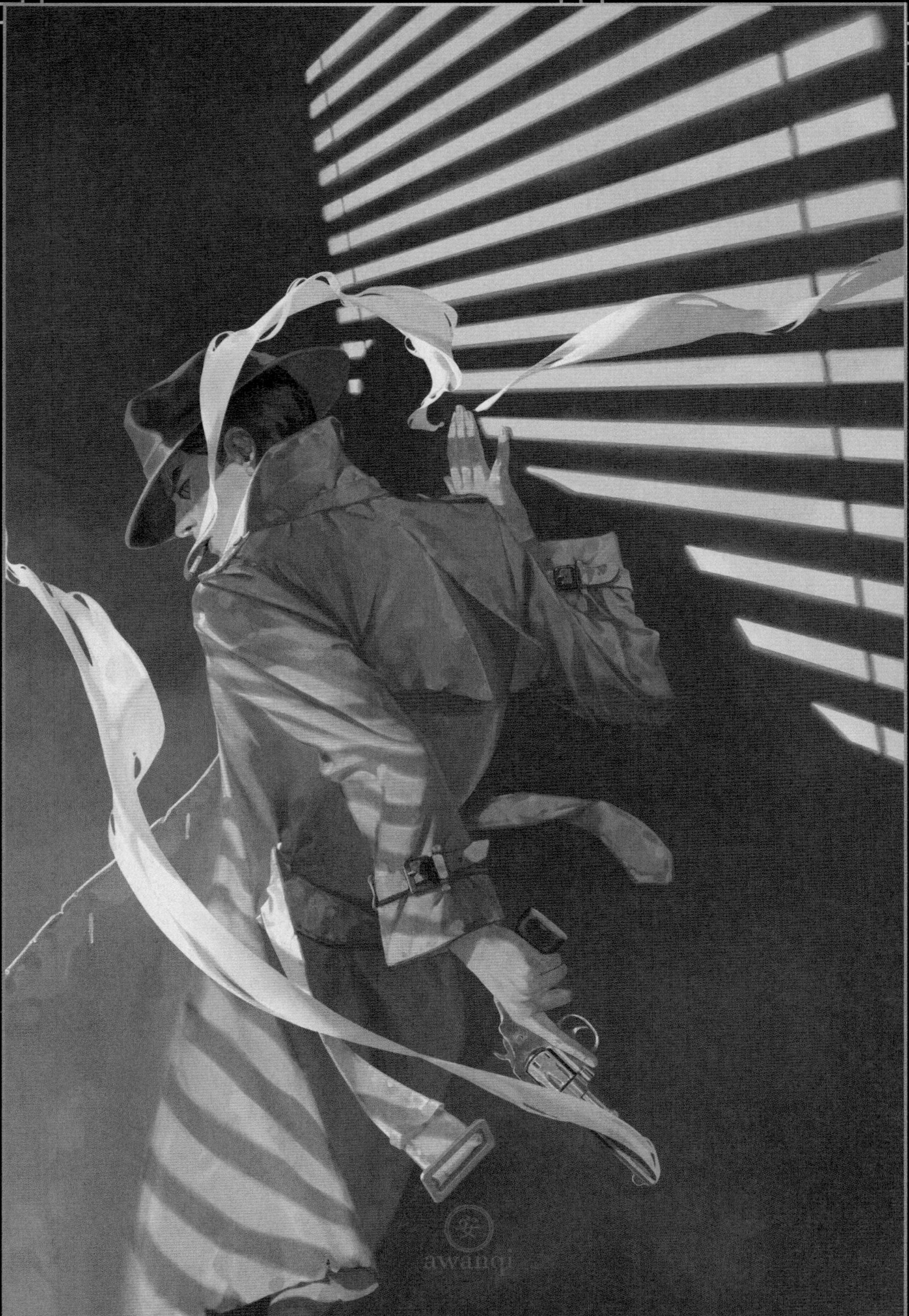
awanqi

ART BY **AWANQI**

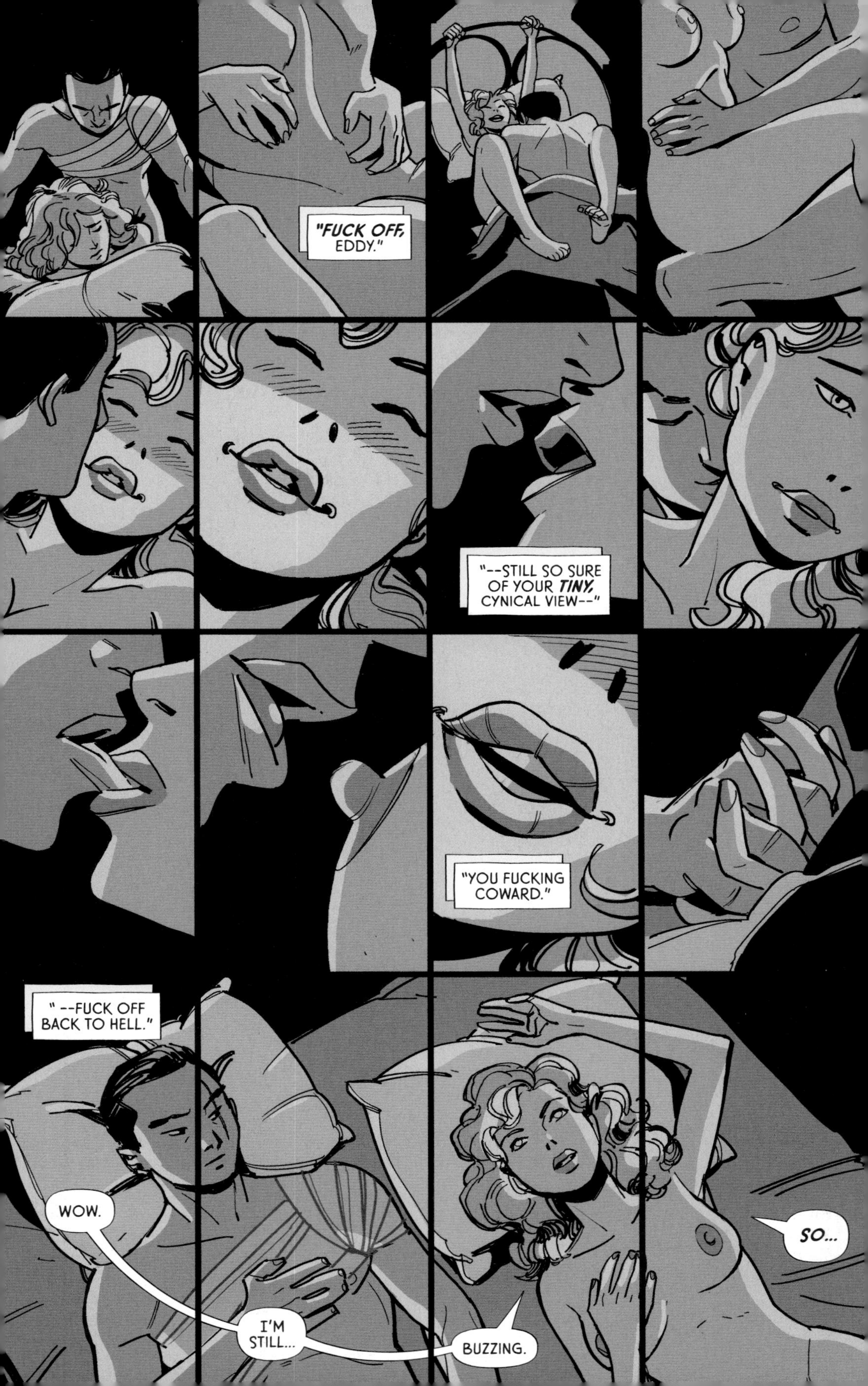
"FUCK OFF, EDDY."
"--STILL SO SURE OF YOUR TINY, CYNICAL VIEW--"
"YOU FUCKING COWARD."
" --FUCK OFF BACK TO HELL."
WOW.
I'M STILL...
BUZZING.
SO...

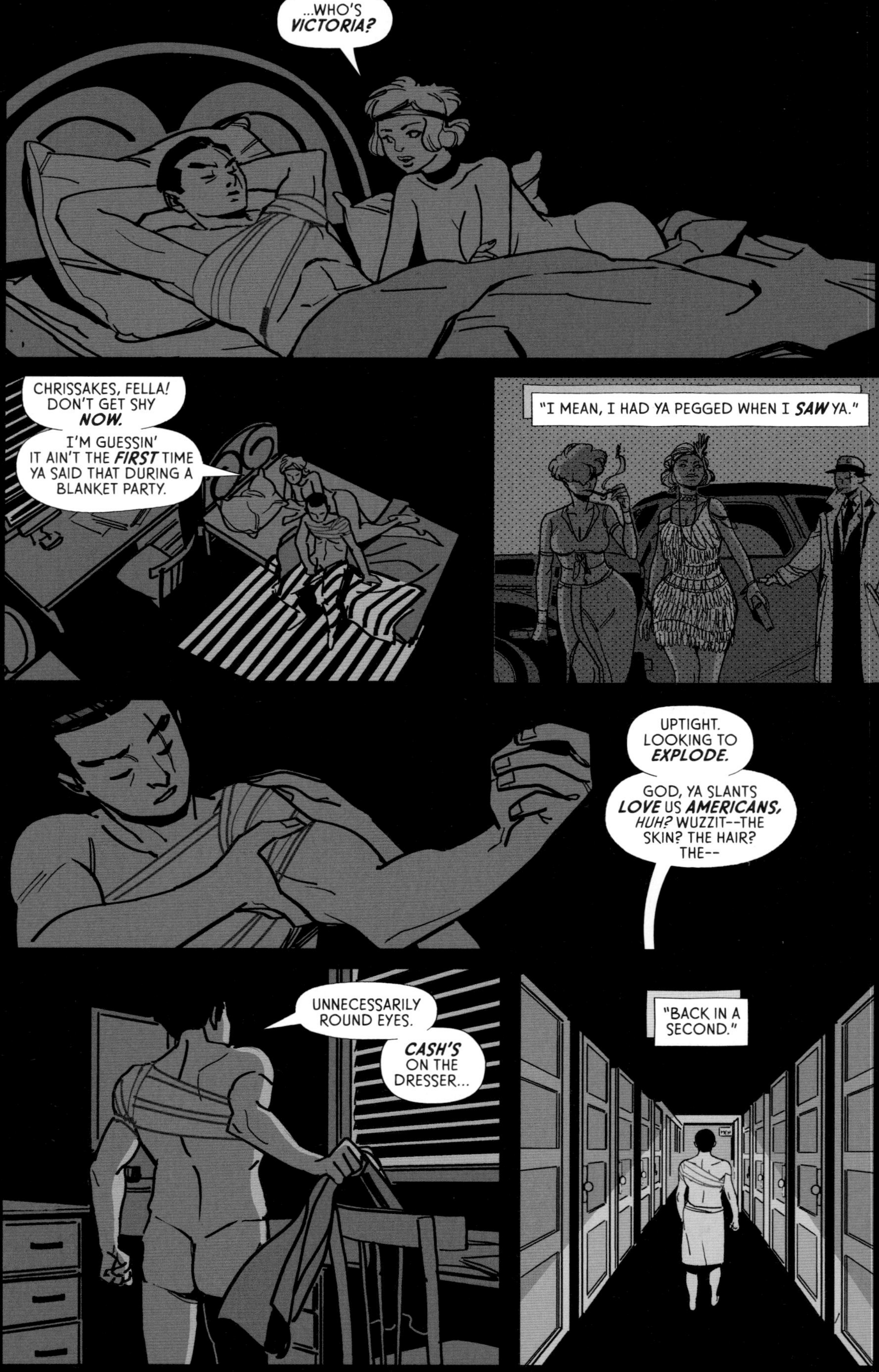
...WHO'S VICTORIA?
CHRISSAKES, FELLA! DON'T GET SHY NOW.
I'M GUESSIN' IT AIN'T THE FIRST TIME YA SAID THAT DURING A BLANKET PARTY.
"I MEAN, I HAD YA PEGGED WHEN I SAW YA."
UPTIGHT. LOOKING TO EXPLODE.
GOD, YA SLANTS LOVE US AMERICANS, HUH? WUZZIT--THE SKIN? THE HAIR? THE--
UNNECESSARILY ROUND EYES.
CASH'S ON THE DRESSER...
"BACK IN A SECOND."

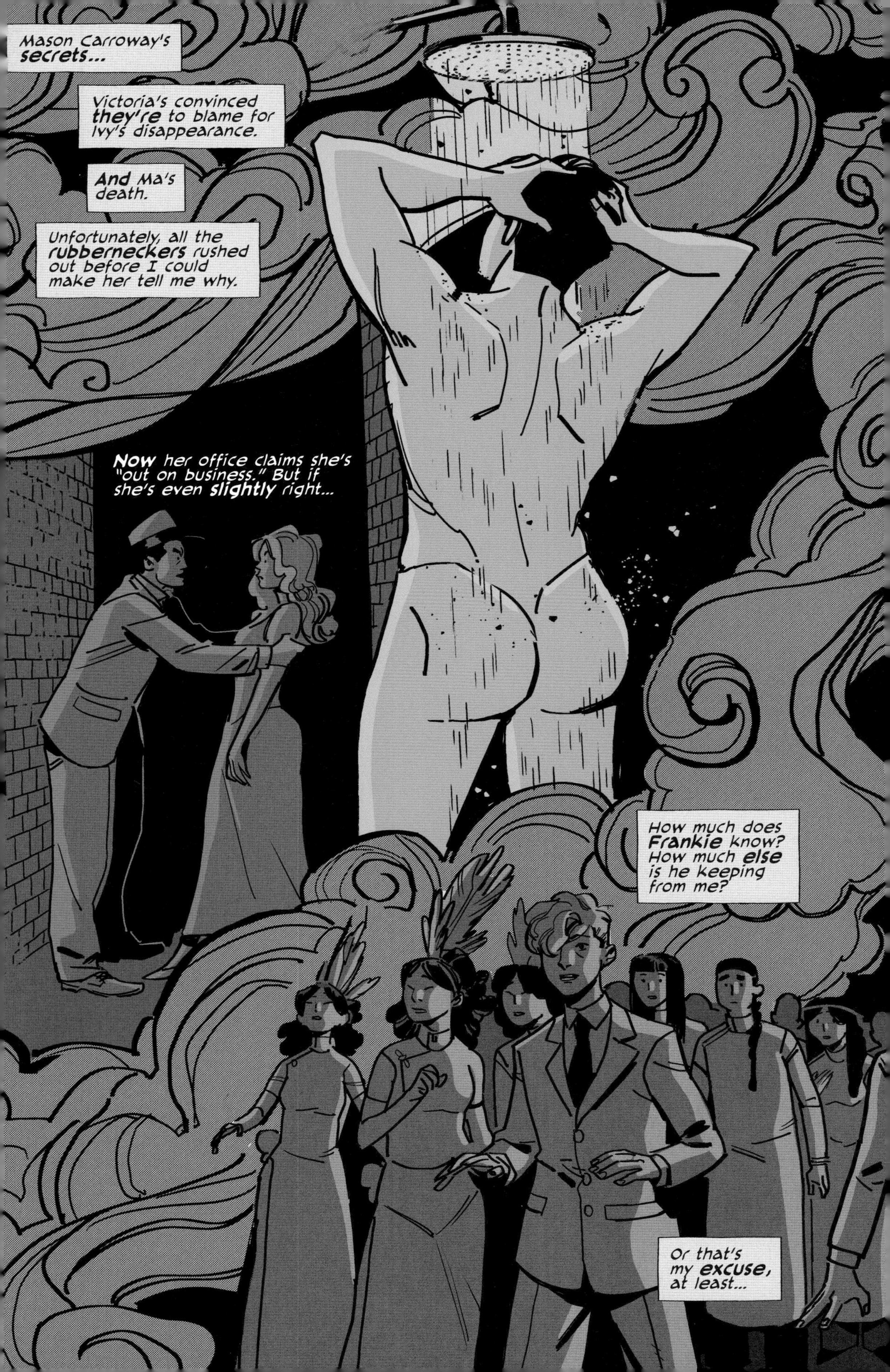

Mason Carroway's **secrets...**
Victoria's convinced **they're** to blame for Ivy's disappearance.
And Ma's death.
Unfortunately, all the **rubberneckers** rushed out before I could make her tell me why.
Now her office claims she's "out on business." But if she's even **slightly** right...
How much does **Frankie** know? How much **else** is he keeping from me?
Or that's my **excuse,** at least...

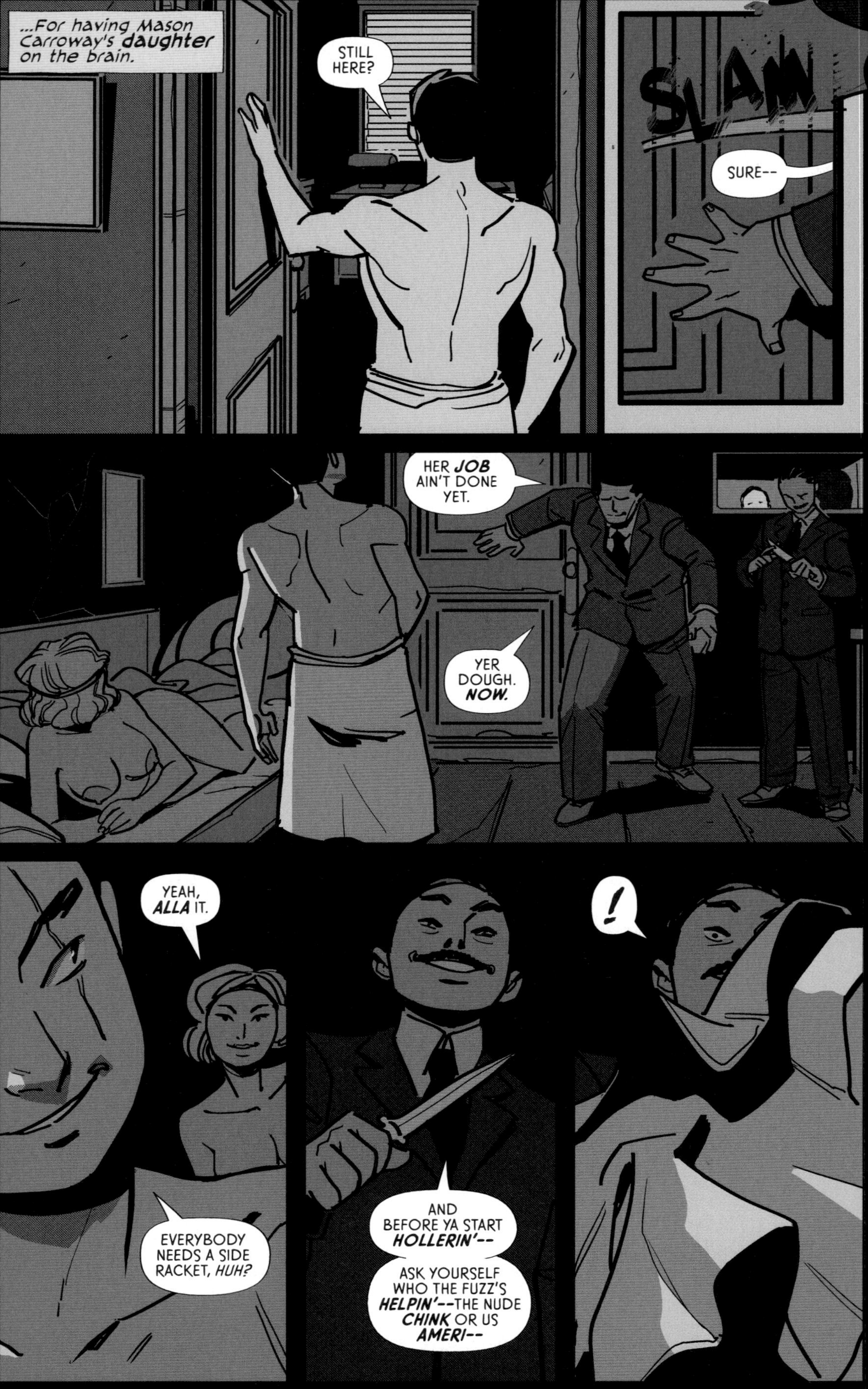
...For having Mason Carroway's **daughter** on the brain.
STILL HERE?
SLAM
SURE--
HER ***JOB*** AIN'T DONE YET.
YER DOUGH. ***NOW.***
YEAH, ***ALLA*** IT.
EVERYBODY NEEDS A SIDE RACKET, *HUH?*
AND BEFORE YA START ***HOLLERIN'--***
ASK YOURSELF WHO THE FUZZ'S ***HELPIN'--*** THE NUDE ***CHINK*** OR US ***AMERI--***
!

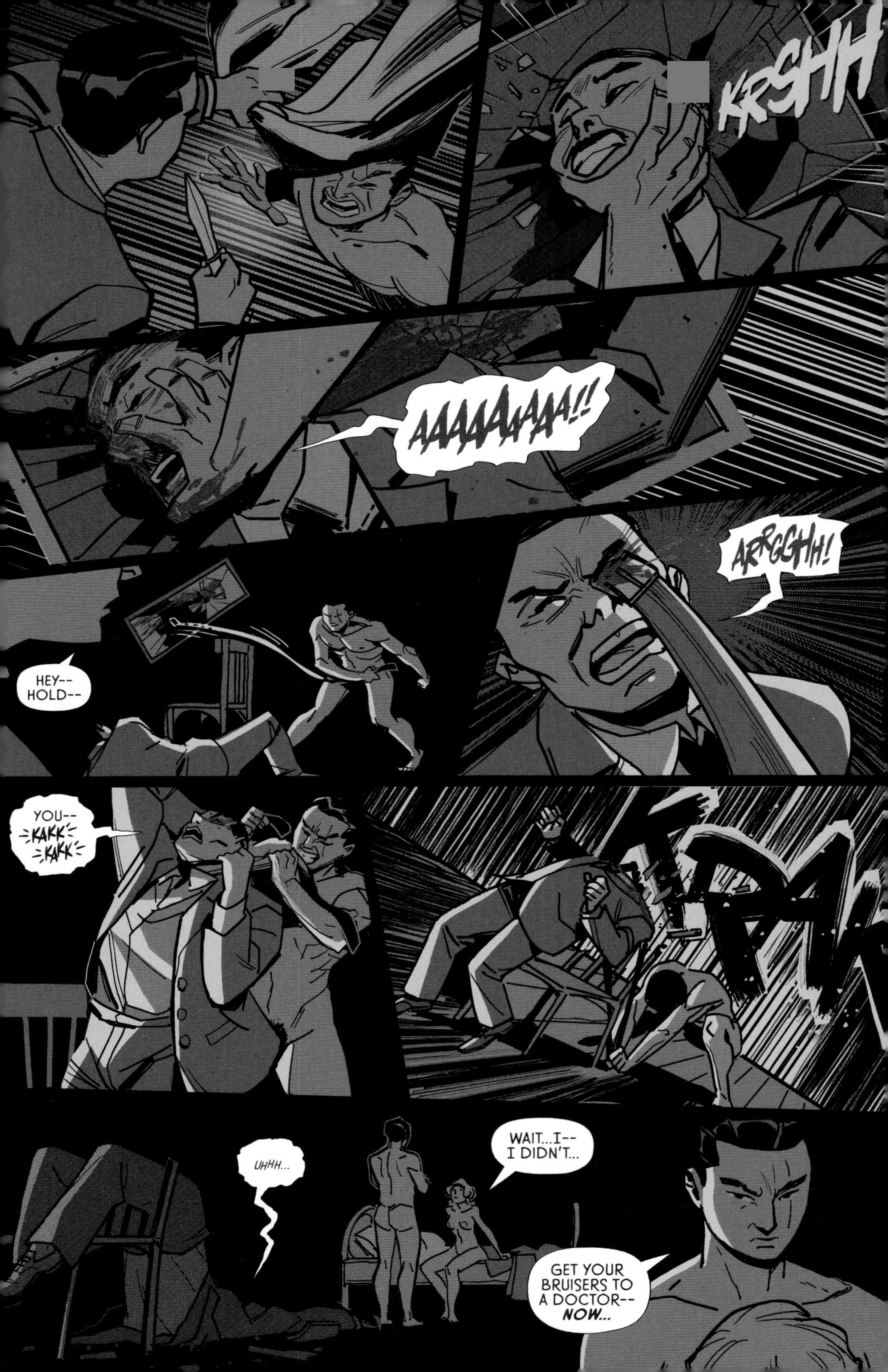
KRSHH
AAAAAAAAA!!
HEY-- HOLD--
ARRGGHH!
YOU-- KAKK KAKK
UHHH...
WAIT...I-- I DIDN'T...
GET YOUR BRUISERS TO A DOCTOR-- *NOW...*

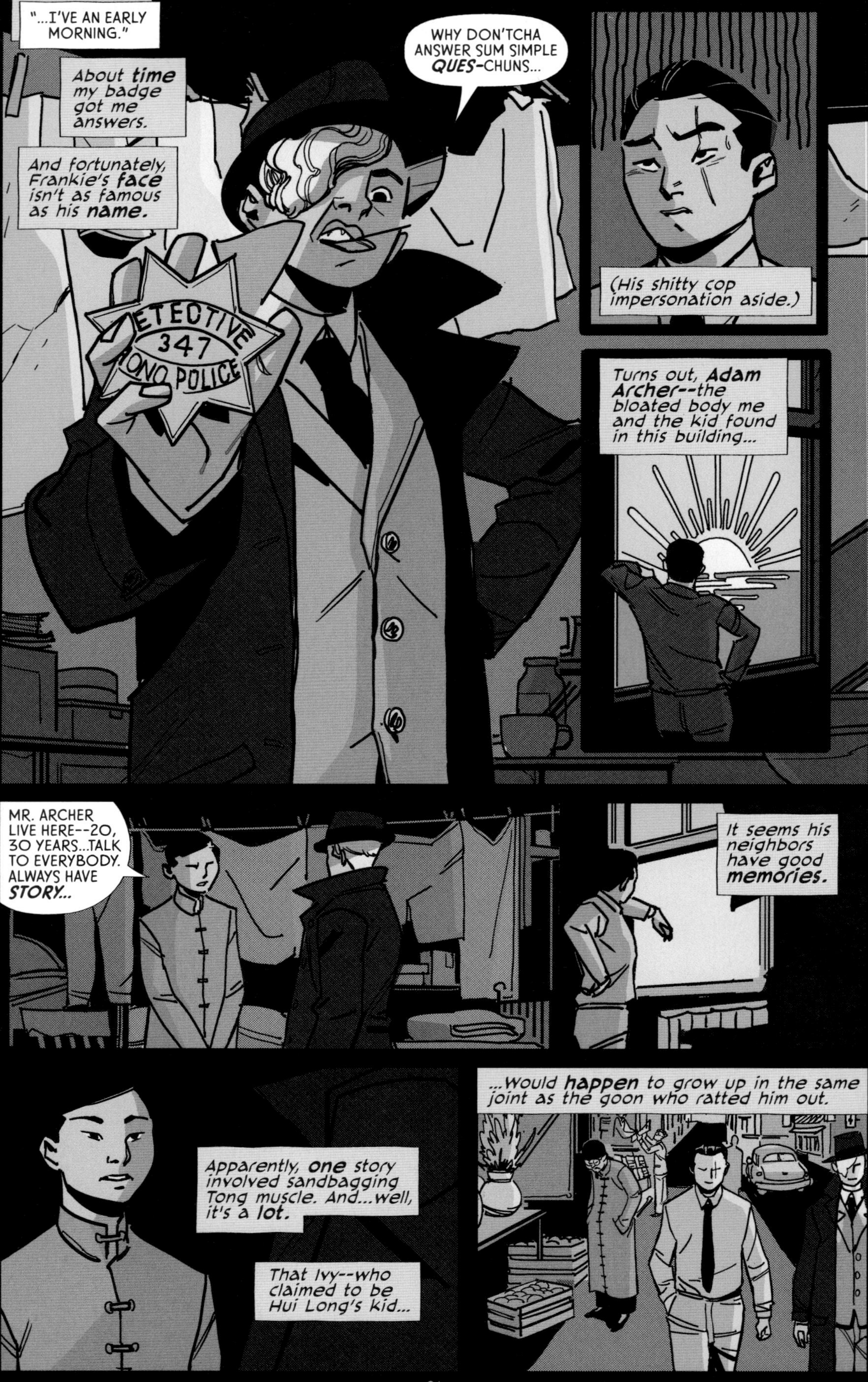
"...I'VE AN EARLY MORNING."
About time my badge got me answers.
And fortunately, Frankie's face isn't as famous as his name.
WHY DON'TCHA ANSWER SUM SIMPLE QUES-CHUNS...
ETECTIVE 347 ONO POLICE
(His shitty cop impersonation aside.)
Turns out, Adam Archer--the bloated body me and the kid found in this building...
MR. ARCHER LIVE HERE--20, 30 YEARS...TALK TO EVERYBODY. ALWAYS HAVE STORY...
It seems his neighbors have good memories.
Apparently, one story involved sandbagging Tong muscle. And...well, it's a lot.
That Ivy--who claimed to be Hui Long's kid...
...Would happen to grow up in the same joint as the goon who ratted him out.

GEEZ, EDDY, IF YOU TOLD ME *DETECTING'S* SUCH A *GAS*--

I'D HAVE HELPED YOU OUT *AGES* BACK.

And suddenly, *my* Frankie's back.

'Cuz although Mason Carroway made his fortune off *sugar refineries*, his life's work was *philanthropy.* A passion he tried imparting to his children.

But Frankie was a *renowned* scoundrel. Constantly in trouble. According to the gossip rags, he knocked up *two* cocktail waitresses just last year.

Everything changed, though, after Mason's heart attack. The help said he straightened up. *Immediately.* It'd be inspiring, if it wasn't also...

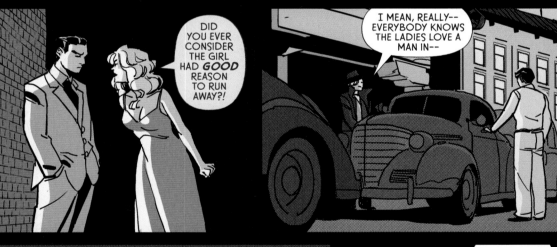

DID YOU EVER CONSIDER THE GIRL HAD *GOOD* REASON TO RUN AWAY?!

I MEAN, REALLY-- EVERYBODY KNOWS THE LADIES LOVE A MAN IN--

SHIT.

I THOUGHT I HID THAT.

GOD, I CAN'T BELIEVE...

WE'VE GOT PICTURES OF--OF...

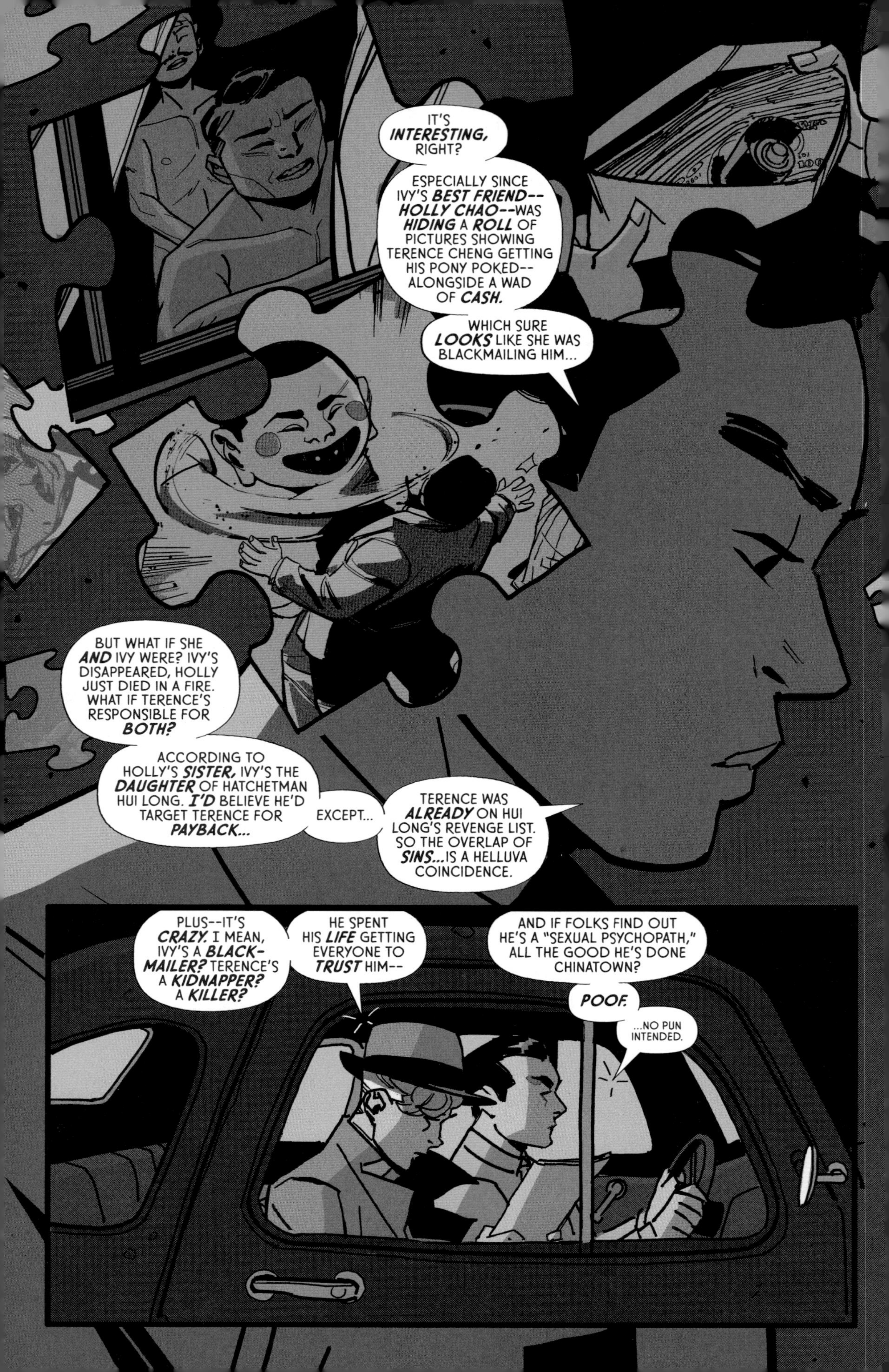

IT'S INTERESTING, RIGHT?
ESPECIALLY SINCE IVY'S BEST FRIEND--HOLLY CHAO--WAS HIDING A ROLL OF PICTURES SHOWING TERENCE CHENG GETTING HIS PONY POKED--ALONGSIDE A WAD OF CASH.
WHICH SURE LOOKS LIKE SHE WAS BLACKMAILING HIM...
BUT WHAT IF SHE AND IVY WERE? IVY'S DISAPPEARED, HOLLY JUST DIED IN A FIRE. WHAT IF TERENCE'S RESPONSIBLE FOR BOTH?
ACCORDING TO HOLLY'S SISTER, IVY'S THE DAUGHTER OF HATCHETMAN HUI LONG. I'D BELIEVE HE'D TARGET TERENCE FOR PAYBACK...
EXCEPT...
TERENCE WAS ALREADY ON HUI LONG'S REVENGE LIST. SO THE OVERLAP OF SINS...IS A HELLUVA COINCIDENCE.
PLUS--IT'S CRAZY. I MEAN, IVY'S A BLACK-MAILER? TERENCE'S A KIDNAPPER? A KILLER?
HE SPENT HIS LIFE GETTING EVERYONE TO TRUST HIM--
AND IF FOLKS FIND OUT HE'S A "SEXUAL PSYCHOPATH," ALL THE GOOD HE'S DONE CHINATOWN?
POOF.
...NO PUN INTENDED.

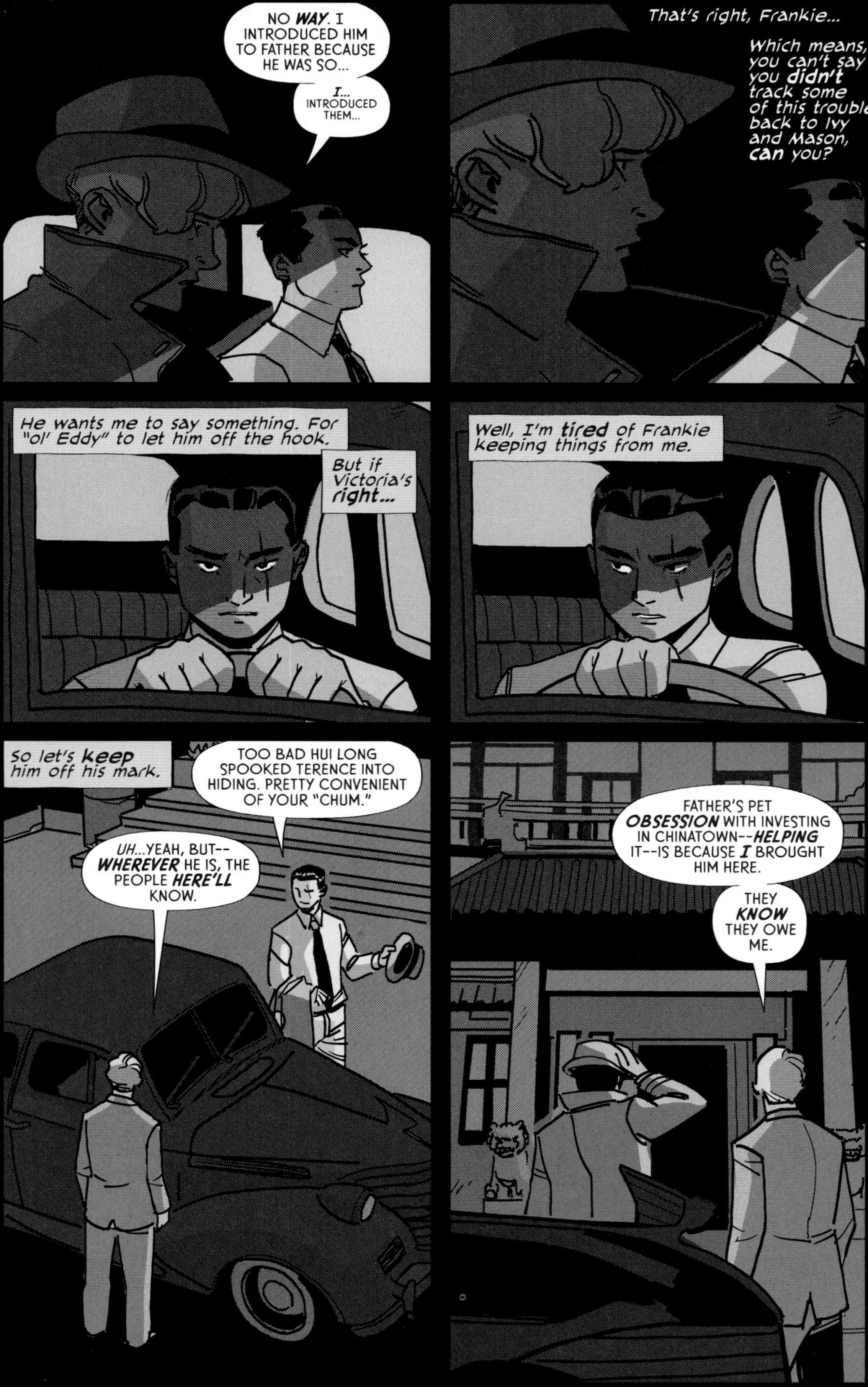
NO WAY. I INTRODUCED HIM TO FATHER BECAUSE HE WAS SO...
I... INTRODUCED THEM...
That's right, Frankie...
Which means, you can't say you didn't track some of this trouble back to Ivy and Mason, can you?
He wants me to say something. For "ol' Eddy" to let him off the hook.
But if Victoria's right...
Well, I'm tired of Frankie keeping things from me.
So let's keep him off his mark.
TOO BAD HUI LONG SPOOKED TERENCE INTO HIDING. PRETTY CONVENIENT OF YOUR "CHUM."
UH...YEAH, BUT-- WHEREVER HE IS, THE PEOPLE HERE'LL KNOW.
FATHER'S PET OBSESSION WITH INVESTING IN CHINATOWN--HELPING IT--IS BECAUSE I BROUGHT HIM HERE.
THEY KNOW THEY OWE ME.

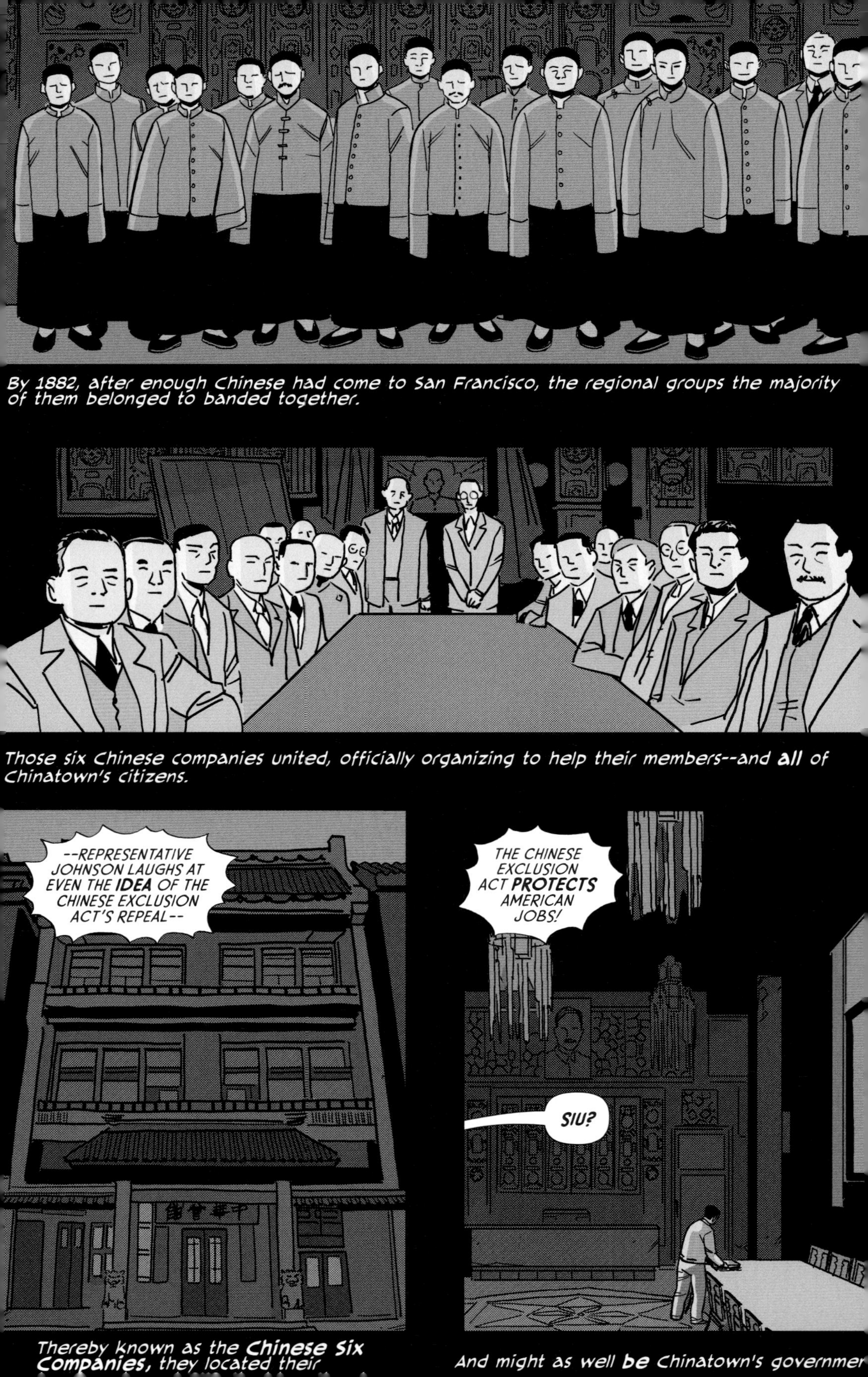
By 1882, after enough Chinese had come to San Francisco, the regional groups the majority of them belonged to banded together.
Those six Chinese companies united, officially organizing to help their members--and **all** of Chinatown's citizens.
--REPRESENTATIVE JOHNSON LAUGHS AT EVEN THE **IDEA** OF THE CHINESE EXCLUSION ACT'S REPEAL--
Thereby known as the **Chinese Six Companies,** they located their
THE CHINESE EXCLUSION ACT **PROTECTS** AMERICAN JOBS!
SIU?
And might as well **be** Chinatown's governmen

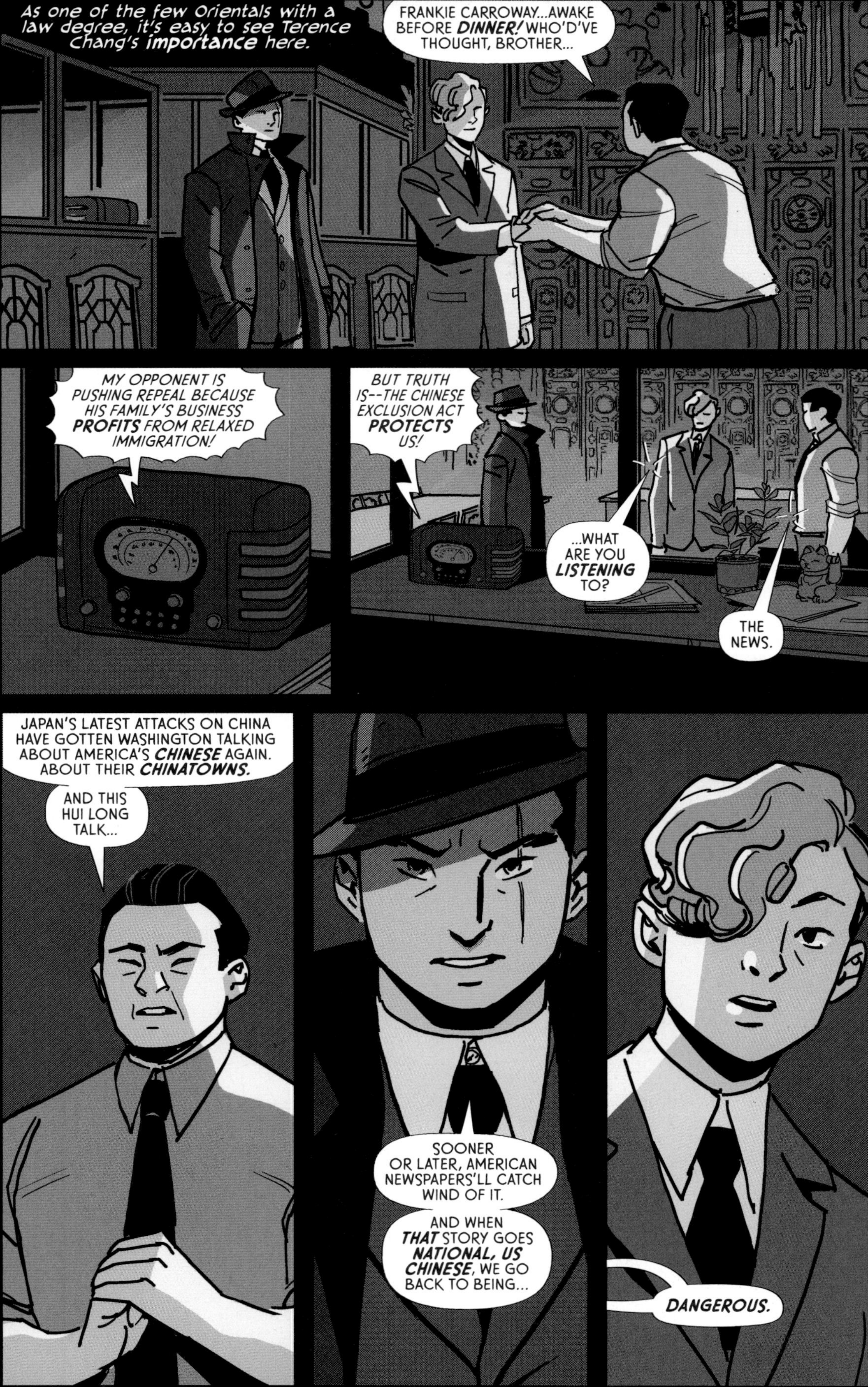
As one of the few Orientals with a law degree, it's easy to see Terence Chang's **importance** here.
FRANKIE CARROWAY...AWAKE BEFORE ***DINNER!*** WHO'D'VE THOUGHT, BROTHER...
MY OPPONENT IS PUSHING REPEAL BECAUSE HIS FAMILY'S BUSINESS ***PROFITS*** *FROM RELAXED IMMIGRATION!*
BUT TRUTH IS--THE CHINESE EXCLUSION ACT ***PROTECTS*** *US!*
...WHAT ARE YOU ***LISTENING*** TO?
THE NEWS.
JAPAN'S LATEST ATTACKS ON CHINA HAVE GOTTEN WASHINGTON TALKING ABOUT AMERICA'S ***CHINESE*** AGAIN. ABOUT THEIR ***CHINATOWNS.***
AND THIS HUI LONG TALK...
SOONER OR LATER, AMERICAN NEWSPAPERS'LL CATCH WIND OF IT.
AND WHEN ***THAT*** STORY GOES ***NATIONAL, US CHINESE,*** WE GO BACK TO BEING...
DANGEROUS.

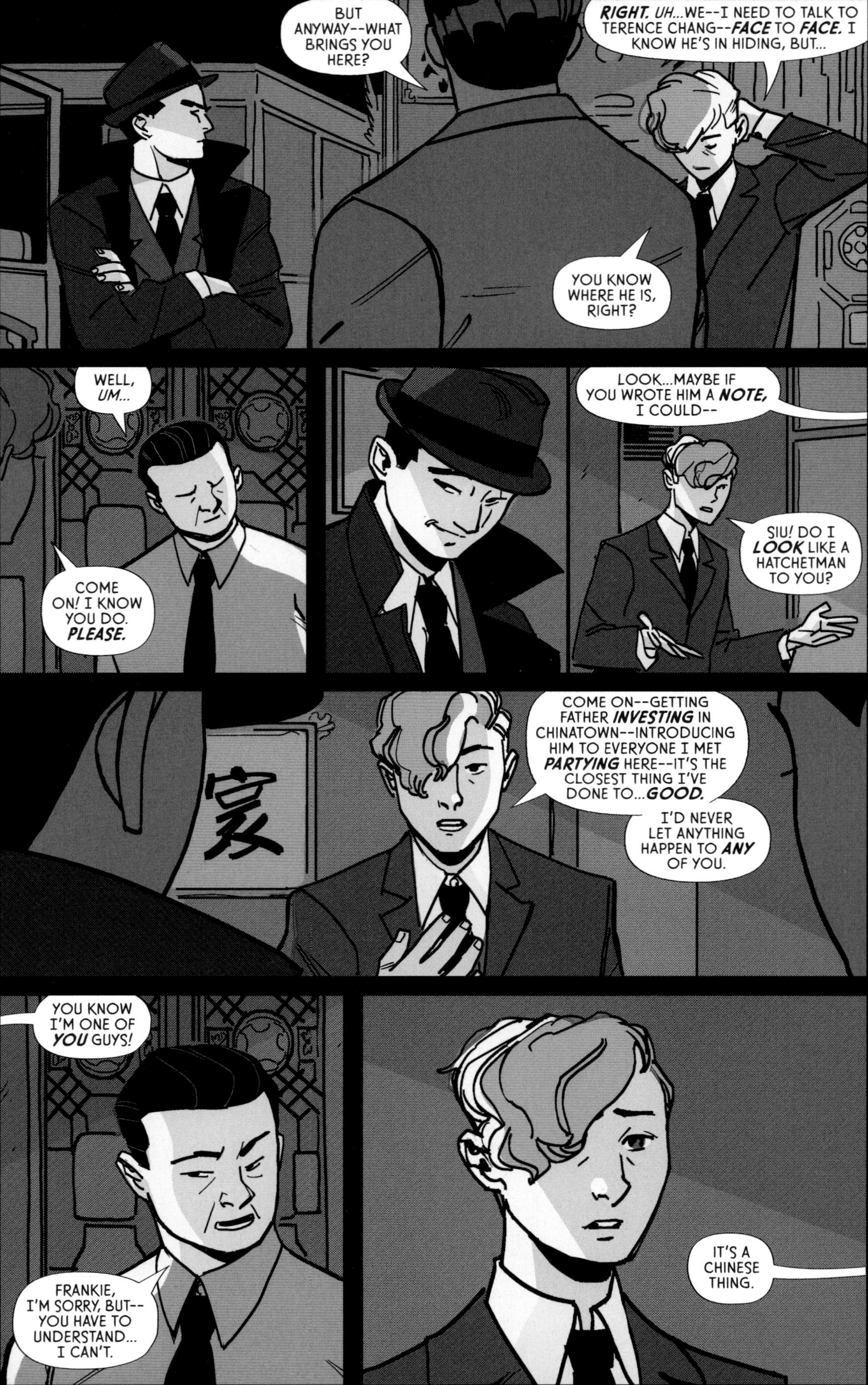

BUT ANYWAY--WHAT BRINGS YOU HERE?
RIGHT. UH...WE--I NEED TO TALK TO TERENCE CHANG--FACE TO FACE. I KNOW HE'S IN HIDING, BUT...
YOU KNOW WHERE HE IS, RIGHT?
WELL, UM...
COME ON! I KNOW YOU DO. PLEASE.
LOOK...MAYBE IF YOU WROTE HIM A NOTE, I COULD--
SIU! DO I LOOK LIKE A HATCHETMAN TO YOU?
宴
COME ON--GETTING FATHER INVESTING IN CHINATOWN--INTRODUCING HIM TO EVERYONE I MET PARTYING HERE--IT'S THE CLOSEST THING I'VE DONE TO...GOOD.
I'D NEVER LET ANYTHING HAPPEN TO ANY OF YOU.
YOU KNOW I'M ONE OF YOU GUYS!
FRANKIE, I'M SORRY, BUT--YOU HAVE TO UNDERSTAND... I CAN'T.
IT'S A CHINESE THING.

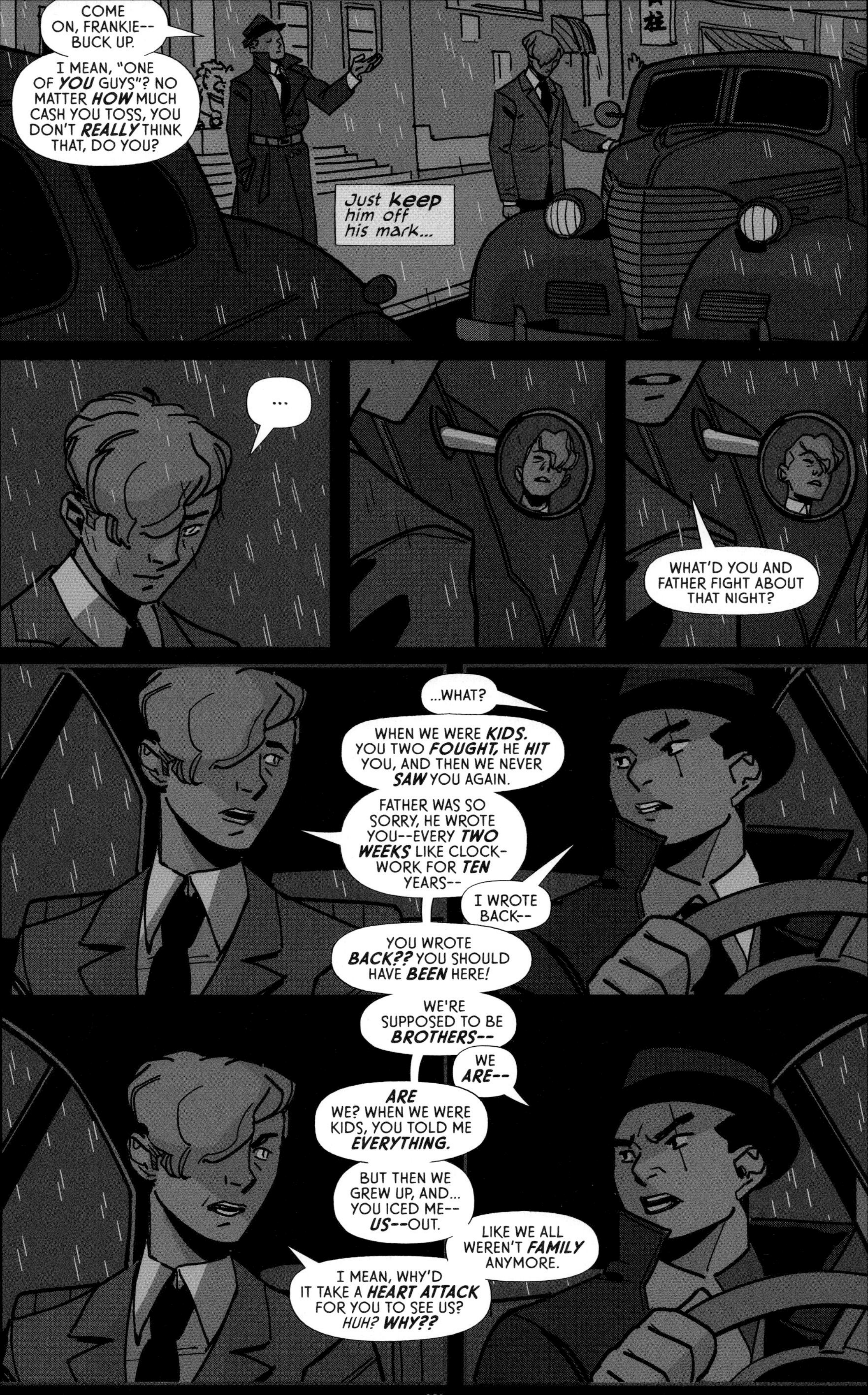
COME ON, FRANKIE-- BUCK UP.
I MEAN, "ONE OF YOU GUYS"? NO MATTER HOW MUCH CASH YOU TOSS, YOU DON'T REALLY THINK THAT, DO YOU?
Just keep him off his mark...
...
WHAT'D YOU AND FATHER FIGHT ABOUT THAT NIGHT?
...WHAT?
WHEN WE WERE KIDS. YOU TWO FOUGHT, HE HIT YOU, AND THEN WE NEVER SAW YOU AGAIN.
FATHER WAS SO SORRY, HE WROTE YOU--EVERY TWO WEEKS LIKE CLOCK-WORK FOR TEN YEARS--
I WROTE BACK--
YOU WROTE BACK?? YOU SHOULD HAVE BEEN HERE!
WE'RE SUPPOSED TO BE BROTHERS--
WE ARE--
ARE WE? WHEN WE WERE KIDS, YOU TOLD ME EVERYTHING.
BUT THEN WE GREW UP, AND... YOU ICED ME-- US--OUT.
LIKE WE ALL WEREN'T FAMILY ANYMORE.
I MEAN, WHY'D IT TAKE A HEART ATTACK FOR YOU TO SEE US? HUH? WHY??

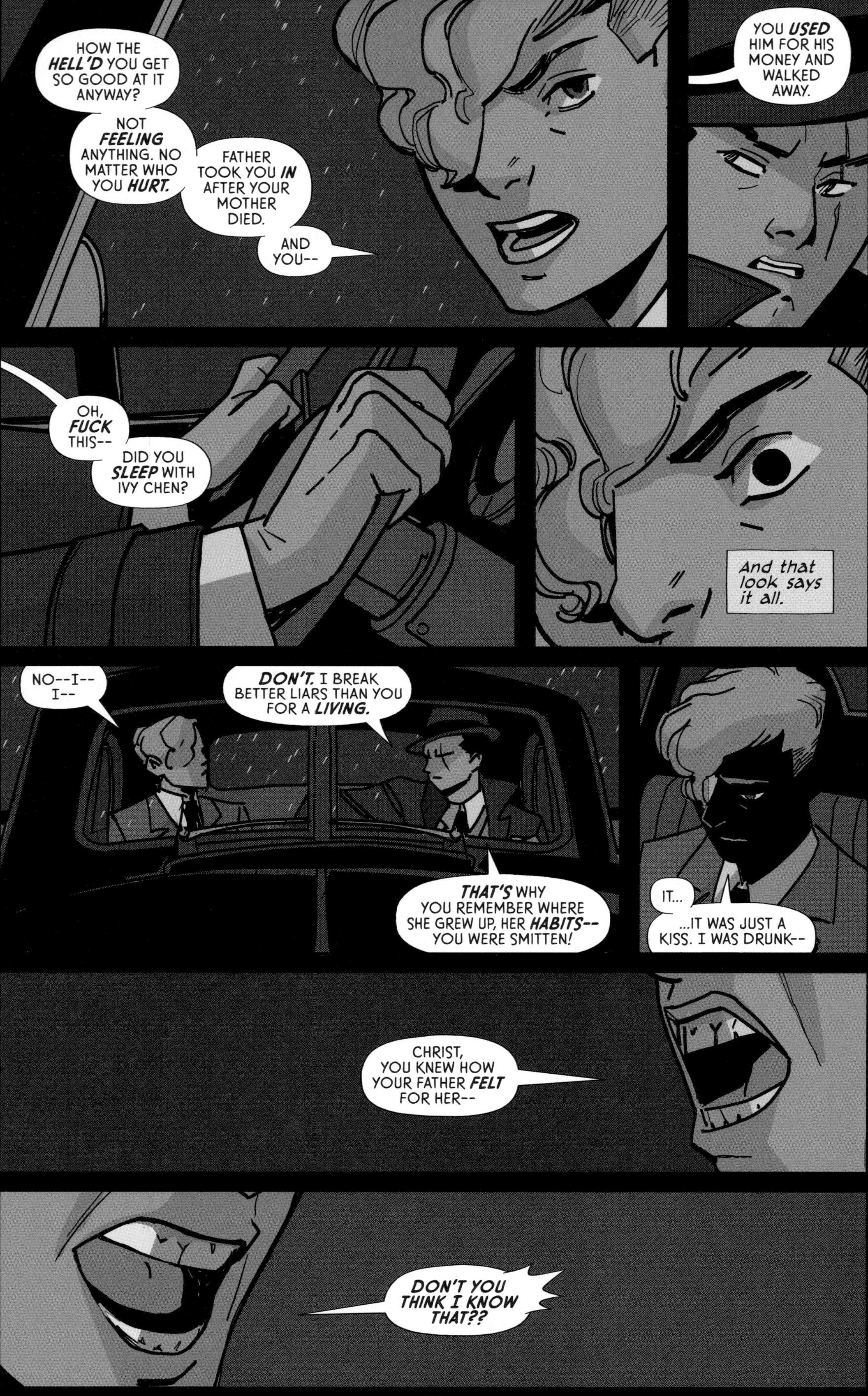
HOW THE HELL'D YOU GET SO GOOD AT IT ANYWAY?
NOT FEELING ANYTHING. NO MATTER WHO YOU HURT.
FATHER TOOK YOU IN AFTER YOUR MOTHER DIED.
AND YOU--
YOU USED HIM FOR HIS MONEY AND WALKED AWAY.
OH, FUCK THIS--
DID YOU SLEEP WITH IVY CHEN?
And that look says it all.
NO--I-- I--
DON'T. I BREAK BETTER LIARS THAN YOU FOR A LIVING.
THAT'S WHY YOU REMEMBER WHERE SHE GREW UP, HER HABITS-- YOU WERE SMITTEN!
IT...
...IT WAS JUST A KISS. I WAS DRUNK--
CHRIST, YOU KNEW HOW YOUR FATHER FELT FOR HER--
DON'T YOU THINK I KNOW THAT??

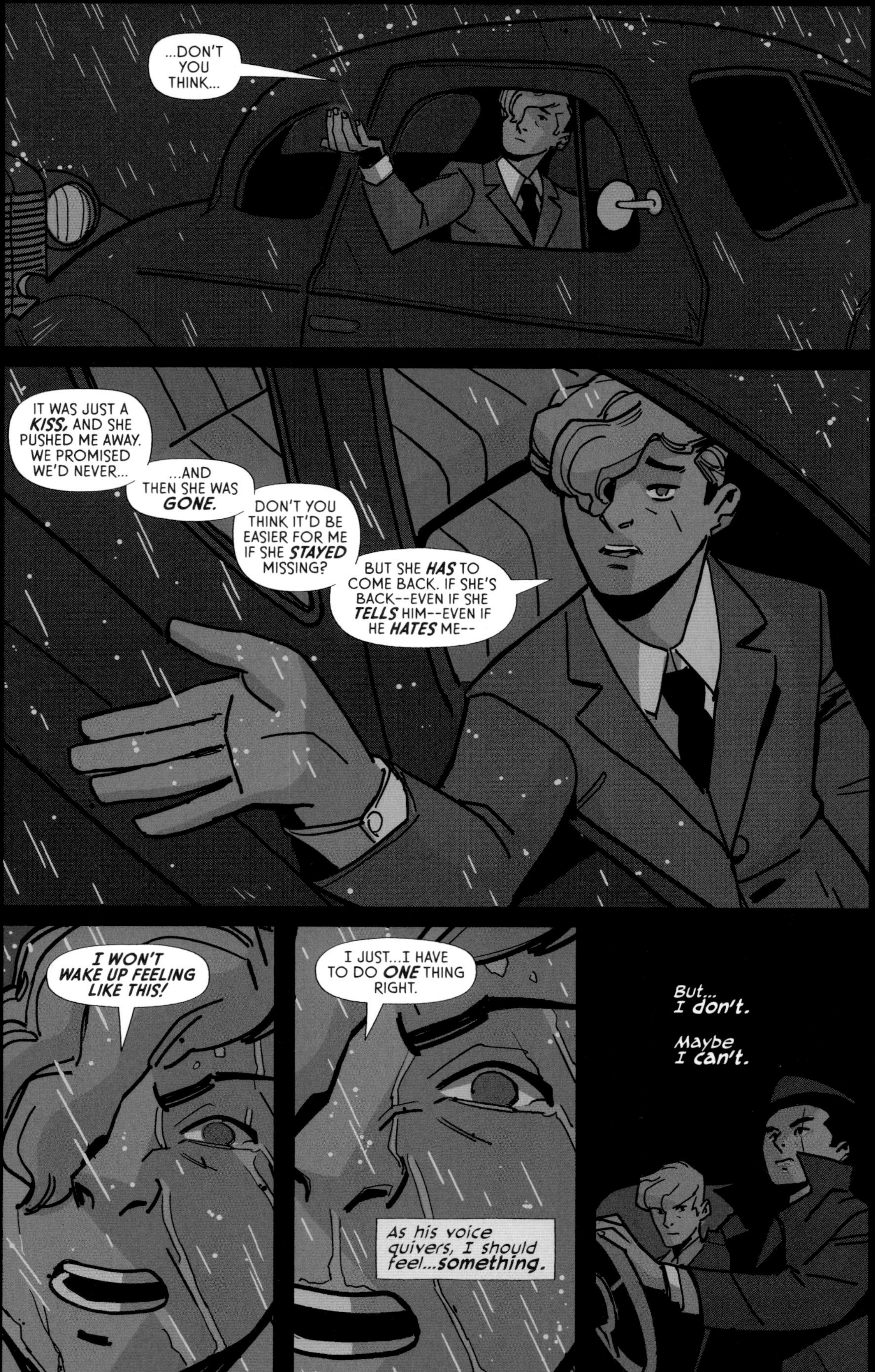
...DON'T YOU THINK...
IT WAS JUST A KISS, AND SHE PUSHED ME AWAY. WE PROMISED WE'D NEVER...
...AND THEN SHE WAS GONE.
DON'T YOU THINK IT'D BE EASIER FOR ME IF SHE STAYED MISSING?
BUT SHE HAS TO COME BACK. IF SHE'S BACK--EVEN IF SHE TELLS HIM--EVEN IF HE HATES ME--
I WON'T WAKE UP FEELING LIKE THIS!
I JUST...I HAVE TO DO ONE THING RIGHT.
As his voice quivers, I should feel...something.
But... I don't.
Maybe I can't.

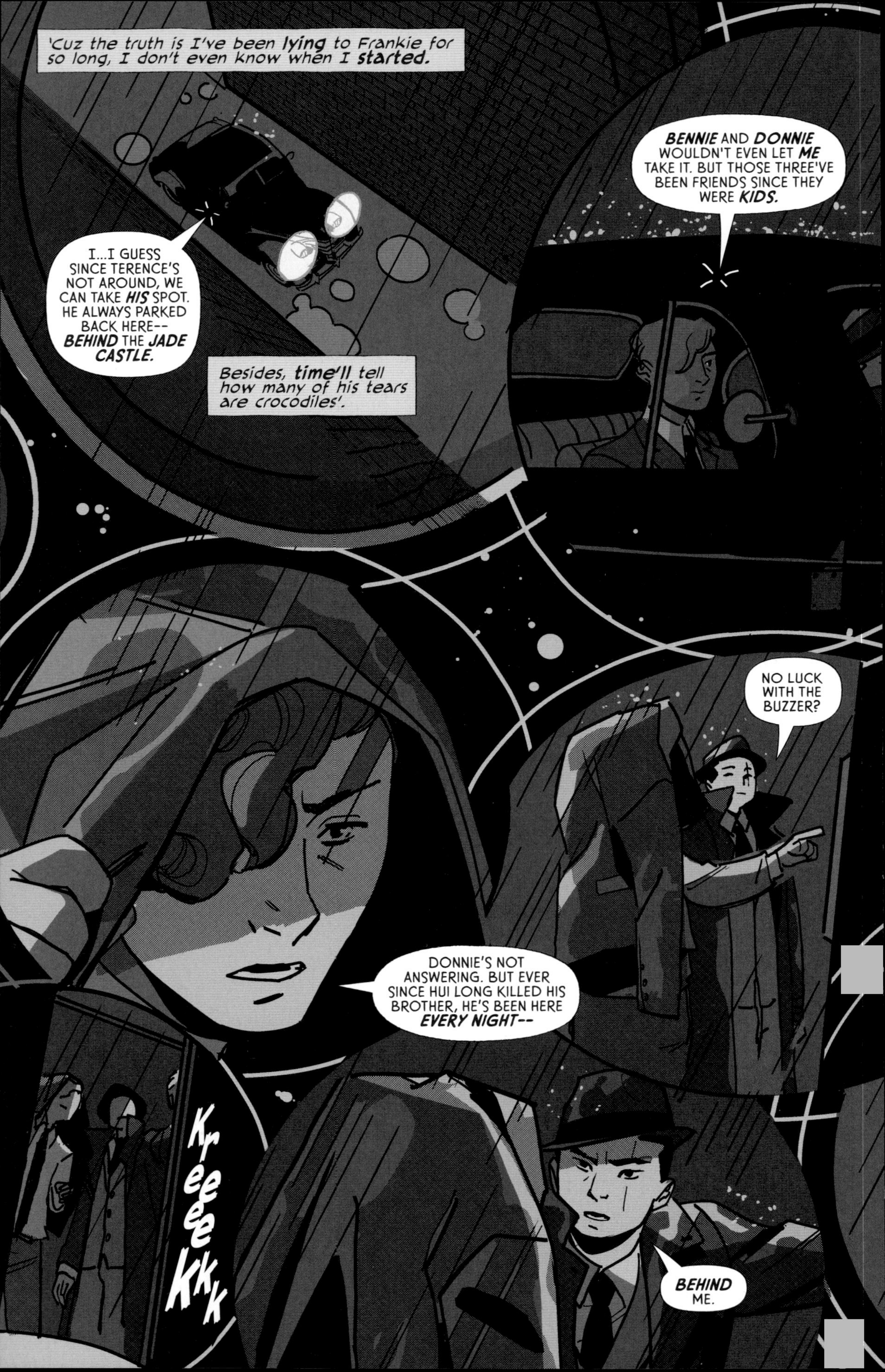
'Cuz the truth is I've been lying to Frankie for so long, I don't even know when I started.
I...I GUESS SINCE TERENCE'S NOT AROUND, WE CAN TAKE HIS SPOT. HE ALWAYS PARKED BACK HERE-- BEHIND THE JADE CASTLE.
Besides, time'll tell how many of his tears are crocodiles'.
BENNIE AND DONNIE WOULDN'T EVEN LET ME TAKE IT. BUT THOSE THREE'VE BEEN FRIENDS SINCE THEY WERE KIDS.
NO LUCK WITH THE BUZZER?
DONNIE'S NOT ANSWERING. BUT EVER SINCE HUI LONG KILLED HIS BROTHER, HE'S BEEN HERE EVERY NIGHT--
Kreeeekkk
BEHIND ME.

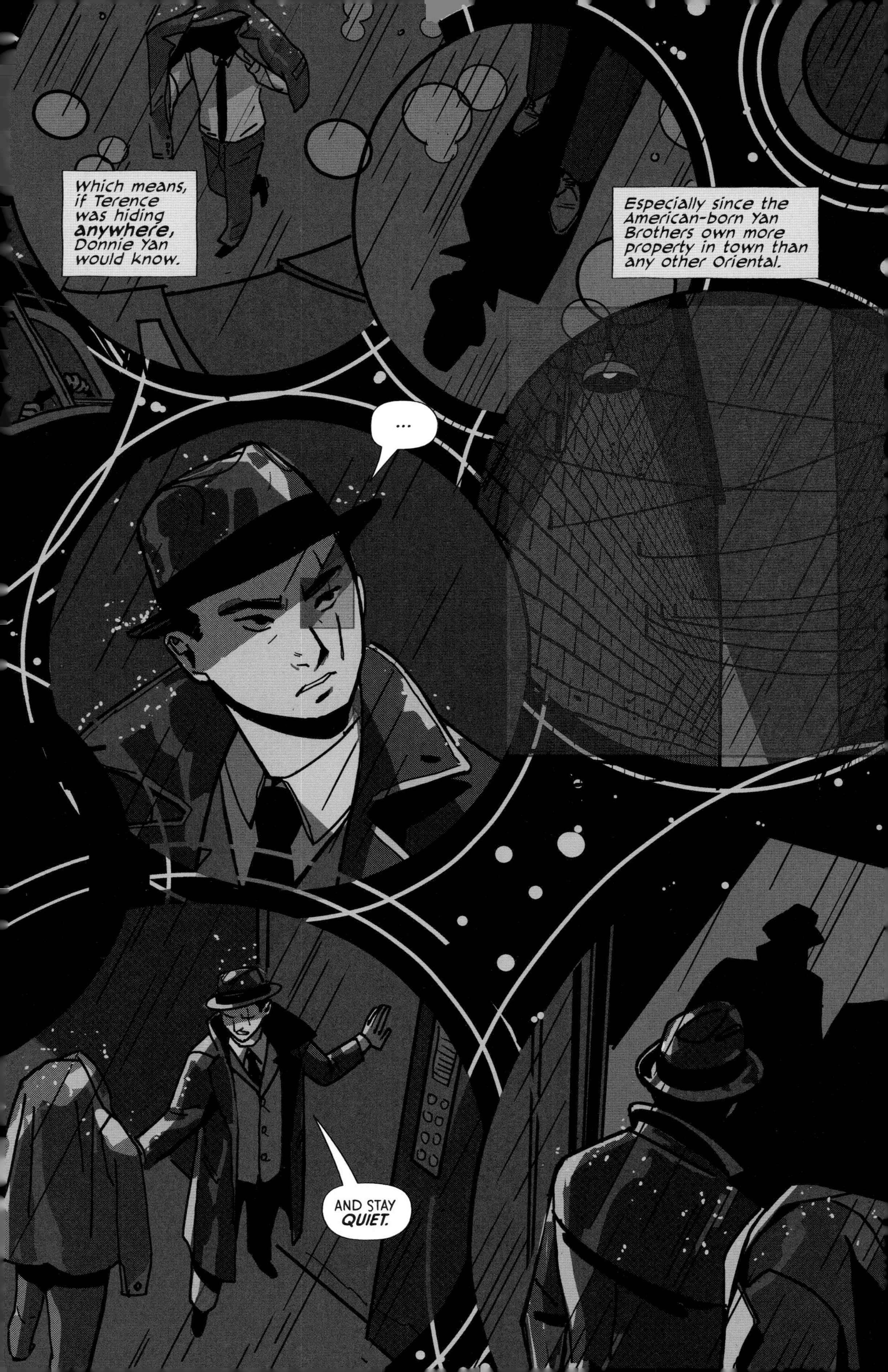
Which means, if Terence was hiding **anywhere,** Donnie Yan would know.
Especially since the American-born Yan Brothers own more property in town than any other Oriental.
...
AND STAY ***QUIET.***

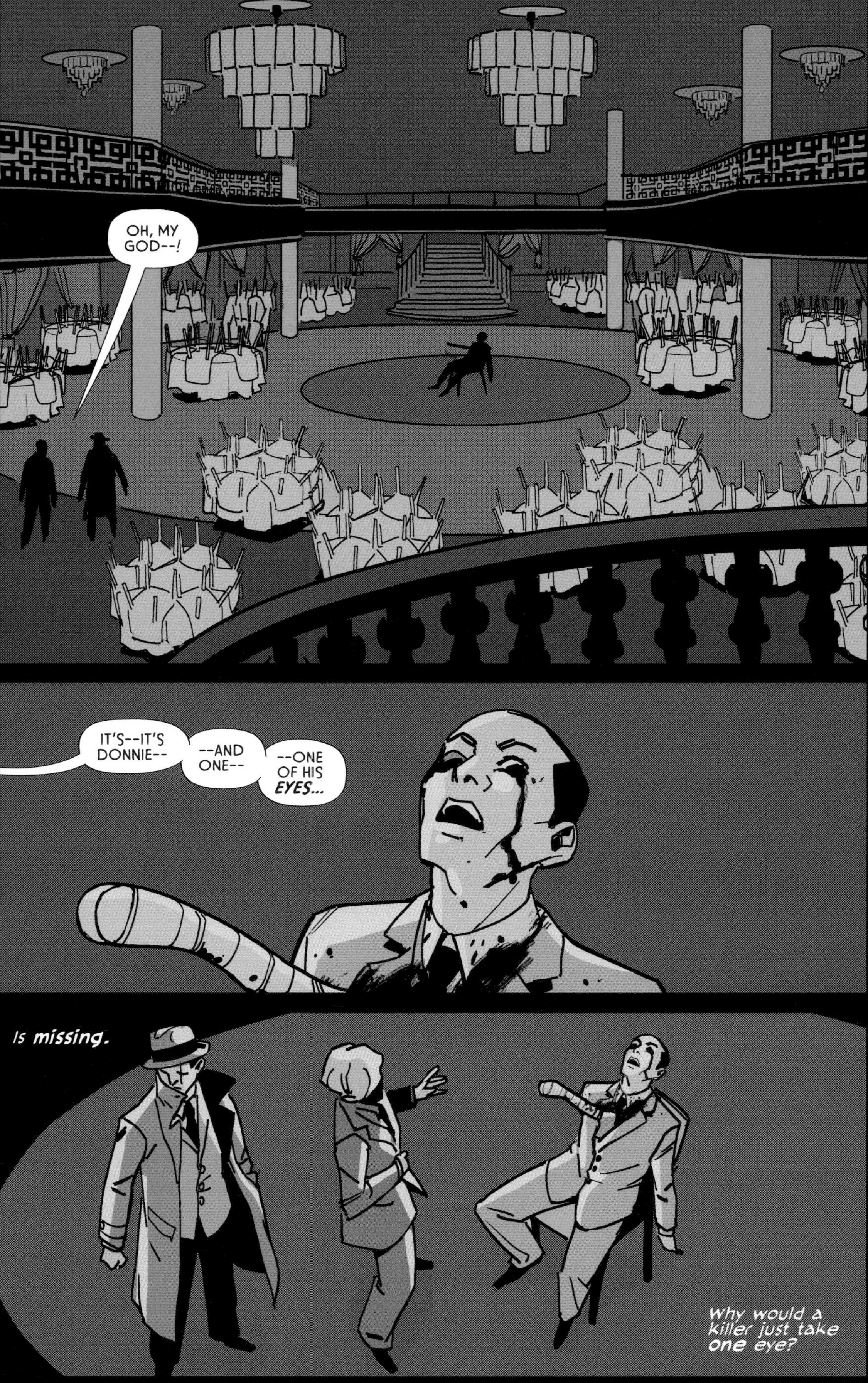
OH, MY GOD--!
IT'S--IT'S DONNIE--
--AND ONE--
--ONE OF HIS EYES...
Is missing.
Why would a killer just take one eye?

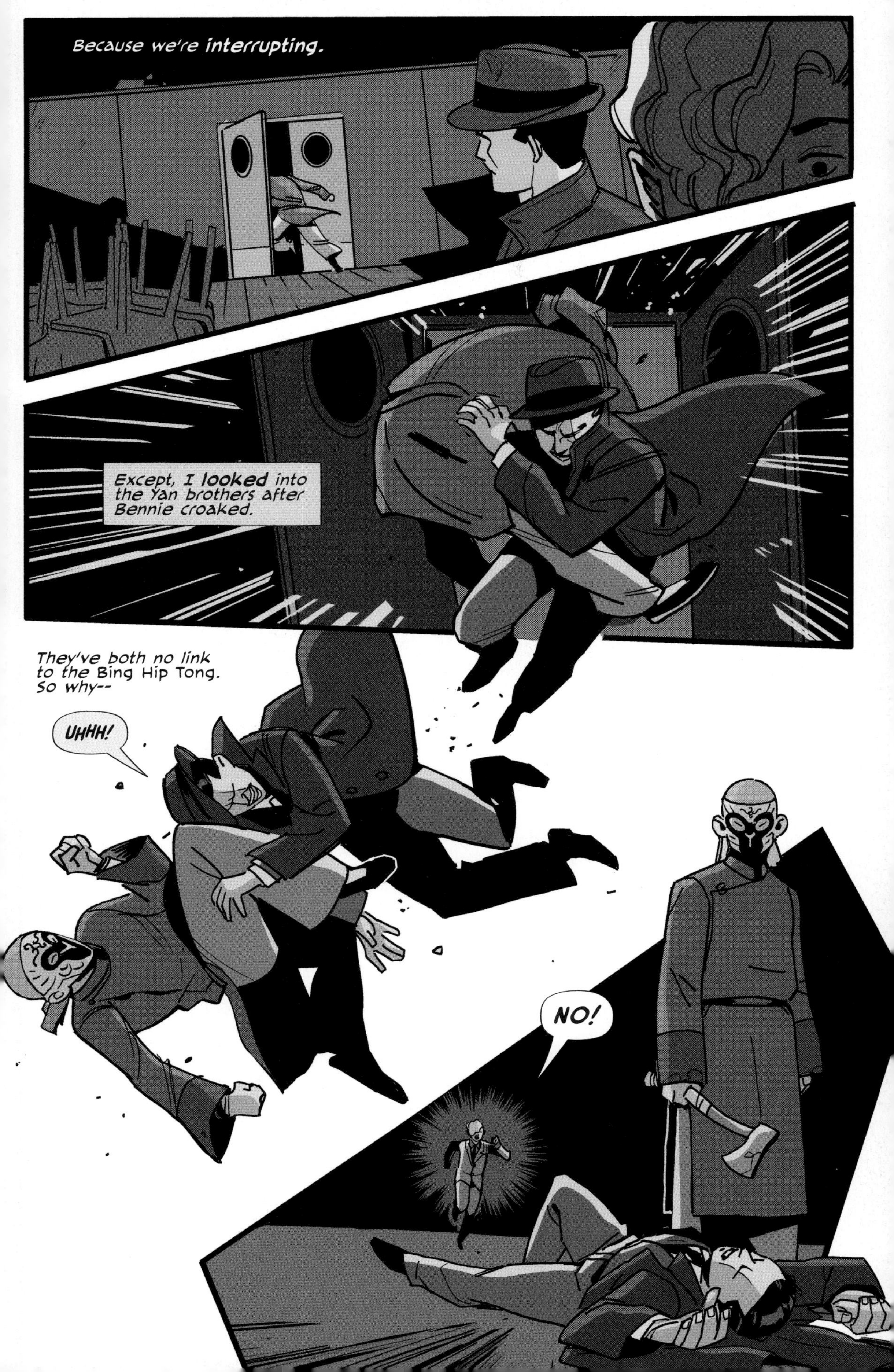
Because we're interrupting.
Except, I looked into the Yan brothers after Bennie croaked.
They've both no link to the Bing Hip Tong. So why--
UHHH!
NO!

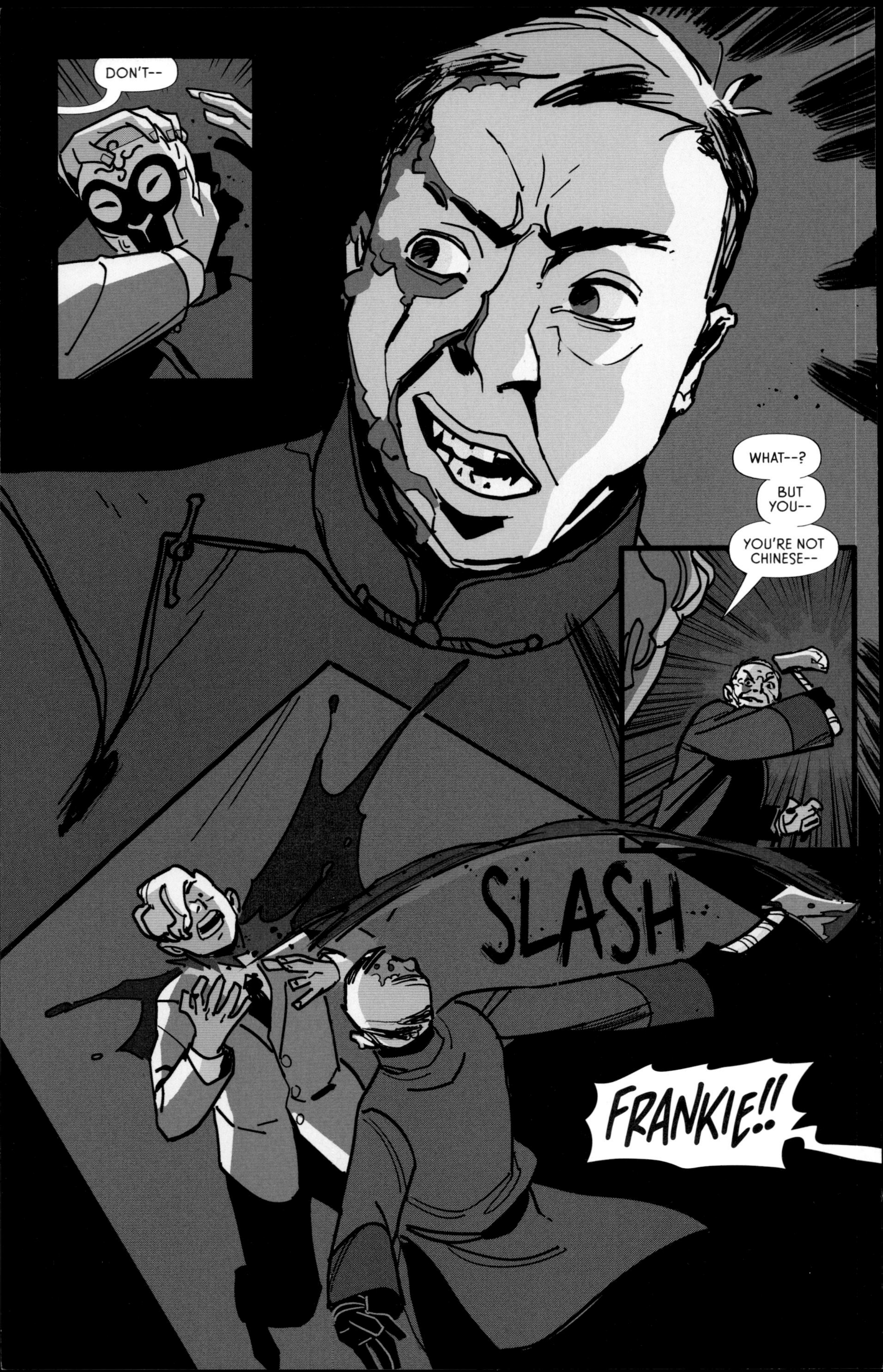
DON'T--
WHAT--?
BUT YOU--
YOU'RE NOT CHINESE--
SLASH
FRANKIE!!

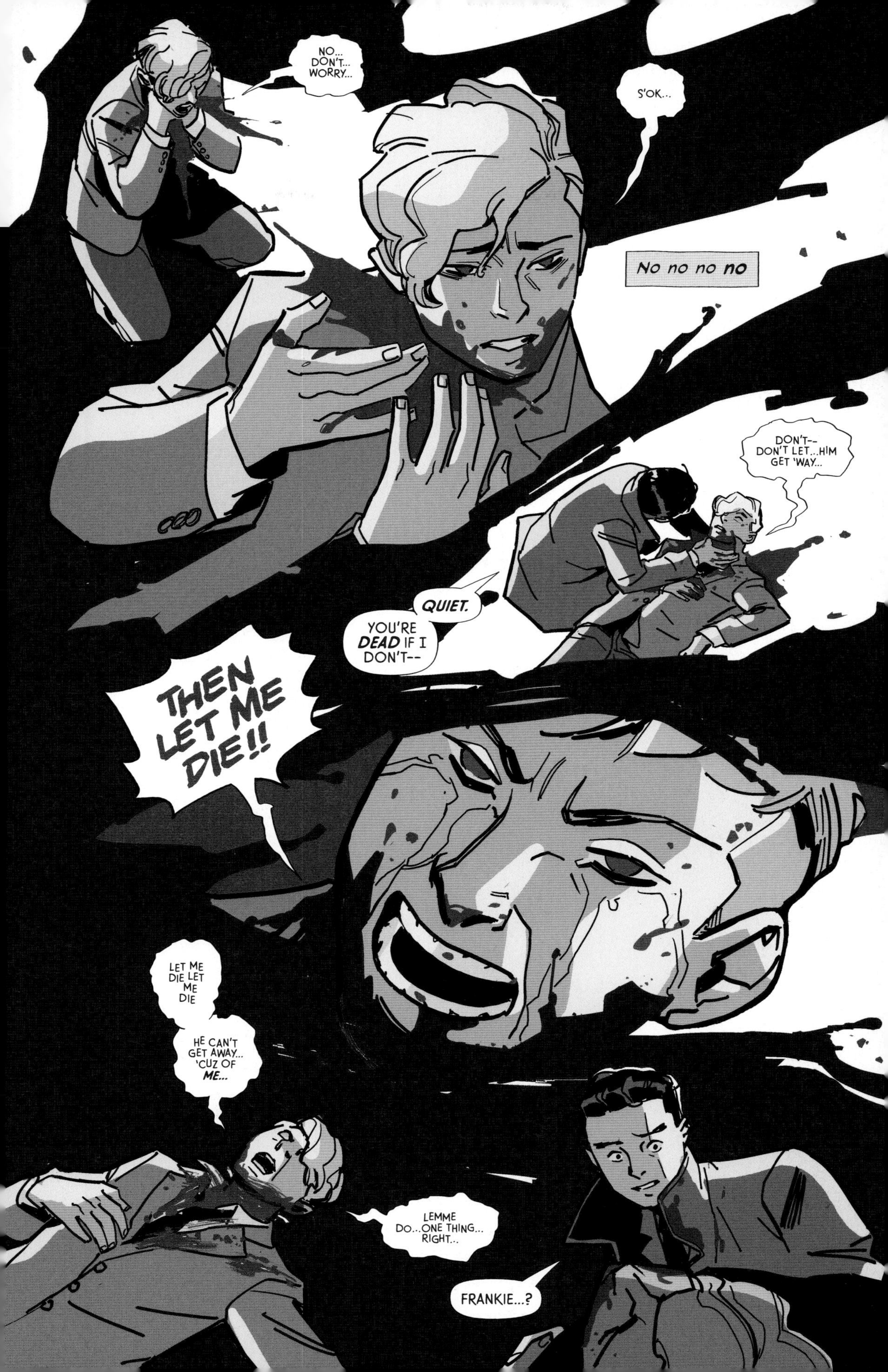
NO... DON'T... WORRY...
S'OK...
No no no no
DON'T-- DON'T LET...HIM GET 'WAY...
QUIET.
YOU'RE DEAD IF I DON'T--
THEN LET ME DIE!!
LET ME DIE LET ME DIE
HE CAN'T GET AWAY... 'CUZ OF ME...
LEMME DO...ONE THING... RIGHT...
FRANKIE...?

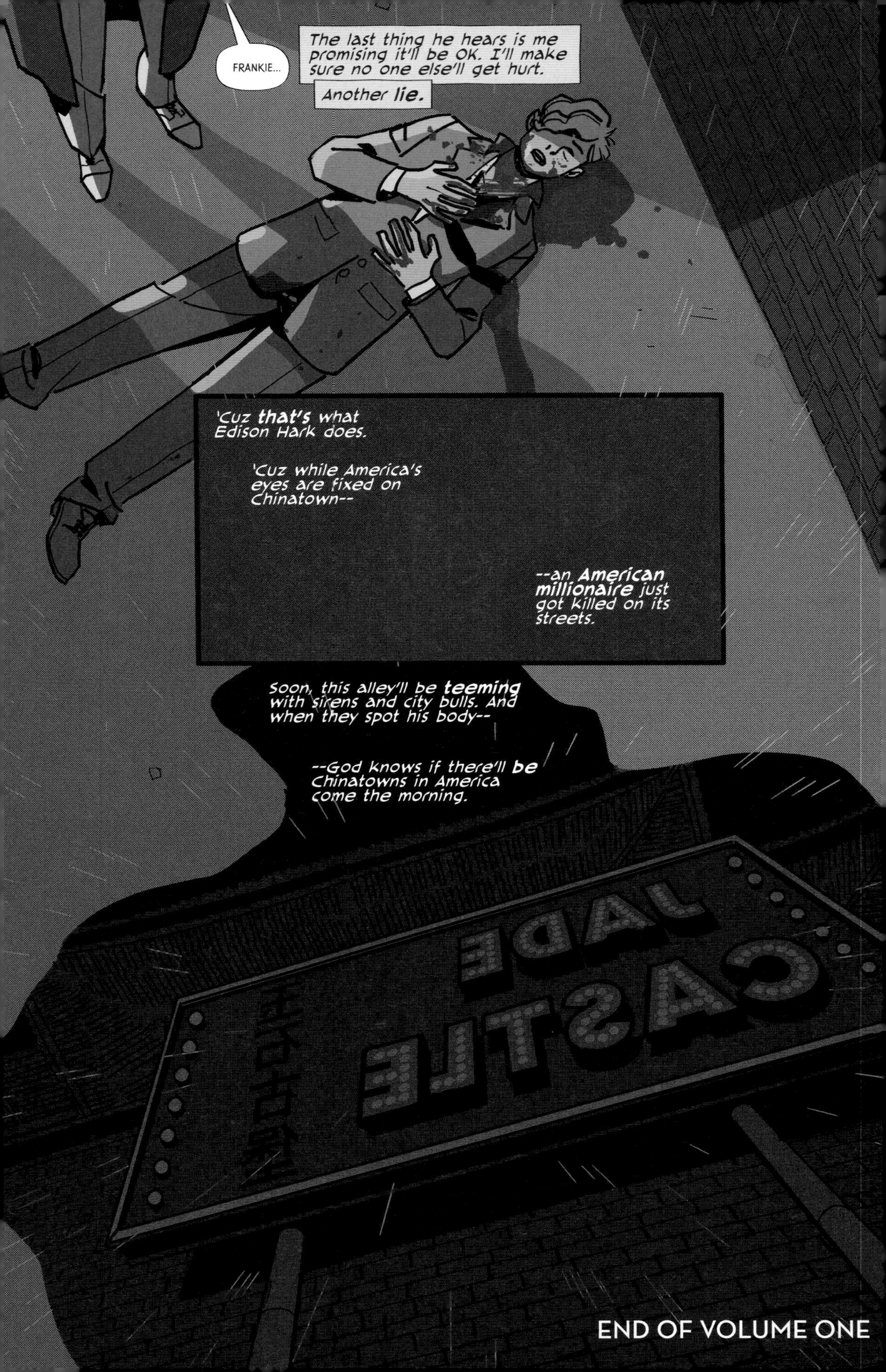
FRANKIE...
The last thing he hears is me promising it'll be OK. I'll make sure no one else'll get hurt.
Another lie.
'Cuz that's what Edison Hark does.
'Cuz while America's eyes are fixed on Chinatown--
--an American millionaire just got killed on its streets.
Soon, this alley'll be teeming with sirens and city bulls. And when they spot his body--
--God knows if there'll be Chinatowns in America come the morning.
END OF VOLUME ONE

HISTORICAL NOTES

THE CHINESE EXCLUSION ACT and ANGEL ISLAND

Context. The primary surge of Chinese immigration into the west coast of America began in the 1850s. The jobs were primarily in mining and railroad construction, but the California Gold Rush also played a part, western America becoming known as the "Golden Mountain" to working-class Chinese who came to the state — like their American counterparts — in the hopes of striking gold and sending money home to their families. Many, of course, didn't, but found payment as cheap labor in dangerous, low-wage jobs.

They were perceived to be driving down worker wages, and America… reacted. In 1854, the California Supreme Court ruled people of Asian descent couldn't testify against a white person in court, which meant a white person could escape repercussions from anti-Asian violence. In addition, politicians campaigned on anti-Chinese platforms with anti-Chinese riots breaking out across multiple American cities in the 1870s. All of it culminated in Congress passing the Chinese Exclusion Act in 1882. While the Act was targeted to keep Chinese laborers out, it would affect all Chinese travelers entering the country, allowing entry to only specific categories of travelers.

This, of course, didn't deter the Chinese from trying to enter the country in the hopes of providing for their families (an estimated 80 — 90% of Exclusion-era immigrants were able-bodied men; approximately seven men for every woman). Many saw immigration as their only way to survive. These banned Chinese would become America's first "illegal immigrants," entering the country through the borders along Canada or Mexico.

Just as immigrants crossing the Atlantic went through Ellis Island, the immigrants crossing the Pacific came through Angel Island. Whereas Ellis Island travelers, however, spent anywhere from a few hours to a few days at Ellis, Asians traveling through Angel — in particular, the Chinese — could spend anywhere from days to years detained.

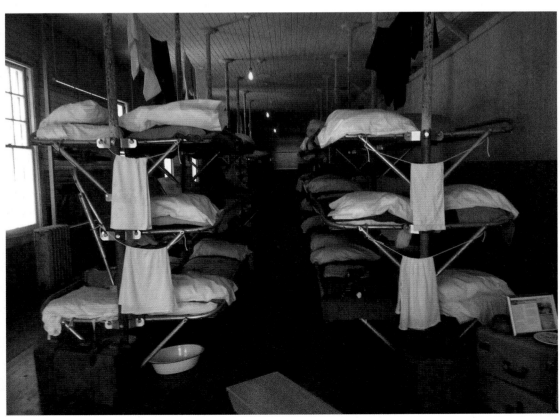

The men's dormitory.

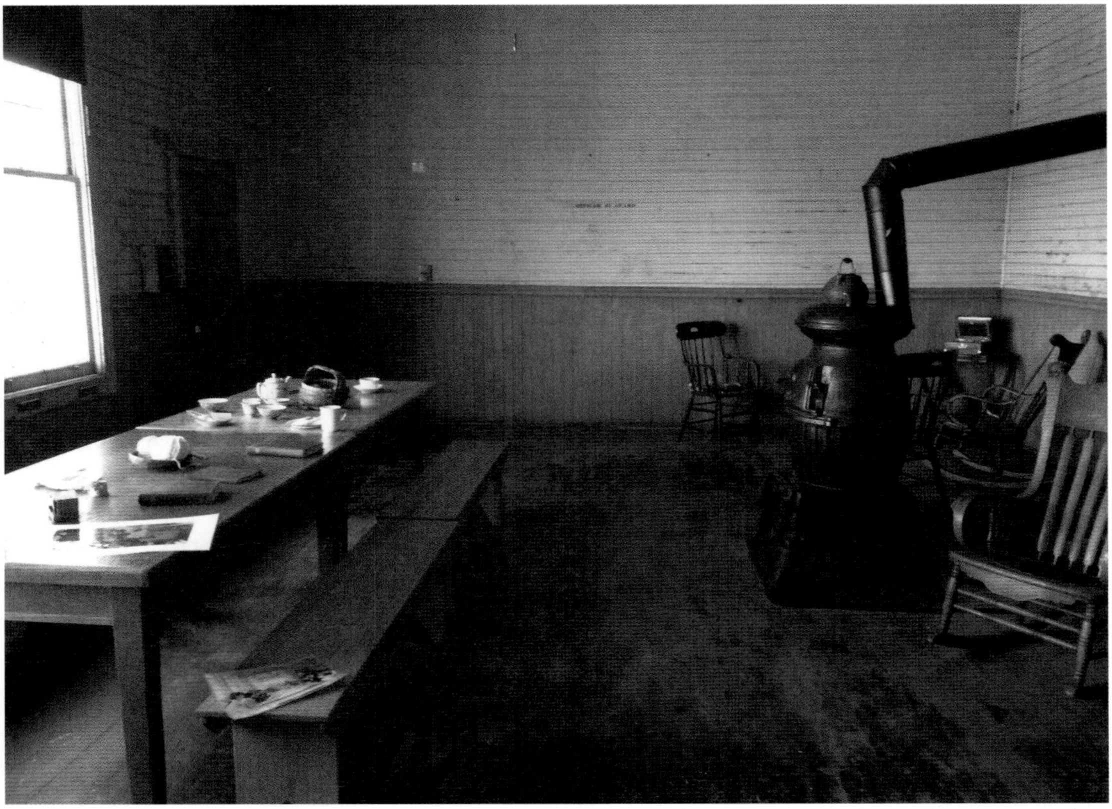

Women's sitting room.

Background. Angel Island is the second largest island in the San Francisco Bay, roughly 6 miles away from San Francisco, making it four times as far as Alcatraz. It began screening immigrants as early as 1891, when worries about the bubonic plague led Angel Island to be a quarantine station where visitors and their baggage were inspected before they could enter the country. Chinese immigrants in particular were believed to be more diseased than Europeans and thereby considered dangerous and contagious.

While the Immigration Station on Angel Island began construction in 1905, it wasn't opened until January 21, 1910, running up until 1940. Different groups were separated upon entry: Europeans were kept apart from the other races. The Chinese were segregated from Japanese and other Asians. Men and women were split into different dormitories – including husbands and wives who were forbidden to see or communicate until they were granted entry into America.

While Angel Island processed immigrants from eighty-four different countries, an estimated 100,000 were Chinese. Each of these travelers had to prove they belonged to one of the categories of Chinese allowed to enter America or risk deportation. In general, however, Chinese immigrants were detained longer than other nationalities.

Proving these travelers hadn't purchased fraudulent papers in the hopes of entering the country illegally was a process that could be as short as less than a week or as long as two years. The median stay for Chinese detainees was sixteen days. During that time, they stayed in large dormitory rooms, some holding over one hundred people. A person's race and class usually determined the intensity of the examination, which meant fewer white Europeans and American citizens were subjected to inspection.

Inside the dormitories themselves, the beds were crammed together, three metal bunks stacked atop one another. At one point in Angel Island's history, visitors hailing from San Francisco inspected the condition of the grounds. The lavatories were found unsanitary, and the hospital inadequate.

Many detainees referred to it as an "island cage," they only being allowed to leave their quarters for meals and a short recreation period.

While they waited, some detainees carved and inked their dormitory walls with Chinese poetry expressing their despair. The Angel Island State Park has preserved two of the original buildings, that poetry still etched there. One example:

The insects chirp outside the four walls.
The inmates often sigh.
Thinking of affairs back home,
Unconscious tears wet my lapel.

Examinations and interrogations. Determining if the Chinese travelers could enter involved a series of examinations and interrogations, processes complicated by a dearth of documentation at the time. Records of Chinese births, marriages, and divorces weren't always available. Many Chinese women in America gave birth at home, leaving their Chinese-American children without birth certificates to prove they were citizens. Complicating matters was how hard immigration

officials found telling the Chinese apart. For a period, in addition to photographs, inspectors even instituted the Bertillon system to identify travelers — a process developed in the 1880s to identify criminals by measuring their forearms, feet, fingers, ears, heads, teeth, hair, and genitalia.

But what officials relied on most were detailed interrogations of the travelers entering the country. While they would range in length, it wasn't uncommon for these exams to span over a hundred questions, delving deep into the minutia of someone's life.

How many windows are in your house? Who lives in the third house of the first row of houses in your village? What kind of feet (bound or not) does the wife have? Chinese immigrants were expected to answer such questions without any signs of hesitation or suspicious behavior. These answers would be cross-checked against testimonies of their "fathers" or people the immigrants offered to vouch for their authenticity. People living in America were obviously the best kind, which meant travelers without relatives or friends in America faced a

The grounds.

A view of the dormitory through the fence.

considerable disadvantage. If any discrepancies were found between a traveler's testimony and their witness, the inspectors assumed the immigrant was entering the country illegally.

Any Chinese-American citizen lacking papers was required to undergo a similar interrogation to re-enter. On top of their testimonies, they could also be judged by whether they dressed enough like an American, how well they recited facts about US history and, of course, how well they spoke English. Unfortunately, until the mid-twentieth century, it was common for Chinese immigrants as well as their American-born children to have little contact with non-Chinese people, tainting the accuracy of any language test.

These interrogations were so extensive that all Chinese immigrants got into the practice of relying on coaching notes, whether or not they were using "real" or "fake" papers. A small business cropped up in China selling coaching books to prospective travelers looking to study up on the most literal type of entrance exam, the topic tested being their own lives.

Exclusion also spawned creative methods of cheating. While visitors weren't allowed to interact with the detainees, some would sneak coaching notes into care packages they left for them — scraps of paper hidden in seemingly innocuous items: Peanuts whose shells were pried apart and glued back together to hide notes inside; oranges which were actually just orange peels carefully wrapped around crumpled up notes and re-glued together. Hollowed out pork buns stuffed with notes. Sometimes these "cheat notes" were even passed along by Chinese kitchen staff feeling sorry for the detainees. Some corrupt immigration guards also got into the action, smuggling notes for a fee.

While the Chinese Exclusion Act would be rescinded in 1943, its creation would impact the lives of all Americans going forward. The Act (and the laws surrounding it) provided America its first example of how to contain undesirable foreigners, initiating the government's first attempts to identify and record them, setting a precedent for the bureaucratic machinery that would eventually create US passports, "green cards," and America's deportation policies.

IMMIGRATION HISTORY TIMELINE

While THE GOOD ASIAN deals primarily with Chinese immigration, it's important to understand America's perception of non-whites, immigrants, and immigration leading up to 1936. Presented below is abbreviated (and admittedly somewhat arbitrary) timeline stringing together some of the most important years, laws, and events which form the story's backdrop.

1790 - The Naturalization Act of 1790 - Granted "free white person[s]... of good character" from other countries a path to US Citizenship, while excluding Native Americans, indentured servants, free blacks, and Asians.

1868 - After the Civil War, the **Fourteenth Amendment** granted African Americans citizenship while establishing birthright citizenship for everyone born in the US.

1870 - The Naturalization Act of 1870 - Extended naturalization to "aliens of African nativity and to persons of African descent" although revoked the citizenship of naturalized Chinese Americans.

1875 - The Page Act - While originally intended to bar East Asian forced laborers, prostitutes, or convicts from entry, the ban was only enforced on East Asian women, effectively banning Chinese women from entering the country.

1882 - The Chinese Exclusion Act - With the Chinese seen as stealing low-paying jobs from Americans, the Chinese Exclusion Act was passed to prohibit all Chinese laborers from entering the country. The Act was intended to last a decade to stop all Chinese immigration with the exception of diplomats, students, teachers, merchants, and US citizens.

1892 - The Geary Act - Extended the Chinese Exclusion Act and required all Chinese residents carry an internal passport / resident permit. Failure to carry one was punishable by deportation or a year of hard labor. In addition, the Act barred the Chinese from bearing witness in court.

1898 - *United States v. Wong Kim Ark* - The Supreme Court case recognizing US birthright citizenship to American-born children of Chinese parents who had a permanent residence in America. This case noted the 14th amendment applied to everyone born in the US, even if their parents were unable to become citizens.

1907 - The Gentlemen's Agreement - An informal agreement between the US and Japan specifying how the US would not impose restrictions on Japanese immigration, while Japan would not allow further emigration into America. Those Japanese in the US could send for their families - resulting in "picture brides," a form of arranged marriages - so Japanese men already in the country could marry.

After Chinese laborers were banned from America, many Japanese had come to the US, taking the low-paying jobs the Chinese once worked.

1917 - The Asiatic Barred Zone extended the impact of the Chinese Exclusion Act to include all of Asia (Japan was already covered by the Gentlemen's Agreement) and imposed a literacy requirement for all immigrants.

1920 - The Cable Act – While in theory designed to grant women their own national identity, the law tied a woman's citizenship to her husband and decreed any American woman who married "an alien illegible for citizenship shall cease to be a citizen of the United States." As a result, any American woman who married a Chinese immigrant would lose their citizenship.

1922 - *Takao Ozawa v. United States* - The Supreme Court case ruling ethnic Japanese were not considered Caucasian and therefore did not meet the Naturalization Act of 1790's "free white persons" requirements, allowing no path to US citizenship for Japanese immigrants.

1923 - *United States v. Bhagat Sing Thind* - The Supreme Court case ruling that while Indians were considered Caucasians by contemporary racial anthropology, they were not seen as "white" in the common understanding, making immigrants from India also ineligible for US citizenship.

1924 - The Immigration Act of 1924, also known as the **Johnson-Reed Act** – Barred Asians and Arabs from entering America, while setting quotas on the numbers of immigrants from the Eastern Hemisphere and reducing immigration from Southern and Eastern Europe. It also banned those ineligible for citizenship from immigrating, which of course applied to Asians. The act provided funding and legal instructions to courts for deporting immigrants while authorizing the formation of the US Border Patrol. According to the US Department of State's Office of the Historian, the law's purpose was designed "to preserve the ideal of US homogeneity."

1924 - The Snyder Act – Granted US Citizenship to Native Americans 148 years after the founding of America.

1930 - Watsonville riots – The Philippines being a US colony at the time, Filipinos were not prohibited from entering America by the Johnson-Reed Act. They and Mexicans migrated to America's West Coast filling jobs previously taken by Chinese,

Japanese, Koreans, and Indians. White men decrying this takeover took to vigilantism to deal with what they called the "third Asiatic invasion." Tensions culminated in a five-day-long riot in Watsonville, California where Filipinos were dragged from their homes and beaten; some were thrown off bridges. This violence inspired anti-Filipino riots across other California cities facing similar frustrations.

1929 – 1936 – Mexican repatriation - A variety of small farmers, progressives, labor unions, eugenicists, and racists had called for restrictions on Mexican immigration, feeling they were taking away jobs and blaming them for exacerbating the Depression. President Herbert Hoover, promising American jobs for Americans, slashed immigration by nearly 90% and launched a mass deportation of Mexicans and Mexican Americans. Roughly 1.8 million men, women, and children were deported, an estimated 60% of those American birthright citizens.

CHOP SUEY CIRCUIT

Although the Jade Castle is fictional, the **chop suey circuit** it represents is not.

In 1936, Charles "Charlie" P. Low opened Chinatown's first cocktail bar — **The Chinese Village**. While locals assumed it'd fail — the Chinese not drinking under moral grounds — white patrons would buoy it, tourists coming for the alcohol but staying for a Chinese singer named Li Tei Ming. And as the bar's popularity grew — reaching standing room only capacity — others copied Low's formula. A slew of Chinese bars popped up, all featuring Chinese entertainment acts, until finally, **Chinese Sky Room** opened in 1937 — America's first Chinese-American nightclub. That led to more copycats and so, the Chinatown nightclub scene was born.

These dine-and-dance venues — now collectively remembered as the chop suey circuit — had a signature formula — food, alcohol, and all-Chinese entertainment, a mix of Chinese showgirls, singers, dancers, acrobats, and magicians. The clubs opened up a renaissance of sorts for Chinese performers. After all, finding work as a Chinese entertainer was hard, their Asian faces being deemed to stand out too much amongst a chorus line or entertainment troop. But with the chop suey circuit's popularity, Chinese dancers became inundated with work — some performing at two or three clubs a night, a few transitioning to work abroad or have their acts recorded for film and TV.

The clubs weren't without their controversy — particularly for the women. Chinese women were raised never to show their arms or legs in public, leading dancers to receive letters characterizing them as loose or whores, telling them they should be ashamed. Recruiting showgirls was so tough, most of the women the clubs hired grew up outside Chinatown — from places as far away as Arizona, Hawaii, and the Midwest. They all came to Chinatown following their hunger to perform — and in the process shattered the stereotypes of what an Asian girl should or shouldn't do.

White patrons came to the clubs looking for an exotic flavor. And while owners and entertainers obliged, it was also important they prove they were just as American as their audience. Some acts would start out in traditional Chinese garb, only to tear them off and reveal Western outfits beneath, as their consequent acts prove they could sing and dance in Western styles just as well as Eastern.

These clubs' popularity skyrocketed through World War 2, as servicemen spent more time in nightclubs and bars. Wartime rationing limiting the amount of goods one could buy left Americans with more money for entertainment. And while the end of the war would result in taxation and unionization (as well as a shift in American priorities) that would hurt the clubs' profitability, the popularity of the chop suey circuit nevertheless changed Chinatown, which in 1936 was still recovering from the Depression. It created a club scene completely run by Chinese Americans, transforming the neighborhood into a tourist attraction and turning a people seen as sideshow freaks into local entertainment moguls.

CHINATOWN TELEPHONE EXCHANGE

According to *Bridging the Pacific* by Thomas Chinn, the **Chinatown Telephone Exchange** was established in 1894 at 743 Washington St with three male operators and 37 telephone subscribers. The original, sumptuously furnished

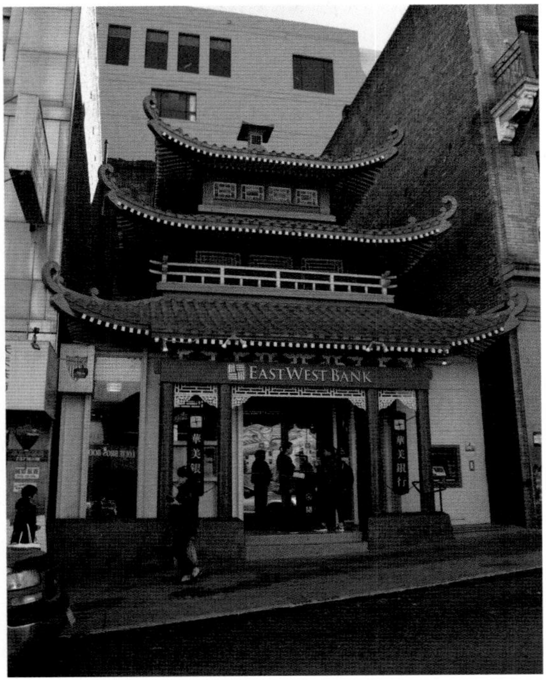
EASTWEST BANK

location featured chairs of carved teakwood inlaid with mother-of-pearl; windows of Chinese oyster-shell panes; and switchboards of ebony.

After the **San Francisco Earthquake of 1906** destroyed the original building, a new one was constructed in 1909 in a pagoda-like building keeping with the drive to create an "Oriental city." It served 800 phones, and by that point, the staff was all-female. Operators were required to have memorized the addresses and 4-digit telephone numbers of everyone in Chinatown. By 1936, the Exchange had 21 operators for the community's 2,200 phones, which included residents, businesses, and public phones. Callers would ring up, asking to be connected to their aunt / uncle / eye doctor, with operators expected to know the numbers to be patched through to.

These operators usually spoke two or three different dialects and were all generally of the same age. The Exchange became a social hub, the women not only growing close, but many even having children around the same time. Automatic dialing forced the Exchange to close in 1948, the building now home to an East West Bank (pictured above).

REFERENCES

For anyone interested in reading more on any of these topics, the following are some recommended sources:

- *Chinese San Francisco 1850 - 1943: A Trans-Pacific Community* by Yong Chen for a general history of the Chinese in San Francisco.
- *At America's Gates: Chinese Immigration during the Exclusion Era: 1882 - 1943* by Erika Lee is probably my go-to text about the topic.
- *Island: Poetry and History of Chinese Immigrants on Angel Island 1910 - 1940, Second Edition,* edited by Him Mark Lai, Genny Lim, and Judy Yung features testimonials from detainees who passed through Angel Island as well as people who worked there and the Chinese poems found on the barrack walls, translated into English.
- *Images of America: Angel Island* by Branwell Fanning and William Wong. Photos from the *Images of America* book series is one of the chief photo-references used in the making of this series.
- *Forbidden City, USA: Chinese American Nightclubs, 1936 - 1970* by Arthur Dong who's probably the authority on the subject of America's chop suey club circuit, the book featuring interviews with many of the club's performers. The book is an off-shoot of Dong's documentary on the subject, likewise titled *Forbidden City, USA*.
- *Carved in Silence* (1987), a documentary by Felicia Lowe about the Chinese Exclusion Act and can be purchased upon any visit to the Angel Island State Park.
- Speaking of which, the **Angel Island State Park** preserves much of this history as well as the original buildings. All pictures shown here were all taken there and run with their permission. Their staff is incredibly helpful and kind, as well as just a google away.
- The CHSA (*Chinatown Historical Society of America*) is located in San Francisco's Chinatown and another fantastic resource for Chinese history. The CHSA has many exhibits chronicling the history of the Chinese in America, including some of the coaching notes passed to Angel Island detainees hidden inside orange peels and peanut shells.

PORNSAK PICHETSHOTE was a Thai-American rising star editor at DC's VERTIGO imprint, his books nominated for dozens of Eisner awards. Currently writing for television and comics, his TV credits include *Marvel's Cloak & Dagger* and *Green Lantern* for HBO Max. His hit graphic novel INFIDEL was selected for NPR's "100 Favorite Horror Stories of All Time."

ALEXANDRE TEFENKGI is a French comic book artist of Vietnamese-Djiboutian descent. He started his career in the European market working with some of France's top publishers. His first international book is the critically acclaimed sci-fi series OUTPOST ZERO for Skybound Entertainment.

LEE LOUGHRIDGE is a devilishly handsome man, despite his low testosterone, who has been working primarily in the comics/animation industry for over twenty years. He has worked on hundreds of titles for all the industry's major publishers, his talents on display on every iconic comic book character from Batman to Punisher to DEADLY CLASS and more.

JEFF POWELL has lettered a wide range of titles throughout his lengthy career. His recent work includes *The Devil's Red Bride, Scales & Scoudrels, Atomic Robo,* and the critically acclaimed INFIDEL. In addition, Jeff has designed books, logos, and trade dress for Marvel, Archie, IDW, Image, Valiant, and others.

DAVE JOHNSON may be best known for his minimalist covers on the noir Vertigo series, *100 Bullets.* He has also done a number of covers for Marvel, DC, and Image Comics. He earned the 2002 Eisner Award for Best Cover Artist and has also been nominated for an Eisner in 2004 and 2021. His work on the critically acclaimed *Superman: Red Son* is also a perennial bestseller.

WILL DENNIS was an editor at Vertigo/DC Entertainment for more than fifteen years, specializing in genre fiction comics and graphic novels. His award-winning titles include *100 Bullets, Y: The Last Man, Joker* and many more. He is currently a freelance editor for Image Comics, comiXology, and DC Entertainment, also writing *The Art of Jock* for Insight Editions.